# From a Drood to a Kill

# From a Drood to a Kill

## Simon R. Green

A ROC BOOK

ROC
Published by the Penguin Group
Penguin Group (USA) LLC, 375 Hudson Street,
New York, New York 10014

USA | Canada | UK | Ireland | Australia | New Zealand | India | South Africa | China
penguin.com
A Penguin Random House Company

First published by Roc, an imprint of New American Library,
a division of Penguin Group (USA) LLC

First Printing, June 2015

LIBRARY OF CONGRESS CATALOGING-IN-PUBLICATION DATA:

Green, Simon R., 1955–
From a drood to a kill: a secret histories novel / Simon R. Green.
    pages cm.—(Secret histories; 9)
  ISBN 978-0-451-41433-5 (hardback)
1. Drood, Eddie (Fictitious character)—Fiction.   I. Title.
PR6107.R44F75 2015
823'.92—dc23 2014048117

Printed in the United States of America
10  9  8  7  6  5  4  3  2  1

Set in ITC New Baskerville

# From a Drood
# to a Kill

This is what you need to know:

First, there are the Droods. A centuries-old family, dedicated to defending Humanity from all the unnatural forces that threaten this world. My family. The Good Guys—more or less. Then, there are all the other very secret organisations, who deal with things the Droods don't have time for or don't feel too bothered about. Groups like the London Knights, the Carnacki Institute, the Soulhunters . . . Good Guys—or good enough. Finally, we have the opposition, hiding in the shadows. The villains, the Bad Guys—only out for themselves and what they can get, and to hell with everyone else. Add to that the monsters, aliens, and general weird shit . . . and we're talking about the world I know.

I'm Eddie Drood, field agent for my family. Doing unto others before they do it to you. Except for when I'm undercover; then I'm Shaman Bond, just another face on the scene, keeping his eyes and ears open. Whichever identity I'm using, I usually have a fairly strong grasp on what's what, and what matters, and whose side I'm on.

I should have known. Nothing's ever that simple. This is the case where everything fell apart, the one when everything and everyone that mattered were taken from me. Because no one ever told me about the Powers That Be, and the Big Game. And what I'd have to do to win.

# CHAPTER ONE

# It's All About the Give-and-Take.
# You Give and I Take.

t was a surprisingly pleasant day. Bright summer sunshine, a cloudless blue sky over sweeping grassy lawns, the cries of peacocks and gryphons loud and clear on the still air. Along with the quiet putt-putt of a steam-powered autogyro chugging by overhead. Just another day at Drood Hall, ancestral home of my long-established family, and training ground for those who would protect the world. I stood outside the main entrance door with my lady love at my side. Molly Metcalf—wild witch of the woods, supernatural terrorist, Hawkwind fan . . . and the only one I trust to always have my back. We looked at each other and grinned.

"Ready?" I said.

"Always," said Molly.

"Once we start," I said, "we don't stop. For anything. Until we get to where we're going."

"Got it," said Molly. "We keep going, no matter what." She looked at me carefully. "Are we really going to do this? Take on the most powerful family in the world, on their own home ground?"

"Isn't that what you always wanted?" I said.

"Hell yes! But are you sure this is what you want?"

"Hell yes," I said.

Her grin widened. "Your family isn't going to know what's hit them."

"Let's do it," I said.

"Love to," said Molly.

I subvocalised my activating Words, and golden armour flowed out from the torc around my neck, covering me in a moment from head to toe in unbreakable, unstoppable strange matter. My family's greatest secret weapon. I felt strong and fast and fully alive, as though I'd just woken up from the long doze of ordinary living. Molly struck a sorcerous pose and was immediately surrounded by coruscating wild magics, spitting and sparking as they discharged on the air. The knight in armour and the wicked witch, determined not to be denied any longer. I raised a golden foot, kicked in the entrance doors, and the two of us slammed into Drood Hall.

Alarms and bells and sirens broke out everywhere all at once, and men and women froze in place along the whole length of the entrance hall, caught off guard. No one ever invades Drood Hall, home to the most feared and respected family in the world. It just doesn't happen. So they simply stood and stared, like rabbits caught in the headlights of an oncoming car, while Molly and I strode on. Two unstoppable forces for the price of one. A few of my family started forward to try to intercept us; some ran away; but most just stood and stared blankly, waiting for someone to tell them what to do.

A handful of security guards finally appeared, charging down the hallway, yelling for everyone else to get out of their way, and armouring up as they came. I didn't slow down, just hit them head on. Some I shouldered aside; others I knocked down and walked right over. They might have been armoured like me, but I was the one with the field training and experience. More armoured guards burst out of side doors. Molly called up vicious storm winds, and they blasted up and down the long entrance hall, picking Droods up and throwing them this way and that. Most of the family either grabbed for something secure to hold on to or ran for their lives. They didn't armour up or reach for weapons. I was seriously unimpressed. It was clear to me that the family needed to run more practise drills so everyone would know what to do when the impossible happened right in front of them. If this had been a real invasion, by outside forces, we would have been in serious trouble.

An armoured Drood blocked my way, reaching for me with golden hands. I hit him hard, slamming my shoulder into his chest. There was a loud clang of colliding metals as he was thrown backwards. I back-elbowed another in the side of the head, and swept the feet out from under a third. And kept going. I wasn't worried about hurting them while they were in their armour, but hopefully I'd knocked the breath out of them and bought us some time. Molly danced happily along at my side, throwing fireworks and concussion spells in all directions, just to keep everyone on their toes.

"Has anyone ever got this far inside before?" she asked.

"It has happened," I replied. "But we don't like to talk about it. Might give people ideas."

Molly was still sending Droods tumbling this way and that with her roaring storm winds. And perhaps enjoying herself just a little too much. Not everyone was armoured. I shot her a hard look from behind my featureless golden mask, realised that wasn't going to help much, and raised my voice to be heard clearly over the howling sirens and alarm bells.

"Take it easy, Molly! These people are family!"

"I know," said Molly.

"My family!"

"Not mine."

"They could be," I said. "One day."

"You say that like it's a good thing."

"Molly . . ."

"Sometimes you want too much, Eddie," said Molly. Not even looking at me. We pressed on, into the heart of Drood Hall.

The Serjeant-at-Arms appeared suddenly before us, wearing his traditional formal outfit of stark black and white. He would have looked very like a traditional old-fashioned butler if it hadn't been for the two extremely nasty-looking guns in his hands. The Serjeant is the first hard line of defence against any hostile intruders, and I was pleasantly surprised that we'd got this far before he turned up to stop us. He immediately recognised both Molly and me, but the guns he had trained on us didn't waver at all. I knew he'd have no hesitation in shooting if he thought it necessary. But I also knew he was so confident in his own abilities, it would never even occur to him that he needed to armour up to protect himself.

So I gave the nod to Molly, and she jabbed a specially prepared aboriginal pointing bone at the Serjeant. And just like that, he was gone. Teleported right out of the Hall and onto the grounds outside. Quite a long way off, to be exact—on the far side of the ornamental lake. By the time he could make his way back to the Hall, this should all be over. One way or another. Molly looked at the pointing bone in her hand. The sheer strain of what it had been asked to do had charred and cracked it from end to end. It's not easy, making a Drood go somewhere he doesn't want to go. Molly shrugged, tossed the bone aside, and we moved on.

We strode quickly through open halls and wide corridors, blasting our way through what little opposition there was. They say you can't go home again, but you can if you carry a big enough stick. The alarms and bells and sirens were deafeningly loud, yet I could still hear armoured feet hammering on polished wooden floors as people headed towards us from all directions. But so far we were still keeping well ahead of them.

The Hall's interior security systems kicked in automatically once we passed a certain point, and all the doors ahead and around us slammed shut and locked themselves to try to contain the problem. With anyone else, that might actually have worked. Molly snapped her fingers at each door we came to, and it leapt open to let us pass. Until the anti-magic protocols activated and that stopped working. So instead I just lowered my armoured shoulder again and hit each closed door like a battering ram, smashing my way through. The heavy wood cracked and broke apart; sometimes the entire door was thrown right off its hinges. The world can be a very fragile place when you're wearing Drood armour.

Concealed trap-doors suddenly fell away in the floor before us, revealing dark, bottomless depths. I knew where they were, so I just stepped around them. Molly walked straight forward across the open spaces, not even deigning to look down, defying gravity as she defied everything else that argued with her. The trap-doors closed behind us with quiet, defeated sounds.

"I have to say, I was expecting your family to put up more of a showing," said Molly. "Something more impressive, like energy weapons or force shields . . . high explosives. That sort of thing."

"My family will be very reluctant to use anything that destructive inside the Hall," I said. "For fear of damaging all the expensive paintings and sculptures we've accumulated down the centuries. Tribute from a grateful and rather scared world. That's what I was counting on. Luckily I don't have that problem. I've never liked the Hall."

"Even though it's where you were brought up?"

"Especially because it's where I was brought up."

I said that very loudly, for the benefit of anyone who might be listening and still planning on stopping us. I wanted them to believe I didn't care how much damage I did. And to be fair, Molly probably really didn't. But I was being careful to do no more damage than I had to—to the Hall, and to my family. Because while I might be mad at them right now, I still had to live with them afterwards. I'd put a lot of thought into this particular home invasion, and it was all about the shock and awe, and moving too quickly for any serious confrontations.

Half a dozen armoured Droods turned up with at least some idea of how to fight and a willingness to get stuck in. Good for them. But I was a trained field agent, with many years of hard experience and all kinds of nasty tricks tucked up my armoured sleeves. I knocked them down and kicked them around, and Molly hit them with eldritch lightnings if they tried to get up. They ended up scattered the length of the corridor, wondering what hit them and whether it was ever going to stop. Poor bastards. They never stood a chance. Which was just as well. Because I would have damaged them if I'd had to. No one was going to stop me this time.

The farther into the Hall Molly and I penetrated, the faster we moved. By the time we approached the centre of the Hall and its hidden core, the Sanctity, we were both running at full pelt. I wanted to leave my family well behind, so there wouldn't be any . . . accidents. I was trying to make it clear to everyone that I was here for a purpose, and determined to get to where I was going. That I had no intention of being stopped . . . and that it really would be better for everyone if they just got the hell out of my way and let me get on with it.

Finally, we rounded a corner and there was the Sanctity, straight ahead of us. At the far end of a long stone corridor. The heart of the Hall, where all the decisions that matter are made. I slowed my pace to a determined stroll, and Molly drifted dangerously along beside me. No more smiles. This was serious business. I felt a sudden harsh tingling in my throat. I'd been expecting that. It was a standard defence, designed to deal with any Droods who went mad or rogue, by taking their armour away from them and pushing it back into their torc.

"Ethel?" I said, subvocalising so only she could hear me.

The warm and friendly voice of the Droods' very own other-dimensional patron and protector came clearly to me, inside my head.

"You know, I really should just shut you down, Eddie. That's what everyone else is shouting at me to do and I do wish they wouldn't. Tell me you have a really good reason for causing this much commotion."

"I have a really good reason."

"Really? Cross your heart?"

"Trust me."

"You know I do. But you don't make it easy."

"I know," I said. "But I do make it fun."

"Yes, you do. I'm looking forward to hearing what this is all about. Hint, hint."

"You'll enjoy it," I said.

"I'd better."

The tingling around my throat went away, and I relaxed, just a little. I'd been fairly confident I could convince Ethel—but it's hard to be sure of anything when you're dealing with an other-dimensional entity.

The way to the great double doors that were the only access to the Sanctity was blocked by two very large armoured guards who stood their ground. They showed no intention of moving or of being moved. I slowed to a casual stroll, with Molly close at my side. She gestured impressively at them, trying to teleport them away, as she had with the Serjeant-at-Arms. But without the pointing bone she hadn't a hope of moving two Droods in their armour. She scowled, and stuck out her lower lip sulkily.

"Come on," I said. "That was never going to work."

"It might have!" she said. "I put hours into researching that spell."

"You didn't really think you could overcome Drood armour all on your own, did you?"

Molly smiled dazzlingly. "A girl can dream, can't she?"

The two guards stepped forward, long golden sword blades extending from their armoured hands. I was glad to see they'd been practising. Drood armour can be reshaped by the will of its occupant, but it takes a lot of concentration to hold the new shape. It was clear from the way the guards stood that they knew what they were doing. They looked practised and prepared, and properly dangerous. Everything a Drood should be. Good for them. I reached through the golden armour at my hip, into the pocket dimension I keep there, and brought out the Merlin Glass. One of the guards had just enough time to say, "Oh shit," before I shook the Glass out to Door size and clapped it quickly over each guard in turn, sending them through the Glass and out into the Drood grounds. Where they could probably have a very interesting conversation with the Serjeant-at-Arms. I shook the Merlin Glass back down to hand-mirror size and put it away again.

"So," said Molly. "That thing has decided to start working again, has it?"

"When it feels like it," I said.

"What would you have done if the Glass hadn't worked?"

"Improvised," I said. "Suddenly and violently and all over the place."

"Always works for me," said Molly. She stopped and looked at me thoughtfully. "Okay, why did the Glass work against the armoured Droods, when my magic wouldn't?"

"It's the Merlin Glass," I said. "Can't help feeling the clue is in the name."

We stood together before the closed Sanctity doors. One last barrier, standing between me . . . and what I'd come for. The alarms and bells and sirens were still giving it their all, and I could also hear a great many feet heading in our direction, but for the moment we had the corridor to ourselves. I looked at Molly.

"You ready to do this?"

"Of course," said Molly. "Looking forward to it."

I tried the door handle, and as I suspected, the door was locked. I raised my voice.

"Ethel! Open the doors, please. If you wouldn't mind. I'd hate to have to seriously damage anything."

"Speak for yourself," said Molly.

I felt as much as heard a quiet, resigned sigh, and then the doors unlocked themselves, swinging slowly open before us.

I strode into the Sanctity with my head held high, Molly moving proudly at my side. The massive open space of the old wood-panelled chamber was almost completely deserted, and suffused with a rose-red glow that emanated from no obvious source. The only physical manifestation of Ethel's presence. Under normal circumstances the rose-red light was soothing and calming to the troubled soul, but I was so full of anger and a deep sense of injustice that I barely felt it. I don't think Molly has ever felt it. She's not a calm person. She stopped just inside the entrance, as the doors slowly closed themselves, so she could block the way against anyone who might come in after us. I walked slowly forward, and there, waiting for me, was the family's new Matriarch. Margaret.

She stood alone, staring defiantly back at me, unsupported by any member of her advisory Council, unprotected by any guards. Margaret was a short, stocky blonde, with hair so close-cropped it was almost military. She wore a battered bomber jacket over seriously distressed jeans, and much-worn work boots with trailing laces. She might have been taken away from her beloved grounds and gardens, and forced to run the family as the next in line; but no one was ever going to make her like it. Or look the part. Margaret had a firm mouth, fierce eyes, and a general air of barely suppressed fury.

"All right!" she said sharply. "You've got my attention. Now what is so important you had to force your way into the Hall and insist on seeing me, even though I already told you I was far too busy? Have you come back to take my position as head of the family by force, Eddie? Like you threatened to, the last time you were here? Because if you want it, you can have it. And I can go back to my gardens. I'm sure they miss me."

"I don't want to run the family," I said, very firmly. I armoured down, so she could see my face and see that I meant it. She relaxed, just a little.

"I hate being the Matriarch," said the woman who not that long ago used to be called Capability Maggie. When all she had to worry about was maintaining the Hall's extensive grounds and gardens. "Far too much responsibility, no time to myself, hardly ever a free minute to stroll round the flower beds and see how the new seedlings are coming along. I'd quit in a minute if they'd let me."

"Hell," Molly said calmly, "I'll take the position, if no one else wants it. Just think what I could do to an unsuspecting world with a whole army of Droods to back me up."

The Matriarch and I both looked at Molly, thought about it, and winced pretty much simultaneously.

"That . . . is a truly disturbing thought," I said.

"You could never take charge of the Droods," the Matriarch said coldly to Molly. "You're not family. Even if you should eventually marry Eddie, which a whole lot of us doubt, that still wouldn't make you one of us. Only a pure-blooded Drood can be Matriarch."

"Yeah," said Molly. "Because that's always worked out so well in the past."

"If we could just tiptoe back into the realms of reality," I said. "We have something important to discuss, Matriarch. I came here to talk to you about something specific, and I will not be stopped or diverted."

"You've made that clear enough," said the Matriarch. "I can't believe you've done this to us, Eddie. Untold damage, injured family members, and chaos everywhere. All because you couldn't be bothered to make a proper appointment, like reasonable people."

"There's no point in being reasonable with this family," I said. "I have tried it, and it never works. Because it takes two to be reasonable."

*"What do you want, Eddie?"* said the Matriarch, meeting my gaze unflinchingly.

"You know what I want! You promised me the family would use all its resources to track down my missing parents! It's been months since they vanished from the Casino Infernale in France, and you haven't come up with a single damned lead!"

"We've been busy!" said the Matriarch. "The world doesn't just stand still because you've got a problem! We have to hold Humanity's hand and blow its nose, and protect it from a thousand different threats it doesn't even know exist, all day and every night, with never a break. And there are, after all, very real limits to this family's time and budget. We deal with the most important matters first. Everything else . . . has to take its place in the queue. Charles and Emily aren't even officially members of the family any more. Like you, Eddie. You walked out on us, remember? Turned your back on family duty and responsibilities so you could run off to work with your precious grandfather in the Department of Uncanny. Who, let us face it, have never been more than second-raters in the secret organisation stakes. And you think you have a right to demand full access to the family's limited time and resources?"

"After everything I've done for this family?" I said. "Damn right I do."

Even I could hear the dangerous chill in my voice. The Matriarch looked away, unable to meet my gaze.

"The general feeling is," she said finally, "that if Charles and Emily are still missing it's because they want to be."

"Don't give me that," I said. "This family can find anyone, if they want to. Ethel!"

"Yes, Eddie!" said the warm, comforting voice, from everywhere at once. "Welcome home! Always good to have you around. You do liven things up so. Did you bring me a present? You know I love presents."

"Yes," I said. "But you're very difficult to buy for. What do you get the other-dimensional entity who is everything? Come on, Ethel. Why can't you just See where my parents are? I thought you said you could See anything, anywhere."

"I can! I can See everything that exists, and a good many things that shouldn't. I can See things you humans don't even have concepts for. But your parents remain . . . stubbornly elusive. They don't have torcs, so I can't track them that way; and when I try to look for them . . . wherever I look, they aren't there. So I can only assume they're no longer in this world."

A cold hand clutched at my heart. "Are you saying . . . they're dead?"

"I didn't say that. There are, after all, all kinds of realities. Some so distanced from this one, or so carefully concealed, that even I can't look into them. My abilities are very limited by my current circumstances. You have no idea what I've given up to take care of you Droods."

"If you want all of our resources turned loose on your private problem, Eddie," said the Matriarch, refusing to be left out of the conversation, "if you want to ask a personal favour from the family, you're going to have to do a favour for the family."

I looked at her slowly, consideringly, and to her credit she didn't flinch.

"I just knew that was coming," said Molly. "Didn't you just know that was coming?"

"A favour?" I said. "Like what?"

The Matriarch stirred uncomfortably, at something she heard in my voice. She chose her words carefully.

"We do have a case pending that the family needs to deal with but that we would prefer to keep at arm's length. Essentially straight forward, but ripe with pitfalls for the unwary. A case that could quite definitely benefit from your . . . special touch."

"Hold it," said Molly. "I've just remembered something I wanted to ask! Do you know what's happening with the Department of Uncanny? Have you heard who's going to be put in charge?"

The Matriarch looked at her. She would have liked to be impatient, but everyone knew there was no point in trying to push past Molly when she had something on her mind. She had a tendency to throw things. Often large jaggedy pointy things. The Matriarch did allow herself a loud sigh, just on general principles.

"As far as I know," she said, "the Government hasn't decided whether they're going to keep Uncanny going, as a separate Department. It was almost completely destroyed, and most of its people killed. The Government might just fold what's left into MI 13, or replace it with something new. I understand Black Heir is very keen to take on Uncanny's responsibilities, and expand their area of influence in the hidden world."

Molly snorted loudly. "Black Heir? That bunch of vultures? Picking over the technological trash aliens leave behind when they have to get the hell out of Dodge in a hurry. They're just looking to increase their power base."

"Well, yes," said the Matriarch. "That's what Government Departments do. I understand there's a lot of interdepartmental jousting going on right now, as everyone fights it out for promotion. There are careers waiting to be made out of situations like this." She looked at me steadily. "Do you still consider yourself part of Uncanny, Eddie?"

"No," I said. "I only went along to be close to my grandfather. Now the Regent of Shadows is gone . . ."

"So who are you with now?" said the Matriarch.

"Remains to be seen," I said, not giving an inch. "Doesn't it?"

"You're family, Eddie," said the Matriarch. "You can always come home." She paused to glare coldly at Molly. "Even if you do bring some baggage with you."

Molly's head came up immediately. "Eddie! Tell me she did not just call me a baggage!"

"She did not just call you a baggage," I said.

"Yes, she did! I heard her!"

"Then why did you ask me?" I said.

"To give you a chance to say the right thing!"

"Now, you know very well I'm never any good at that," I said. "Can't we all just agree that everyone must have misheard and move on?"

Molly was still pouting dangerously, so it was probably just as well that the Sanctity doors burst open and the Serjeant-at-Arms launched himself into the Sanctity, armoured up and guns in hand, ready for action. And then he stopped, and looked around, as he realised there was no obvious trouble going on. He saw I wasn't wearing my armour any more, and immediately armoured down himself, rather than be outdone by me in the calm-and-controlled stakes. The guns in his hands remained pointed at me and Molly. We both made a point of appearing conspicuously unimpressed, while being careful to make no sudden moves. They were very big and very impressive guns.

"Stand down, Serjeant!" the Matriarch said loudly. "I am perfectly safe, and completely in control of the situation!"

The Serjeant didn't look like he believed a word of that, but he nodded reluctantly, and the guns disappeared from his hands. He drew himself up to his full height, looking more than ever like the world's most dangerous butler, and glowered coldly at me and Molly. We glared right back at him. Never show a moment of weakness to anyone in my family. They'll only take advantage.

"If it was up to me, I'd have you shot on sight," the Serjeant said flatly. "Every time you come home, Eddie, you bring trouble with you. When you aren't starting it yourself. I demand to know what has happened to the black box the previous Matriarch left you in her will! The contents of which could supposedly put you in complete control of this family, against all opposition!"

"Oh, that box," I said. "It's around somewhere. I'm sure I could put my hand on it if I felt I needed to."

"It belongs with the family!" said the Serjeant-at-Arms.

"But it was left to me," I said. "If my grandmother had wanted you to know about it I'm sure she would have told you."

"You must know you can't be allowed to keep it," he said. "It's an open threat to the family! What if someone else got their hands on it?"

"Who's going to take it from me?" I said.

"You can go now, Serjeant," said the Matriarch in her most commanding voice. "I need to speak privately with Eddie. And Molly. You need to go calm the family down and check out the security situation. Make sure no one tries to take advantage and sneak in while we're all . . . distracted. And for God's sake shut those bloody alarms off! Can't hear myself think!"

The Serjeant made a quick gesture with one hand, and all the alarms and bells and sirens shut down. The sudden peace and quiet was an almost physical relief. The Serjeant scowled at me, and then at the Matriarch.

"He broke into the Hall! Threw the whole family into confusion, did all kinds of property damage, and made a joke of our defences! Are you really going to let him get away with that?"

The Matriarch stood her ground and stared him down. "Yes. I am. Because if you hadn't let internal security become so slack, this would never have happened. He should never have been able to get this far! I'd say we owe him our thanks, for demonstrating so clearly all the shortcomings in our current defences. It's high time we ran more practise drills."

"I thought that!" I said.

"I know," said Ethel. "I heard you."

The Serjeant-at-Arms stared at the Matriarch with a look of betrayal, then abruptly turned around and stomped out of the Sanctity. Not quite slamming the door behind him.

"That man desperately needs more fibre in his diet," said Ethel. Just a bit unexpectedly.

"Can we please now return to the subject at hand?" said the Matriarch. "Because the case I was talking about is just the tiniest bit urgent."

"All right," I said. "What is this new mission that I'm so perfectly suited for?"

"And if it's so straightforward," said Molly, "why does it have to be Eddie?"

"Because there are . . . complications," said the Matriarch.

"Of course," I said. "Aren't there always? What kind of complications are we talking about? Things or people?"

"Let's just say I could use a Drood who isn't really a Drood," said the Matriarch.

"Ah," I said. "Are we talking plausible deniability?"

"Possibly," said the Matriarch. "If this should go wrong, suddenly and horribly and embarrassingly wrong, I don't want the repercussions coming anywhere near this family. It doesn't matter if you do something to upset the Government, they already hate and loathe you, with good reason. But I have to work with these people. The days when we could just tell Governments what to do are, unfortunately, behind us. Thanks to you."

"You're welcome," I said.

"You took away our authority! You neutered the family!"

"I saved our soul!" I said, not backing down an inch. "We were only ever meant to be Humanity's shepherds, not their owners! I did what was necessary to prevent us from becoming worse than the things we fight. Now, what kind of case are we talking about, exactly? Bearing in mind I still haven't committed myself to anything yet."

"Just a simple infiltration and information-gathering assignment," said the Matriarch. A little too smoothly for my liking.

"Good," I said. "Because there's something important I need to tell you first."

The Matriarch looked quickly from me to Molly, and back again. "This isn't going to be anything good, is it?"

"I have decided," I said, "that from now on . . . I'm not going to kill anyone. I have had to do that too many times. I am a field agent, not an assassin."

The Matriarch looked at me searchingly, not sure where this had come from or where it was going. "Has something happened, Eddie? You've killed your fair share in the service of this family and never said anything before."

"More than my fair share," I said. "More than enough."

The Matriarch looked at Molly.

"Don't look at me," said Molly. "I haven't changed my mind. He's the moral one here."

"This case calls for an agent's skills," the Matriarch said carefully. "Nothing more."

"All right," I said. "Give me the details."

"Then you'll do it?"

"Give me the details."

"The Prime Minister made contact with the family, earlier this morning," said the Matriarch. "Begging for our help. World leaders might like to boast to each other that they're free from Drood influence these days, but they still know who to run to when it all goes pear-shaped. Ethel, be so good as to play back the recording of my conversation with the Prime Minister."

"Hold everything," I said. "Ethel, since when have you been recording conversations inside Drood Hall?"

"Welcome back, Eddie! I knew it had to be you, once I heard all the alarms. This place is always so much more fun when you're around. Run the question by me again. I must have missed something. Why shouldn't I be recording conversations?"

"You've been recording *everything*?" I said pointedly.

"Well, not everything. Just the important things, that the Matriarch wanted an official record of, for the family files. I have eyes and ears everywhere, after all, and infinite capacity, so . . ."

"We are only talking about things that take place in a public setting," said the Matriarch.

"I haven't forgotten all those long, boring lectures of yours, about respecting people's privacy, Eddie. Even if no one has properly explained the concept to me yet. Or what it's for."

"Show me the recording," I said. "But we will be talking more about this later."

"Oh joy. Wildly looking forward to it. I'll bring popcorn."

A vision appeared, floating on the air before us like a disembodied monitor screen. I didn't ask Ethel how she was doing it. On the few occasions when I have been unwise enough to ask questions like that, I've rarely understood the answer. And when I have, I've usually ended up wishing I hadn't. She is an other-dimensional entity, after all, a Power from Beyond. That's all I need to know. Though I would quite like to understand exactly why Ethel has chosen to stick around here, in our limited reality, just to be near my family.

One side of the vision showed the Matriarch sitting calmly behind her desk, in her office, while the other showed the Prime Minister sitting at his desk in his office. She seemed entirely relaxed; he didn't. The Prime Minister was trying hard to look like a man of High Office and a World Leader, but he couldn't seem to meet the Matriarch's steady gaze for more than a few moments at a time. I got the feeling he was more distressed about the situation he was in than about having to beg the Droods for help. Something had seriously upset the man. And not just because he must know that if we did agree to help him out, he was going to have to pay a high price for it in the future. The Prime Minister started speaking, and I listened carefully.

"You have to do something!" said the Prime Minister. "Important secret information is being leaked from our most secure listening centre."

"I take it we're talking about one of those places where the Government spies on people who'd be very upset if they ever found out they were being listened to," said the Matriarch.

"Well, quite," said the Prime Minister. "The majority of the information being leaked from this particular station is of a highly sensitive nature, and it seems clear that only a very important person could be doing it. Because only that sort of person would have access to this level of classified data. We need a Drood agent to go in undercover, find out what's going on, and put an immediate stop to it."

The Matriarch smiled, briefly. "I think we can arrange that. Which particular listening centre are we talking about?"

"The very latest, and most important," the Prime Minister said quickly. "The most up-to-date establishment in the country. We spent a great deal of money on Lark Hill. We can't afford for it to fail so soon. It's our most wide-ranging eavesdropping operation, unofficially called the Big Ear. Their purpose is to monitor all forms of communication. They have a new extremely powerful and most secret device that allows them to listen in on absolutely everything without being detected. Phones, e-mails, computers—everything! Nothing is safe from this new device. The Big Ear is officially tasked and licensed to listen to everyone. Public and private, no exceptions. Including, of course, the most secret and secure information from every kind of source."

"No wonder you came to us," said the Matriarch. "If the people of this country find out that you've been spying on them . . ."

"It's for their own good," said the Prime Minister. "For their own protection."

"They might not see it that way."

"Which is why they must never know." The Prime Minister tried a knowing smile, but quickly let it drop when he realised it wasn't working. "We need a Drood field agent to go in and investigate the situation inside the Big Ear, because we can't trust anyone inside the centre and we can't call on anyone from the usual security organisations. Because they're not supposed to know the Big Ear even exists. We need to know if someone inside Lark Hill is selling secrets for money, or politics, or for what they think is a higher morality. The last thing we need is for this kind of information to show up on WikiLeaks! God save us from well-meaning people . . ."

"And," said the Matriarch, "you're worried about this new device of yours."

"Of course we're worried about the new device!" said the Prime Minister. "Sorry! Sorry . . . Didn't mean to raise my voice, but I'm really very concerned. If some disaffected person has gained access to it . . ."

"If we agree to do this," said the Matriarch, cutting firmly across his carefully rehearsed speech, "you will agree to owe us. I will tell you what and I will tell you when. And you don't get to whine about it."

The Prime Minister nodded immediately, trying his knowing smile again. "Of course! Understood. Yes. I'll leave it to you to sort out the details, shall I . . ."

The Matriarch cut off the connection; and the vision disappeared from the rose-red air.

"He expects this to go wrong," I said. "He wants someone from outside in the frame, to lay the blame on."

"Of course," said the Matriarch. "He's a politician. But I need you to do this, Eddie. Partly because we need the present administration to owe us a favour, something we can hold over them in the future— and partly because I want to know more about this new eavesdropping device they have that can do so much. They shouldn't have access to anything that powerful."

"Why do you want me specifically?" I said.

"Because you are not officially part of this family at present. Every-one knows you're affiliated with the Department of Uncanny. Which should make it just that little bit harder for the mud to stick, if it starts flying. If . . ."

"If what?" said Molly.

"If I knew that, I could send one of my own people," said the

Matriarch. "There's clearly something going on at the Big Ear that the Prime Minister isn't telling us, so . . . go in and sort it out, Eddie. Do whatever you have to, to get to the heart of things and put this right. While doing your very best to keep the family out of the line of fire. I've already made arrangements with the Armourer to sort you out a suitable cover identity with all the proper paperwork. You can go in as a security consultant from some real but minor organisation that won't even know its identity has been hijacked until it's too late. Do this favour for the family, Eddie . . . and you'll get what you want."

Molly looked at her suspiciously. "You couldn't have known Eddie was going to turn up here today. What would you have done if he hadn't been available?"

"I do have other off-the-books field agents," said the Matriarch. "Any number of them could handle an assignment like this. But . . . none with your experience, Eddie. Just in case it becomes necessary for you to do something . . . drastic. And, Eddie, you have to do this on your own. You can't take Molly with you. The Prime Minister would have a shit-fit if he even thought the notorious Wild Witch was anywhere near his precious new listening centre."

Molly sniggered loudly. "They've probably got special security in place just to detect my presence. Lots of places have. All right, I get it. You're on your own, Eddie. But you will tell me all about it afterwards, won't you? If you know what's good for you."

"Ah, the joys of a continuing relationship," I said. "So, I can go in as an expert supplied by British Security. A term vague enough to cover a multitude of sins, while still being sufficiently impressive and intimidating. As long as I appear to have all the proper clearances, and the implied authority that goes with them, no one at Lark Hill will challenge me. The Prime Minister will have informed them by now to expect someone. I'll just tell them I'm there to check their internal and external security measures, make sure they're up to regulations. There's always someone checking something."

"Remember, no one at the Big Ear is to even suspect we're interested," said the Matriarch. "We don't want the leak to take fright and run before we know how much damage they've done, and who they've talked to."

"Teach your grandmother to juggle eggs," I said. "Now, what did the Prime Minister tell you that you're not telling me? What makes the Big Ear so important to us, that we need to get involved?"

The Matriarch chose her words carefully. "Officially, the Big Ear was created to spy on terrorists, but really it's there to spy on people. All the people, all the time. So the Government can know what they're doing, what they're talking about, and what they're planning . . . so those in power can stop any trouble before it can get started."

"Trouble?" said Molly, frowning darkly.

"Anything that might make trouble for the Government," said the Matriarch.

"Listening to everyone, public and private?" I said. "Is that even legal?"

"If the Government does it, it must be legal," said the Matriarch. "They make the laws."

"And we don't like Governments that get above themselves," I said.

"No," said the Matriarch. "We don't. But I'm more interested in this marvellous new device they have that allows them to listen in on absolutely everything. Even we don't have anything that wide-ranging. I need to know what this device is, Eddie, and where they got it. In case we decide they can't be trusted with it. At the very least, I expect you to come back with a full set of plans so the Armourer can duplicate it."

I looked at her thoughtfully. "This new Prime Minister is a bit frisky, isn't he? Contacting you directly out of the blue and asking for a favour? There used to be whole layers of protocol for people like that to go through before they got to you."

"In the old days, he wouldn't have dared," the Matriarch agreed. "But things have changed. You changed them. As long as he's still sufficiently respectful, and scared, I'll settle for that."

"What," I said carefully, "are my instructions for this mission? Exactly?"

"Find out the source of the problem," said the Matriarch, just as carefully. "And then do whatever you feel necessary to bring the situation to a close."

"Ah, good," I said. "Nothing at all ambiguous there. But remember, I won't kill."

"I'm not asking you to kill," said the Matriarch. "Just asking you to spy."

"All right," I said. "I'll take the case. As a favour to you. But this is conditional on your agreeing that the family will use all its resources to locate my mother and father."

The Matriarch nodded quickly. "Agreed. We will find them, Eddie. Wherever they are. After all, no one can hide from us."

"Charles and Emily have managed pretty well so far," said Molly.

"Only because we didn't really care," said the Matriarch. "But I have a condition of my own, Eddie. And I'm afraid I'm not in a position to negotiate about this. Before you leave on your mission you must hand over the Merlin Glass, into the family's keeping."

"Of course," I said.

The Matriarch looked at me. "What?"

"I'd already decided to give the Glass to the Armourer," I said. "The damned thing's been acting up so much recently, it's no use to me any more."

"You're being very reasonable," said the Matriarch, clearly looking for the catch, and disturbed because she couldn't see it.

"I am being reasonable," I said, "so that you will be reasonable. Don't give me reason to regret it."

Molly came forward to stand before me. She planted both fists on her hips and glared right into my face. "That's it? After all we went through to break you free from your family so we could make a life together? You're ready to go back and work for them again?"

"Only because I have to," I said. "To get what I want."

"Give me time and I'll find your parents!" said Molly. "I have resources your family never even dreamed of. People will talk to me who would never talk to them!"

"I'm not sure my mother and father have time," I said. "They've been gone too long. No arguments, Molly. I've made up my mind."

She sniffed loudly. "That's what you think. There will be words, later."

"I'm sure there will," I said.

The Matriarch started to say something. Molly and I both looked at her, and she thought better of it.

"I'll go see the Armourer," I said. "You can ask me one more question before I go, Matriarch. Because I'm feeling generous."

"You do still have the black box, don't you?" said the Matriarch.

"I know where it is," I said.

"What's inside the box?" said the Matriarch.

"Sorry," I said. "That's two questions."

"You're keeping the box so you can always come back and take control of the family," said the Matriarch. "If you ever decide you disapprove of what we're doing."

"I'd rather not," I said. "Been there, done that, and hated every moment of it. I don't ever want to be Patriarch again—unless you make me."

"So I only get to be in charge as long as I keep making decisions you agree with?" said the Matriarch.

"Think of me as your conscience," I said. "With a really big stick. Because, God knows, this family needs one."

"Who gave you the right to sit in judgement on us?" said the Matriarch.

"Ask my parents," I said. "Or Molly's."

I left the Sanctity, with Molly at my side. Ethel called out a cheerful good-bye and closed the doors firmly behind us. I looked quickly down the corridor, but it was still empty. Molly and I both let out a long sigh of relief, grinned at each other, and strolled off arm-in-arm.

"I thought that went rather well," said Molly. "I told you that you'd have to make some kind of agreement with the Matriarch to get what you wanted. In fact, I think you got off lightly."

"Just the one case, and a simple investigation at that?" I said. "Very lightly."

"I don't think I approve of this Big Ear listening centre," said Molly.

"You're right," I said. "Only Droods can be trusted with that kind of power. Because we don't care what people think. It's probably for the best that I'm taking this case; I'll be able to find out what's really going on in there. And shut the whole place down, if necessary, just on general principles."

"What kind of amazing new device could they have that could do so much?" said Molly. "I mean, listen in on everyone, simultaneously?"

"Could be recovered alien tech," I said. "Black Heir has a long history of cleaning up things left behind after unauthorized close encounters. There's always the possibility they made a present to the Prime Minister of something they shouldn't have so they could get first shot at taking over the Department of Uncanny."

"Vultures," said Molly.

"It's a dirty job, but someone's got to clean up the trash," I said. "Still, you're not wrong; there's a limit to just how much reverse-engineered alien tech we can allow out in the world. Which could be just the excuse I need to pull the plug on Lark Hill."

"If you don't, I will," said Molly. "I will go there myself and hit the Big Ear with shaped curses, high explosives, and general insurrection."

"For you subtlety is just something other people do, isn't it?" I said.

"I'm really not keen on you working this case alone," said Molly. "You need me with you, to watch your back and keep you grounded. Especially in morally dubious places like the Big Ear. You know they always design that kind of building in a circle, so everyone can stab each other in the back at the same time. Watch yourself, Eddie. They'll all have something to hide, and really good excuses to keep you away from what you need to see, in the name of protecting their own territory."

"I did spend several quite successful years working as the Drood field agent in London," I said. "Long before I ever teamed up with you. I think I can manage just the one case on my own."

"Those were the good days, back then," said Molly.

"When we weren't trying to kill each other," I said. "For being on a whole bunch of different sides."

"Ah yes," said Molly. "Spies and secrets and lashings of violence. Happy times."

We shared a smile.

"So," I said, "what will you be doing while I'm gone? And please tell me it won't involve shaped curses, high explosives, and general insurrection."

"I'm sure I can keep busy," Molly said innocently. "I might go visit with my sisters. Isabella and Louisa are off on vacation together at the moment. I do need to talk to them. You're not the only one with unfinished family business, you know."

"Where are they?" I said. "Or shouldn't I ask, because the answer would only upset me?"

"It's usually best not to when the two of them get together," Molly conceded. "They always do so much more damage when they're together. But just now they're relaxing, on a grand tour of darkest Africa:

holidaying in a hidden world packed with dinosaurs and weird shit; visiting with the fabled Lord of the Crater."

"I met him once," I said. "Years ago, when he came to London in hot pursuit of one of his dinosaurs that had been kidnapped. A charming fellow, I thought—for a heavily armed barbarian in a loincloth." I stopped abruptly, and Molly stopped with me. We looked at each other for a long moment. "Molly, have you told Isabella and Louisa that your parents were killed by my grandfather, the Regent of Shadows? On orders from somewhere inside the Drood family?"

"Yes," said Molly. "We don't keep secrets from each other, like you do. Well, yes, of course we do; we're sisters. But not the things that really matter. So, yes, they know, but we haven't had time to sit down and discuss it properly as yet."

"The Regent is dead," I said. "And the chances of finding out whoever gave my grandfather his orders . . . are remote. It was a long time ago, Molly. Let the past stay in the past."

"How can I," said Molly, "when it will insist on intruding into the present?"

# CHAPTER TWO

# You Do What You Can for People. But It's Never Going to Be Enough.

went down to the Armoury. The family keeps it safely tucked away in a great stone cavern carved out of the bedrock deep under the Hall's West Wing. So that when things go wrong, as they inevitably will, usually in a loud, messy, and horribly destructive way, the damage it does to the Hall above can be strictly limited. The Armourer, along with his merry crew of highly intelligent and only slightly disturbed lab assistants, is responsible for researching and producing all the weapons, gadgets, sneaky items, and mean tricks that make it possible for those of us out in the field to do our job. The family armour is good; hell, the armour's amazing . . . but it can't do everything.

The Armoury is one of the few places in the Hall that actually feels like home to me. Everywhere else just reminds me of the harsh discipline, brutal schooling, and endless authority of Drood family life. Everything I ran away from, first chance I got. The Armoury, on the other hand, is where I used to hide out when I was supposed to be properly busy somewhere else; hanging out with the only member of the family who really had time for me. The Armourer—my uncle Jack.

When I finally passed through the heavy blast-proof doors and emerged into the long series of connected stone chambers that make up the Armoury, I was immediately struck by how unusually quiet and well organized everything seemed, compared to the barely controlled chaos I was used to encountering. Sudden lights still flared brightly, and chemical stinks hung heavily on the air. Lightning crawled across one wall like sparking ivy, and black smoke drifted quietly over what remained of a workstation after the latest unfortunate incident. But no one was paying me any attention. I could usually rely on the odd smile and nod, and even a cheerful wave or two, from the lab assistants in their charred and chemical-stained lab coats. They approved of me, mostly, seeing in me the same rebellious attitude they all cultivated as a matter of pride. But today, no one even looked up as I passed them by, all of them conspicuously intent on their work. There was none of the usual standing around in groups, discussing things at the top of their voices and inevitably coming to blows, none of the usual trying things out on each other. It was all very . . . calm, and disciplined. I hardly recognised the place.

Of course there are always going to be a few rogue elements. Two assistants were having a Drood-off, standing facing each other in their armour and trying to outdo each other as they shaped and reshaped their golden strange matter through an effort of will. Experimenting beyond the usual basic humanoid form, seeing just how extreme and grotesque they could become while still holding things together. Golden demons became gleaming angels, switching quickly from horrible propensities to amazing proportions, rocking back and forth as they added extra limbs or shaped exotic weapons out of their armour. But the new shapes inevitably faltered and fell apart, as the wearer's concentration wavered. The more outré the form, the harder it was for the occupant to hold all the various elements in his mind at one time. One assistant became suddenly top-heavy and fell over. I left them to it.

Farther in, a small group of lab assistants was forming a search party to locate another assistant who'd finally perfected his new invisibility field but had suddenly stopped answering their questions. They moved through the Armoury with outstretched arms, trying to find him. Of course, there was always the possibility that he'd just sneaked out of the Armoury and was hiding somewhere else, giggling a lot. It was what I would have done.

Two female assistants were fighting it out in the battle circle, with depleted-uranium knuckle-dusters, and shimmering force shields on their arms, while a small group of onlookers took careful notes and made a series of quiet bets. Not far away, two young male assistants were playing sock-me-rock-me with two giant stone golems. I'm almost sure there was a practical purpose in there somewhere.

And down at the firing range, one assistant had armoured up and transformed one golden arm into something very like a bazooka. While everyone else hid behind things, he aimed carefully and fired off a strange matter projectile. The far end of the firing range disappeared in smoke and fire, while the recoil blasted the assistant right off his feet and sent him flying backwards half the length of the Armoury, crashing through a whole bunch of things along the way. Some people just won't be told. There was general merriment from those watching, and some applause.

I found my uncle Jack sitting slumped in his favourite chair, before his usual work-bench. Which seemed a lot less crowded than usual, though his computer was still wrapped in long strings of mistletoe and garlic, for no obvious reason. The back of the Armourer's chair bore the legend *Sudden Experiments Make God Jump*. He didn't seem to be working on anything in particular, which was unusual for him. The Armourer lived for his work. But now Uncle Jack was just sitting there, staring at nothing, his gaze far away. I said his name a few times, and he slowly turned his head to look at me. He seemed older, tired. A stick-thin man with a pronounced stoop, a bald head, and harsh features. The bushy white eyebrows were still the same, but his normally steely grey eyes seemed oddly vague. His lab coat was sparkling clean and freshly starched, without any of the chemical burns or bullet holes that he usually wore as badges of honour. He looked at me for a long moment, and then seemed suddenly to recognise me. He smiled broadly, his gaze snapping into focus as his head came up, and just like that he wasn't some tired old man any more. He looked like my uncle Jack again.

He shook my hand firmly, mine almost disappearing inside his oversized engineer's hand, and he sat up straight in his chair. He was wearing a blank white T-shirt under his coat, with none of his usual disturbing messages on it, and that worried me, obscurely. The Armourer liked his T-shirts to make a statement, usually something offensive and wildly inappropriate. His own small rebellion against authority. I sat down on the edge of his work-bench, because I knew that always annoyed him. I waited for him to tell me off, and when he didn't, I was so shocked that I immediately got up again. I found a spare chair and pulled it over so I could sit opposite him, while wondering how I could tactfully ask what the hell was the matter with him.

"Welcome back, Eddie," said the Armourer. "Good to see you again. You don't come home nearly often enough. This is your home, you know. You belong here. Not gallivanting about with well-meaning second-raters like the Department of Uncanny. Yes, yes, I know, your grandfather did good work there. But they were only ever a Government Department. We Droods have the whole world as our responsibility. More and more, it seems you only ever come home when you want something from us. Why are you here now, boy? What do you want from me this time?"

"Didn't the Matriarch tell you?" I said carefully.

"What? Oh yes . . ." He leaned forward and scrabbled through a few desk drawers, before finally coming up with a packet of assorted papers that he thrust carelessly into my waiting hand. He settled back in his chair and smiled easily at me.

"There you go, boy. Standard all-purpose legend; all the paperwork and IDs you'll need to properly impress everyone at the Big Ear. Just fill in whatever username you decide to go with in all the appropriate places, and add whatever authorizing signatures you feel necessary. Just scrawl something—they never check. All pretty generic stuff. Just flash it around and glare at people a lot, and you'll be fine."

A really loud bang echoed from the far end of the Armoury. The multicoloured spaghetti of tacked-up electrical wiring danced on the walls, the lights flickered, and the floor shook. No one looked up. In the Armoury, explosions and worryingly loud noises were just business as usual. So I was genuinely surprised, and actually a bit worried, to see the Armourer jump and flinch, just a little.

I retrieved the Merlin Glass from my pocket dimension and handed it to the Armourer; he just took it from me absently and put it on his work-bench without even looking at it.

"That's the Merlin Glass, Uncle Jack!" I said.

"I know!" he said. "What do you want me to do with it?"

"The damned thing's been acting up so much recently, I'm not sure I trust it any more," I said. "It seems to be developing a mind of its own. Which is never a good thing in a device you need to depend on in the field. I thought you might be able to do . . . something with it."

"I'll look into it," he said solemnly, and then raised a bushy eyebrow at me. "I have to say, I'm surprised you're handing it over so casually, after you made such a fuss about not giving it up the last time you were here."

"I'm giving it to you," I said. "Not to the family. I trust you."

"Well," said the Armourer, "that's nice . . ."

I looked at him thoughtfully. "Uncle Jack. I've been thinking a lot about the Merlin Glass' origins just recently. The last time I saw the Independent Agent, Alexander King, he said he gave you the Merlin Glass. In return for a device he could use to turn off Drood armour by remote control."

The Armourer snorted loudly. "As if I'd ever give him anything he could use against the family. King lied. He did that a lot."

"So where did you get the Merlin Glass?"

"From the London Knights."

"Well, where did they get it from? How did they get their hands on something given to our family by Merlin Satanspawn himself? And why did they give it back to you?"

The Armourer smiled briefly. "You should ask them. Ah! Look who's here! Good boy . . ."

There was a loud clattering of steel paws on the hard stone floor as a large metal dog came padding forward to join us. A good five feet tall at the shoulder, it was all gleaming Art Deco steel curves, with a sculpted metal hound's face and glowing red eyes. It looked sleek and powerful, and strong enough to crash through any wall that had the nerve to get in its way. I'd seen something very like it before; in fact, I'd destroyed the original. Back when it was a robot attack dog, defending Area 52 in the Antarctic. I'd brought the pieces home as a present for Uncle Jack. I knew he liked jigsaws. It seemed he'd finally found time to put the dog back together again; along with his own improvements. The Armourer did so love to tinker. He made a fuss of the robot dog as it sat down heavily before him, its long steel tail hammering loudly against the stone floor as it raised its metal head to be scratched. I wasn't sure which of them was humouring which. The Armourer grinned at me.

"Eddie, this is Scraps.2. Much better than a real dog. I haven't been able to have a real pet for years and years. Not since the first Scraps exploded. It's not safe down here for real animals. For any number of reasons. Scraps.2 is much more . . . hard-wearing." He grinned nastily. "He gives the assistants a good run for their money and helps keep them on their toes. Don't you, boy? Eh? Who's a good dog!"

Scraps.2 was looking at me thoughtfully. He appeared to have a great many sharp metal teeth set into his powerful jaws, and a definite sense of barely restrained menace about him. I sat very still.

"Don't worry," the Armourer said cheerfully. "I scrubbed his memory cells really thoroughly before I rebooted his AI. Just in case."

"Then why is he looking at me like that?" I said. "If he doesn't remember what happened to the old him?"

"I don't know," said the Armourer. "Instinct?"

"What does he do here, exactly?"

"He keeps me company! He's very intelligent . . . though for a first-class robot dog AI, he does seem to be having remarkable difficulty with the simple concept of *Fetch!*"

"Perhaps he's just too smart to," I said.

The sound of loudly disagreeing lab assistants rose suddenly in the background. Followed almost immediately by the sound of energy weapons discharging, followed by explosions, muffled screams, and really bad language. Scraps.2 lurched abruptly to his feet, his eyes glowing brightly as his metal ears pricked up, and then he padded determinedly off to investigate.

"That's right, boy!" said the Armourer. "Off you go! You sort them out! Don't take any nonsense from them . . ."

"So!" I said. "What are you working on at the moment, Uncle Jack?"

"Oh, nothing much," he said. "Just sitting here. Thinking . . ."

"But you're always working on something!"

"I've been making a list," said the Armourer, looking vaguely at the papers scattered across his work-bench. "Of all the things I created for this family, down through the years. How many have become standard, useful items—like the Colt Repeater, or the portable door. And how many just worked for a while, then developed problems. And how many turned out to be something that just seemed like a good idea at the time. And you know what, Eddie? In the end . . . I don't think any of them really mattered. A well-trained agent is what makes all the difference out in the field. The man, not the weapons."

"I couldn't do the job without your help, Armourer," I said. And I meant it.

And then I got distracted, as a large eyeball fitted out with membranous batwings went fluttering past, pursued by a determined-looking young woman with a large butterfly net. Everyone else ignored them.

"Why do you encourage your assistants to work on such weird stuff, Uncle Jack?" I said.

"Because you never know what might come in handy someday," said the Armourer. "And it encourages them to think outside the box. Some of them are so far outside the box they can't even see the box from where they are." He stopped, and looked at me for a long moment. "They're a good bunch, Eddie. They do good work. But I'm still worried because I haven't been able to find a suitable replacement among them. Someone to take over from me, so I can retire. The assistants come and go, all the good boys and girls . . . excellent minds, but never anyone special. They mean well, and they turn out impressive work, sometimes, but . . . none of them seem to have that special spark."

He gestured with an only slightly shaky hand at two figures standing really close together, leafing through a thick file of reports. I recognised them immediately. Maxwell and Victoria, the Armourer's two most impressive and most irritating students. First-class scientific minds, and so in love with each other they couldn't help but get on everyone else's nerves. They would insist on sharing their happiness with the whole world, whether the world wanted to know or not. They were both almost indecently young for such senior assistants—barely into their twenties. The Armourer sighed loudly.

"Look at them! Love's young dream, and masters of mass destruction. Brilliant weaponeers, when they can stop cooing at each other. And they're the best I've got. I brought them in to help carry the load. To keep things running, while I'm . . . busy, thinking. I'm feeling old, Eddie. I get tired. I take naps. Maxwell and Victoria are good organizers—but have they got that special something that makes them Armourer material? They'd better have. There's no one else . . ."

"You've never complained of feeling old before," I said.

"Yes, I have. You just didn't want to hear it. Like everyone else in this family. *Oh, the Armourer's good for a few more years yet, so let's pile on even more work, and more responsibilities* . . . But I think I've done enough. It's time for me to put down the load and walk away. Well past time, in fact. My best years are behind me, Eddie; that gets clearer every day. It's . . . difficult, to look back at the kind of work I used to be capable of and know I'm just not up to it any longer. I can repair things, even improve on them sometimes. Like Scraps. But I can't innovate any more. I don't have the spark these days . . . But I can't stand down, can't let the family down, until I'm sure I've found a suitable replacement."

"Come on, Uncle Jack," I said uncomfortably, struggling to find the right thing to say. He was scaring me now, talking like that, but I didn't want him to see how worried I was. "You've got years of good work in you yet."

"Not many," said the Armourer. His large engineer's hands came together in his lap and held on to each other, as though for comfort. "I'm older than I look, Eddie. I'm wearing out, at last. Worn thin . . ."

He looked slowly round the Armoury, at his quietly hardworking assistants. "I used to know every inch of this place. Had a hand in everything that was going on. Knew who everyone was and what they were working on. Who needed encouraging and who'd profit most from a good kick in the arse . . . Now, I don't even recognise half of them. All the assistants from my generation are gone. And most of the generations in between. Which is as it should be; no one is ever supposed to stay a lab assistant. One way or another, they move on, hopefully to better things, in the family. You need to be young just to stand the pace here. I can't help feeling . . . I've outstayed my welcome."

I decided it was well past time to change the subject. Before he depressed the shit out of both of us.

"So!" I said brightly. "What new toys have you got for me this time, Armourer? What new guns and gadgets to help me brown-trouser the enemy?"

"Nothing," he said flatly. "If you really feel you need something, go talk with Maxwell and Victoria. They handle all that sort of thing these days. But you don't need my toys, Eddie. You never did, really." He broke off and gave me a long, careful look. "I heard what you said in your little talk with the Matriarch."

"You were listening in?" I said.

"Always. It's a matter of self-defence in this family. Forewarned is forearmed in the Droods. So I have to ask what's happened, Eddie. Something must have happened for you to decide so suddenly and so definitely that you're not going to kill again out in the field. To be just an agent, never an assassin. So what was it? What happened to change your mind? You've always known the ultimate sanction is always going to be part of the job."

"It shouldn't have to be," I said.

The Armourer nodded slowly. "Killing does take its toll. No matter how good the reason, or how great the cause. The ghosts . . . mount up. That was one of the reasons I retired from fieldwork, back in the day. Talk to me, Eddie. What changed your mind?"

His gaze seemed sharp and fully focused for the first time, as he gave me all his attention.

"You might say I was made to see things differently," I replied. "A sudden insight into what I do, and why I do it. And I didn't like what I saw."

The Armourer considered this. "I killed my fair share and more when I was a field agent. Rushing around Eastern Europe, trying to hold things together in that coldest of Cold Wars. All of them people who needed killing . . . There's no doubt in my mind that the world is a better, safer place for them being gone. But I never did it as often as your uncle James. The legendary Grey Fox . . . some say the greatest field agent we ever had. He always was more of an assassin than an agent. By his own choice. It seemed to come so easily to him. It never came easily to me. I did what I had to, when I thought it necessary, but I was never so . . . casual about it. James never gave it a second thought. But then, he never was one for looking back.

"Which is probably why he left so many bastards scattered across the world. Half the up-and-comers in secret organisations and hidden bunkers have his eyes, or his smile. I keep thinking we should do more for them. Bring them in, bring them home, into the family fold. Not leave them out in the cold. I do try to keep in touch with as many of them as I can."

He didn't mention his only son, Timothy. Who went rogue and became Tiger Tim. I ended up having to kill him. So I didn't mention him either.

"Was Uncle James . . . always like that?" I said. "A natural-born killer for the Drood family?"

"No," said the Armourer. "Not always. But after he lost his one true love, Melanie Blaze . . . well, he was never the same after that. She was a marvellous woman. A great adventurer in her own right. Lost in the subtle realms, on some very secret mission I never did get to the bottom of. I sometimes think, when he lost her . . . the best part of your uncle James was lost too. All he cared about after that was getting the job done."

"Did the family never try to find Melanie Blaze?" I asked.

"Not hard enough," said the Armourer. "Now talk to me, Eddie. Tell me what has happened."

"Molly and I paid a visit to the Department of Uncanny," I said. "Just to pay our respects, to the place where my grandfather fell. Along with so many other good people."

I told my uncle Jack the story of what happened there. A story I could never tell anyone else.

The hidden entrance to Uncanny lies in the shadow of Big Ben. Two armed policemen stood guard outside that very inconspicuous door, and I was a little surprised at how many of the everyday people passing by seemed completely unmoved by the presence of armed police on a London street. That's still pretty rare in Britain. But I suppose it's just a sign of the times. I headed straight for them, with Molly striding happily along beside me, and the police officers moved calmly but firmly together, blocking the way to Uncanny's hidden door. They weren't actually pointing their guns at us just yet. Which, given Molly's short fuse, was just as well. And then they clearly recognised us and ostentatiously lowered their guns. The one on the left actually saluted.

"Eddie Drood and Molly Metcalf, good morning to you both, sir and madam," he said respectfully. "We were advised you might turn up, and we have been given orders to allow you to pass."

"How very fortunate," murmured Molly, smiling sweetly.

"You know who we are?" I said, to the policemen.

"Not as such," he said quickly. "We were shown your photos and told to get the hell out of your way. It has been made very clear to us that we don't need to know anything about the door behind us or any of the people who might want to go through it."

"We don't want to know," said the other officer. "Some of us like to sleep at night."

"Very wise," said Molly. "If you knew what we know about what happened here you'd never sleep again."

"Don't mind her," I said. "She's just being herself. Has anyone else tried to go in today?"

"Not today, sir," said the first officer. "It's my understanding that the whole building has been very thoroughly emptied out and cleaned up over the last few weeks. All important resources cleared away, all bodies removed. You don't need to worry about disturbing anything. The forensic people have been and gone. We're just here to keep any poor innocent souls from wandering inside. You take as long as you like, sir and madam. We'll see you're not interrupted."

"Did you know any of the people who worked there?" said the other officer.

"Yes," I said. "My grandfather used to run the Department. He was killed there, along with everyone else."

"Sorry for your loss, sir," said the first officer. And give the man credit; he tried to say it like he meant it.

And then both officers stepped carefully back, out of our way. I headed for the entrance, and Molly hurried to catch up with me. I was a little disappointed that no one else had shown an interest. I had been hoping my father and mother might show up, once they heard the Regent of Shadows was dead. But apparently not.

I made a point of going in first, and Molly made a point of shouldering past me. Just to make it clear she was quite capable of protecting herself. I let her, since the entrance lobby was quite clearly deserted. The first time Molly and I had been there, it had seemed a cheerful enough setting, with flowers in vases, and restful colours, and nice paintings on the walls. Now everything was smashed and broken. The paintings had been ripped off the walls and torn to pieces. The comfortable furnishings had been reduced to wreckage and kindling. It had the feel of vindictiveness and spite, as much as vandalism. Dark bloodstains everywhere—old blood, long dried. Soaked into the thick carpet and splashed across the walls. No one had cleaned up; it was still a crime scene.

"I wonder what they did with the bodies?" said Molly, peering quickly about her, entirely unmoved and unaffected. She didn't believe in being sentimental about people she barely knew. "I hope they've been buried properly. The last thing this place needs is the unquiet dead wandering around, disturbing the peace."

"Heroes lie in anonymous graves," I said. "Comes with the job, and the territory. But not the Regent. Grandfather's body was recovered by the Droods. He was still one of us, after all. So the Matriarch sent in a special team to retrieve the body and take it back to the Hall."

"That was good of them," said Molly.

"Not really," I said. "They were just being practical. Drood DNA contains far too many secrets and mysteries to be allowed to fall into enemy hands. Or even the hands of people who might become our enemies at some future time. My family always thinks ahead. That's how we've survived so long. At least Grandfather Arthur got to go home at last. That's something, I suppose."

Molly frowned. "I don't remember receiving any invitation to his funeral."

"That's because there wasn't one," I said. "No ceremony, no get-together. It was all taken care of very quietly, very quickly. Because Arthur had dared to walk away from the family. And to make things even worse, he had become fairly successful on his own terms, without Drood help. So the family just did what was necessary to put him to rest. I didn't even know it had happened until it was over. Or I would have been there. Which is probably why they didn't tell me. Or you."

"Your family . . . ," said Molly.

"Trust me," I said. "I know." .

We walked on, through empty corridors and open rooms. It was all very quiet, since we were the only living things left to make any noise. It was like walking through a battlefield after the opposing forces had clashed and moved on. Signs of violence everywhere: broken floorboards, kicked-in doors, smashed-in walls. The sight of blood and the smell of death. The Drood from Cell 13 and his vicious clone army had made a slaughterhouse out of the Department of Uncanny.

"What about special weapons, and objects of power?" said Molly quite casually. "All the sensitive information in the computers?"

"All of it gone," I said. "Transferred to safe locations. Just in case anyone had any ideas about looting . . ."

"Oh, perish the thought," said Molly, grinning. "I wouldn't dream of such a thing. No. Not while there was anybody watching . . . Where do you suppose it's all gone?"

I gave her a look, and she shrugged prettily.

"The Government will only lock it away, Eddie. You know that. They won't appreciate what they've got. Not like I would."

"My family removed all the heavy-duty stuff, while they were here," I said. "Things we felt the Government couldn't be trusted with. Or isn't supposed to know even exist. There are special protocols in place, even for disasters like this. In fact, probably especially for disasters like this. I'm sure everything else has been locked up in the usual secret depositories. Until it can be shared out, among the other secret organisations. They'll all be struggling to fill the gap with Uncanny gone, and they'll need all the help they can get. This is just an empty place now. Waiting for new occupants. A new identity and a new purpose."

"Do you think they're going to rebuild the Department of Uncanny?" said Molly.

"Probably not," I said. "It failed."

And then we both stopped abruptly and looked around, as we heard someone moving about. Quiet, furtive sounds. The police officers had been quite certain that no one else should be here. We were supposed to have the place to ourselves. So whoever was in the building with us had no right to be there. I looked at Molly, and she smiled brightly.

"Maybe someone didn't know there's nothing left to loot . . ."

She concentrated, and invoked a quick-and-dirty tracking spell. A glowing green arrow appeared, floating on the air before us, pointing the way to the intruder. Molly set off briskly, and the arrow moved on ahead of her. I hurried to catch up. As far as I was concerned, barging in here uninvited was like desecrating a grave. Good people died here. The Department should have been left in peace. If there were ghouls or vultures rooting around here, I would make them suffer for their temerity. We followed the glowing arrow as it led us through empty corridors and past empty rooms, into the heart of Uncanny.

"Who could have got in here without being noticed?" I murmured to Molly. "There's only the one entrance, and that's been continuously guarded."

"All it takes is a moment's distraction," said Molly, just as quietly. "And may I remind you, you are listening to the voice of experience here."

"But they must know there's nothing left worth the taking," I said. "People have been in and out, carrying stuff off, for weeks."

"Hope springs eternal in the heart of the burglar," said Molly. "There's always the chance they missed something. Perhaps something very secret and very important that wasn't officially here . . ."

"Unless . . . this is one of the unquiet dead," I said. "Some very powerful individuals died here. If the forensic people missed something—if they didn't follow all the proper procedures—there could still be someone moving around. Some remnant or revenant, stumbling around and wondering where everyone else went. Not realising they should have moved on . . ."

"You and your imagination," said Molly. "Far more likely it's a burglar."

The arrow finally came to a halt outside the closed door to my grandfather's office. Where he was murdered. The arrow flickered, then disappeared. It had taken us as far as it could. A slow chill crawled up my back. I knew the Regent wasn't in there. My family said he'd been put to rest, and I believed them. But still . . . of all the places the arrow could have brought us . . . Molly moved in close to the door, and listened, and then beckoned urgently for me to come and join her. I leaned in close beside Molly, and listened. There was definitely someone moving around inside the room.

My grandfather was dead. I'd seen the body. With the great bloody hole in his chest, where that ancient and powerful jewel Kayleigh's Eye had been torn out by brute force. The only way it could be taken. I knew there was no way the Regent could be in his office. But a part of me still hoped, because it just didn't seem right that such a good man could be gone and not leave something of himself behind. For those who loved him.

Molly straightened up, gestured sharply at the door, and it sprang open, flying all the way back to slam against the inner wall. I charged into the office, with Molly beside me. And there, frozen in place by shock and surprise, caught searching through the drawers of the Regent's desk, was an entirely unremarkable young man. He gaped at me and Molly, and then straightened up quickly, backing away from the desk with both hands raised to show they were empty. He was wearing a cheap, ill-fitting suit, without a trace of character in it. It went with his face.

"I know you!" he said suddenly, in a harsh, cracked voice. "Oh yes. I should have known, should have expected . . . Eddie Drood! And Molly Metcalf! The runaway Drood and the wicked witch of the woods! I've read your files. Did you know they had files on you here? Not that there was much in them, of course. And what there was, was pretty contradictory. But then, that's Droods for you. And witches. But you don't know who I am, do you?"

"No," I said. "Who are you, and what the hell are you doing here? If you do know me and Molly, then you know better than to hold out on us."

He drew himself up and sneered haughtily. "I used to be a Shadow. One of the Regent's old Shadows, from the organisation he used to run before they lured him away to Uncanny. He took most of the Shadows with him when he moved; but he didn't take me."

"What are you doing here?" I said. And although I could hear how cold my voice was, he didn't flinch one bit.

"What are *you* doing here, Drood?" he said, lowering his hands so he could stuff them in his pockets and slouch defiantly before me.

"You have no business being here. You went away and left him, left the Regent and all his people here to die . . . at the hands of your own kind."

"That's not what happened," I said. He drew himself up haughtily.

"What are you doing in the Regent's office?" said Molly. "Bearing in mind that I am getting very tired of this, and am only moments away from turning you into something small and squishy, with your testicles floating on the top, and then Riverdancing on them."

He sneered at her, too. "I didn't come back to avenge the fallen Regent. Or mourn his death. No, I just needed to be sure he really was dead. For my own peace of mind. He was a great man, you know. Everyone said so. Including him . . . But not always. No, not to everyone. Not to those he considered unworthy . . . I didn't let him down! Not really. But he still wouldn't take me with him to Uncanny. In fact, he told me to stay away. Gave orders that I was to be turned away from his door if I did show up! Not that I would have. I have my pride . . . He should have cut me some slack! I tried so hard. Really hard. But he was just so old-fashioned in his thinking. He didn't understand . . . that you can't be strong all the time . . ."

I looked at Molly. "Are you following any of this?"

"So far, it just seems to be *whine whine whine*," said Molly.

I glared at the young man behind the Regent's desk. *"Who are you?"*

"I'm Marcus Turner," he said. "And you've never heard of me. It's not fair. It's not fair! I was going to be someone; everyone said so. Including him! The Regent of Shadows told everyone I was going to be someone important someday! But he betrayed me. Offered me the world, and then snatched it away again."

"Why?" I said. "Why would he do that?"

"Because I dared to disagree with him! Because he was old, and limited in his thinking! He couldn't see the big picture . . . Not like me. I made him the Regent of Shadows, you know. I made that possible. I was the one who found Kayleigh's Eye for him. And you don't even want to know how far I had to go to find the awful thing and bring it back. All the things I had to do . . . all the blood on my hands . . . Mine! Not his! I was entitled to something for myself. I was! For everything I went through, for him . . . I said to him, I said, we should break the Eye up, shatter the stone into a thousand pieces, so we could all have a shard. So all the Shadows could be untouchable, and unstoppable. We could have changed the world . . . But he said no! He said he'd seen where that led, with the Droods. He lied. He just wanted the Eye for himself. Old fool! We could have been greater than the Droods!"

"I am starting to follow this," I said. "But I really don't think I like where it's going."

"He let us down," said Marcus. "He let us all down. So I tried to take the Eye back, for myself. Who had a better right? But he stopped me, kept the Eye for himself, and had them throw me out. Out into the cold." He shuddered suddenly, and wrapped his arms around himself, as though to hold himself together. "But I fixed him. I fixed him . . . oh yes! I got the word out. On the one way the Eye could be taken from him, after he'd fused it to his chest. He thought he was untouchable, but I knew better!" He giggled suddenly—a high, nervous, disturbing sound. "I had my revenge! On him, and his whole precious Department! The life he built without me . . . That should have been mine. I wish I could have been here to see it when they came for him. When they all came crashing in, and it all came crashing down." He glared at me suddenly. "He did die, didn't he? Tell me the Regent died! I need to hear you say it. Tell me I didn't make all of this happen for nothing . . ."

"You're responsible for all this destruction?" I said.

He shrugged quickly. "I got the word out. To the Drood they don't like to talk about. And he did what I couldn't."

"Hundreds of good men and women died here!" I said.

He shrugged again. "If you can't hurt the one you hate, hurt the ones you can reach. Did he die with the others? Did the Regent die? Talk to me! I need to know!"

"The Regent was my grandfather," I said. "I found his dead body, right here in this office. He was a great man!"

"To you, maybe." Marcus was breathing hard now, his eyes wild. "But then, you're just as bad as he was. Eddie Drood . . . I've read your file. All the lives you destroyed to get your own way. To serve your nasty little family. And you dare look down your nose at me? He probably gave you all the breaks I never had. The breaks that should have been mine!"

"Why?" said Molly. "Why should the Regent have given you all these breaks?"

"Because he was my grandfather too!" shouted Marcus, his face crimson. "Oh yes! The Grey Fox wasn't the only one who left a trail of bastards behind him. I . . . am a bastard's bastard. Never good enough for a torc, only a quarter Drood . . . And never good enough for dear old Grandpa. But I showed him . . ."

"You're really claiming you're responsible for the Regent's death?" said Molly. "For everything that happened here? Why would you say that when you must know people will be lining up to kill you for it?"

"Because I want the world to know! I want them to know what he was really like, to his own grandson! I'm not afraid of anyone. I'm not afraid of you! Screw you! I fixed him, and I'll fix you too! I didn't just find Kayleigh's Eye; I went back and found another Eye!" He ripped open his shirt, to reveal a glowing gem fused to his bare chest. "See? You can't touch me!"

Molly looked at the gem thoughtfully, then snapped her fingers loudly. The gem stopped glowing, and fell away from Marcus' chest. It hit the floor with a dull thud.

"Fake," she said. "Not even a little bit convincing."

Marcus stumbled back a step, snarling and clawing at his chest. His eyes were wide and unblinking.

"How did you get in here?" I said. "Past the policemen on duty?"

"I have my ways!" said Marcus. "Special ways! Secret ways! You can't stop me!"

Molly ignored him, looking at me. "What are we going to do with him? Slap him down, drag him out of here, and hand him over to the authorities?"

"I suppose so," I said. "Even if he really did do everything he claims, he's just too pathetic for anything else."

"I am not pathetic!" shouted Marcus, actually stamping one foot in his rage. "I am a Shadow! And I came here armed!"

His right hand came forward, suddenly full of a heavy, glowing blade. It burned with a sick yellow flame. He swept the blade back and forth before him, grinning widely as it left crackling trails of unnatural energy on the air behind it. He laughed breathily.

"This is the Devil's Dagger! I found it! It can cut through anything, penetrate any defence. Even your amazing armour, Drood. I was going to use it on the Regent if he had survived . . . but you'll do. Or your bitch!"

He lunged forward, the glowing blade aimed right at Molly's heart. I armoured up and put myself between him and Molly. And as the glowing blade shot forward, I punched my armoured fist through his chest, and out his back. He stopped dead, looked down, and made a small sound. And then all the light went out of his eyes, and he just hung there, dead, transfixed on my golden arm. I pulled it back, and he fell limply to the floor. Blood dripped thickly from my fist. The Devil's Dagger was still in his hand, but it wasn't glowing any longer. It didn't look like much. Molly leaned over for a quick look.

"Another fake," she said. "No real threat, after all. Don't feel bad, Eddie. You did what he wanted. He wanted to die."

"I know," I said.

I looked at the Armourer, sitting opposite me. "And that is why I'm so determined never to kill again, Uncle Jack. Don't you see? It doesn't matter what he might or might not have been responsible for. I wanted to kill him. I was looking for some excuse to kill the man who killed the Regent of Shadows before I even had the chance to get to know my grandfather properly. I killed Marcus Turner because I could. Because I wanted to. And I don't think . . . I should be able to do that."

"Eddie . . ."

"How's Maggie settling in as the new Matriarch?" I said. Because although I was ready to talk to the Armourer about what I'd done, I wasn't ready to hear *him* talk about it. He saw the look in my eyes, and went along with the change in subject.

"She's doing surprisingly well. I suppose bullying all those gardeners for years was actually special training for running the family. She's showing a real aptitude for getting people to work together. Something about the position always seems to sober the person who assumes it. Much like your grandmother, Eddie. I'm told she was quite the bright young thing in her day. Always dancing and drinking and laughing . . . Yes, I know. Hard to imagine, isn't it? The position, its duties and responsibilities, does take its toll."

"Being a Drood takes its toll," I said.

"Yes. It does," said the Armourer. "But I still wouldn't swap it for anything. No one else gets to lead the kind of life we do."

"Which is sometimes good, and sometimes bad," I said.

"But always glorious," said the Armourer.

We shared a smile.

"Maxwell and Victoria, Uncle Jack?" I said. "Really? They're your best bet for replacing you as Armourer?"

"They both have first-class minds," the Armourer said firmly. "Underneath . . . And they're certainly a lot better at organising this place than I ever was. Look around you! We haven't had a major fire or an unfortunate transformation in weeks . . . And at least they've got each other. That's important. They won't end up married to the place, and the job. Like I did."

"You've had a life, outside the Armoury," I said. "Even though you weren't supposed to. I know all about your little trips to the Nightside and what you got up to there."

"No, you don't," said the Armourer. "Or you wouldn't be talking about it so casually. But, yes, I did get around . . . for all the good it did me."

He looked away from me, and his gaze fell upon a piece of discarded tech, lying on his work-bench. He scowled fiercely at it.

"There! You see? Look at that! That's what I'm talking about! Do you know what that is? Neither do I . . . I know I put the damned thing there, but I don't have a single clue as to what it is or what it's for. I must have known what it was when I put it there to work on, but now . . . I can't remember. There's so much I don't remember these days . . . And I just can't seem to give a damn any longer. When the family Armourer doesn't care, Eddie, it is definitely time to find a new Armourer."

"You've got years in you yet, Uncle Jack," I said.

"Perhaps. But not as Armourer. I've stretched myself too thin, boy, gone on too long. Extended my working life through questionable choices . . . There's always a price to be paid for such decisions. And the longer you put off paying it . . ."

I decided to change the subject again. If only because the Armourer looked seriously close to feeling sorry for himself.

"There's something important we need to talk about, Uncle Jack."

"Oh dear," said the Armourer, fixing me with a steady gaze from under his bushy white eyebrows. "That sounds serious. Did I forget your birthday again? I'm sorry, but I'm not good with birthdays. I don't even remember my own. Of course, at my age you don't celebrate birthdays—you survive them."

I waited patiently for him to run down, and then pressed on. "This isn't about me. It's about Molly, and her parents, and what happened to them. We need to talk about what you know, Uncle Jack. About the family's really secret agents. The ones who take on the kinds of missions the family can't officially acknowledge. Because we might be ashamed of them."

"Sometimes that kind of thing can be necessary," the Armourer said steadily. "I learned that the hard way, during the Cold War. You have to be prepared to make the hard, necessary choices. You do the things your enemy can't or won't do. It's the only way you can stay ahead of them, and maintain the upper hand. And then, afterwards, you live with it. We've all made all kinds of sacrifices for the family. And the very secret agents . . . are a necessary evil. Your uncle James used to run them. After he died, I inherited them. They trusted me, inasmuch as they trust anyone. I only know what they want me to know. They pretty much run themselves, following basic policy set down . . . long ago. So the rest of us don't have to know what they do in our name."

"Not even the Matriarch?"

"Especially not the Matriarch. She can't know what they do. She can't ever know. So that if necessary, she can plausibly deny it. These agents are . . . a family within the family. I don't even know how many of them there are. I'm just the contact point. They only put up with me because I supply them with what they need."

"The point is," I said, "would they know about the Regent's execution of Molly's parents? Would they have been the ones who gave the Regent his orders?"

The Armourer considered this for a long moment, and then shrugged tiredly.

"You know as well as I do, Eddie . . . this family has secrets like a dog has fleas. Nothing personal, Scraps. Scraps? Where has that dog got to? I'll see what I can do, Eddie. Ask a few questions . . ."

"You don't know anything yourself?"

The Armourer glared at me. "Don't you think I would have made it my business to know who made my father a murderer? I never knew anything about it—until you came back from Trammell Island and told me."

"You could ask them!"

"It's not as simple as that! There are departments within departments, and people who don't even talk to themselves about what they know. All I can do is see if some of them will talk to me."

"If what they do is so shameful," I said, "we shouldn't be doing it. The last great secret I uncovered, about how the Heart made our old armour, almost destroyed the family."

"Exactly," said the Armourer. "I'm not sure we could survive another upset like that. Some things have to stay secret. Because some things that may be necessary can never be forgiven."

I waited, but he had nothing more to say. In the end, I just nodded and got ready to go.

"Take the Bentley," he said suddenly. "You always loved that old car. She's yours."

"What?" I said. "You mean your Bentley? That classic old car?"

"I never get the chance to take her out these days," said the Armourer. "And she should be out in the world. She wasn't made to sit around in a garage. She needs to be enjoyed, appreciated . . . But mind you, take good care of her! And then she'll take good care of you."

"Well," I said, "she's got to be easier on the nerves than the Scarlet Lady. You know, the car the Regent gave me?"

"Oh yes," said the Armourer, "I know all about the Scarlet Lady. Including a few things she doesn't know I know. You wouldn't get me behind her wheel on a bet."

"Where did the Regent get her, anyway?"

"Not sure anyone really knows. Way I heard it, she just turned up at Uncanny one day, they took her in and gave her a saucer of milk, and then found they couldn't get rid of her."

"They adopted her?"

"More like she adopted them." The Armourer sat up straight suddenly, and glared at the piece of tech on his work-bench. "Yes! I remember now! Just a few touches, a bit of fine-tuning, and you'll be ready to rock! Off you go, boy; I've got work to be getting on with . . ."

I nodded good-bye and made to leave. Without looking up from what he was doing with the piece of tech, the Armourer raised his voice.

"Remember, Eddie. Anything for the family. Because the family goes on, when we can't."

I was heading for the exit when Maxwell and Victoria emerged from a side aisle to intercept me. They both still seemed impossibly young, but something in the way they looked and the way they held themselves now put years on them. We moved quietly to one side, out of the Armourer's line of sight, so we could talk together. Max was tall and dark and handsome, Vikki was tall and blonde and beautiful. Their lab coats were a pristine white. They looked like they should be starring in a Harlequin Romance. They nodded and smiled to me, diffidently. They hadn't assumed the authority of the Armourer yet.

"I gather he's told you," said Maxwell. "We're going to be the Armourer."

"Both of us!" said Victoria. "We're awfully proud, of course."

"Equals, working together," said Maxwell. "Though Vikki's the real genius, truth be told."

"Oh hush, Max! You're putting yourself down again, and I won't have it."

I couldn't help noticing they were holding hands. Though they did seem unusually solemn, for them.

"How did your uncle Jack seem to you?" Maxwell said carefully.

"Did he . . . make sense?" said Victoria. "Most of the time?"

"Why shouldn't he?" I said.

They looked unhappily at each other.

"Well," said Maxwell, "he isn't always himself these days."

"He has good days, and bad days," said Victoria. "Sometimes on the same day."

"How long has this been going on?" I said.

"Oh, not long!" said Victoria. "It was all very sudden, wasn't it, Max?"

"Very sudden," said Maxwell. "It was like . . . the last of his strength just ran out. And he's been running on fumes ever since."

"Look after him," I said.

"Of course, of course!" said Maxwell.

"As much as he'll let us," said Victoria.

"There must be something you can do for him!" I said, more loudly than I'd intended.

"If there was anything to do, we'd already be doing it," Maxwell said steadily. "But there's a limit to how often you can patch something . . ."

"Your uncle has already done an awful lot to himself," said Victoria.

"And since he won't talk about that, we can't help," said Maxwell. "If there was anything left to do, I think he'd already have done it."

"And in the end," said Victoria, "we're Armourers, not miracle-workers."

"When did all this start?" I said. "The . . . deterioration? He seemed fine just a few months ago!"

Maxwell and Victoria looked at each other again, choosing their words carefully.

"We're pretty sure he's been hiding it for a while now," said Maxwell.

"But he's been having off days for some time," said Victoria.

"You just weren't here to see them," said Maxwell. "That's why he asked us in. To carry some of the weight for him. His condition has deteriorated surprisingly quickly."

"It's worse when he gets confused," said Victoria, "and doesn't realise how bad he's got."

"He forgets who the Matriarch is," said Maxwell. "Or he'll ask for a lab assistant who hasn't worked down here in years."

"Just the other day," Victoria said quietly, "he asked for your uncle James . . ."

"It's always sad when the mind goes first," said Maxwell. "When the man outlives the legend . . . And he is quite a lot older than he appears."

"He should have retired long ago," said Victoria. "But he did things to himself so he could keep going. Out of a sense of duty."

"If he could be persuaded to retire . . . ," I said, "do you think he might improve?"

Maxwell and Victoria didn't need to look at each other. They both looked at me with kind but implacable eyes.

"Without knowing what he's done to himself," said Maxwell, "we can't know how fast he'll run down."

"But he can't have long," said Victoria. "I think he's happier here. Keeping himself busy."

"We're ready to take over," said Maxwell. "If he could just . . . learn to trust us, I think that might take some of the pressure off him."

"But . . . his mother, Martha, was sharp as a tack, right up to the end!" I said.

"She was a most remarkable lady," said Maxwell.

"Aren't you both just a little young to be the Armourer?" I said.

"How old were you?" said Victoria. "When you left Drood Hall to be a field agent?"

I looked around the Armoury—the quiet, well-organized, mostly smooth-running operation that had replaced everything I knew and remembered.

"This place won't be the same without him," I said.

"It will be different," said Maxwell.

"It will be better," said Victoria. "But we'll do our best to keep the old man occupied, and useful, for as long as we can."

"He still has much to contribute," said Maxwell. "If only he'd stop hitting his computer with that hammer . . ."

"Has he seen a doctor?" I said.

"He wouldn't go," said Maxwell. "So we sneaked one in, and he scanned your uncle Jack from a distance. Unfortunately, after everything the Armourer has done to himself, the readings didn't make any sense."

"Even the very best clockwork winds down eventually," said Victoria.

"The old order changes," said Maxwell, "but the family goes on."

I was on my way out of the Hall, actually headed for the front door and the grounds, when the Serjeant-at-Arms appeared suddenly out of nowhere, to block my way. I stopped, reluctantly, and glared at him.

"Really not in the mood, Cedric," I said.

"You rarely are. But the family comes first. Always."

"What do you want?"

"The Matriarch has decided on a new official policy for all field agents," said the Serjeant. "And you are back with us, as a field agent, are you not?"

"For now," I said darkly.

"From now on, all agents operating in the field must keep in regular contact with the family, through an individual designated handler. That means regular updates, a steady flow of two-way information, and readiness to obey new orders and instructions as necessary."

"I don't need a handler!"

"It has been decided," said the Serjeant. "All agents in the field. No exceptions."

"I used to have a handler," I said. "Penny. She was murdered by Mister Stab."

"After you brought him into the Hall," said the Serjeant.

"Don't push your luck, Cedric," I said. "Really. Don't."

"Your new handler is Kate," said the Serjeant. "She's on line now, waiting to talk to you."

"Hi!" said a bright and cheerful young voice, through my torc. "I'm Kate! I'm right here! Think of me as your backup and support,

Eddie. I'm here to see that you have whatever you need. I can provide information, weapons, and tech, and even have the cavalry ready to ride in at a moment's notice. But you need to keep me updated on everything that's happening, Eddie, so I can learn to anticipate your needs. Oh, I just know we're going to have such fun, working together!"

"Oh, this can only go well," I said.

# CHAPTER THREE

# From Out of the Past

O utside of the main entrance, waiting for me, was the Armourer's Bentley. I stood there for a long moment, staring at it, transfixed. Just the sight of that magnificent old car was enough to take my breath away. It wasn't simply a superb example of restored period technology; it was a work of art in its own right. Sleek and powerful, and very deadly. Though of course that last point really went without saying; this was the Armourer's car, after all.

A lovingly restored 1930s open-topped, four-and-a-half-litre, racing green Bentley with red leather interiors. And an Amherst Villiers supercharger under the long, gleaming bonnet. Along with God alone knows what else, after the Armourer finished working on her. Back when he was a field agent, Jack drove this Bentley all over Eastern Europe, all through the heights and depths of the Cold War. Stamping out supernatural bush-fires, stopping wars before they could get started, and keeping the lid on all manner of unnatural things. My uncle James might have the reputation, as the internationally feared and respected Grey Fox; but Jack did good work too, in his own quiet and often very final way.

Somewhat to my surprise, I found that the Serjeant-at-Arms had followed me out of the Hall and was standing beside me, staring

admiringly and just a bit wistfully at the Bentley. I wasn't used to seeing him display his emotions so openly. We stood together a while,
looking at the car.

"I do miss my old 1930s Hirondel," I said finally. When it became
clear that somebody was going to have to say something, and it clearly
wasn't going to be him. "Marvellous old car. My tribute to the Armourer's Bentley . . . But after I had to destroy her, back when I was on the
run from the family, I never felt right about replacing her with just
another Hirondel. She was one of a kind . . . And as the family does so
love to say, never look back."

The Serjeant nodded solemnly. "Of course. All you'll ever see are
all your old sins and regrets, piling up behind you. Which is why I
don't even keep a photo album. But the Bentley is a special case. One
of the family's official treasures . . . I can't believe the Armourer just
handed her over to you! Especially considering the appalling condition you brought her back in, the last time he let you drive her."

"Be fair," I said. "I had just been attacked by armed men and gun-
ship helicopters from British intelligence."

"Excuses, excuses . . ."

I looked at him. "The Armourer only just gave her to me. News
does travel fast around here, doesn't it?"

"In this family?" said the Serjeant. "If we could only harness the
speed of gossip inside Drood Hall, we'd have a faster-than-light
stardrive overnight."

"Were you and the Matriarch listening in during my talk with the
Armourer?" I said.

"Of course not. The Armourer would never stand for it. He can be
very old-fashioned about some things—and it's never wise to upset
someone who has a whole Armoury of weapons at his fingertips."

"Would he even know?" I said. "If it was Ethel doing the listening in?"

"He'd know," said the Serjeant. "Even in his current . . . somewhat
distracted state."

"You're right," I said. "He would know."

"Why did he give you the Bentley?" said the Serjeant; not even trying to make it sound like a casual question.

"I don't know," I said, quite honestly.

The Serjeant actually smiled, just for a moment. "She really is an amazing car . . ."

"All the very best hidden extras," I said, "for the agent out in the field who doesn't want to be stopped by anyone or anything. Bullet-proof chassis; machine guns fore and aft, firing explosive fléchettes at two thousand rounds a minute—"

"EMP-proof," said the Serjeant, cutting in. "Spell-proof, curse-proof, and impervious to all known forms of unnatural attack. Back when I was just a boy, I used to love paging through the operating manual when it was put out on display in the Library. Damn thing was the size of a phone book . . ."

"A lot of us kids did that," I said.

"And we all dreamed of being field agents," said the Serjeant. "Doing great and glorious things in the service of the family. Going out into the world, and being wild and free and glamorous, like the Grey Fox." He stopped, and looked at me. "You do know the cigarette lighter button actually fires the hidden flame-throwers?"

"Yes," I said. "And I know about the Overdrive, that can send you sideways through Space, taking short cuts through adjoining dimensions. I tested the Bentley out quite thoroughly the last time I drove her."

"No wonder she came back in such a mess," said the Serjeant. He looked at me suddenly and sharply. "You gave the Armourer the Merlin Glass, didn't you? That's why he's given you the car!"

"Uncle Jack can be very thoughtful," I said.

"I should have known . . . Why did you give him the Merlin Glass when the last time you were home, you were so determined not to return it to the family?"

"You might think the Armourer has the Glass," I said, "but I couldn't possibly comment. You could ask the Armourer if he has the Merlin Glass. Go on; ask him. See how far it gets you."

"This family . . . ," said the Serjeant. "It's a wonder to me we're all still talking to each other."

"So," I said, "do you still dream of being a field agent, Cedric? Rushing around the world being dangerous and glamorous? Like me?"

"We all have dreams when we're children," he said steadily. "Most of us grow up, and grow out of them. I am perfectly content being Serjeant-at-Arms. I get to protect the whole family from outside and inside threats. But I would still love to drive the Bentley, someday."

And I surprised myself then, by looking at him and nodding slowly. "You know, you could come with me for a ride, Cedric. If you like. We could take her out for a little spin, open her up and see what the old girl can do. I've got some time before I have to go off and save the world. Again."

He looked at me, and smiled again, briefly. "Thank you, Eddie, but I have to say no. I am tempted, but I have my duties to perform. Protecting the family."

"That's not what I'd call it," I said. "You enforce family discipline, and that should not be taken as any kind of compliment. It's your job to stamp out dissent inside the Hall and put a stop to any emerging signs of independence in the young. You're just as much a thug and a bully as your predecessor."

"Thank you," said the Serjeant. "I do try."

"Come on, Cedric, admit it! Really you think you should be the one running this family, because only you know what's best for it! You'd kill to be Patriarch!"

"No," he said. "I've never wanted that. I know my limitations. I have no ambitions beyond keeping the family safe."

"But what if I gave you the contents of the black box?" I said. "What if they really could put you in charge, despite what anyone could do to stop you?"

"I would destroy whatever was inside that box," he said flatly. "Whatever it turned out to be. Because no individual should possess that kind of power. The Matriarch only runs this family because we allow her to. She can set all the policy she likes; we're the ones who decide how it's carried out. Checks and balances . . . keep the ship of family on an even keel. I really don't care whether you approve of me or not, Eddie. I only ever do what is necessary to hold the family together." He met my gaze steadily. "You only have to look at what certain members of this family have become once they got the scent of power in their nostrils. Or see what others get up to, out in the field, away from a healthy sense of discipline, to be aware of what Droods might become without family concerns to rein them in."

"It's time I was going," I said. "When I find myself starting to agree with you, I know I've been here too long."

"Take good care of that car," said the Serjeant. "The Bentley is irreplaceable; unlike you. In her time, she's given far more good service to this family than you ever have."

"I'll bring her home safely," I said. I couldn't help but smile. "Who would have thought it? After all this time, it turns out we do have something in common after all."

"We're Droods," he said. "We are always going to have more in common with each other than with anyone outside the family."

"See?" I said. "You had to go and spoil the moment."

"It's what I do," said the Serjeant-at-Arms.

I strode over to the Bentley, and the bright green driver's door sprang open before me. I sat down behind the big, broad steering wheel, and the door quietly closed itself again. Proof, if proof were needed, that the Armourer meant for me to have the car. She wouldn't have done that for anyone else. Seat belts snapped into place around me, across the waist and the chest, strapping me firmly into my seat. Because when this car starts moving at speed, you can't afford to be caught unawares. The Armourer installed the seat belts; 1930s

Bentleys didn't have them. It was a simpler, more reckless age then. I hit the press-button ignition, and a whole bunch of glowing dials and instruments lit up, the whole length of the polished beech-wood dashboard. It was like looking at the bridge of the starship *Enterprise.* I hadn't a clue what most of them meant; it had been a long time since I'd paged through the operating manual. The massive engine purred like a great jungle cat under the long green bonnet, and then roared happily as I slipped the car into gear and stamped hard on the pedal. The Bentley surged forward, harsh acceleration pressing me back in my seat as we sped down the gravel drive, leaving the Hall behind. In the rearview mirror I could just make out the Serjeant-at-Arms staring wistfully after us before he turned away and went back inside the Hall. Back to his duty.

I slammed the Bentley through the Drood Hall grounds, and all heads turned to watch us pass. The gardeners and the security staff, the boys playing football and the girls riding winged unicorns, even the peacocks and gryphons. Some of the younger Droods waved, and a few even saluted. Though I knew better than to think any of those salutes were for me. The Bentley was just that kind of car. Family history, in motion.

I poured on even more speed as I reached the end of the long gravel drive and the massive iron-barred gates loomed up before me. I didn't slow down—and they didn't open. Because they weren't really there. The gates were just an illusion, as long as you're a Drood. Seen from the other side, they're an unbroken stretch of high stone wall covered in ivy. A Drood can pass right through, as though it is all just so much mist and shadow; anyone else will have a really nasty collision. We're not keen on visitors. They rarely mean anything good.

The Bentley glided through the closed iron gates like so much fog, and out into the narrow country lane that leads away from Drood Hall. And the moment I was out, and free from the constraints of family, I hit the control for the Bentley's Overdrive. It's a small red button on top of the gear stick. With an embossed tip, so the driver can find it by touch without looking. For if it's dark, or you're being shot at. You could tell everything in the Bentley had been designed by a man used to the pressures and demands of operating in the field. Where there's nearly always someone, or something, trying to kill you.

I had no intention of driving all the way to the Lark Hill listening centre, along hours of congested motorways and minor back roads, not when there was a much quicker alternative to hand. The Bentley came with super-prescient sat-nav. It didn't depend on information from satellites for global positioning; it just knew. The car's onboard computers used quantum description to plot short cuts through adjoining dimensions and territories, to take the car straight to the required destination. The Armourer did try to explain the theory behind this to me once, and I had to beg him to stop. I was afraid my brains were about to start leaking out my ears. I know enough to drive the car; I don't need to know how it all works.

I didn't even need to input coordinates for the Big Ear; it seemed the Armourer had already done that for me. Which suggested he'd already decided to give me the car, some time before . . . My uncle Jack might be slowing down, but he was still several jumps ahead of everyone else. It was good to know there were still some things in life you could depend on. The Bentley's computers calculated the quickest route to the Big Ear, through the smallest number of side dimensions, and then something on the dashboard chimed prettily to let me know we were ready to go.

(Don't ask me where the Bentley keeps her extensive computer systems; everything under the bonnet is a mystery to me. Never meddle with the Armourer's work. And besides, an old lady like the Bentley is entitled to keep a few secrets to herself.)

I braced myself as the whole car began to shake and shudder, and then she shot forward like a scalded cat. The Bentley accelerated so fast she broke the walls of Time and Space, and left the world behind. The surrounding countryside elongated into a long streak of distorted colours, as reality itself stretched and snapped, and just like that . . . we were somewhere else.

The world I knew was replaced by another, and then another and another in swift succession, as the Bentley drove sideways through dimensions. The familiar English countryside was replaced by a tropical jungle, complete with huge trees, dark shadows, and awful lurking things watching balefully from the gloom. Then the jungle was a desert, was a mountain pass, was a great stony waste. Day and night switched back and forth, flickering wildly, as worlds snapped by in a slipstream of motion. I drove under dark purple skies full of strange constellations, where the stars spun like Catherine wheels. The air was full of strange sounds and disturbing voices. A whole city sang a single great song, in harsh, dissonant harmonies. It snapped off abruptly as the world changed around me, replaced by a massive choir of whale songs, as I drove the Bentley through a great school of banana yellow whales, flying through the rain clouds. Followed by a terrible screaming of insane children plotting mass murder, and then one great Voice, impossibly distinct and utterly inhuman, speaking my name . . . until the Bentley accelerated even faster and left it all behind.

Different realities shot past like so many shop-window displays, Dopplering away behind me as I clung fiercely to the steering wheel with both hands. I knew better than to actually try to steer; the car knew where it was going. I just kept a careful eye on the view ahead of me in case we needed to defend ourselves. I didn't even try to slow down when things loomed up suddenly before me; I trusted the Bentley to dodge anything that needed dodging and drive right over everything else. The faster we moved, the happier I was. There was always the chance Something might notice me, take an interest in me, and try to follow me home. It's never a good idea to attract the attention of

Forces from Outside. I have heard stories of what happens when they decide to meddle with people . . .

Differing details accumulated in the worlds I passed through, until I barely recognised my surroundings. A series of strange cities swept by, everything from tall metal structures with flashing lights and flying machines buzzing around the tallest towers like pollinating insects, to huge tomblike castles with human-sized insects scuttling up and over the pitted stone walls, to shapes so abstract I couldn't make any sense of them. Fortunately, the Bentley never stuck around in any of these unnatural places long enough for us to interact with anyone who might try to impede our progress. Anyone or anything.

We left the cities behind, and passed through a series of forests. Bitter green foliage, then blood-red, then a sickly organic mess of purple and pink . . . The skies were still flickering from day to night and back again, flaring through a series of painfully bright colours. Sometimes I was driving up the side of a mountain, pressed right back in my seat, and sometimes I was dodging in and out of a labyrinth of sleazy back alleyways. Once, briefly, I was underwater. Dark green waters, with glowing fish everywhere. Not that I was concerned; the Bentley maintained its own special presence, its own scientific laws of reality, no matter where it happened to be. Nothing could touch or affect me, inside the Bentley. I couldn't even feel the deep ocean I was passing through. A pack of huge blue-grey sharks, each of them twice the size of the Bentley, swam alongside the car, sweeping in close to study me through dark, dead eyes. I let my hand drift nearer to the gun controls, just in case. But the Bentley passed on to another dimension long before the sharks could make up their minds about us.

We were driving across a wide-open stony expanse, miles from anywhere and entirely untroubled by any evidence of life, when the Bentley's alarms went off. Which came as something of a surprise to me, as I didn't even know the Bentley had alarms. A great blast of warning sound filled the car, and I would have jumped out of my skin if I hadn't been held so firmly in place by the seat belts. The alarm sounded like one of those emergency klaxons I used to hear in old submarine movies; they went off when the depth charges were getting a bit close. I looked quickly around me, trying to spot the problem, but the stony waste had been replaced by a blur of stretched colours, as we shot through worlds too quickly for them to register. The Bentley's long bonnet jerked back and forth before me, as though the car was no longer certain of where we were going. I looked at the dashboard instruments, but none of the wildly flashing lights meant anything to me. And then a voice came suddenly to me, speaking calmly and reassuringly through my torc. My handler, Kate, from back at Drood Hall.

"You've been hauled off course, Eddie," she said briskly. "The family has been tracking you from the Operations Room, and a whole bunch of emergency protocols just kicked in. People are running around in here like you wouldn't believe. Are you all right, Eddie?"

"Depends," I said. "Talk to me! What's happening?"

"You've changed direction completely, inasmuch as that means anything where dimension-hopping is concerned, but it does seem clear that you're not going where you were going. And that the Bentley isn't in control of your journey any more. Which is . . . disturbing. Nothing we know of should be able to seize control of the Armourer's Bentley from outside. That car has the same kind of shields and protections we use to defend Drood Hall. Sit tight, Eddie; a lot of very smart people are working really hard on what to do next. It should be possible for us to block out the exterior influence and return control to the Bentley."

"Good to know," I said. "Any chance you could shut off the alarm klaxon? Because the bloody thing's deafening me."

"Oh yes! Of course! Sorry!"

The blaring racket shut off, and I could hear myself think again.

"Have you told the Armourer what's going on?" I said. "Has he got any ideas?"

"Apparently he's having a little nap," said Kate. "And it's proving rather difficult to wake him . . ."

"Terrific," I said.

The scenery outside the Bentley was just a smear of chaos and a blur of motion, constantly changing. I had no idea where we were, or where we might be going. I wrestled with the steering wheel, but it wouldn't budge an inch. Same with the pedals under my feet. I even tried to access the onboard computers by shouting loudly at them; but they weren't listening to me. I was just a passenger, along for the ride. Of course, strictly speaking I always had been, but I hadn't minded so long as I thought the Bentley knew what she was doing. I even leaned on the handbrake, which was supposed to be the emergency stop for the Overdrive, but I couldn't move it. (I could have armoured up and used the extra strength, but I didn't want to risk breaking the thing off.) The Bentley wasn't responding to me at all any more. Someone else was in charge. And I really didn't like that idea at all.

"We're still tracking you, Eddie," said Kate. "You appear to be travelling farther and farther from the fields we know. Or at least recognise. Out beyond the spatial dimensions, and into . . . other realms."

"That does not sound good," I said. "Hold it—if I've travelled that far, how is it I'm still able to hear you?"

"We're connected through Ethel," said Kate. "Apparently, spatial dimensions don't mean anything to her. And no, I don't understand that either."

"Any idea what it is that's taken over the Bentley?" I said, trying hard not to sound in any way worried. "Or how that's even possible?"

"Has to be an Outside Force," said Kate. "Some Power, or Domination . . ."

"You're guessing now, aren't you?"

"Pretty much," said Kate. "Head of Operations just wanted me to keep you calm and reassured and in the loop . . . How am I doing?"

"Don't you have any good news for me?"

"We're working on it . . . Ah!"

"What?" I said suspiciously. "What do you mean, *ah*? That did not sound like a good *ah* to me!"

"Eddie, according to what Ethel is telling us, you've left the spatial dimensions completely," Kate said slowly. "Frankly, we're all amazed she can still See you. We haven't been able to track you for some time. She says you have now entered the subtle realms. You have heard of them . . . ?"

"Of course!" I said, scowling hard as I racked my brains for half-remembered lessons from my youth. "Yes! The subtle realms are the in-between places. Unfinished realms, where nothing is necessarily certain and physical properties aren't properly nailed down at the edges. Where the very laws of reality are strange, changeable, unreliable. And I think I felt a lot happier before I remembered all that. We're talking . . . broken universes, improved universes. Insane universes! I am getting really very quite worried now."

"Regions of Magic and Chaos," said Kate. "Where everything is always changing, just because it can. Eddie, can you still hear me? You're moving farther and farther away from anywhere we understand."

"I can still hear you," I said, as calmly as I could. "We're still connected, thanks to Ethel. Can she do anything to bring me back?"

"Ah . . . she says not."

"Why isn't she talking to me herself?"

"She says . . . because she can't interact with you directly without directly affecting you, which would be a really bad idea in your current surroundings. Whatever they are."

"Okay," I said. "Something has just rolled down the inside of my leg, and I'm really hoping it's sweat."

"You're not alone, Eddie. We're all here with you. Working really hard to bring you back from the subtle realms."

"Does Ethel know anything about what kind of people might be living in these places?"

"She says no people. As such. But apparently, there are sometimes . . .

visitors. Those who delight in such conditions. I get the distinct impression we're not talking about anyone you'd want to meet."

"Story of my life," I said. "Any advice?"

"Everyone here in Operations has your back," said Kate. "We're pulling up all the information we have on the subtle realms . . . In the meantime, see if you can do anything to regain control of the car, Eddie. You have to break free from whatever it is that's drawing you on. Trust me—you're not going anywhere you'd want to go."

"I already tried that! The Bentley isn't responding to any of her controls! I've been taken, Kate. Kidnapped. And I have to wonder . . . why me? And why now?"

"You have to try something, Eddie! We're losing you!"

I hit every switch and button on the dashboard, including the cigarette lighter that actually worked the flame-throwers, but nothing happened. And then all the lights on the beech-wood panel went out and didn't come back on again. Even the ones I hadn't touched. All the Bentley's systems had been overridden by the Outside Force. I told Kate, and then she was quiet for a worryingly long moment.

"We've had the Bentley's operating manual brought up from the Library to Operations," she said finally. "We're working our way through it as quickly as we can, but it is, after all, a very large book. With no index. Apparently . . . whatever it is that's happening was never meant to happen. Was never supposed to be possible . . . You wouldn't believe some of the protections the Armourer put in place . . ."

"I was worried Something Big and Nasty might take an interest in me, and try to follow me home," I said. "But it looks more like Something Really Powerful has taken a liking to me and is transporting me to its home. Either to adopt me or to put me in a petting zoo."

"You have an appalling imagination, Eddie," said Kate.

"Comes from working in the field so long," I said. "Where the worst possible scenario comes as standard."

"As long as you stay inside the Bentley, you should be safe enough," said Kate. "The operating manual is very firm on that. The car creates and maintains its own reality to protect and preserve the driver."

"I know that!"

"No, Eddie, please listen! This means something! The Bentley imposes its own scientific laws of reality on its immediate surroundings. A bubble of normal Space and Time, wherever you are. The car contains traditional cause and effect, and linear Time, no matter what's going on around it. So whatever happens, Eddie, *don't leave the car.*"

"Got it," I said.

And then I was rocked savagely back and forth in my seat, the belts cutting into me, as the Bentley's speed suddenly dropped away. As though we were crashing through a series of invisible barriers. I clung on grimly to the steering wheel with both hands, sudden lurches slamming the breath out of my body, until quite suddenly the world returned. Through the windshield, I could see perfectly normal Earth-style conditions ahead of me. The steering wheel was suddenly responsive under my hands again, and I hit the brake, slowing us down some more.

I was driving under a dark sky full of unfamiliar constellations and a really big full moon. I turned on the Bentley's headlights, and a blast of pure white light illuminated the scenery ahead. I was driving across endless open moorland, in the middle of nowhere. It all seemed very normal, ordinary, sane. Just another place. Had I really come so far just for this? The ground was bumpy and uneven, rocking the Bentley from side to side, but it seemed firm enough. I slowed down even more, so I could get a good look at my new surroundings. But there was only the moor, and the night, for as far as I could see in any direction.

"Hello? Kate?" I said. "Can you still hear me?"

"Yes, Eddie, I'm right here. But Operations can't track you any longer, and Ethel says she can only See you very dimly, from a distance."

"Am I out of the subtle realms now? I mean, back in the spatial dimensions at least? Because it all looks . . . solid enough."

"I'm afraid not, Eddie. Which means you can't trust anything you see."

"Can you find me a way home?"

"Ethel says . . . not. You're going to have to track down whoever brought you to wherever you are and persuade them to send you home again."

"So I'm on my own, then," I said. "No chance of backup, no one to turn to. Situation entirely normal, for a field agent."

I drove on, across the moor. There was a lot of light in the night, from the stars and the full moon, while a strange glow suffused the drifting mists, but even so I couldn't see a horizon anywhere. The moor just seemed to go on forever. It did all seem very real, and comfortingly solid, after everything I'd passed through on the way here. And it certainly didn't look anything like the chaotic realms I'd been warned about. My computers were back, so I tried the Bentley's short-range sensors, but they just basically threw up their electronic hands and indicated that the whole situation confused the hell out of them.

The fog curled increasingly thickly all around me, giving me only glimpses of my surroundings. Mud and mire, and thick tufts of dark vegetation, along with open stretches of standing water. I just kept going, hoping to reach someplace that made sense. Off in the distance, something was howling. My first thought was *wolf*, and then, *not quite*. There was something distinctly *off* about the sound. Werewolves, perhaps? The car's machine guns had special backup ammunition for special creatures: silver, wood, cursed and blessed bullets . . . but not a lot.

It occurred to me that given how much noise the Bentley's engine was making in the quiet night, there was no way of hiding where I was. So I might as well announce my arrival and let my kidnapper know I was here. I leaned heavily on the car's horn, and the loud blaring sound carried defiantly on the still air. It was immediately answered by more wolfish howling. It sounded a lot closer.

The Bentley lurched dangerously, as she ploughed through bog and mire, and unseen deep muddy furrows. I put my foot down and hung on grimly. The car kept going. Dark waters splashed up against the sides of the car, and even over the bonnet. And then I realised from the smell that it wasn't water. It was blood. I was driving across moorland soaked in blood. I turned on the windscreen wipers and hunched down in my seat. The car was supposed to protect me against all unnatural threats, but I wasn't sure whether the blood qualified. Maybe blood in the mud was natural here. And then I pulled a face, as I realised I was going to have to clean the car when all this was over. And caked dried blood can be a real pain to remove.

A massive circle of ancient standing stones loomed up out of the mists on my right, and despite myself, I slowed down to get a better look. There were more circles, inside the main circle—dozens of them, grey pitted stone menhirs, standing tall in the night. And every single one of the many stones was spattered with old dried blood. As though uncountable human sacrifices had been made in this place, under these stones, long ago. Like some terrible primeval machine, designed for slaughter. And I couldn't escape a very definite feeling that there was something moving, silently observing, from inside the circles. Hidden in the shadows, watching me with bad intent. I couldn't make out any specific shapes, but then, I wasn't sure I wanted to. I put my foot down again, and the car lunged forward. As I moved away, leaving the standing stones behind, the giant menhirs in the outer circle started spinning like a roundabout, round and round, faster and faster. And then all the inner circles began spinning round in opposing directions, until all the standing stones were sailing round and round like some out-of-control machine.

I drove on, keeping a careful eye on the stones in my rearview mirror, until I was sure I'd left them behind.

Not long after that, a cemetery loomed up on my left-hand side, and once again, against all my better judgement, I slowed down to look the place over. It appeared to be an old-fashioned burying ground, surrounded by low stone walls and a single pair of tall iron-barred gates. Which were, of course, standing wide open. I brought the Bentley to a halt outside the gates. The mists had thinned right out, as though to make sure I had a good view. I could see some distance into the cemetery. It was all broken crosses and shattered headstones, and a great many dark, gaping holes in the ground. Graves that had been opened and dug up, or perhaps burst out from within. Just looking at the place was enough to raise all the hairs on the back of my neck. Another bad place. And once again, I had the strongest feeling that someone or something hiding inside the cemetery was watching me from the shadows. I also had a strong feeling that I should get out of the car and go into the cemetery and investigate. So I didn't. Some impulses you just know aren't going to lead you anywhere good. I turned the wheel and hit the gas, and accelerated away from the cemetery.

Never leave the car.

The fog thickened again as I moved on, curling and roiling in the Bentley's headlights, glowing all around me with a sullen pearlescent light. The electric light couldn't seem to penetrate far into the mists, but I was still damned if I'd slow down. That didn't feel at all safe. It was hard to judge distances on the moor with no landmarks. No way to tell how much of it I'd crossed, or how much more there was to go. The whole setting had a dreamlike quality. The howling of the wolves was getting closer, now on this side, now on that. And above the wolves I could hear the wind howling, gathering its strength, building a storm. But although I could hear the wind, I couldn't feel the smallest breath of it inside the car. The Bentley was still protecting me from everything in this world.

A massive old-fashioned house appeared abruptly in the car's headlights, not far ahead of me. I swung the car around, and once again slowed down for a good look. If only because there was so little else to look at in the desolate open moorland. The house stood alone, in the dark. There was no road or drive leading to it. The house was huge, towering above me, with dozens of windows on several floors. It looked to be even bigger than Drood Hall. And the look of the place, the feel of it, was just . . . wrong. It didn't feel like a house, or a home; it felt like a tomb. A place of the dead.

Light blazed fiercely from the dozens of windows. More light spilled from the open front door. A sick, yellow, feverish light. Unhealthy. I could see human forms standing silhouetted against the windows, outlined by the fierce light. Moving slowly, ominously. And someone, or perhaps something, stood in the open doorway to watch me pass. It was big, filling the whole doorway, and there was something really wrong about the way it stood and held itself. Not human. Or at least, not human enough. Again, I felt an almost overwhelming impulse to stop and get out of the car, to go inside the house and find out what the hell was going on in there. I forced the impulse down, sped up, and drove on. Getting out while the getting was good.

Only this time, the house came running after me.

It seemed to just sweep along beside the Bentley, shooting silently over the moorland, maintaining the same distance from the car. I slammed my foot down hard, and the Bentley surged forward. The house kept up with me, racing along, the figures still standing silhouetted in the blazing windows, the dark presence still filling the open front door. A whole house moving like a ship under sail. Pursuing me silently, menacingly, as though we had unfinished business. I was just starting to think about reaching for the car's weapons systems when the house began to lose speed, and just like that it fell behind me as the Bentley roared on. When I looked for the house in my rearview mirror, it wasn't there any more. No sign to show it had ever been.

It occurred to me then that someone was trying to scare me. That this moor, this whole world, had been set up just to terrorise me. As though I was driving through an old Hammer horror movie. The standing stones, and the cemetery, and the old dark house—they were all standard horror icons. I laughed out loud. I had seen far scarier things in my time as a Drood field agent. And besides, I used to love all those old Hammer movies. Used to really enjoy staying up late of an evening when I was a kid, watching a horror double bill on late-night television. Sitting on that battered old sofa, with Uncle Jack on one side and Uncle James on the other. Feeling scared and excited and utterly safe. We must have watched every film Hammer ever made, along with most of the Amicus and Tyburn films too. I can still remember my uncle Jack getting quite excited when he saw that *Quatermass and the Pit* was coming on; and saying to me *You're in for a real treat with this one, Eddie.* And how right he was.

I used to love watching Peter Cushing and Christopher Lee, as Frankenstein and Dracula and the Mummy. And not forgetting that amazing classic *The Abominable Snowman.* Which I later discovered to be a lot closer to the truth than most people realise. You wouldn't think Droods would go in for fantasy horrors, given the truly weird shit we have to deal with every day . . . but there was a certain comfort to be found in watching Hammer's old-fashioned morality plays. Where Good and Evil were always so clear-cut . . .

So I just drove along, across the open moor, under the strange stars and the unfeasibly large full moon, listening to the wolves howling in the distance . . . and quite enjoying myself. Until a young woman ran desperately into the glare of my headlights. The mists seemed to curl back, to show her to me more clearly. A young woman, running with all the speed that terror and desperation could lend her. Tall and slender, with long dark hair, wearing a ragged white gown that shimmered in the moonlight. *How very traditional,* I thought. Until she turned her head to look at me, gazing wide-eyed into the light of my car's headlights, and I saw how scared she was.

She looked back over her shoulder at what was chasing her. I looked too, and finally I saw what it was that had been howling. A great pack of oversized hounds were chasing the girl, pursuing her across the uneven ground with appalling speed. Closing in on her. The young woman looked at me pleadingly and ran on. I changed direction and sent the Bentley hurtling forward, putting the car between her and the approaching wild things.

The moment the Bentley got between the hounds and their prey, the pack turned on me. They moved quickly to surround the car, running silently alongside, matching the car's speed effortlessly. Up close I could see they were huge, monstrous things, with taut, veiny skin and bulging muscles, jumping and leaping effortlessly over the mires and the ditches. And because they were so close I was finally able to see what was most monstrous about them. They had no heads. An old joke bubbled up inside me, almost hysterically. *How do they smell?* Hell, how did they see, to follow their prey?

They surrounded my car in moments, pressing in close from all sides.

The dogs in front looked to be getting too close to the running woman, so I opened fire with the Bentley's machine guns. The front-mounted cannon hammered deafeningly on the quiet, explosive fléchettes slamming into the hounds over and over. The impacts hit the dogs hard, throwing them this way and that, slowing them down but not stopping them. No blood flew up from any of the hits, and I couldn't make out any wounds or injuries. At this range the explosive shells should have blown the damned creatures apart. I switched to silver bullets, and then blessed and cursed ammo, all to no effect.

The headless hounds pressed in even closer now, threatening the car from every side. I reminded myself that the Bentley's chassis was spell-proof. If these things were the magical creatures they seemed, they shouldn't be able to get inside the car. They must have sensed that, because none of them tried to leap over the low-slung doors. Instead, they threw themselves against the sides of the car, hurling their great bodies into the metalwork with appalling force. The impacts shook me like a rag doll in the driving seat, as the hounds slammed the car back and forth, trying to force the Bentley away from their prey. I heard the sides of the car buckle, and then groan loudly as the metal forced itself back into shape. The Armourer does good work.

I turned on the car's emergency force shield. Powerful energies sparked and shimmered on the night air all around the car, but they didn't even slow the hounds down. The creatures just charged in again and again, slipping effortlessly through the force shield. So I turned it off. It used up a lot of power, and I couldn't risk draining the battery so far from home.

The headless hounds hit me hard, from both sides at once, and I had to fight to control the steering wheel and keep the car on course. I'd almost caught up with the running woman. And so had the first of the hounds. I hit the cigarette lighter, and fierce yellow flames belched out of the front of the car, enveloping the nearest dogs. They fell away, rolling on the soaked ground to put out the flames, and then they were up and running again, entirely unharmed. What kind of creatures were these?

One of them put on a burst of speed and got in ahead of me. It turned abruptly, and came straight at me. I put my foot down, intending to run the thing over, but it leapt into the air at the last moment and gained a purchase on the long green bonnet. Its heavy clawed paws scrambled for purchase, but somehow it held its balance, and advanced towards me. Up close, the lack of a head wasn't the least bit funny. The creature reeked of menace, and bloodlust. I slammed on the brakes, and then jerked the steering wheel hard left and hard right, but it didn't throw the hound off.

It forced its way forward, jumping up onto the windscreen and blocking my view, its massive front paws holding it in place. The metal frame buckled under the hound's weight, but the windscreen glass held. I armoured up one hand and arm, and grabbed hold of the hound's left leg, just above the paw. It felt reassuringly hard and solid and real, in my grasp. I clamped down with all my armoured strength, and the dog howled horribly. I hauled the hound off the bonnet and threw it away. It went tumbling through the air and crashed to the ground yards away, somewhere behind me. And even as I drove on, I couldn't help but think, *How can it howl, when it doesn't have a head?*

I grinned despite myself. These things might be disturbing, and really tough, hard-to-kill sons of bitches, but my armour could still deal with them. It was good to know there was something I could depend on in this ever-changing world.

I realised I'd lost track of the running woman, and looked frantically around for her. She was right ahead of me, running headlong with the complete lack of grace that showed she was on her last legs. As I looked, she fell suddenly, sprawling full length on the muddy ground. I slammed on the brakes and hauled the wheel right round, and the Bentley screeched and churned to a halt just short of her. I had to armour up to protect myself, to keep the seat belts from cutting me in half. I shouted to the young woman to get up and get in the car. She tried to get up, then cried out and fell again. She'd broken something. And the headless hounds were almost upon us.

"They're coming!" I yelled. "Get in the car! I'll get you out of here!"

"I can't!" she yelled back miserably. "Please! I'm hurt! Help me!"

I threw open the driver's door, the seat belts retracting automatically. I got out of the Bentley and hurried forward to stand between the fallen young woman and the advancing hounds, ready to take them all on, if necessary. And just like that, everything changed. The woman stopped her piteous crying and looked at me with a cold triumph. I stared at her stupidly as she rose easily and unaided to her feet. The headless hounds came running forward to surround us, forming a great circle, cutting off all hope of escape. They didn't look like pursuers any more. They looked like they'd caught what they were really after. The young woman in her long, shimmering white gown stood before me, tall and arrogant and in command. And I realised at last that she was the bait in the trap, and I was the sucker. I looked back at the Bentley, but several of the headless hounds had already moved in to block the way.

"Kate?" I said, through my torc, "can you hear me?"

But there was no response from my handler. I'd broken the connection when I left the reality generated inside the Bentley. I should have remembered. *Never leave the car.*

The young woman seemed to shrug, and her appearance changed in a moment. She was still tall and slender, but now she was wearing black motorcycle leathers—jacket and jeans and boots—covered with steel studs. Her face was high-boned and narrow, with her long, straight black hair hanging down on either side of it, and her skin was unnaturally pale. Her eyes glowed golden, without any trace of pupil, and her ears were pointed. If all that hadn't been enough, the aristocratic arrogance that she radiated would itself have marked her as an elf. She smiled at me with slow, cold satisfaction at having put something over on a mere human. Elves live to mess with humans; it's all they've got left.

The headless hounds stood up suddenly on their hind legs, and all of them were immediately elves. No transformations, no shape-shifting; just the dropping of a glamour. They were all smiling, and not in a good way. Which is pretty much what you'd expect from an elf. They smirked at one another and sneered at me, but it was still hard for me to take them too seriously . . . because they were all dressed in the height of Elizabethan fashion. Tights and doublets and thick pleated ruffs. Probably because that was the last time anyone had taken elves seriously. They all wore enchanted weapons at their sides. Glowing swords, and axes, and wicked daggers. I thought about the Colt Repeater on my hip, and then thought better of reaching for it. At least until I had a better idea of exactly what was going on here.

I folded my armoured arms across my golden chest and stood as tall as I could. "I should have known!" I said loudly. "You do so love to play games, don't you? So, whose little elves are you? To whom do you owe allegiance? Queen Mab? Or King Oberon and Queen Titania? Are you of the Sundered Lands, or Shadows Fall? And I feel I should point out that Mab is quite definitely dead. And this time she won't be coming back."

"We serve no one," said the elven lady; in a cold, harsh, thrilling voice. "We are all of us independent agents here. Free spirits, rogue elves."

"Ah!" I said, as a sudden insight hit me. "That's what you're doing here, in the subtle realms, so far from the Courts . . . You're on the run! You're hiding out!"

"What's that to you?" said the elven lady, smiling slowly, like a cat with a mouse caught between its paws. "What can it matter to you who we are, and who we once were? Do you think knowing such things will save you?"

"Do you really think you can kidnap a Drood and get away with it?" I countered. "To take on one of us is to take on all of us. And even Oberon and Titania in their place of power would hesitate to anger the entire Drood family."

"We are elves! We dare anything! Especially when your precious family doesn't have a clue where you are . . ."

I thought about mentioning Ethel, and then decided not to. You never know when you might need a trump card, or information to bargain with.

"There are long-standing pacts in place," I said carefully, "Historical promises and agreements, made between the Drood family and elven royalty. Or can it be that you no longer acknowledge these pacts? Have the elves of this place forsaken honour?"

The elves standing around stirred angrily, only to fall still again as the elven lady glared quickly about her.

"Your family made those agreements with the old Courts, with Mab and Oberon and Titania," she said. "We have all of us renounced those Courts, and are no longer bound by anything they may once have agreed to."

"Okay," I said. "Let's try something else. What am I doing here? Why bring me to this place, so far from anywhere?"

"Show me your face," said the elven lady. "It has been a long time since I have seen your face."

I was pretty sure I'd never seen her before, but I armoured down anyway. I could always bring it back if I needed it. But the moment my golden armour disappeared into my torc, and I stood revealed before them, a great roar of surprise went up from the elves, and the elven lady looked at me with something very like shock.

"You're not Jack Drood!"

I had to raise an eyebrow at that. "Never said I was . . ."

The elven lady scowled at me dangerously. So did all the others. I glared right back at them. Never show any sign of weakness in front of an elf. They'll only take advantage.

"What are you doing, driving Jack Drood's car?" said the elven lady accusingly.

"I'm Eddie Drood, Jack's nephew," I said. "He gave me the car."

She shook her head slowly. "You . . . are Edwin, son of Jack's sister Emily? The last time I saw you, you were just a babe in arms."

"What?" I said. "You knew me, as a child?"

"Yes. And here you are now, grown to a man's estate." The elf lady shook her head slowly. "How many years have passed, back on Earth?"

"Since when?" I said. "How long have you been here?"

"You were two years old," she said. "I was there for your birthday. And that was the last time I saw Earth."

"Ah," I said. "Then it's been thirty years."

The elves all looked at one another, but I couldn't read the expressions on their faces.

"Time moves differently in the subtle realms," said the elf lady. "We forget that at our peril. I am Melanie Blaze, Eddie. I was married to your uncle James."

I looked at her blankly for a long moment, honestly at a loss for what to say. Of course I knew her name, and her story. Of the one woman James truly loved; how she was never accepted by my family; and how she disappeared forever on a mission to . . . the subtle realms. At least now I knew why my family had never accepted the marriage. In the past, elves and Droods have defied tradition to get together in spite of all taboos and prejudice, the Blue Fairy being the most obvious result. But for the family's greatest field agent, the legendary Grey Fox, to declare that he intended to marry a pure-blooded elf . . . No wonder they still wouldn't talk about it. I realised that Melanie Blaze was still staring coldly at me, and I hurried to bring her up to date on the major changes in the family since she'd disappeared. Ending with the news that my parents, Charles and Emily, were missing and I was looking for them.

"Would you happen to know where they are?" I said. "Have you seen them . . . here?"

"No," said Melanie. "They're not here."

"I never knew you were an elf," I said.

"Few ever did," said Melanie. "Your family saw to that. Droods aren't afraid of anything—except a scandal inside the family. Anything that might make them look weak—and human. Even though James and I were properly married. We had a special ceremony, at Saint Jude's Church in the Nightside. Your uncle Jack was best man. Saint Jude is the patron saint of lost causes; it seemed appropriate. But your family would never accept that, so James could never take me home. Finally the family sent us on an urgent mission together. We thought that meant something. It did, but not what we thought. It should have been simple enough—a quick incursion into the subtle realms in pursuit of a rogue Drood who'd gone missing with a weapon she'd stolen from the Armageddon Codex."

"I never heard anything about that either," I said.

Melanie smiled briefly. "Your family does love its secrets. They sent us . . . because we were considered expendable. We tracked down the rogue Drood: Catherine. But if she ever had a Forbidden Weapon, she didn't have it when we caught up with her, here. She had something else, though, something really nasty. And she didn't hesitate to use it. Perhaps because she used it here, it nearly killed James, despite his armour. I had to send him home, and then stand my ground and duel Catherine to the death. When that was over, most of my power was gone, and I had drifted too far into the subtle realms. I was trapped here. I waited for James to return and rescue me. Or for the family to send help. But no one ever came."

"They said you were lost," I said. "And James . . . didn't know how to find you again."

"Did James ever speak of me after I was gone?" said Melanie.

"Not so much, to me," I said. "But I know he never forgot you. Never gave up looking for you."

"How can you know that?"

"From Uncle Jack."

She nodded slowly. "I like to think of James still looking for me. That he never gave up on me."

"I don't think the family helped much," I said. "Uncle Jack tried, of course, but . . ."

"How is Jack?"

"He's the family Armourer now," I said. "Has been for years. He's getting ready to retire."

"Hard to think of Jack as old," said Melanie.

I wanted to ask her how old she was, but this didn't seem the right time, so I approached the question obliquely.

"Are elves really immortal?"

"No," said Melanie. "We do die, eventually. James knew I would outlive him, but he loved me anyway. And I knew he would pass through my long life like a mayfly, but I loved him just the same. I thought . . . we'd have more time together."

"Why are you still here?" I said. "In this place? Surely your power must have returned by now?"

"Don't you like this world?" said Melanie. "We fashioned it just for you. The world of your dreams. Your darkest dreams."

"I love it!" I said cheerfully. "Just like the old Hammer films Uncle James introduced me to."

"Yes," said Melanie. "He did like them. I never understood that."

"I'm not surprised," I said. "It's a human thing. What's it like here usually?"

"You wouldn't like it," said Melanie. "You wouldn't recognise it. A place of elven dreams and desires."

"Would Uncle James have recognised it?" I said.

"No," said Melanie. "There were things, parts of me, that I could never share with him. He knew that."

I looked around at the silently watching elves. "Where did all your . . . companions come from?"

"The elves have always had a taste for the soft worlds," said Melanie. "Their chaotic nature appeals to us. And a world like this can be a good place to get away from it all. Down the long years the elves came here, looking to lose themselves . . . for their own reasons."

"You do know . . . James is dead," I said carefully. "Has been for some years now."

"Of course I know," said Melanie. "How could I not? I knew the moment it happened. We were always close. That's why I never made any attempt to leave this place. What would be the point? I had no reason to go home. Because it wouldn't be home without James. This world is good enough for me."

"Where are we exactly?" I said.

"A place of refuge," said Melanie. "For broken hearts and broken spirits, and those who wish to remain lost."

She didn't seem to know that Molly and I were responsible for James' death—and I didn't see any good reason to tell her.

"You thought I was Jack," I said. "When you saw the Bentley . . . after bringing it here. What do you want with Jack?"

"I hadn't thought of him in a long time," said Melanie. "He was kind enough to me, I suppose. Didn't give a damn whether the Droods approved of James and me or not. But he never came to find me, so . . . Then I caught a glimpse of his famous old chariot, speeding so dramatically through the adjoining spatial dimensions, and I remembered. I reached out with my magics and brought the car here. Because I have a use for Jack. Back when I knew him, he was fascinated by the possibilities of Time Travel. And I thought he must have a working device by now. So I would persuade him to use it, and take us back through Time, to save James. Make it so he never died. And then I could go home again, to him."

"Never work," I said quickly. "The Droods have never believed in Time Travel. Mostly because the few times we've tried it, it's gone really badly wrong." I didn't tell her about the Time Train, and Alpha Red Alpha. It would only have complicated things. "Trust me; Uncle Jack doesn't have a working Time machine! Really! The family doesn't allow meddling with Time."

"Jack will work something out, for me," said Melanie.

"That's not going to happen!" I said. "Don't you think Jack would already have gone back and saved James if he could?"

"He just needs the proper motivation," said Melanie. "I may not have him, but I have you. I shall send a message back to Drood Hall, explaining that. And making clear all the terrible things I will do to you if Jack doesn't do what I want. I will be cruel, to be kind to myself. I will have my beloved back again. Or the Droods can have you back in pieces."

"You really believe you can hold a Drood against his will?" I said.

"This world, this reality, exists because we made it with an effort of will," said Melanie. "We have control over it, and everything in it. Including you. There's no way out, Eddie."

It was my turn to fix her with a cold smile. "You've been away too long, Melanie. Things have changed. To start with, you don't know how my family feels about me. They wouldn't send you a dead dog in return for my safety." I stopped, and looked at her thoughtfully. "Indulge my curiosity; how were you able to kidnap the Bentley, snatch it out of the spatial dimensions, and bring it here? I was given to understand that was impossible, because of all the protections the Armourer built in."

"The Bentley was always James' car as well as Jack's," said Melanie. "So of course he gave me the secret override codes, for emergencies." She turned to look at the other elves. "Take him down. Hold him securely. Hurt him if you have to, but don't kill him. We need him alive, as a bargaining chip."

"You think James would have wanted this?" I said.

"James is gone," said Melanie. "And after the way your family treated me, I have no time for any of you. I will do whatever it takes to get my James back. He can forgive me afterwards." She glared at the other elves. "Don't just stand there! Take him captive!"

"Not going to happen," I said.

She ignored me, turning to the elf nearest her. "Contact Drood Hall. Tell them what they must do."

The elf nodded, then disappeared. Melanie Blaze looked at me coldly.

"Surrender," she said. "It will go easier for you."

"Sorry," I said. "I'm a Drood. You should remember that we've never given a damn for doing it the easy way."

I subvocalised my activating Words, and my armour flowed out and over me in a moment. I concentrated, and heavy spikes rose on my arms and shoulders. A long golden sword blade extended from my right hand. The elves murmured loudly, staring at me, fascinated.

This was new to them. They only knew the old inflexible Drood armour; now they had to wonder what else this new armour could do. Melanie studied me carefully.

"Your armour is . . . different," she said. "Changed radically since my time. Strange matter! Interesting. Strange matter comes from places like this."

I did wonder then if that meant Ethel might come from a place like this . . . but I made myself concentrate on the matter at hand. I reshaped my armour to make it more martial-looking and more threatening, and the watching elves murmured loudly again. I swept my golden blade back and forth before me.

"Take me down," I said. "Go on, give it a try. See how far it gets you."

The elves stepped forward, drawing their enchanted blades. Slender swords and heavy axes that shone brightly in the night, crawling with elven magics. Anywhere else, I would have backed my strange matter armour against any number of elven blades; but this wasn't anywhere else, and I wasn't sure of the ground rules here. If the elves really had fashioned this world through willpower alone, it could be that the rules were whatever they decided the rules were. But on the other hand . . . I was here now, and I had a pretty strong will of my own. The elves moved in, and I braced myself.

The nearest elf launched himself at me, moving impossibly quickly, raising his glowing battle-axe and swinging it down with vicious force. I put up my golden sword to block it, and the enchanted blade shattered against it, falling away in a dozen pieces. If strange matter really did come from around here, apparently it had the home advantage. The elf cried out in shock and horror as his axe fell apart, and then he backed quickly away from me. The other elves looked at him, and then at one another; and made no move to approach me. I swept my long golden blade back and forth, waiting.

"There's only one of him!" Melanie said loudly. "And an army of you!"

"One Drood is enough," I said.

And then the elf who'd disappeared, sent to make contact with Drood Hall, suddenly reappeared. He hurried forward and spoke quietly and urgently with Melanie. And just like that, all the strength and purpose went out of her. She looked older, and terribly tired. Almost haggard. She gestured sharply at the other elves and they sheathed their weapons. Then Melanie Blaze looked at me.

"It's over," she said. "You can go, Eddie. It doesn't matter any more."

"What?" I said. "I don't understand. What's happened?"

"Go home, Eddie."

She gestured briefly and a Door appeared, not far from the Bentley. A Door back to the spatial dimensions. I could tell. I looked at the elves standing between me and the car, but they were already walking away. I pulled my sword back into my golden glove and hurried over to the Bentley. I sat behind the wheel and armoured down, as the seat belts snapped into place. I fired the car up and headed for the Door. Before Melanie could change her mind.

I looked for her, but she'd already disappeared. One by one, the other elves were blinking out of existence. I steered the Bentley carefully through the open Door. The soft world was already starting to fade away; turning into something else. Something I was pretty sure I'd rather not see. I kept my gaze away from the rearview mirror, and gunned the Bentley.

And wondered if I'd ever find out what the hell that was all about.

# CHAPTER FOUR

# Keeping an Ear on the World

A blast of brilliant sunlight hit the windscreen as the Bentley roared through the Door, out of the subtle realms, and back into the world. A long country lane stretched away before me, bounded on both sides by low stone walls. I slammed on the brakes, but I had the whole road to myself. Even the fields beyond the walls were open and empty, just grazing land for a few incurious cows. The sun was bright, the sky was blue, and everything looked reassuringly real and solid again.

I took a moment then to access the Bentley's computers and have them flash up a detailed local map on the inside of the windscreen. The Bentley only looks old-fashioned; the Armourer would never send an agent out into the field without everything he needed to get the job done. It quickly became clear that the Door had delivered me just a few miles short of the Lark Hill Centre, home to the Big Ear. Which raised a couple of rather interesting thoughts.

The first being, how did Melanie Blaze know where I was going? I never told her . . . though I suppose she could have hacked my car's computers. Elf magic prides itself on being sneaky. And second, if she could open a Door directly back to this reality, she wasn't trapped in the subtle realms. She could have come home anytime. Perhaps she was telling the truth after all. That this world just wasn't worth it without my uncle James in it. I shut down the information on the windscreen and headed for Lark Hill. I still had a mission to complete.

Kate's voice rang suddenly in my ear. "Eddie! Eddie, can you hear me?"

"Yes! Yes, I can hear you! Now will you please turn down the volume before you have me off the road and into a hedge!"

"Well, where the hell have you been?" said Kate at a more reasonable level. "We've all been on tenterhooks since you went quiet. What's been happening?"

"Beats the hell out of me," I said. "Let's just say I got lost for a while. I'm back now. I'd settle for that if I was you."

"Eddie . . ."

"I'm almost at the Big Ear."

"Already? What kind of short cut did you take?"

"Really don't want to talk about it," I said.

"Keep in contact," said Kate, after an only slightly ominous pause. "I can only advise you properly if I'm kept in the loop."

Her voice went blessedly quiet, and I was left to concentrate on my thoughts and my driving. If I had to have a family overseer, I was going to have to work out some kind of off switch so I could call the inside of my head my own. I wasn't sure why I hadn't told her about Melanie Blaze. I think it was because the family just didn't need to know. She was none of their business any more.

I followed the long, curving country lane as it passed between fields full of waving corn and hulking farm machinery, until finally it took a sharp turn to the left and cut across a wide-open moor. After a couple of miles of almost nothing, the road came to a sudden halt before a pair of massive steel-mesh gates standing upright and alone in the middle of nowhere, completely blocking off the road. Barbed-wire fences extended away in both directions. No name, no warning signs—just two uniformed soldiers carrying automatic weapons. They took up positions in front of the gates as I approached, covering me with their guns.

I eased the Bentley to a halt and gave the two soldiers my best *I have every right to be here* smile. I took my time pulling out my prepared documents, since both soldiers had the look of men who wouldn't re-act well to sudden movements. One soldier shouldered his weapon, came forward, and took his time sorting through my papers, one page at a time. I wasn't worried. The Armourer always did good work.

I'd already decided this wasn't a case for Shaman Bond, when I'd filled in the details earlier. His reputation wouldn't be of any use in a situation like this; in fact, it would probably be enough to get me shot on the spot, just on general principles. The Big Ear might specialize in security work, but it was still a military establishment. So for this mis-sion I was using an old family name, Sebastian Graves. He had a tradi-tion of turning up at places where absolutely no one would be pleased to see him.

The soldier finally nodded reluctantly and handed the papers back to me. I accepted them with a *told you so* smile, and he stepped back and gestured to his companion. The other soldier opened the gates, stepped quickly back, and actually saluted me as I drove through. I approved of that. I don't get saluted nearly often enough.

The road carried on for another half-mile, and then dropped sharply away before me, plunging down into the earth through a steel-walled tunnel illuminated by harsh fluorescent lighting. The roar of the Bentley's engine was painfully loud in the enclosed space. Some-body should have told me Lark Hill Centre was an underground bunker. I contacted Kate.

"The information was there, in the briefing notes," she said pa-tiently. "But you didn't bother to read all the way through, did you?"

"I may have skimmed," I said. "I really don't like underground bases . . . They're always so much harder to fight your way out of. I was expecting some kind of high-tech establishment, with big windows and lots of antennae and dishes and things . . ."

"You quaint old-fashioned thing, you," said Kate.

The tunnel finally levelled off and opened out into a vast underground garage half full of assorted military vehicles. A small group of uniformed soldiers was waiting for me, before the only obvious exit. I goosed the Bentley's engine just enough to make it roar, and then screeched to a halt right in front of the soldiers. A few of them actually flinched. I shut down the engine and took my time getting out of the car. I didn't want these military types to think they could hurry me.

Half a dozen soldiers immediately surrounded the Bentley, covering me with really big guns. They'd noticed the dark blood from the soft world splashed across the car's sides and bonnet. Their commanding officer stood his ground and looked me over with open disapproval. A large man, with a barrel chest and broad shoulders that strained his spotless uniform to the breaking point. Well into middle age, with close-cropped iron-grey hair and a face deeply etched with the harsh lines of experience, he looked like he ate spies for breakfast and crapped bullets. I just knew we weren't going to get on. I gave him my most charming smile, but he only thrust out a hand for my identifying documents.

I handed them over, and he took his time working his way through them, checking every detail against information already listed on his clipboard. Clearly looking for something out of place, so he could deny me entrance to his precious base. I'd met his type before. Hard-core military, determined not to be pushed around by some mere civilian. I leaned casually against the Bentley and smiled meaninglessly at the soldiers. They just stared steadily back, watching me carefully, still covering me with their guns. The commanding officer finally reached the last page in my documents, checked the very last signature, and scowled fiercely at me before reluctantly handing the papers back.

"Commander Donald Fletcher, Mister Graves. I am in charge of this installation."

"Good to meet you, Commander," I said, still smiling remorselessly. "What nice tunnels you have. And a really big garage. Can't help noticing those are all military vehicles—not a civilian car anywhere."

"This is a military base," said the Commander. "We don't get many visitors. Security is paramount at Lark Hill. Your papers appear to be in order; I'll check them again against the security computers once we get inside. I can't allow you access to the more secure areas of this installation until you provide fingerprints, a retina scan, and a DNA sample."

"That . . . is not going to happen," I said. "You don't have the security clearance for that kind of information."

He smiled, for the first time. "Then you're not setting foot inside my base."

"Try to stop me," I said. I wasn't smiling any more. "You've seen my authority, Commander. I could shoot you, right now, and no one would even slap my wrist afterwards. Or, more pertinently; I could make one phone call and have you removed as Commander of Lark Hill. Your own soldiers would frog-march you out of here. You've seen my papers; for as long as I'm here, I outrank you. Commander."

He glared at me, at a loss for anything to say. He knew I wasn't exaggerating. The documents the Armourer provided were unimpeachable. The soldiers were watching the Commander out of the corners of their eyes. He must have noticed, because he nodded stiffly to me, stepped back, and indicated the exit behind him. The door swung open, and the soldiers fell back on two sides to form an honour guard for me to walk through.

I made a point of not noticing or caring, turned back to the Bentley, and activated the car's security system. The Bentley made a series of loud and ostentatiously dangerous noises, then settled down again. Like a predator pretending it was asleep.

"I'll have someone park your car out of the way," said the Commander.

"No you won't," I said. "No one touches this car but me. She can look after herself. And don't let anyone get too close. I haven't fed her recently."

The soldiers looked at the Bentley, and then looked quickly away again. Because they could all feel the car looking back at them, in a thoughtful sort of way. The Commander shook his head disgustedly. He was clearly old-school military, with no time for anyone outside the recognised chain of command. Which left him vulnerable to people like me, who operate outside the system and don't give a damn. Fortunately, he thought I was just another security expert, and I was determined to keep it that way for as long as possible. People in authority tend to clam up once they know they're in the presence of a Drood.

The Commander led the way through the open door. I looked hopefully at the honour guard of soldiers, in case they felt moved to salute me, but none of them did. Beyond the door lay just the kind of high-tech establishment I'd been expecting. Brightly lit corridors, gleaming white walls, all very calm and peaceful, with surveillance cameras everywhere. I had no doubt there would be more-sophisticated systems operating as well, hidden away from the naked eye.

People hurried back and forth, nodding to the Commander and shooting suspicious glances at me, all of them doing their best to look as though they were on their way somewhere important, to do something vital, and possibly even urgent. I wasn't fooled. I knew that look. It was the same expression I used to put on when I went striding purposefully through Drood Hall as a teenager, pretending to be frightfully busy so the family wouldn't find me some real work to do. Interestingly, none of the people I passed were soldiers. No military uniforms, just cheap suits and the occasional white lab coat. Scientists and technicians, the lot of them. The Big Ear might be a military installation, but its work was still strictly scientific in nature. Despite all the airs and graces the Commander gave himself.

Give the man his due; he went out of his way to give me the grand tour. I was taken in and out of endless offices and workrooms, where people sat in long rows, staring fixedly at computer screens or listening to headphones, occasionally bursting into flurries of sudden movement as they entered new information into the system. Dozens of men and women, watching the world and making long notes as to what it was up to. Studying video feeds, listening in on conversations, reading endless streams of e-mails. Doing their best to put it all together and make useful connections. Sorting out the dangerous wheat from the babble of chaff.

No one spoke to anyone else. They were doing important work, and they took it all very seriously. I indicated to the Commander how impressed I was, and he nodded curtly.

"We run a tight ship here, Mister Graves. Everyone knows their job and gets on with it."

"And this centre's job is to listen to everyone?" I said. "Every communication, public and private? No exceptions?"

If a note of disapproval had entered into my voice, the Commander chose not to hear it. "Of course," he said flatly. "Security threats can come from anywhere. We need to know everything."

"What about people's right to privacy?"

"Their right to be protected must come first."

"Your new device must make that a lot easier," I said.

"It does. We've been covering the same ground for years, but the Big Ear gives us fuller access, in a far more efficient way."

I would have liked to say something about the moral implications of spying on people you're supposed to be protecting. But I really couldn't. Not when my family listens to the whole world, every day. We do it for a much greater cause than national security—but we still do it.

The grand tour came to an end at the security control centre, where monitor screens covered the whole exterior and interior of Lark Hill. Short- and long-range sensors observed the surrounding countryside twenty-four hours a day. I leaned in for a close look at one screen, showing the soldiers guarding the gates I'd passed through earlier. The screen next to it seemed to be showing a bare expanse of open countryside. I looked at the Commander.

"That is what lies on top of this centre," he said. "Off-limits to the general public, of course. Protected by land mines, and other nasty hidden surprises, to discourage visitors."

"Do the locals know that?" I said.

"Of course not," said the Commander. "No one outside this base knows. If anyone knew, they wouldn't be surprises, would they? We're miles away from the nearest town, and the perimeter is fenced and guarded. No one has any good reason to be out there."

"Has anyone ever actually got inside the centre?" I said.

"No," said the Commander, with a certain pride. "And we are determined to keep it that way. Security here is top-notch. First-rate."

"Then how is important information getting out?" I said.

"We don't know! We're on top of every form of communication that goes in or out of Lark Hill! It's impossible for anyone to make contact with the outside world without going through several layers of oversight. But someone is alerting and warning off the very people we've identified as security risks. It has to stop!"

The Commander escorted me to his very private and secure office, set behind a steel door that opened only to the right numbers punched into a computer keypad. Which he was careful to block from me with his body. He needn't have bothered. Never met a keypad my armour couldn't crack. The office turned out to be unsurprisingly spartan, with not even a single family photo on his neat and tidy military desk. The Commander sat on a hard-backed chair on his side of the desk, while I settled myself on the equally uncomfortable visitor's chair facing him. For a while we just sat and stared at each other. In the end, the Commander leaned forward across the desk to fix me with his steely gaze.

"We're going to have to work together, Graves. The situation here has become unacceptable. Our country's safety is at risk. It appears . . . somebody working inside this centre has betrayed us. As soon as we identify someone as worthy of our attention, someone here tells them they've been found out. Warning them! So they can run bleating to their lawyers, or the media—or just disappear."

"You're sure this is an inside job?" I said, just to show I was paying attention. "There's no chance someone could be intercepting your communications? Maybe even tapping into the Big Ear itself?"

"No. Completely impossible. We checked, of course, but no, it has to be one of our people. All the military personnel were personally selected by me—men and women I'd worked with before. I trust them implicitly. So that leaves just the civilians. Scientists, technicians, computer people, and security. But they were all exhaustively vetted before they were allowed anywhere near Lark Hill! So it can't be them either."

"Perhaps someone here isn't who they're supposed to be," I said.

The Commander shook his head. "We've checked everyone's fingerprints, retina scans, and DNA. Twice."

"I'll run my own checks," I said. "Just in case."

"You were invited in to come up with new ideas," said the Commander, "not cover old ground."

"This new device of yours," I said. "The Big Ear. I'm going to need to see it at some point."

"No," the Commander said immediately. "I don't care what your papers say; you don't have the necessary clearance. No one gets to see the Big Ear except me."

I didn't argue. I could see he wasn't going to budge. I fed him a few cheerful platitudes, told him not to worry because I was on the case now, and said I'd take a walk around the centre to get the feel of things. The Commander wanted to send a couple of soldiers with me. I politely but firmly declined. I rose to my feet, and he did too. We didn't shake hands. I left his office, and the heavy steel door closed firmly behind me.

I strolled through the brightly lit corridors, nodding amiably to everyone I passed, and they all avoided my gaze and hurried away. No one wanted to draw attention to themselves. I did think about grabbing a few at random, slamming them up against the nearest wall and asking a few pointed questions, but I didn't see the point. The Commander was right; security in Lark Hill was airtight. Cameras everywhere, no blind spots, all kinds of hidden surveillance systems . . . So the problem had to be with the only new element: the Big Ear. Someone must have got to it.

I made a point of popping into various offices and just hanging around, chatting aimlessly, letting people get used to me. Making it as clear as I could that I wasn't on any kind of witch hunt. Gradually, people started to open up and talk to me. They all seemed honestly puzzled as to how the information was getting out. They all had their own theories too, but none of them amounted to much. There were the usual suggestions as to who might be behind it—agents of a foreign power, someone doing it for the money, or even some over-principled whistle-blower doing it for WikiLeaks. All perfectly plausible, but no one was able to suggest how it could be done.

The one thing that did emerge, very clearly, was that none of them had ever seen the Big Ear. They'd all been locked in their offices and workrooms the day the device was installed by outside contractors. And the device and its room were strictly off-limits to everyone but the Commander. *So who operates it?* I asked. And the answer came back: *We think it operates itself.* One technician lowered his voice to a whisper as he told me that even the approaches to the device's room were protected by seriously extreme security measures. One man had been killed, early on, just for taking a wrong turn and ending up where he shouldn't have been. The Commander hadn't even tried to cover it up. Just let it stand as a warning, and an object lesson.

I went back to wandering through the corridors, heading nowhere in particular, thinking furiously. It was clear the centre's security was as much about keeping an eye on people inside Lark Hill as on people outside. Nothing happened here without someone knowing all about it. Whoever was beating the system had to know every detail of how Lark Hill operated, from the inside out. Including the Big Ear. Which meant I had to see the device for myself. I always love it when my first instincts turn out to be right. I contacted Kate.

"Way ahead of you," she said briskly. "I'm sending you Lark Hill's floor plans. Don't tell the Commander; he doesn't know we've got them. We've already worked out where the Big Ear is, but . . ."

"Oh, it's never good when you hesitate like that," I said. "But what?"

"Well, it is rather odd. The first thing we looked for was the kind of power levels necessary to run something as powerful as the Big Ear would have to be, and there don't appear to be any. Whatever kind of device this is, it doesn't follow any of the expected design parameters. No energy drain, no connections to the rest of the centre's technology; and no one to operate it. Which suggests . . ."

"It's not technology as we know it," I said. "Not from around here . . ."

"Exactly. So find out what it is, Eddie. And if need be, take it away from them."

"I've been told there are lethal levels of protection in place, defending the device," I said.

"Oh yes. All sorts."

The floor plans arrived through my torc. I looked quickly around to make sure no one was watching, then sent a trickle of strange matter up the side of my face to form a pair of golden sunglasses over my eyes. The floor plans appeared floating on the air before me. I studied the plans just long enough to memorise the quickest route to the device, then let the sunglasses run back into my torc.

"I'm going to need a distraction," I murmured to Kate. "Something to keep everyone occupied while I pay the Big Ear a quick visit."

"No problem," said Kate. "The comm people tell me they're ready to hit Lark Hill with a blast of electronic chaff—enough useless information to temporarily override all their systems without seeming like any kind of attack. We don't want them to shut down the centre, after all. So make this quick, Eddie."

"Right, then," I said. "I'll just pop in for a peek and then piss off again."

Just around the corner from the Big Ear's corridor, and all its hidden deadly protections, I leaned against the wall and put my phone to my ear. Marvellous invention, the mobile phone. Never been a better excuse for standing around, apparently doing nothing. Everyone just assumes you're listening to someone. A quick glance around the corner was all it took to confirm that there were heavily armed soldiers patrolling both ends of the corridor. I let Kate know I was in position, and immediately every alarm bell and siren and flashing light in the centre went off at once. People came running from all directions, glaring wildly about them, then heading for their prescribed panic stations, at speed. At speed, while still being very careful to avoid all approaches to the Big Ear, of course. I put my phone away, and took another quick peek round the corner. The armed guards were still standing their ground. Which was a pity—for them.

I subvocalised my activating Words, and my golden armour flowed out and over me in a moment. I felt stronger and sharper, as though I'd been kicked fully awake. I shot round the corner and took out both guards at my end of the corridor with two solid taps behind the ear. The guards at the other end realised something had happened, but I was off and running before they even had time to raise their weapons. I raced down the corridor at inhuman speed, driven on by the unnatural strength in my armoured legs. I was just a golden blur to the startled soldiers, right before they were suddenly unconscious too. When the guards finally woke up, none of them would be able to explain to the Commander what had happened.

I stood well back from the door that led to the Big Ear and looked it over carefully. I didn't worry about the security cameras; Drood armour is invisible to all surveillance. How else could our field agents operate today? We move unseen through the world to do what we have to do.

The lethal security measures were very well hidden; I couldn't see a sign of them anywhere. I kicked in all my mask's filters, and then discovered the pressure pads cunningly concealed in the floor, the hidden panels in the walls over robot gun emplacements, and the hidden panels in the ceilings for poison gas nozzles. The Commander really wasn't taking any chances. I considered the situation carefully. I couldn't hang around too long. The Commander would be bound to check in with his soldiers during an emergency alert, and he'd send serious reinforcements when the guards didn't answer.

The most obvious solution was to just stomp on the pressure pads and trust my armour to protect me, but that would confirm that someone had been here. Someone the lethal levels didn't bother at all. So, step around the pads. But when I stepped carefully past the first pad, the others immediately rearranged themselves into a whole new pattern. Which was just downright sneaky. So I hopscotched my way past and around the pads, my mask's filters allowing me to dodge them all no matter how fast they moved.

I can be sneaky too.

I stood in front of the door and looked it over carefully. Fairly ordinary-looking, with another computer keypad lock. I grinned under my mask. Good enough to keep most people out, but I'm not most people. I pressed a golden fingertip against the keypad and sent a filament of strange matter leaping into the electronic system. It took my armour only a moment to find and input the right entrance code, and then the door swung quietly open before me. And no, I don't know how the armour does that. My armour does a lot of things I don't understand, and I discovered long ago that there was absolutely no point in asking Ethel questions concerning the marvellous armour she provides for my family. The answers only make my head hurt. I stepped quickly inside the room, and the door closed and locked itself quietly but firmly behind me.

I appeared to be standing inside someone's parlour. Quiet, comfortably old-fashioned, with padded chairs and chunky furniture, and more doors leading off to other rooms. Fresh flowers in vases, nice prints on the walls, and a pleasantly patterned carpet underfoot. A little old lady was sitting in a chair, knitting something shapeless, her gaze far away. She wore a baggy sweater over a simple dress, and big fluffy slippers. Her hair was grey, and tightly curled. Her face looked well-worn, but not unhappy, with bifocal glasses pushed right down her nose. In front of her chair stood a simple coffee table, bearing a computer laptop chattering importantly to itself. The old lady didn't appear to be paying it any attention.

I armoured down, so as not to alarm her. My torc would still conceal me from the room's surveillance systems. The old lady looked at me, smiled vaguely, and put her knitting down in her lap, to give me her full attention. The computer kept working on its own.

"How nice," she said, in a pleasant, slightly reedy voice. "A visitor! I don't get many visitors, these days. Just Commander Fletcher, and he only ever wants to talk business. Let me see now . . . Yes! You're Eddie Drood . . . Nice to meet you, Eddie. I'm Gemma Markham. They call me the Big Ear. I was hoping for something a little more dramatic, but . . ."

I got it immediately. There was only one way she could have known who I was so quickly.

"Hello, Gemma," I said. "You're a telepath, aren't you? There is no device, no great computer, just you. Listening in on everyone with your mind."

"That's right, dear," she said. "Would you like a nice cup of tea?"

"I wouldn't mind," I said.

I pulled up a chair and sat down opposite her, as she poured me tea from the china service set out on a side table. She offered me a plate of bourbon biscuits too, but I declined. Molly's got me watching my weight. No wonder the Commander didn't allow anyone else in here . . . Gemma and I sipped our tea and chatted politely. The Drood secret agent and the telepath who could overhear everyone in the country. In the most secret room of an underground bunker. Some days I love my job.

"Are you here to rescue me, dear?" said Gemma, blowing on her tea to cool it.

"I don't know," I said. "Do you need rescuing?"

"Do you know, I rather think I do. Not that I'm in any danger, you understand. Everyone has been very kind. But I'm not allowed to leave these rooms. Not ever. It's a nice little flat, very comfortable, I'm sure, but it's not what I agreed to."

She told me her story. Gemma was the Big Ear, and always had been—a telepath powerful enough to listen in on every person in the country. She didn't need to read or hear their communications; she plucked the thoughts right out of their heads. The Government told her they needed her to find terrorists, to stop them before anyone could get hurt. So of course she volunteered straightaway. Because she was of that generation who understood duty and responsibility. But life at Lark Hill turned out to be very different from what she was told.

She agreed to spy on dangerous people who presented a real threat to national security. People with murder on their minds. But once the Government had her firmly in place, locked away in her hidden rooms, deep underground . . . they changed the deal. They told her they wanted her to listen in on everybody. On all the ordinary, everyday people. So they could find out who the troublemakers were. People who opposed the Government, or didn't believe the things the Government wanted them to believe.

"And they weren't just talking about illegal things," said Gemma. "It was all politics, and not rocking the boat, or making waves. Or drawing attention to things the Government didn't want people to know about. Well, I wasn't having that. I couldn't defy the Commander and his own private army, but I could reach out to people who were in danger and warn them."

"So . . . you've been the leak, all along?" I said.

"Yes, dear. It seemed the right thing to do."

"You really can hear everyone?"

"Oh yes . . . My mind has become ever so much stronger since they introduced me to that machine. The one on the table there. I listen to people, and the device listens to me, sorting out what it has been pro-grammed to consider important. Special key words and phrases. I don't pay much attention. Most of the time, most people aren't think-ing anything interesting. Sometimes the Commander wants me to concentrate on some particular person, or organisation, and that can be quite exciting. I have detected a great many terrorists planning aw-ful things. I was glad to be able to put a stop to that. To have saved lives . . . But mostly it seems the people in charge are just going after ordinary, everyday people. Because they can. And that isn't at all what I agreed to."

"How long have they kept you locked up here?" I said.

"Almost a year now. Ever since I realised they'd lied to me. I told them I wasn't interested in politics. I told them I wanted to leave, wanted to go home. And they just smiled and told me that I could never be allowed to leave, because I would be far too valuable to any foreign power." She sniffed loudly. "Too valuable to the Government, they meant. I should never have voted for that man. But he seemed such a nice, clean-cut sort . . . I could have refused to work for them, but I could see in the Commander's head that he was already thinking of threats to my family. And worse things . . . so I just carry on. Pointing out the bad people and helping the ordinary people when I can.

"They've made me very comfortable here, but it does get a bit lonely. I was promised that my family would be able to visit, but that was just another lie. Only Commander Fletcher comes here, and I won't talk to him. Just on principle. He did try bribing me—offered me all kinds of things. But I know my Bible stories. I know what it means when they offer you the whole world if you'll just bow down and worship them."

"You're never allowed out of here?" I said. "Not even for exercise?"

"Don't need much exercise at my age, dear. They say all this security is to keep me safe, from terrorists who'd try to kill me if they ever found out what I can do. But they're just afraid that if I ever did get out, they'd never get me back in. And they're right!" She stopped, and looked at me thoughtfully. "I'm surprised they haven't come dashing in here to arrest you just for talking to me."

"They can't see me," I said. "Or hear me. They probably think you're just talking to yourself."

"I hoped someone would come looking for me," she said wistfully. "My family must be very worried . . ."

"Can't you listen in on them?" I said.

"Oh, I couldn't do that! I'd never intrude on my family's privacy."

"Why did you decide to start contacting people and warning them?"

She shrugged briefly. "Because it's the right thing to do. And because it's the only form of rebellion left to me. I only warn those people who seem to be in danger and haven't done anything wrong that I can see. Not terrorists, just people with minds and opinions of their own. Which never used to be a crime. So I warn them. Because as far as I'm concerned, they're the kind of people I was brought here to protect."

"Do you want me to break you out?" I said. "I could, if you wanted.

I'm a Drood; you must have seen in my mind what my armour is capable of. My family would protect you. No one messes with the Droods."

"No thank you, dear," said Gemma very firmly. "If I really wanted to leave I don't think anyone here could stop me. I could make someone open the door, and even escort me out. And anyone who tried to stop me would end up wishing they hadn't. But I'm doing important work here. If it wasn't for me looking after the nation, people really would die . . . And I won't have that. I am keeping my country safe, and that means more to me than this . . . inconvenience." She looked at me steadily. "Would you try to take me out of here by force, against my will?"

"No," I said. "That's not how I work. I think I'll go and have a word with the Commander. Express my displeasure. I'll see you later, Gemma."

"Thank you, Eddie. That would be nice. Good-bye, dear."

She took up her knitting again and went back to staring into space while the computer before her worked furiously, making a list of everyone's secrets. I armoured up and returned to the corridor, carefully locking the door behind me again. Because she did need protecting, after all.

I armoured down once I'd left the danger zone outside the room, and strode quickly through the corridors. People took one look at my face and hurried to get out of my way. Which was just as well. Gemma was right. I couldn't just take her away, not when she was doing such necessary work. People might suffer or die if Gemma wasn't there to protect them. Remove her from Lark Hill and I could be crippling this country's ability to defend itself from terror.

But on the other hand, I was damned if I'd let the Government bully an old woman and keep her as a slave.

I stood outside the Commander's door and knocked politely. His voice came through a grille above the keypad.

"Not now. I'm busy."

I armoured up, smashed the keypad with my golden fist, kicked the door open, and strode into his office. He jumped to his feet behind his desk, outraged, and then his jaw dropped as he took in my armour. I stood before him, golden arms folded over my gleaming chest. The Commander started to reach for the gun holstered on his hip, and then had the good sense to stop himself.

"I should have known," he said bitterly. "Of course they'd send a Drood. Who else could they trust with a situation like this . . . No wonder you had such authority!"

"What were all those alarms about?" I said innocently.

"An attack on our communications," he said. "Not the first time it's happened. The enemy is always testing us."

"Which enemy?" I said.

"Does it matter? We're spoilt for choice, these days. That's why the Big Ear is so vital to this country's defences."

"You mean Gemma Markham."

"Of course you'd find out. Drood. Yes, I mean her—and the device. She's nothing without that machine. It made her the telepath she is today."

"About that," I said. "Gemma isn't too happy with the way she's being treated."

His jaw dropped again. "How the hell did you get in to see her?"

"I'm a Drood, remember?"

"You can't have her," he said bluntly. "She's ours. We found her; we made her! She's a vital part of this country's national security!"

"You don't need her," I said. "You've got my family. We've been protecting this country for centuries."

"But we can't always rely on you," said the Commander, regaining some of his composure. He sat down behind his desk again. "You aren't always here. You get distracted. Running off to fight your secret wars against God knows what and forgetting all about us. Our everyday concerns and dangers. But you don't need to worry about Gemma Markham. We are aware there is a problem with her, and there have already been serious discussions, at very high levels, on how best to control her. The current thinking seems to indicate some kind of lobotomy. Surgical, chemical, psionic. For the moment, my superiors are understandably reluctant to do anything that might interfere with the goose's ability to deliver golden eggs . . . But we'll work something out."

He was actually smiling, and I was just a moment away from kicking him through the nearest wall. But he was only the man in the chair, carrying out orders. No wonder the Prime Minister went bleating to the Matriarch when he saw his precious secret being endangered. Who else could he trust with a secret like this? Taking down the Commander wouldn't help Gemma. So I just turned my back on him and stalked out of his office.

I armoured down and went wandering through the corridors again. I always think better when I'm walking. Several corridors later, I was no nearer an answer, so I contacted Kate and filled her in on everything I'd discovered.

"Where the hell did they find such a powerful telepath?" she said immediately. "One we knew nothing about?"

"I think that's down to the device," I said. "Whatever it turns out to be. It made her what she is."

"Well, where did they get such a powerful device? That we knew nothing about?"

"It's not like there's any shortage of black markets for strange and unnatural tech," I said. "The point is, what do you want me to do?"

"The Matriarch will have to consult with her advisory Council," said Kate. "Don't go anywhere, and don't do anything. We'll get back to you."

And that was when all the alarm bells and sirens and flashing lights went off again. People went running in all directions again, this time looking even more upset. Soldiers came hurrying down the corridor, guns at the ready, looking for someone to use them on.

"I heard that!" said Kate. "What have you done, Eddie?"

"Wasn't me, for once," I said. "And since it's not you, this time, I'd better go and investigate."

I armoured up and started down the corridor. No point in trying to hide that I was a Drood any more. But I did have my armour soak up the noise that my metal feet made on the floor, so no one would know I was coming. Nobody can sneak around like a Drood field agent. I peered into the security control centre. Everyone looked up, and a whole bunch of them had something very like a coronary as they took in my armour. I raised a placating hand.

"It's Sebastian Graves," I said. "Security, remember? Now someone talk to me. What's happened?"

One of the braver souls gestured for me to come over and look at his monitor screen. I leaned in beside him, and he shied away from my armour despite himself. I pretended not to notice. The screen showed a view of the steel-mesh gates I'd passed through on my way in. They'd been flung wide open, and the armed soldiers were lying on the ground, quite dead.

"I'm not getting any life signs on the short- or long-range sensors," the tech guy said grimly. "Nothing to show who could have done that. The guards never even got a shot off, and whoever did it passed through all our lethal defence measures without triggering any of them. Which is supposed to be impossible. They could already be inside Lark Hill! Whoever they are, they're a real pro."

"Like a Drood," said another tech from a safe distance away.

"No one is that good," I said.

"Someone is definitely inside the centre," said the first tech. "Several guards are not reporting in, from the perimeter inwards . . . Someone is heading towards the looked-down room and the Big Ear device! How is that possible? How could they even know where it is?"

"Like you said," I murmured, "a real pro . . . Come to steal the device—or destroy it."

"Can't you do anything?" said the tech.

"I'll go defend the device," I said. "In the meantime, lock down all the entrances and exits. Since you can't rely on the cameras to track our intruder, try boosting the microphones . . . Maybe you can hear him moving even if you can't see him. And keep everyone else well away from the Big Ear! Soldiers would just get in the way while I'm working."

"The Commander already sent troops to defend the corridor," said the tech. "We haven't heard anything from them."

"And you won't," I said. "Real pros eat soldiers for breakfast."

I went running back through the corridors, heading for the locked-down room and Gemma Markham. It could be anyone at all, coming after her. You don't shut down terrorists without making a lot of enemies. Or it could be someone who wanted the Big Ear working for them. I began to pass dead bodies. Technicians at first, and then soldiers, lying scattered the length of the corridors. Guns lay discarded on the floor. Whoever took these people down did it so efficiently that they never knew what was happening. None of the dead men or women got a chance to defend themselves. So—not just a spy. A professional assassin as well.

I stopped to check a few of the bodies. They'd all been killed in the same way. A single stab wound from behind.

I came to the Big Ear's corridor, and stopped abruptly. I couldn't see anything, but I was sure I'd caught a glimpse of surreptitious movement out of the corner of my eye. I put my back against the nearest wall. My armour should protect me from a knife in the back, but I didn't feel like taking any chances. I looked quickly back and forth, but no matter how fast I turned my head, I couldn't see anyone. I stood very still and listened. I was sure there was someone else in the corridor.

When you've been in the field as long as I have, you learn to trust your instincts. I activated all of my mask's filters and enhancements—and suddenly there he was. Right in front of me. Standing very still, studying me thoughtfully, holding a long slender knife in one hand. *Got you*... I turned my golden mask to look at him directly, and his head came up as he realised I could see him. He nodded respectfully, then walked confidently forward to join me. He didn't lower his knife.

He was an old man, probably tall once but stooped now and more than fashionably thin. Most of his gaunt face was hidden behind a black domino mask. His formal tuxedo hung loosely about him, and he also wore a heavy black opera cape and a gleaming top hat. He should have looked ridiculous, wearing such an old-fashioned outfit in a modern setting, but somehow he didn't. Something in the way he wore the outfit made it clear that these were his working clothes. And while age might have slowed him down, it hadn't affected his professional style. This old man had already killed a great many people, just to get this far, most of them trained soldiers.

I looked at the outfit and knew who he was. Who he had to be. My uncle James had talked about him. I inclined my golden head respectfully.

"Do I have the honour of addressing that venerable French spy and assassin, the premier villain of Paris, the legendary Fantom?"

He smiled quickly and bowed briefly in return. "Indeed you do, monsieur Drood. Might I inquire . . . ?"

"I'm Eddie Drood. I believe you knew my uncle James."

"But of course! The legendary and renowned Grey Fox! Yes, indeed; many the years we spent, chasing and being chased across the rooftops of Paris. And sometimes through the underground, or the sewers . . . The fox and the hare. It was like a game we played, except the stakes were real. Money and secrets and honour . . . I would take something, and he would do his best to take it from me. Sometimes he won, sometimes I won. But it was really all about the chase. I think he would have killed me if he could have. I would certainly have killed him. But somehow that never happened. Now the old Grey Fox is gone . . . Without him, I tired of the game. The streets and rooftops of

Paris are no doubt so much safer as a result, but I can't help feeling they have lost something of their glamour."

"I know why you're here," I said. "But why are you wearing your old outfit?"

"A matter of style," said the old villain with dignity. "It reminds me of the good old days, when everyone dressed up to do battle. Put on a persona, choose a mask and an outfit, and go out into the world to play the greatest game of all. People just can't be bothered these days, my young friend. You are the Grey Fox's nephew, yes? I have heard of you, Eddie. A fine adversary."

"That's close enough," I said. And the Fantom stopped his stealthy advance.

"Your uncle trained you well," he said, smiling. "I feel . . . you will not be persuaded to let me pass."

"I'm a Drood," I said. "I'm here to stop you. It's what we do."

"But I came prepared, monsieur Drood! You see this cloak; it belonged to the original Fantom of the Paris Opera. It enables its wearer to walk unseen, in plain sight. How else was he was able to run around that crowded old opera house without being observed? And see this knife! A very special blade, I assure you. Fashioned from the very first Madame Guillotine, from the time of the Terror. Bathed in the blood of a thousand executed aristocrats, it has become so sharp it can cut through anything! Perhaps even the legendary Drood armour."

"So," I said, "you sneaked up on people while you were invisible, and stabbed them in the back. Not exactly worthy of the legend of the old Fantom."

"But no, monsieur Drood! That is exactly what a thief and spy does! He comes and he goes, and no one knows, until it is far too late. I was often pursued by your uncle, and occasionally thwarted in my plans, but never once was I captured!"

"Then what are you doing here now?" I said. "No one's heard anything of the Fantom in years. We just assumed you'd retired."

"And I had!" said the Fantom, with a sudden flash of anger. "Being a spy and a villain is a young man's game. I carried on longer than I should have, for pride's sake, but eventually . . . even legends grow old, and slow. I gave up the name and the legend while they were still something I could be proud of. For many years now, I have served my country quietly as an accredited member of the French Embassy staff, here in London. Nothing like being an old thief to help guard against young thieves. And there is nothing like knowing where all the bodies are buried to make you a player in the diplomatic game.

"And I was happy, monsieur Drood. Happy! Content to be a respected elder statesman, whose opinion was still sought and valued. And then this Big Ear of yours ruined everything! This new device that sees everything, hears everything. I could not allow myself to be found out, to have my past revealed. There is no forgiving some of my old sins. My friends and colleagues would disown me, my old enemies would come after me for retribution! I had no choice but to come here and destroy your precious Big Ear before it could destroy me. I had retired, damn you! I was no threat to anyone! Why couldn't you just leave me in peace?"

"The Big Ear knows everything," I said carefully. "But why should you feel singled out? Why would they care about you?"

"Because I am the Fantom! I was the nightmare they could not wake up from! Never captured, never interrogated! Of course they would come after me, after all the things I did!"

"No one's so vain as an old spy and villain," I said.

"Perhaps, monsieur Drood. But I could not take the chance. The Big Ear must be destroyed."

"You're a myth," I said. "A piece of espionage history. A story in old books. You should have stayed that way."

He looked at his domino-masked reflection in my golden mask, and some of the strength seemed to leave him. Suddenly he looked . . . like an old man playing dress-up.

"You're right," he said. "I should never have come here. Just let me go, monsieur Drood. I will leave here, leave England, disappear. No one will ever see me again."

"I would like to," I said. "But I'm afraid that isn't possible."

"Why not?"

"How many people did you kill to get this far?"

He shrugged angrily. "I don't know. As many as I needed to. They were just soldiers! Just . . . functionaries. They don't matter!"

"People always matter," I said.

"You have killed people, have you not, Eddie Drood?" the Fantom said coldly. "People who had to die? People who needed killing!"

"Sometimes," I said. "When I had no other choice. But always for a greater cause. Never to protect my own interests."

"You're so like your uncle," said the Fantom. "Just another self-righteous Drood."

He swirled his long opera cloak about him, and just like that he was gone. I couldn't see him anywhere, even through my mask's filters. I stood very still, listening, in case he did the sensible thing and made a run for it. But there was no sound of rapidly departing feet, so I boosted my hearing through the mask, holding my breath so I could concentrate on the smallest sounds in the corridor. I heard him breathing, heard the rasp and rustle of his clothes as he moved, heard every faint footstep as he advanced on me. I let him come, knowing he had that very sharp blade in his hand, trusting to my armour to protect me against even that awful weapon.

The knife came slamming into my side out of nowhere and skidded harmlessly across my armoured ribs in a shower of sparks. I let out a breath I hadn't realised I was holding and clamped down on where I knew his arm had to be. The Fantom cried out despite himself as my armoured hand crushed his arm. I took the knife away from him and snapped the blade in two. The broken pieces appeared in mid-air, falling to the floor. I grabbed the Fantom's cloak and hauled it off him, and he appeared before me, glaring sullenly through his black domino mask, cradling his hurt arm. I let the cloak fall to the floor.

"Go on, then, Drood!" the Fantom said defiantly. "Kill me! Do what your legendary uncle could not, and prove yourself a man!"

"No," I said. "I don't do that any more."

There was the sound of a gunshot. The bullet hit the Fantom in the back, driving him forward into my arms. He didn't cry out. He looked more puzzled than hurt, like an old man who'd fallen and didn't know why. I held on to him as his legs gave out, and he tried to say something, but all that came out of his mouth was blood. I armoured down, still holding on to him. He seemed such a small and fragile thing. He looked up into my face, still struggling to say something, some last words worthy of a legend, but he died before he could. I lowered his body to the floor, straightened up again, and glared down the corridor at the Commander.

"You didn't have to do that! He was just an old man, no threat to anyone!"

"He was the Fantom," said the Commander. "A notorious uncaught criminal. A threat to the security of this establishment!"

"He was just an old man, afraid of his past catching up with him," I said tiredly.

"He knew about the Big Ear," said the Commander, finally holstering his gun. "He knew too much to ever be allowed to leave. If I hadn't shot him, he would have spent the remainder of his life in solitary confinement. You might say I did him a favour."

"No," I said, "I wouldn't say that."

"What would you have done, Drood?"

I didn't have an answer for him.

The Commander went back to his office, after giving orders for his men to come and take away the body. I waited with the Fantom until the soldiers turned up. It didn't feel right to leave him alone, in a strange place. The soldiers gathered him up with brisk efficiency and carried him off. There wasn't much left of the old man to weigh much. They left his top hat behind, lying on the floor. It looked lost and sad, on its own. I left it there, and walked away. Legends shouldn't grow old. And they shouldn't die from being shot in the back. Even though so many do.

To my surprise, I soon caught up with the Commander. As though he'd been walking deliberately slowly, waiting for me.

"What should I do with the body?" he said, not looking at me. "Send it back to the French Embassy?"

"No," I said. "It would only embarrass them. Just dispose of it. Legends should disappear without trace."

"No," said the Commander. "I think a lot of people are going to want evidence that the legendary Fantom is finally dead."

He increased his pace and strode off down the corridor. I watched him go. The idea of the Fantom's body being shown around the espionage community, as some kind of exhibit or trophy, suddenly made me so angry I determined there and then to bring the whole damned centre down around the Commander's ears.

"Kate!" I said. "Are you still there?"

"Of course, Eddie. I'm always here. Has something happened? You sound upset."

I filled her in on the Fantom, and the manner of his death. "Has the Matriarch decided on her official policy yet?"

"Yes, Eddie. The Matriarch authorizes you to take all necessary actions to remove the telepath and the device from Lark Hill and bring them back to Drood Hall. They're both far too valuable, and too dangerous, to be left outside the family's control."

"So Gemma Markham gets to swap one prison for another," I said. "That's not what I had in mind when I offered her sanctuary with my family."

"We must all do what we have to," Kate said carefully.

"And if taking her away from Lark Hill puts this country's security at risk?"

"They managed without her before. And they always have us."

"Not always," I said. "What if she doesn't want to go with me?"

"Explain the situation to her; tell her that it's for the best."

"And if she still says no?"

"You are authorized to use all necessary measures, Eddie."

There was a great deal I felt like saying, but I didn't. I thought hard.

"I've had an idea," I said. "Put me in touch with Ammonia Vom Acht."

"What?" said Kate. "Her? Are you sure?"

"Do it," I said. "I need her."

There was a long pause. Ammonia Vom Acht was perhaps the most powerful telepath in the world, currently married to the Drood Librarian, William. She didn't stay at the Hall; she couldn't. Too many voices, pressing in on her. But they would know how to contact her. Ammonia's voice rang suddenly inside my head, so loud it rattled my fillings.

"What do you want, Eddie? I'm busy. I'm always busy."

"You'll want to hear this," I said. And I told her about Gemma Markham, and the device, and what they were doing at Lark Hill.

"Where the hell did she come from?" said Ammonia. She sounded honestly startled, even shocked. "I never even heard of the woman! And I know, or know of, everyone on the psionic scene. If only in self-defence . . . Telepaths that powerful don't just appear out of nowhere, Eddie. Could she have been artificially produced? Her mind and powers strengthened by this device, whatever it is?"

"Looks that way," I said. "I remember a scientist who was supposed to have made some real breakthroughs in the mind/machine interface. A Herr Doktor Herman Koenig. Molly and I fought over him, back in the day, when we were on different sides. But he's been dead for years."

"Can't be him, then," said Ammonia. "But others could have carried on his work. Found a way to produce their own telepath and make a slave out of them. That was always my greatest fear . . ."

I remembered when the Great Satanic Conspiracy kidnapped Ammonia and held her prisoner in Castle Shreck. They did bad things to her before my family rescued her.

"The Commander has been talking about . . . controlling Gemma," I said. "He used the word *lobotomy*, and not in a good way."

"That's it!" said Ammonia, her harsh voice painfully loud inside my head. "I am going to mind-wipe everyone at Lark Hill!"

"Please don't," I said quickly. "Most people here don't even know Gemma exists! They're doing important work—discovering terrorist plots, saving lives. I just want to help Gemma, not shut the place down. I could do that myself. I was hoping you might have some other idea . . ."

"Hold everything," said Ammonia. "I've been looking the base over, and I've just locked on to what the Commander is thinking. Eddie, you have to get to Gemma, right now! The Commander has decided to kill her! He believes you're going to take her away, and he'd rather have her dead than share his secrets with the Droods. He's heading there now . . . No. I've lost him. I can't read him any more; he's shielded somehow. You have to save Gemma!"

I was already off and running, charging through brightly lit corridors at inhuman speed, drawing on all the speed my armour could generate. My pounding metal feet made dents and holes in the floor. I shot past people so quickly they seemed like statues to me, frozen in place. I called up the centre's floor plans on the inside of my mask again, to calculate the quickest route to Gemma's locked-down room. It took me only a moment to realise she was just too far away. I'd never get to her before the Commander did. So I changed direction, smashing through the intervening corridor walls, hammering through the fragile physical world in a straight line to Gemma's room. When I take the power of my armour upon me, the world might as well be made of paper.

I blasted through the last wall, and there was Gemma's room, right before me. The door had been left open. The Commander was already there. I ran straight for the door, not even trying to avoid triggering the pressure pads in the floor. Gun emplacements swung out from inside the walls and opened fire on me. Gas nozzles emerged from the ceiling and filled the corridor with a thick yellow smoke. And acid sprays I hadn't even noticed doused me with steaming fluids. My armour took it all in its stride. I didn't even slow down. My armour absorbed the bullets, while the acid rolled harmlessly off, dripping down to eat ragged holes in the floor. My mask protected me from the curling yellow gas. I hit the door with my shoulder, and slammed it right off its hinges. It hit the floor hard, and I walked right over it. I needed to make a big entrance to distract the Commander from whatever he was doing.

I finally came to a halt, not even breathing hard, just inside the room. The Commander was standing beside Gemma Markham, who was still sitting calmly in her chair, her knitting in her lap. She seemed entirely unconcerned by the Commander's presence or my sudden entrance. The Commander's head whipped round, and he glared at me silently. There was something not quite right about his cold, unblinking gaze and the taut, strained way he held himself. As though he was nerving himself to do something irrevocable and unforgivable. Gemma smiled reassuringly at me.

"Please don't concern yourself, Mister Drood; I'm quite unharmed. Can you please talk to Commander Fletcher? I fear he's not in his right mind . . . and might be about to do something unwise."

"Shut up!" said the Commander. The gun in his hand was aimed at Gemma's head. He was wearing a strange crown on his head, all stubby tech and glowing crystals. I'd seen similar devices before; they shielded the wearer from psionic attacks. He was breathing erratically. "She can't be allowed to leave here, Drood. She knows far too much . . . You didn't come here to save my command, did you? You came here to steal her, and the machine! Well, you can't have them. They're vital to national security."

"She can protect this country wherever she is," I said, doing my best to sound calm and rational. Because one of us had to, and it clearly wasn't going to be him. "I think she'll be a lot safer with my family."

"You can't guarantee your family wouldn't trade her to someone else," said the Commander. "If there was something the Droods wanted more, or if they just thought it was in their best interests. Who knows who she might end up with? And what if she chose to leave the protection of your family? Would you hold her against her will? Or would you make her work for you? . . . No, the government has invested millions in Gemma Markham, and that machine. They belong to us!"

"I won't let you kill her," I said.

"I will kill her, rather than let you take her," he said flatly. The gun in his hand didn't waver at all, pressed into the tight curls on her head. "And you can't stop me, Drood! Even you're not fast enough to intercept this bullet!"

I considered the point. My armour is fast, but . . . I couldn't put Gemma at risk. So, when in doubt, be sneaky. I armoured down, and the Commander relaxed, just a little, as I stood openly before him. He thought I was helpless. He turned his gun on me. But I'd kept my right hand armoured, down at my side, out of sight. I concentrated, just as his finger tightened on the trigger, and a long golden blade shot out of my glove, extending so quickly he never saw it coming. The tip of the blade sliced through the gun, cleaving it neatly in half. The severed part fell away, dropping to the floor; and the Commander stared at it blankly. And while he was looking at that, I raised the tip of the long blade and inserted it neatly under the edge of his crown. I flipped it off his head, and it fell away.

"Thank you, Mister Drood," said Gemma.

And just like that, all the expression went out of the Commander's face. He just stood there silently, his eyes empty. I looked at Gemma.

"Oh, don't worry, Mister Drood," said Gemma. "He's not dead. I just let him hear what I hear, all the time. But he doesn't have the device to help him make sense of it. He's lost among the voices. I'll bring him back—in a while. And by then he should have a better understanding of what it's like to be me. Hopefully, it will give him an insight, make him more reasonable."

"And if it doesn't?" I said.

"Then I'll make him be reasonable," said Gemma Markham.

Some people are more frightening than others. I carefully withdrew the long golden blade into my glove and looked at the laptop computer set out before her.

"You can't have it," said Gemma. She'd taken up her knitting again. "I don't need rescuing, young man. I have decided to remain here, now that Commander Fletcher is no longer a threat. I'm actually very comfortable, and I am doing vital and important work. Which is nice at my age. I'm sure everyone here will be much more reasonable about letting my family visit and the like. After they've seen what I've done to Commander Fletcher.

"Now I can concentrate on what I came here to do—locating terrorists and putting a stop to their plans. I'm sure I can rely on you and your family to prevent the Government from sending in another bully like Commander Fletcher. Can't I?"

"Of course," I said. "Are you sure . . ."

"Yes," she said. "Please don't come here and bother me again, young man. I'm where I'm supposed to be. Doing good work."

I had to smile. I do love it when a case works out for the best.


I went back down into the garage. The Bentley was waiting patiently, right where I'd left her. I contacted Kate to tell her I'd resolved the situation. Without major bloodshed, for once.

"You have to come home, Eddie," said Kate. "Right now."

"Oh, come on," I said. "I agreed to help the family out on just the one case. What's so damned urgent?"

"Come home, Eddie," she said. "Please. There's been a death."

# CHAPTER FIVE

# Good-bye, Uncle Jack

And so I came home, for the Armourer's funeral.

I drove the Bentley hard, following the shortest route through the side dimensions that the on-board computers could come up with. I kept my foot pressed down, my hands clenched tight on the steering wheel, not stopping for anything, and the old car smashed through world after world like so many curtains in stage plays I had no interest in watching. Through a place where mountains sang to one another, to another where great swarms of multicoloured manta rays swam through the sky, diving in and out of the clouds. A world where the trees walked was replaced by another where rainbows burst up out of the ground like fountains under pressure. Purple skies, green skies, dark skies, studded with blazing stars in insane patterns. I had no eyes and no time and no care for any of them. They were just things I had to get through, things that stood between me and getting home. The last of the spatial dimensions was suddenly shouldered aside by a great blast of familiar light, of brilliant Summer sunshine; as I returned at last to the world I knew.

I reappeared inside the Drood Hall grounds, just past the closed front gates, burning along the path at such speed that I sent showers of gravel flying in all directions. I finally eased up on the accelerator and hit the brake, and the Bentley slewed dangerously back and forth for several heart-stopping moments before I got it under control again. I continued on up the long entrance drive at a more civilised speed, and pulled out my mobile phone. I needed to talk to Molly. She'd spelled my phone a while back, so I could always be sure of reaching her, no matter where in the world or out of it she might be. She took her own sweet time answering, just to make it clear she wasn't always at my beck and call. She never liked being interrupted when she was off on her own. But we had promised each other long ago that no matter what was happening in our lives we would always take each other's calls.

"What is it, Eddie?" Molly said finally. "Can't it wait? I'm busy. Seriously busy."

"I need you to come back to the Hall, Molly. Right now."

"What? You have got to be kidding. Why in hell would I want to do that?"

"The Armourer is dead."

"Oh, Eddie." Her voice changed in a moment. "Of course, sweetie. Don't you worry. I'll be right with you."

Her voice cut off. I put the phone away and drove on. I rounded the last great curve and brought the Bentley screeching to a halt right in front of the main entrance. Molly was already standing there, waiting for me. I shut down the engine, shrugged out of the seat belts, and then just sat there, for a long moment. Breathing hard. It took real strength to summon up the determination to get myself out of the car. Because once I did that, I was admitting it was all real. That I had come home because Uncle Jack was gone. But I did it; because I knew Uncle Jack required it of me. The moment I stepped away from the Bentley, Molly was there in my arms. Pressing up against me, her cheek against my chest, holding me tight.

"It's all right, Eddie, I'm here. I'm here. I've got you."

I wanted to say something, but I couldn't. I held on to her just as tightly. The only thing left in my life that I could depend on.

After a while, we let go of each other and stood back. I managed a small smile for Molly, to show her I was okay. Even though I wasn't. She looked searchingly into my face, and then just nodded. We didn't say anything. There'd be time for talk later. For now, there were things we had to do.

I headed out onto the great open lawns stretching away before the Hall, with Molly close beside me. She locked one arm through mine, so that even when I wasn't looking at her I'd know she was still there. The lawns were covered with people, rank upon rank, row upon row. It seemed to me I'd never seen so many of my family assembled in one place before. It looked like every Drood in the Hall had turned out for the occasion. To pay their respects to the memory of the family Armourer. No one was wearing black, though. We don't do traditional mourning. We follow our own traditions in death, as in everything else.

And it was only then that I understood why Melanie Blaze had let me go so abruptly from the subtle realms. The elf she sent to make contact with my family must have returned with the news that Jack was dead. Time moves differently in the subtle realms . . . So there was no point in Melanie holding on to me any longer. No Jack meant no Time machine. Her last chance to be reunited with James, gone forever. She could still have killed me or held me captive, but she let me go, sent me home. Perhaps as one last gesture to a man she respected.

I joined the crowd and people fell back, making room for me and Molly to walk through to the front row. Where the Matriarch was waiting. She nodded courteously to both of us, then stepped forward and patted me on the arm with surprising gentleness.

"Thank you for returning so quickly, Eddie. Sorry to rush you, but you know we couldn't put this off."

"Why not?" Molly said truculently. "Why did you have to drag Eddie back here in such a rush?"

"It's the Drood way," said the Matriarch, still looking at me.

"What happened?" I said. "I still can't believe he's dead. I was just talking to him in the Armoury, before I left. He seemed fine."

"Did he?" said the Matriarch. "Are you sure?"

"Well . . ." I stopped, and thought back, and things I hadn't under-stood at the time began to make a kind of sense. "He did seem . . . tired. And not entirely himself."

"Talk to Maxwell and Victoria," said the Matriarch. "They found him."

She summoned them forward. They nodded quickly, to me and to Molly. They both looked pale and drawn, shocked—and so much younger outside of the Armoury. They were hanging on to each other in the same way Molly and I were. And probably for the same reason.

"We found him sitting at his work-bench," said Maxwell. "Quite dead. He looked . . ."

"Very peaceful," said Victoria. "No sign of any distress."

They were trying to be kind. I let them.

"The doctors are quite sure it was a massive heart attack," said Max-well. "Very sudden. With any luck, he didn't know anything about it."

"No signs of foul play," said Victoria. "The doctors checked very thoroughly. At the autopsy."

"There had to be an autopsy," said Maxwell, glancing at Molly. "Because a man like Jack Drood makes a great many enemies. As a field agent, and as Armourer. We wanted to be sure . . . But there was nothing. Nothing at all."

"Then why are you rushing into his funeral so quickly?" said Molly. "If there's nothing to hide?"

"Because things have to move forward when a Drood dies," said the Matriarch. "I have already appointed Maxwell and Victoria as the new family Armourer. Because the work must go on."

"You must know we didn't want the job," Maxwell said to me ear-nestly. "Vikki and I have never been . . . ambitious."

"We were perfectly happy, just keeping things running," said

Victoria. "But we are ready to take over. It's what we've been train-ing for."

"And it's our duty," said Maxwell.

"Anything, for the family," said Victoria.

And I remembered the last thing my uncle Jack said to me before I left. *Anything, for the family, Eddie. Because the family goes on, when we can't.* And I had to wonder whether Jack had been trying to tell me something . . .

"It was a heart attack," said the Matriarch. "He was a lot older than he looked, you know. He . . . did things, to himself. Down through the years. Most of them entirely unauthorized. So he could carry on as Armourer. Long after anyone else would have retired."

Molly kept a tight hold on my arm through all of this. Pressing it so tight against her side I could feel her breathing. It felt like she was the only thing holding me up. My head felt strangely light and far away, as though I might just drift off at any moment. And there was a simple great ache in my chest, as though someone had punched the heart right out of me.

The Matriarch and Maxwell and Victoria finally stopped talking and stepped back to give me some space. They looked at one another, but I couldn't read the expressions on their faces. It did seem to me that there were things I should be saying, should be doing, but I couldn't think what. I was just dazed. Lost. Molly moved in closer so she could stare into my face. She looked worried.

"It's all right to cry, Eddie," she said quietly. "It's all right, if you need to. No one will stare."

"No," I said. "I don't cry. Not ever. I just don't. Because I discovered very early on that crying didn't help. The bad things still kept happen-ing when I was a child, and my parents never did come back, no matter how much I cried. So I just . . . stopped. What was the point?"

"It might be good for you," said Molly. "Make you feel better."

"No," I said. "It wouldn't."

"Then I'll cry for you," said Molly. And she did, with quiet, respectful dignity. And apparently quite genuinely.

"I'll never see my uncle Jack again," I said. "Never talk to him again. Never have him place one of his big engineer's hands on my shoulder when he wanted to make a point."

"You've lost people before," said Molly, sniffing back her tears.

"Not like this," I said. "Uncle Jack was always there, from my earliest childhood. I could depend on him to always be there. I really thought he'd go on forever. That even after I was gone he'd still be the Armourer . . . He and Uncle James were the nearest things I had to father figures. And I killed one of them and disappointed the other."

"James would have killed you," Molly said carefully, "if I hadn't finished him off first. And Jack was never disappointed in you."

"That's not what it feels like," I said. "I have to find my parents now. Charles and Emily. They're all I've got left."

"You've got me," said Molly.

I managed a small smile, for her. "Yes," I said.

"Isabella and Louisa wanted to come with me, to pay their respects," said Molly. Tactfully changing the subject. "But we all decided that probably wasn't a good idea. All three of the Metcalf Sisters, in one place? We didn't want to make your family feel nervous, at such a delicate time. Besides, somebody would be bound to say something, and Iz or Lou would be bound to overreact, and before you know it there's frogs hopping everywhere. Which is bad, especially at a funeral."

"You were right," I said. "Drood funeral services are always only for the family. There'll be a wake later, somewhere else. For friends and colleagues."

One of the family vicars came forward to start the service. Rather younger than I expected, but granted a certain gravitas by the old family robes and vestments, which hadn't changed a bit since Tudor times. His voice was calm, confident, and reassuring, as he read from his Bible the old words of comfort and farewell. I didn't recognise him, but then, we're a big family. And I haven't felt the need to attend family services since I got old enough to say no and make it stick. I pretty much gave up on prayer when I gave up crying, and for the same reason: because it didn't help. These days, when I do feel the need to pray, I do it directly. I don't feel the need for an intermediary. Ritual has never been a support or comfort to me. Probably because there's always been far too much of that in the family.

Molly leaned in close beside me, so she could murmur in my ear. "I'm surprised your family has vicars."

"We have everything we need," I said quietly. "We have to be totally self-sufficient, because we can only trust and depend on each other. He's Protestant, of course, because Droods won't stand for any outsider having authority over us. But that's as far as it goes. We don't do denominations."

"Are your family's funerals always this . . . big?" said Molly.

"No," I said. "This is special. A much-larger-than-usual gathering; for an important and much-loved member of the family."

I couldn't help but contrast this well-attended ceremony with the rush job the family had made of my grandfather's funeral. Arthur Drood, the legendary Regent of Shadows, had been put to his rest with almost indecent haste. Because he committed the cardinal sin of walking out on the family, and being successful outside it. I had to wonder what kind of send-off I would get when my time came.

All the gryphons and peacocks who normally wandered the grounds had gathered together in small groups on the outskirts of the crowd, watching the proceedings with big eyes and quiet solemnity. Not a sound out of any of them, as though they understood what was happening. And perhaps they did. You don't get ordinary gryphons and peacocks on Drood grounds.

I looked around me, at all the Droods, standing with heads bowed in their quiet, respectful ranks and rows. I didn't know or even recognise most of them. It occurred to me, then, that I wasn't even sure just how many Droods there were these days. So many had died in the recent wars and battles. Fighting the Hungry Gods, and the Accelerated Men, and the Immortals. And so many others. I looked from face to face . . . and a sudden thought struck me, squeezing my heart with a cold hand. Might some of them be the very secret agents Uncle Jack and I had talked about? The family within the family, specialising in deniable operations that only he had access to? Would it take something like the Armourer's funeral to bring them out to show themselves in public?

And then an even worse thought came to me: could any of these very secret and secretive agents have been responsible for the Armourer's death? If anyone could make a sudden death look like a natural heart attack, it would be them. Could they have done it to shut down our proposed investigation into them? Because he was ready to start asking awkward questions, on my behalf? Did I get my uncle Jack killed? That thought was too awful to bear. I couldn't breathe for a moment; then I relaxed, just a little. No. They wouldn't do that. I was almost sure they wouldn't do that. Because the Armourer was their only link with the rest of the family. They needed him, to get the things they needed to do their jobs. Things only the Armourer could supply. So who would they turn to now? Maxwell and Victoria? Should I say something to them? Or might those very secret agents turn to me? As the only truly independent Drood left in the family?

I realised I was only thinking these things so I wouldn't have to think about what was happening in front of me. So I pushed the thoughts aside and gave the funeral my full attention. Uncle Jack was what mattered. Everything else could wait.

I looked around the massed ranks of family mourners again and was relieved to see a few familiar faces. The Librarian, William, was standing not far away. All dressed up in his formal Sunday best, and looking very ill at ease in it. At least he wasn't wearing his usual fluffy white bunny slippers. His assistant, Yorith, was right there at his side, keeping a watchful eye on him. Since I had brought William home from the Asylum for the Criminally Insane, he was a lot more together than he used to be, but his thoughts did still tend to wander, and so did he. Standing on William's other side was his wife, Ammonia Vom Acht. A short, pugnacious bulldog of a woman. Except she wasn't really there, of course. Just a sending, a telepathic projection. Ammonia would have been allowed in, as the Librarian's wife, but she wouldn't have been able to stand being among so many people for long. Crowds got past her mental defences, and then she couldn't keep the voices outside her head.

"Hello, Eddie," said a quiet, very familiar voice. I looked round and saw a short, rather plump young woman with straight black hair and heavy-framed spectacles smiling tentatively up at me. She held herself somewhat stiffly, as though to compensate for her lack of inches. Her formal clothes didn't suit her, though I would have been hard-pressed to say what would. She took in my blank expression and smiled quickly.

"I'm Kate!"

"Of course you are," I said. "Molly, this is Kate."

"I'm Eddie's controller," said Kate, thrusting out a hand for Molly to shake. Molly looked at it for a moment and then clasped the hand briefly.

"She's my contact," I said. "New ruling from the Matriarch; all field agents have to have their own personal contact with the family. For information, backup, and the like."

"Really?" said Molly. "How nice."

The two women glared at each other. I could tell they'd taken an immediate dislike to each other. I could feel frost in the air between them.

"Strictly speaking," said Kate, her cold gaze fixed on Molly, "this is a gathering for family members only."

"Molly is with me," I said. "That makes her family."

"You're not married to her yet," said Kate. "And a lot could happen before that. You need to think about which side you're on, Eddie."

"I have," I said.

Something in the tone of my voice must have got through to Kate, because she stopped glowering at Molly and looked uncertainly at me.

"Ah. Well," she said, "I won't bother you during the funeral. We can talk later."

People were already frowning at us, for raising our voices during the vicar's service. Kate backed quickly away, disappearing into the nearest collection of family members. Molly looked at me.

"Controller?"

"In her dreams," I said.

"I suspect that may be the problem," said Molly.

"What?"

"We'll talk about it later."

"Looking forward to it," I lied.

Molly stared around her. "I have to say, I'm really impressed at the size of the turnout. Is this . . . everybody?"

"Not everybody," I said. "There's still a skeleton staff on duty inside the Hall, manning the sensors and defences, just in case anyone should try to take advantage of the situation."

Molly nodded at the Librarian. "William's looking almost . . . normal. At least he didn't bring his giant white rabbit friend with him."

"The Pook?" I said. "He might be here. Being tactfully invisible."

"No," said Molly, "I'd See him."

"Have you any idea what he is?" I said.

"He's the Pook," said Molly.

"Okay . . . ," I said.

I turned my attention to a small group of people standing to one side, keeping themselves very much to themselves. I knew who they were, who they had to be. Such a varied assortment of types and attitudes could only be James' assorted illegitimate offspring. The Grey

Bastards. Unacknowledged and unaccepted by the family—though that didn't stop us making use of them when we needed people who operated in their murky twilight worlds. I shouldn't have been surprised there were so many of them; you can't swan around the world the way the legendary Grey Fox did, seducing one and all, and not leave a trail of illegitimate children in your wake.

I'd met a few of them. Maurice Levallier, Le Freak. Charlotte Karstein, the Wilderness Witch. Monkton Farley, consulting detective. And so many others, whom I knew by name or reputation. All of them here for Jack. He always had time for them. He kept in regular contact with a surprising number of his nephews and nieces, looking out for them as best he could. I had to wonder why so few of them had been brought home, into the arms of the family. Certainly Uncle Jack had always been ready to go to bat for them, down through the years, convinced that it was wrong for us to leave them out in the cold.

I moved over to the Matriarch, and quietly put the question to her. She shrugged quickly, as though irritated by such a question on such a formal occasion, but answered me anyway.

"Most of them have been contacted and offered sanctuary at one time or another. Usually on Jack's urging. And most of them politely, and sometimes not so politely, turned us down. They value their independence—perhaps because that's all they have that's rightfully theirs. They like to maintain a distance from us, though not so much that they won't take work from us when it's offered. As long as the money's right. We would never turn away anyone in need, Eddie, as long as they have Drood blood in them. Now hush, please; pay attention to the service."

The vicar was winding down, coming to the end of his reading. I went back to looking round at the family. All the lab assistants were there, still wearing their white lab coats with all the usual chemical stains, electrical burns, and bullet holes, like so many proud battle scars. A great many older members of the family stood with them, also wearing lab coats, just for the occasion. Men and women who had been the Armourer's assistants once, before moving on to take up other forms of service in the family. Few stay in the Armoury for long. It wears people out and burns them up, very quickly.

The rows of mourners suddenly opened up, falling back to allow the coffin to be brought forward. It glowed brightly in the Summer sunshine; formed from the golden strange matter of my uncle Jack's armour. Complete with a bas-relief representation of the Armourer, lying stretched out on the coffin lid, with a calm, composed face and his arms folded neatly across his chest. The golden figure looked very peaceful, very dignified. I barely recognised him. I wasn't sure Jack would have approved of this. He certainly never gave a damn about appearing dignified while he was alive.

"You still haven't explained," Molly murmured, "why your family felt the need to hold this funeral so quickly. When did the Armourer die exactly?"

"Just this morning, apparently," I said.

"Then what's the rush?"

"There's no body inside that coffin," I said. "He would have been cremated immediately after his autopsy. Nothing suspicious or sinister about that; it's standard family procedure. You have to remember, it's all about Drood DNA. We can't risk a Drood body, even the smallest part of it, falling into enemy hands. Or even potentially enemy hands. Which is pretty much everyone who isn't family."

"Why?" said Molly, frowning. "What makes your family's DNA so special?"

"We have all been changed," I said carefully. "First by the Heart, and then by Ethel, so we could bond with our armour. Only we can wear the torc, and summon the armour. So even if a torc should fall into enemy hands, they couldn't use it."

"Then you're not fully human?" said Molly, smirking suddenly. "That would explain a lot . . ."

The lab assistants, past and present, formed a long corridor of white coats, two rows of bowed heads for the golden coffin to be carried through, as a mark of honour and respect. The coffin itself was being carried by six very favoured assistants. Chosen by lot, because they would all have volunteered for the Armourer. Several assistants at the back of the crowd fired off a bunch of assorted experimental weapons in salute. From the look on the Matriarch's face, they hadn't cleared that with her first. No doubt they meant well, but I thought it sounded a bit ragged. They should all have agreed on the same weapon. But then, getting lab assistants to agree on anything is like herding cats. It can be done, but only with lots of rough language and the liberal use of a cattle prod. A choir of assistants sang "My Country, 'Tis of Thee," a cappella. One of Jack's favourites. Followed by "Moon River."

Molly leaned in close to me again. "I've never thought to ask before: is there any particular thing you'd like sung at your funeral, Eddie? Or haven't you thought about it?"

"Of course I've thought about it," I said. "I'm a field agent, and damn few of us survive to reach retirement age. Many's the stakeout I've passed, occupying myself with all the details of my funeral. I want lowered flags, and fireworks, and a day of general mourning. I want rent clothes and lives ruined forever. And as I'm put to my rest I want everyone to sing that hardy old perennial 'Remember You're a Womble.' Just to annoy everyone. They'll all be going, *Oh, that must be very significant. It must have meant something special to him.* But, no, it's just me having one last laugh. In fact, if people listen carefully they'll probably be able to hear giggling from inside the coffin. What about you, Molly?"

"I want 'The Witch,' by the Rattles," Molly said firmly. "It was an old Sixties hit, and my mother's favourite song when she was a kid. Either that, or Redbone's 'Witch Queen of New Orleans.' My mother was always singing that when I was little."

"I'm sensing a theme here," I said. "They're both very you."

She grinned. "It's either that or 'Kick Out the Jams Motherfucker.'"

People on all sides were glaring openly at us. So Molly and I glared right back at them.

Next came a flyby overhead, as several female lab assistants in white coats rode across the sky in an organized display, on white winged unicorns. It all looked very impressive, as they swept back and forth in carefully executed patterns, though I was just a little bit worried about the danger of sudden unicorn droppings. I also wondered when they'd found the time to practise all this before the funeral. Unless this was just something people in the family learned for special occasions. I used to know about things like that; maybe I had been away from the family for too long. The flying unicorns finished their display and fluttered down to the ground, to be replaced by a grand aerial procession of steam-powered autogyros, modernistic hellicars, and a whole bunch of brightly glowing flying saucers. I thought it all looked splendid.

The six chosen lab assistants carefully lowered the golden coffin to the ground before the Matriarch and the vicar and stepped back, surreptitiously massaging their aching shoulders. The vicar said a few last words, closed his Bible, and bowed his head. There was a pause. The Matriarch turned to me.

"Would you like to say a few words, Eddie?"

I looked at her, and then at the golden coffin. And at the bas-relief figure on the lid that didn't look anything like Jack. I stepped forward and the family watched silently. I thought I knew what I wanted to say, but my throat just closed up and I couldn't get the words out. In the end, all I could manage was "Good-bye, Uncle Jack."

And then I just stood there, unable to say or do anything, until Molly came and took me by the arm again and led me gently away.

The Matriarch made a speech. All very nice, and very formal; nothing that mattered. I didn't listen. And then we all looked round sharply as something exploded out of the artificial lake at the other end of the grounds. The Matriarch broke off, because no one was paying her any attention. We were all staring at the lake, where a great fountain had risen up out of the frothing, bubbling waters, sending huge ripples coursing across the disturbed surface. The fountain rose up and up, and then bent over suddenly and rained down onto the shoreline. It quickly formed into a pale blue human figure that strode forward across the lawns to join us.

As it drew nearer, it became clearer; the figure was a woman, made entirely from water. The outer shape remained solid, though its movements sent slow tides surging back and forth inside it. The family fell back, to allow her to approach the golden coffin. Up close, we could all see heavy drops of water dripping continuously from her chin, like tears. The Matriarch bowed to her respectfully, and we all followed suit. It isn't often that the undine in the lake takes on human form and favours us with her presence.

"Jack Drood," said the undine, in a soft, bubbling voice. "I was fond of him. He was kind to me."

We all waited, but she had nothing more to say.

The ceremony continued. The Matriarch finished her speech, the vicar said a few last words, and the golden coffin disappeared quite suddenly. Leaving in its place a small golden urn.

"The urn contains Jack's ashes," I explained to Molly. "They'll be scattered across the grounds, in some place that was special to him."

"Are we supposed to . . . ?" said Molly.

"No," I said. "The Armourer's ashes are the responsibility of the next Armourer."

Maxwell and Victoria came forward and picked up the urn between them. They both seemed surprised at how light it was. They turned to address the family.

"We will sprinkle the Armourer's ashes among a particular copse of trees, down by the lake," said Maxwell.

"He used to walk there with his wife, Clara," said Victoria. "She has already been put to rest in that place, and now he gets to join her. So they can be together again, at last."

I was a bit upset that I hadn't known about that. It seemed to me that I should have known about something so important to Jack. But then, there was a lot about my uncle I didn't know. I'd always known that.

"Droods have been put into the grounds of Drood Hall for centuries," I said to Molly. "So we can become a part of the trees and the grass and the flowers. One way or another, none of us ever get to leave Drood Hall."

The undine suddenly lost her shape and became a fountain again. People fell back as she blasted up into the air, arcing high across the Summer sky. She rained down onto her lake and disappeared back into the waters. Not leaving even a single ripple on the surface.

"She didn't stay long," said Molly.

"I'm surprised she stayed as long as she did," I said. "I've never known her to turn out for a funeral before."

"Look!" said Molly. "She left us a rainbow."

And so she had—a great brilliantly coloured bridge, sweeping across the sky from one side of the grounds to the other.

"Our ways may seem hard to the outsider," said the Matriarch, and everyone turned back to look at her again. "But they are necessary. For the protection of the living, as well as the dead. Be at peace, Jack Drood. Be at peace, the family."

Everyone bowed their head, and then they all turned away. The crowd started to break up. The Matriarch came over to join me and Molly.

"I take it Eddie has explained to you about Drood DNA, Molly," she said. "Even though he shouldn't have? Of course he has . . . In the past, we have tried other ways of dealing with our dead. There was Iain, for example, who persuaded the Matriarch of his day that we should experiment with taxidermy. Unfortunately, as it turned out, Iain didn't always wait for his subjects to be entirely dead before he started his work."

"What happened to him?" said Molly.

"He was cremated," said the Matriarch. "Alive. Along with all of his . . . creations."

"Where did the Armourer's coffin go?" said Molly.

"Back to Ethel," I said. "All torcs, and all armour, return to her. Because she is the source of our strange matter, after all. The urn will disappear, after Maxwell and Victoria have finished with it."

"You know," said Molly, "this probably isn't the right time to ask questions like this, but . . ."

"But you're going to anyway," I said. "Because propriety has never stopped you before. Go on; what is it?"

"Well," said Molly, "it's just . . . how does an invisible and immaterial presence like Ethel produce entirely material things, like the torc and the armour? I mean, where does all the strange matter actually come from?"

"Good question," I said. "Basically, Ethel can do all the amazing things she does because she's not from around here. Inasmuch as I, or anyone else in the family, is able to understand what she says on the subject . . . Ethel comes from a higher level of reality. You could say she's realer than us. Realer than our world, or our reality. It's not that Ethel won't explain herself; it's more that I don't think any of us are equipped to understand her answers."

"But . . . ," said Molly.

"There's always a but with you, isn't there?" I said. "But what?"

"But if she's so very godlike and far above Humanity, what is she doing here, hanging out with the likes of us?"

"Another very good question," I said. "And one that would almost certainly keep me up at nights worrying, if I thought about it too much, which I try very hard not to do. I can't help feeling that if we ever do discover the real reasons for Ethel being here, we're really not going to like them." I looked at the Matriarch. "Would you care to add anything?"

"I wouldn't dare," said the Matriarch. "The torcs and armour go back to Ethel. That's all we know, and all we need to know. For our own good."

"It's a pity she couldn't be here," I said.

*I am here!* said Ethel's voice from out of the air around us. *In spirit, anyway.*

"I thought you could only manifest in the Sanctity," said the Matriarch.

*Whatever gave you that idea? I'm flexible . . .*

"The body has been cremated, and you have his armour," said Molly. "So there's nothing left of the Armourer now. You don't even have a tombstone to visit, Eddie. Shouldn't there be a memorial wall somewhere, with the names of the honoured dead on it? For those who have fallen in battle, fighting the good fight, protecting Humanity?"

"Too many Droods die," said the Matriarch quite calmly. "The wall would soon be full, and the grounds would be overrun with tombstones. As a family, we've never been sentimental. We can't afford to be. We always look forward. Not back."

"How do you feel about that, Ethel?" said Molly. "Hell, how do you feel about death? Ethel?"

We waited, but there was no response.

"I think she's gone," I said. "A fine time to discover our otherdimensional benefactor has a sneaky side . . ."

"The Armourer will have his photo in the entrance hall," said the Matriarch. "And yes, before you ask, Eddie, I have made it my business to see your parents' photo reinstated in its rightful position there. It should never have been removed. Someone was just being petty. You get that sometimes, in families."

I looked around, at the departing members of my family. It was easier to see faces now that the ranks and rows were breaking up and everyone was going his own way. I kept hoping to see my parents in the crowd somewhere. I'd been sure they would turn up for the funeral, for the Armourer's sake, if not for mine. But there was no sign of them anywhere. It seemed they were still missing . . .

The ceremony had come to its proper close, and Maxwell and Victoria were now the new family Armourer. The family goes on . . . Married teams were not unusual in the position, but it had been quite a while. It was the kind of job that usually suited an enthusiastic loner. Like my uncle Jack . . . had become.

Scraps.2 was sitting quietly on his own. The robot dog had been there all along, watching everything with his glowing red eyes. I wasn't sure how much he'd understood about what was happening. I pointed him out to the Matriarch.

"Who's going to look after the Armourer's dog now?" I said.

"Oh, don't worry," said Maxwell, moving over to join us. "Victoria and I have already decided he can stay with us. In the Armoury."

"We'll look after him," said Victoria.

Scraps.2 rose to his feet and padded unhurriedly over to join them. He didn't seem too enthusiastic about the idea, but it was hard to read anything in his inflexible metal face. Maxwell and Victoria headed off to find the right copse to scatter the Armourer's ashes. Scraps.2 started after them, and then paused and turned his head to look back at me.

"Don't worry, Eddie," he said. "I'll look after them."

He padded after Maxwell and Victoria, and I just stood there and watched him go. It wasn't just that this was the only time I'd ever heard him speak; it was that Scraps.2 had spoken with his master's voice.

With the funeral over, the family broke up and everyone disappeared. Moving quickly off in different directions, going about their various business. In small groups, in couples, or on their own. As families will.

Most of them went straight back to the Hall, of course; back to work. Because the family's work was always waiting. The Grey Bastards disappeared through a series of briefly manifesting Doors. And a few of us just went wandering off through the grounds, to commune with nature for a while. Everyone mourns in their own way.

The Matriarch made a point of staying with me, for a few last words. Molly stuck close beside me.

"I have to say, I'm not pleased with your handling of the Big Ear business," the Matriarch said flatly, "but I suppose you did the best you could, in a difficult position. I'm definitely annoyed that the Prime Minister tried to use us to clean up his mess. I really must ring him up later and put the hard word on him. I haven't had good reason to make a world leader cry like a baby, so far."

"It is one of the perks of the job, as Drood Matriarch," I said solemnly.

"And I am most definitely not pleased that this Gemma Markham is doing the kind of job only Droods should be allowed to do," the Matriarch said loudly. "Only we get to listen in on everybody, because only we can be trusted. And because mostly we don't care. Eddie, you were ordered to bring the device here. Along with the telepath."

"I couldn't remove the device from Lark Hill," I said steadily, "because Gemma needed it to do her job. And I didn't feel right about removing her, in case I crippled this country's ability to defend itself from terrorists."

"You don't get to decide policy like that," said the Matriarch.

"I do when you can't make up your mind in time," I said. "It really doesn't matter. We don't need the device itself. Now that we know the government acquired it from Black Heir, we can lean on the organisation to find out where they got it, what they know about it, and how it works. Because you can bet they examined that device top and bottom, and inside and out, before they handed it over. And . . . now we know Black Heir has ambitions to become a Major Player in the hidden world. To be the new Department of Uncanny. Forewarned is forearmed."

"Would that necessarily be such a bad thing?" said the Matriarch. "Somebody has to take over. Work isn't being done that needs to be done, and someone has to take up the slack. At least Black Heir is a known organisation. They're ambitious, but we can live with that."

"What matters is they didn't tell us about the device, and what it can do," I said. "And they should have."

"Good point," said the Matriarch. "I can see I'm going to have to make another phone call, and make someone else cry hot tears of bitter shame before I'm through."

We all walked back to the Hall. Along the way, we met up with the Serjeant-at-Arms. He presented the Matriarch with a thick sheaf of papers, and she leafed quickly through them as we walked.

"A lot of people have sent their regards . . . ," she said. "Friends, and colleagues, and even a few enemies, from all over the world. And from a few places not anywhere in the world. The Armourer did get around . . . Word has got out very quickly, to the supernatural and the super-science communities. Jack knew a great many people outside the Hall, even though strictly speaking he wasn't supposed to. And yes, Eddie, I do know all about his clandestine visits to the Nightside, and the London Knights, and a whole bunch of other places very much off-limits to members of this family. The previous Matriarch knew too. It never seemed worth making a fuss over. As long as he was . . . discreet, we thought it better to just let him go, rather than have a confrontation. Which might have led to us having to lay down the law and him defying us."

I thought about that. "Do other people in the family . . . ?"

"Of course," said the Serjeant-at-Arms. "Don't ask, don't tell. And above all, don't get caught."

"The Armourer touched the lives of a great many people," said the Matriarch, still working her way through the thick sheaf of papers.

"One way, or another . . . He was the last of the Old School Droods. Blunt instruments of Drood policy. A lot of people are going to miss him. A pity we couldn't allow some of them to attend the ceremony . . . but it just wasn't practical. We can't have outsiders at a Drood ceremony, in Drood grounds."

"I'm here!" Molly said immediately.

"Believe me," said the Serjeant, "we noticed."

"We made an exception for you," said the Matriarch. "Because we have to."

"Damn right," said Molly.

"There'll be a wake, in a few hours, for friends and colleagues and . . . others," said the Serjeant. "At the Wulfshead Club. We've hired the place exclusively for the evening. Should be quite a do."

"We'll head over there later," I said to Molly.

"Of course," she said. "And then we'll see the old man off properly."

I stopped, and everyone else stumbled to a halt. They looked at me, as I looked out over the wide, sweeping grounds.

"You go on," I said. "I'm not going back to the Hall, just yet. I think . . . I need to be by myself for a while. Take a little stroll around the grounds. Do some thinking."

"Of course," said the Matriarch. "We'll talk more later, Eddie."

"Looking forward to it," I lied.

She moved on, with the Serjeant-at-Arms. Already forgetting me as they discussed existing business, and what the change in Armourer might mean to the family, and how it would affect ongoing operations. I found I felt a bit annoyed about that. It seemed disrespectful, with Jack only just dead. But the family goes on. Molly leaned in close and kissed me on the cheek.

"Go for your walk, Eddie. Take your time, say your good-byes. I'll head on over to the Wulfshead, make sure they're arranging things properly."

She stepped back and disappeared. Gone in a moment. The air

crashed in to fill the empty space where she'd been standing. I looked
at where she'd been thoughtfully. It wasn't supposed to be possible for
an outsider to just teleport out of Drood grounds without permission.
The standing defences and protections should have prevented it. But
then, that was Molly for you. Always ready to do the impossible and
make it look easy.

I wandered off into the grounds, across the great grassy lawns, past
the huge flower beds with their intricate patterns of unusual and unnatural blooms. A large eye composed of almost unbearably colourful
flowers winked slowly at me as I passed. Most of the family were gone
now, and even the gryphons and peacocks had returned to their usual
stomping grounds. Raucous noises floated on the still air as they made
their presence known. I walked on, taking my time, not heading anywhere in particular. I was thinking about my uncle Jack. I wished we'd
talked more. I wished I'd listened more. So many things I meant to ask
him, or tell him, but I never did, because I always thought there'd be
another time. Until suddenly there wasn't.

I passed a small copse of quite unremarkable trees, not far from
the lake, and there in the quiet patch of shade Maxwell and Victoria
were taking it in turns to scatter Jack's ashes from the small golden
urn. They were being very solemn, and very efficient about it. Scraps.2
watched them work, lying on his back with all four metal legs in the
air, for all the world like a real dog. I left them to it.

I wandered here and there, thinking about this and that, and
couldn't seem to make up my mind about anything. It was all too sudden, too raw . . . like a wound that needed time to heal. An important
part of my life had been torn away, and that would take some getting
used to.

I finally wound up standing before the great burial mound at the
rear of the grounds, under which lay the dragon's head I had brought
back from Castle Frankenstein. I think he knew I was coming to see him

before I did. He addressed me from inside his mound, the warm, friendly voice booming inside my head, expressing his regrets over Jack's passing. Of course he knew the Armourer was dead. He was a dragon.

"Your human lives go by so quickly," he said. "Mayfly moments, flickering through history . . . It amazes me you ever get anything done in such a short time. I shall miss Jack Drood. He did a lot for me. And he often came out here to talk to me. We learned so much from each other."

"What did you talk about?" I said.

"We had a lot in common," said the dragon. "We'd both seen the world change in so many ways since we were young. And we both understood that it's never too late to make your mark."

I thought about that, all the way back to the Hall.

Finally, because I'd run out of reasons not to, I went back into the Hall. I didn't want to talk to my family, or share my private memories of the Armourer with them, but I knew it was required of me. Not by my family—I didn't give a damn what they wanted—but because my uncle Jack would have expected it of me. He was always very firm on duty and responsibilities and family obligations. The upholding of family traditions. Except for when they got in the way of what he believed needed doing.

I found William the Librarian waiting for me just inside the entrance hall. He stood alone, still in his good suit, looking uncomfortable but determined. I looked around, but there was no sign anywhere of his assistant and part-time keeper, Yorith.

"I sent him away," said William, without having to be asked. "You and I have private business, Eddie."

"We do?" I said politely.

"Oh yes! Very definitely yes. Do we? Yes."

He looked firm and focused enough, but there was still a certain vagueness in his eyes. I nodded slowly.

"Shouldn't we be attending some terrible prepared buffet, with cold finger food and people making forced small talk?" I said. "That is what usually happens after a funeral, isn't it?"

"Knowing this family, by now they'll have descended on the free food like a swarm of locusts," said the Librarian. "Let them. You and I have something far more important to do."

"Oh yes?" I said, still being as polite as I could. "Like what, exactly? What could be so important now?"

"We have to clear out Jack's room," William said firmly. "Sort through his belongings and possessions, decide what to keep and what to throw away. Because Maxwell and Victoria are waiting to move in."

Of course. I understood. It's family tradition that when someone high up dies, their replacement takes over straightaway. In all private, as well as public, matters. It's the only way some of us ever get a better room. There would be a whole series of upheavals in the Hall now, with people dragging suitcases and crates up and down the hallways as everyone moved up one. So I just nodded, and followed William up the stairs, all the way to the top floor. A room on the highest floor of the Hall was a mark of the exalted status the family afforded Jack, and not just as Armourer. He'd served the family in so many ways, for so many years. It's all about seniority and respect.

Jack's room turned out to be cosy and comfortable, with a large window and a really nice view out across the grounds. I knew people in the Hall who would kill for a window, with or without a really nice view. I stopped just inside the door and looked the room over. Decent-sized if characterless furniture, white walls, and a grey carpet. It all seemed very . . . tidy. As though Jack had hardly made an impression on the space.

William wandered around, looking at things, picking them up and putting them down again. After a while he realised I hadn't moved from the door, and he stopped to look back at me.

"He wasn't ever here much, you know. Spent all the hours he could down in the Armoury. Even kept a cot there, for emergencies. He did love his work . . . It was different, I think, back when he had Clara. Do you remember his wife, Clara?"

"Not really," I said. "Did you know her, William?"

"I think so," he said. "My memories still tend to come and go, but . . . yes, I'm pretty sure I knew her. A pleasant enough sort. You know, he should have had this carpet cleaned. Look at the state of it . . ."

"I haven't been here in years," I said. "Not since I was a kid. But nothing seems to have changed much. Why are we doing this, William? Why does it have to be us? Shouldn't something like this be down to the Matriarch, or the Serjeant?"

"We get to do the honours," said William, "because we were his friends. We knew him best."

"You were his friend?" I said. "I never knew that."

"Jack . . . liked to compartmentalise his life," said the Librarian. "Kept things, and people, separate. Easier to keep secrets that way."

"Secrets?" I said. "What kind of secrets?"

But William was already off again, bumbling around the room with vague eyes, as though expecting to see something he couldn't quite remember.

I moved slowly forward, to look at the Armourer's bed. It was still unmade, the blankets thrown back from where he'd got out of it just that morning. There was even a dent in the pillow, from where his head had rested. It seemed wrong to me that so many things could just go on when my uncle Jack didn't. The world should have stopped, at least for a while, when he died. It was as though the world didn't care. Didn't realise what a marvellous thing it had lost.

"Your uncle Jack left you something," William said suddenly.

"Yes, I know," I said. "The Bentley."

"No," said the Librarian. "I meant this . . ."

I looked around. William was holding out an object to me, wrapped in rough cloth. The kind of rag Uncle Jack always kept handy to mop up spills. I took the object from the Librarian and carefully unwrapped it. And of course, it was the Merlin Glass. The silver-backed hand mirror looked innocently back at me. I studied the Glass for a long moment, and then looked at William. He shrugged quickly.

"Jack had it delivered to me, in the Library. Don't ask me how; it was just . . . suddenly there. With a note saying I should get the Glass to you if anything should happen to him. I don't think it was any kind of presentiment; he was just being cautious. Which is always a good idea, with something as powerful as the Merlin Glass. Can't risk it falling into the wrong hands, hmm? According to the note, he hadn't had time to do any work on the Glass . . . Presumably you know what that means."

I nodded and put the Glass away in my pocket dimension. And then I carefully folded the piece of cloth and tucked that away too. Because it was the last thing Uncle Jack ever gave me. Of course, he would never have approved of such a gesture. He was never sentimental. I looked at William.

"Does the Matriarch know about the Glass?"

"Oh, I'm sure I'll get around to telling her," said the Librarian. "Eventually."

"Maggie is taking her new role as Matriarch very seriously," I said. "She won't like things being kept from her."

"Tough," said William.

"I don't want you getting into trouble on my behalf."

"If the Matriarch is ever dumb enough to raise her voice to me," William said calmly, "my wife will make Maggie think she's a chicken. For a whole week. Besides, I'm crazy. Everyone knows that. I can't be expected to remember everything. And I don't. Really! I have witnesses!" He grinned at me. "Which can be a very useful mask to hide behind, on occasion."

His voice was calm and rational. His face was everything a normal face should be. But there was still something about his eyes . . . I decided it was probably best to move on. William must have seen something in my face, because he nodded quickly.

"Is the Merlin Glass broken?" he said. "You really are very rough with your toys, Eddie."

"It's been . . . acting wilful, just recently," I said.

"Oh, that is never good in an inanimate object," William said cheerfully. "I'll do some research once I'm back in the Library. Dig through some of the family's oldest annals and see what I can turn up on the Glass' earliest history. Maybe I can finally discover just why Merlin Satanspawn made us a gift of the Glass in the first place. I mean, after all, the man didn't exactly have a reputation for kindness and generosity. The clue is in the name."

"Thank you," I said.

"Think nothing of it! I won't . . ." He stopped, and fixed me with a thoughtful look. "But you must know you are going to have to give the Glass back at some point. Picking an open fight with the Matriarch is rarely a good idea."

"Oh, I don't know," I said. "It's never stopped me before."

"But this is a new Matriarch," said William. "And as you have already noted, Maggie is very serious about her responsibilities."

"Nothing ever really changes in this family, William," I said. "You should know that."

"You've changed things."

"Yes. I have. But I have to wonder how much, and how long the changes will last."

"Well," said William, "if you will keep going away . . ."

"Maintaining a distance is all that keeps me sane."

"I know just what you mean," William said solemnly. "Why do you think I spend so much time in the Library?"

I looked around the room again. "They're all gone now," I said. "Grandfather Arthur, and Grandmother Martha. Uncle Jack and Uncle James. The Grey Fox's sons, Harry and Roger. And Jack's only son,

Timothy. Tiger Tim, rogue Drood and villain. I killed him, even after Jack asked me not to."

"I've read the report," said William. "You did what you had to."

"Doesn't make it right."

"Jack understood."

"Did he?"

William looked away. "The family goes on . . ."

"That's not the point! The point is . . . the only close family I have left now are my parents. Charles and Emily. Still missing; presumed dead by most people."

"I don't believe that," William said firmly. "And neither should you. First rule of the secret agent business: if you don't see the body, they're almost certainly not dead. And even if you have seen the body, they could still be faking it. You mustn't worry, Eddie. They'll turn up." And then he stopped and looked at me sharply with his cool, fey eyes. As though he knew so much more than I could ever know, or hope to understand. "Are you sure you still want to find them? They betrayed you at Casino Infernale. Traded away your soul in a game of chance and then disappeared before they could be called to answer for it. Those are not the actions . . . of good and loving parents."

"They didn't betray me," I said steadily. "I don't believe that, and neither should you. And even if they did, they're still my mum and dad. I'm sure they had their reasons. They're still out there, somewhere. And I will find them. I have to."

"We do seem to have lost a lot of Droods lately," said William. He sat down on the edge of the unmade bed and kicked his heels idly. "It's been a hard few years for the family. Our victories may have been great, even significant, but we have paid for them with the blood and suffering of our bravest and our best. Still, look on the bright side, eh? At least the Hall isn't so crowded any more. We won't have to move anytime soon. I really wasn't looking forward to that."

I looked at William. He didn't seem to be joking.

We sorted through Jack's few belongings. There weren't that many. He never did care much for . . . things. Not outside of the Armoury, anyway. There were only two framed photographs, on the small bedside table. One showed Jack with his wife, Clara, not long after they were married. It was a carefully cropped close-up of just the two of them, with no background. Could have been taken anywhere. Tellingly, there was nothing in the photo to link them to the Droods, or to Drood Hall. Just two not-so-young people, smiling happily at each other, obviously very much in love.

I thought the other framed photo would be of their son, Timothy, perhaps when he was just a child. Instead it turned out to be a photo of me. Smiling broadly into the camera. I picked it up and looked at myself. It was hard to believe I'd ever been that young. I recognised the image immediately. The Armourer took the photo on the day I left Drood Hall for the very first time. Full of hope and ambition and confidence, with no idea how my life was going to turn out. I was so happy then, and so impatient to be off and put the family behind me. William moved in beside me.

"You look . . . very keen," he said.

"Couldn't wait to be on my way," I said. "All I wanted then was to run away from home and never have to see any of my family again. I never knew Jack kept this photo all this time."

I put it down on the bedside table. I could feel my throat closing up again.

Jack's bookshelves were packed from end to end—not with science books or weapons manuals, but with dozens of old science fiction magazines from the Fifties and Sixties. *Analog, F&SF, Galaxy* . . . And a complete set of Arkham House first editions. They all looked very well read. I had to smile. I loved the idea of my uncle Jack sitting down after a hard day's work and relaxing by reading the grim cosmic horror tales of H. P. Lovecraft.

"Would you like those?" said William. "I'm sure he'd want them to go to someone who'd appreciate them. The Matriarch would just sell them all off. I understand this kind of thing can raise a bundle on eBay."

"Yes," I said, "I'd like them."

"No problem! I'll hide them away in the Library," said William, "until you're ready to pick them up. Who'll notice a few more books in a Library, hmm?"

"He doesn't seem to have any films," I said. "No DVDs or Blu-rays. Not even any laser discs, and I know he had a complete set of Hammer films on those."

"He kept all his favourite films and television shows on his computer," said William. "Though don't ask me when he ever found the time to sit down and watch them. Don't worry, I've already removed all his porn."

He winked at me roguishly, and once again I had no idea at all whether he was joking.

I opened up the heavy old-fashioned wardrobe that took up half a wall. Inside were a dozen freshly laundered white lab coats, all of them positively crackling with starch. Hanging side by side, ready for use. Along with a dozen pairs of identical grey slacks, and a dozen pairs of freshly shined black shoes. So he could just reach out and take the next in line when he needed it, without having to think about it. He never could be bothered with things that didn't matter to him. His thoughts were always somewhere else.

"Who did his T-shirts for him?" I said suddenly. "I don't see any here, but every time I met him, he always seemed to have a new one, saying something appalling."

"It was a competition," said William. "The lab assistants got to make suggestions, and Jack would wear the ones he liked most. The winning assistant was honoured by being allowed to wear one just like it. I'm told competition was very fierce."

"I never knew that," I said. "What else didn't I know about him because I couldn't be bothered to ask?"

"You can't know everything about anyone," said William.

"I should have tried."

"You're too hard on yourself, Eddie."

"Somebody has to be," I said.

"Jack's clothes will be recycled among the family," said William. "Nothing is ever wasted. Same with all of his belongings, except for whatever you and I decide we might like for ourselves."

"We get first pick?" I said.

"We get the only pick. No one else is interested. The family doesn't do sentiment, remember?"

"What about his lab assistants?" I said. "Past, and present? I mean, I understand there were some he was . . . closer to than others."

"Ah! You mean the ladies! His lovers!" William dropped me another roguish wink. "I think they'll probably lie low. Won't want to draw attention to themselves. Probably just as well. Last thing we need in here is a major catfight. Not so much bad language and hair-pulling . . . more like improvised weapons and depleted-uranium knuckle-dusters! Really not good, in such a confined space . . . No, let sleeping lab assistants lie, I think. Oh, don't look so shocked, Eddie. Your uncle was a much-loved man. Especially on weekends. He was old, not decrepit. And he was always discreet. Ish. If anyone does come forward, quietly, I'll see what I can do."

"It's all such a rush," I said. "No time to think . . ."

"You know the family likes to do this quickly. Like ripping off a Band-Aid. Get the pain over with as quickly and efficiently as possible. And move on."

It didn't take us long to sort through Uncle Jack's belongings. When we'd finished, we stood by the door and looked round the room one last time. I didn't know what to say.

"You don't have to wait around for the removal people if you don't want to, Eddie," said William. "If you'd find that . . . difficult. I can take care of things."

"I have to do this," I said. "It's my duty."

"This isn't duty, boy," said William. "It's a privilege. You've already done everything your uncle would have expected of you."

"He didn't have much to leave behind," I said. "Just a room full of bits and pieces. Not much to show for a life of service to the family."

"The measure of a man isn't his possessions," said William. "It's his legacy."

"The Armoury?"

"No, boy. The family he protected. And you. He helped make you the man you are today. Didn't he?"

"Yes," I said. "He did."

# CHAPTER SIX

# It's Not a Proper Wake Until Someone Does Something They Shouldn't

The Bentley was still waiting patiently outside the main entrance to Drood Hall. I'd broken all kinds of rules by leaving her there, but no one was going to mess with one of the Armourer's best-known and much-loved creations. In fact, quite a large admiring crowd had gathered around the car, and I received a great many jealous and downright envious looks as I settled down behind the wheel again. I smiled happily on one and all, in a not at all smug way, and then fired up the engine and drove away, scattering the fans like a flock of chickens. I drove round the side of the Hall, then round the back, and straight into the Drood garage.

The heavy doors in front of me were quite definitely closed. I put my foot down hard and the Bentley leapt forward. She's a lot like me; tell her you can't go somewhere, and nothing on earth will stop her going there. The garage doors slid smoothly aside at the very last moment, providing just enough room for the Bentley to pass between them without actually scraping the paint off her bodywork. I could have stopped outside, sounded my horn, and waited politely, like a good little Drood, but I really wasn't in the mood. I rarely am, when I'm home. Being around my family does that to me. And I absolutely wasn't in the mood so soon after Jack's funeral.

I brought the Bentley to a sudden halt just inside the doors, because there wasn't anywhere left to go. The Drood garage is really just a long, wide shed, packed from end to end and from side to side with more assorted forms of transport and death on four wheels than the human mind can comfortably cope with. And not just the famous ones, of which there are always a few. Just sitting there in the Bentley, I could see the Nineteen Sixties Black Beauty, a shocking pink Rolls-Royce, and the only occasionally successful Lotus submersible. Thick shafts of golden sunlight dropped down from massive skylights in the vaulting roof, shining brightly back from the highly polished metallic exteriors of hundreds of exotic vehicles, all of them ready for use at a moment's notice. Provided you could show the garage chief all the proper paperwork and a chit personally signed by the Matriarch.

I shut down the Bentley's engine, wrestled my way out of the seat belts, and got out of the car. I leaned back against the long green bonnet and waited for someone to notice me. I really should have gone through proper channels and bowed down to the mechanics and engineers until they were satisfied I had a right to be there, and then let them summon the garage chief . . . But I didn't trust my self-control. All it would take was one wrong word, or even a look, and there would be harsh language, arse-kickings, and bad temper all over the place. Goodwill and cooperation would go right out the window. No. Much better to start as you mean to go on—stubborn and intractable, with a side order of pigheaded.

I looked around me, taking in rows and rows of cars and motorbikes, rescue vehicles and attack craft, tanks and field ambulances and camouflaged surveillance trucks. We've got at least one of everything you can think of because you never know from day to day just what the family is going to need in order to stay on top of everything. My family has always worked on the principle *Better to have it and not need it than need it and not have it.*

But the garage isn't there just for the field agents; the family is always ready to hire out specialized vehicles and equipment to other people and organisations in our line of work. For a suitably eye-watering fee, of course; along with secret information, or the promise of future favours. We could afford to do it for free, out of the goodness of our hearts, but then no one would respect us.

The garage chief came striding through the parked rows to join me. Frowning so hard it must have hurt her face. Sandra used to be one of my uncle Jack's lab assistants, until it became clear she was interested in working only on things that went really fast. So the then Matriarch made a virtue out of a necessity and promoted Sandra sideways, to work in the garage. It took only a few years before Sandra was garage chief, and very much in charge. Tall, statuesque, and burning with far more nervous energy than was good for her, Sandra had a face that would have been pleasant enough if she ever stopped scowling, under an unrestricted mop of curly red hair. Her dungarees were covered in fresh and old oil stains along with a great many other less easily identifiable discolourations. She believed in running things from the ground up, and positively delighted in getting her hands dirty. She planted herself in front of me, stuck both fists on her hips, and glared at me meaningfully.

"You've got some nerve, Eddie."

"So they tell me," I said pleasantly. "Hello, Sandra. You're looking . . . very yourself. Blown up anything interesting recently?"

"What do you want, Eddie?"

"Just dropping off the Bentley."

"You haven't broken her *already*?" Sandra pushed past me to look the car over, like a mother whose child has just returned from school in the company of an axe murderer. "Jack should never have left you this car! You don't appreciate her! I would have looked after her properly. Respected her! You've never respected anything in your life!"

"That is one of my more appealing qualities," I murmured. "Unclench, Sandra, before you strain something. The Bentley's fine. She just needs a good look-over. I did push her pretty hard, racing back here for the funeral."

Sandra sniffed loudly, to make it clear I was not in any way forgiven. "Don't think I've forgotten the mess you made of the Bentley the last time the Armourer let you drive her. Took us weeks to beat the dents out of the bodywork."

"Cars are meant to be used," I said. "And the world can be a very unforgiving place when you do the kind of work I do. If it was up to you, none of these vehicles would ever leave the garage in case someone breathed on them the wrong way."

"You're so sharp you'll cut yourself one of these days," growled Sandra. She patted the Bentley's bonnet encouragingly. "Don't worry, baby; Mama's here to protect you from the nasty man."

She yelled to her people, and a whole bunch of them came hurrying forward from all sides at once. They crowded round the Bentley, making excited noises and muttering barbed comments they only thought I couldn't hear. They soon had the car up on the hydraulic ramp, so Sandra could check the underside for damage. I stood back and let them get on with it. I have all the mechanical aptitude of King Kong in boxing gloves. I can break things just by looking at them wrong.

Sandra darted back and forth underneath the Bentley, shining a hand torch into all kinds of nooks and crannies I hadn't even known were there. The first thing she found was a long-stemmed rose, wrapped round and round the rear axle. She put on a pair of really heavy leather gloves, took a firm hold on the thorny stem, and pulled the thing free with a series of harsh, vicious jerks. I leaned in close for a better look, curious to see what I'd picked up. You're bound to acquire the odd hitchhiker when you take short cuts through the side dimensions. Sandra made a pleased, satisfied sound as she pulled the rose free, and then said something really unpleasant as the thorn-covered stem lashed out at her. It whipped tightly round her arm and did its best to force jagged thorns through her reinforced sleeve. The blood-red rose hissed loudly at Sandra, its thick, pulpy petals curling back to show vicious teeth. Sandra glared right back at it, entirely unimpressed. She took a firm hold on the stem with her other hand, unwound the thing one curl at a time, and then broke its neck just below the flower. The long stem stopped thrashing immediately, and the rose screamed shrilly. Sandra threw the flower on the floor and stamped on it, hard. The rose went quiet, and Sandra nodded stiffly.

"I've seen worse," she said. "Let's see what else you picked up along the way, Eddie."

"It's not like I offered it a lift," I said.

She ignored me. Further inspection turned up an extra exhaust pipe that had no business being where it was. Sandra looked at it thoughtfully, and gestured for two of her people to pry the thing loose with long-handled screwdrivers. It took them a while, because it really didn't want to budge; but when the pipe finally came away it immediately changed shape, becoming a long metallic snake that shot straight for the throat of the nearest mechanic. Sandra stabbed it neatly through the head with her screwdriver, piercing it in mid-air, and then threw it down and pinned it to the hard stone floor. The metallic snake refused to die, whipping back and forth, but it couldn't escape . . . as long as the cold iron of the screwdriver held it firmly in place.

"Another hitchhiker," said Sandra. She wasn't even breathing hard. "Just pretending to be a length of pipe, hoping not to be noticed, until it got a chance to drop quietly off and make a run for it. Hugh! Denny! Get the blueprints for the Bentley! We're going to have to go over this car inch by inch to make sure everything is what and where it's supposed to be."

While they were waiting for the blueprints to turn up, Sandra had her people spray the metallic snake with freezing nitrogen. The snake fought the foam's effects till the last moment, turning into half a dozen increasingly impossible things, until the terrible cold finally knocked all the fight out of it. Sandra then pulled her screwdriver free, and her people moved quickly in to deposit the snake in a reinforced container with a lead-lined interior, before taking it away for further study. Sandra then turned back to me, and glared at me accusingly.

"Where the hell have you been, Eddie?"

"The subtle realms," I said.

"Then you've only yourself to blame. Some places should be declared permanently off-limits to all sane and rational beings. Hello, what have we here?"

Everyone else surrounding the Bentley took several steps back, upon hearing those words. Sandra crouched down, looking closely at the mud dripping off the underside of the car. Not to be outdone, I crouched down beside her. Bits of mud on the floor were writhing and seething, humping slowly and deliberately away from the car.

"Interesting . . . ," said Sandra. "Psychegeography; living materials, from a world where every part of it is alive and conscious . . . Usually with bad intent. You do get around, don't you, Eddie? Come on, people! Get your arses back here! I want every single bit of this unnaturally mobile shit caught, collected, and locked up in seriously secure containers so it can be sent away for analysis. And God help any of you if you miss one little bit."

Her people made themselves very busy. Secretly, I think they quite liked being shouted at. Sandra straightened up again, so I did too. She shook her head slowly.

"We are not here to provide you with a cleaning service, Eddie."

"Come on," I said. "Admit it. You're having fun."

She looked around to make sure no one was watching, and then shot me a quick grin. "You do tend to brighten up an otherwise dull day, Eddie."

"How long before I can have the car back?" I said.

"Oh, she'll be ready by the time you're back from the wake," said Sandra. "Sink a few cold ones for me. He was the best, your uncle Jack; you know?"

"Yes," I said. "I know."

I nodded a quick good-bye and headed for the garage doors. Sandra yelled after me.

"Hey, Eddie! You're supposed to be close to the new Matriarch! Talk to her! Tell her we need a decent budget to do a proper job. You can't work miracles every day on the cheap! Are you listening to me, Eddie?"

I kept walking. Some fights you just know you shouldn't get caught in the middle of.

Once I was safely outside the garage, I retrieved the Merlin Glass from the pocket dimension I keep in my pocket, shook the Glass out to Door size, and stepped through. The Glass dropped me off in a very familiar dark alleyway outside the Wulfshead Club. I shivered despite myself, moving from the warmth of a Summer's day to the chilly twilight of a London evening. The Glass worked perfectly, for once, which was just as well, because I wasn't in the mood to be messed with. Perhaps the Glass could sense that. It shrank down to a hand mirror again, and I tucked it away in my pocket. I looked carefully around me. There was no one about in the alley to note my arrival; the Merlin Glass is always very good about choosing just the right moment.

The alley was full of shadows, lit only by the single amber street light at its far end. It all seemed very quiet; even the roar of passing city traffic sounded eerily muffled, suppressed. Harsh neon from the adjoining streets barely penetrated a few inches into the alley. It was a lonely, separate place, by design. The alley existed only to give access to the Wulfshead Club.

The narrow passageway was a mess, as always, with piles of genuinely disturbing garbage scattered the length of it. Deliberately never cleaned up, to discourage the wrong sort of people. Some of the garbage seemed to be moving, and not in a good way. And I was pretty sure it wasn't going to be anything as obvious as rats. I gave the garbage plenty of room as I headed for the only door, set flush in the left-hand wall.

The shiny wet brickwork was covered with layer upon layer of old overlapping graffiti—the usual threats and warnings, boasts and sarcasm. Names of old gods and new street gangs, monsters and messengers. The usual gossip and intelligence, from the hidden world. From the ones who know . . . There was one example of very recent graffiti, right next to the door. The paint still looked wet. *Eye Can See You.* Oddly ominous, and just a bit worrying . . .

I stood before the dully gleaming metal door. Solid silver, with no sign or name; either you knew this was the entrance to the Wulfshead Club, preferred drinking hole and gathering place of like-minded souls in the supernatural and super-science community, or you had no business being there. The silver was deeply etched with threats and warnings in angelic and demonic script. You can find all kinds at the Wulfshead. The Management don't care which side you're on; they just want your money. The door had no handle. I placed my left hand flat against the metal, which felt uncomfortably warm to the touch. Organically warm. The door swung slowly back, and I retrieved my hand with a certain amount of relief. If your name isn't on the club's approved list, the door will bite your hand off. I didn't think it could get to me past my Drood armour, but I wasn't in any hurry to find out the hard way.

I strode through the open door with my head held high and my nose in the air, as though I wasn't bothered at all. Never show weakness in front of your enemies. Or your friends.

Inside the Wulfshead Club, it was all bright lights and loud noise, the cheerful roar of a great many people determined to have a good time. It's almost obligatory to be cheerful at a wake, or you'd never get through it. I was pleased to see the place looking so crowded; I always knew my uncle Jack had a great many friends and colleagues, but it was good to see so many of them had turned out for the occasion. It isn't always possible, given the kind of lives we lead. Music from the Fifties and Sixties—Jack's favourite period—pumped out of hidden speakers. I recognised a compilation of John Barry themes, from old James Bond movies. Someone's idea of a sense of humour.

The walls were covered with a series of massive plasma screens, usually showing secret and embarrassing scenes from the lives of the rich and powerful, just for a laugh; but they'd all been turned off. To-night was all about Jack Drood, not the outside world. I headed for the long bar, which took up half the far wall. A gleaming high-tech structure, it looked more like a modern art installation than anything functional. But if you can name a drink, or even describe it, you can be sure you'll find it at the Wulfshead. Everything from Atlantean Ale to Angel's Urine, from sparkling holy water with a mistletoe chaser to Chernobyl Vodka (for that inner glow). From the frankly perverse to the seriously terrifying, from the entirely illegal to the utterly unnatural. Rumour has it the Wulfshead's mysterious Management keep their bar stock securely locked up in a separate dimension. Because they're afraid of it. The dozen or so barmen serving behind the bar all looked exactly the same, because they were. The Management clone them.

I spotted Molly half-way down the bar, chatting with her sisters, Isabella and Louisa. The world's most dangerous hen party. I called out Molly's name, and even through the loud music and raucous chatter, she heard me immediately. She spun round, saw me, and yelled my name joyously. She headed straight for me, barging through the packed crowd with simple determination and much use of her elbows. No one objected. Because even the kind of people who drink at the Wulfshead have more sense than to annoy a Metcalf sister. Molly broke through the last few people, hugged me hard, kissed me harder, and grabbed my arm so she could drag me back to the bar.

"Have a drink!" she said loudly. "Hell, have several! I am! All drinks are on the house, courtesy of your family, for the duration of the wake. I hope you brought a toothbrush and a change of clothes because I plan on being here for some time!"

We finally made it to the bar, and Molly drank thirstily from the glass in her hand before banging it down on the bar top, in front of the nearest barman.

"Another Hemlock Wallbanger, if you please, barman! With a mandrake chaser. And another bag of pork scratchings. What are you having, Eddie?"

I had already decided that one of us was going to have to pace ourself, and since experience suggested it definitely wasn't going to be Molly, I settled for my usual bottle of chilled Beck's. My family had hired this club for as long as needed, and this particular crowd looked determined to do Jack Drood's memory justice and see him off in grand style.

"We should really have held this do at Strangefellows," said Molly. "Your uncle always did most of his drinking in the Nightside. But I suppose there are limits . . ."

"Oh, there are," I said. "Really. You have no idea. I did once visit Strangefellows, with Walker. As Shaman Bond. Can't say I cared much for the place . . ."

"Of course not," said Molly. "Far too much fun going on there for you."

"I know how to have fun!"

"Only since you met me."

I decided it was probably safer not to disillusion her. I put my back to the bar, alongside Molly, and looked out over the club. There were lots of familiar faces present, many of them the kind of people you meet only at weddings or wakes. Or when you're trying to kill each other. I took a long pull at my nice cold Beck's and smiled easily on one and all. I was the only Drood present, because people like these wouldn't have felt at all safe or comfortable about discussing the Jack Drood they knew in front of his family. Because Uncle Jack . . . got around. I was allowed in only because everyone there knew how close I'd been to the Armourer. So, no Droods. My family can be tactful when we have to.

But almost immediately I saw one face that shouldn't have been there. Cedric Drood, the family's Serjeant-at-Arms. The only Drood who could break the rules with impunity, because he was responsible for enforcing them. He was dressed so casually I almost didn't recognise him; instead of his usual traditional butler's outfit, he was wearing a Sex Pistols T-shirt over very distressed jeans, and Doc Martens boots. Much about his personality suddenly became clear. But he actually did have every right to be at Jack's wake; I knew for a fact that he was one of the few other Droods who regularly went off the reservation, to meet and drink with people he shouldn't. I was sure that if pressed, Cedric would claim he did such things only so he could gather useful gossip and intelligence for the family. But then, as a wise woman once said, he would say that, wouldn't he? I could remember a time when I was the only Drood who got out and about; but perhaps I only thought that.

Cedric was drinking and laughing openly with people who genuinely didn't seem to care that he was a Drood. It's not often that that happens. In fact, the Serjeant seemed to be on friendly and even familiar terms with a great many people. I was actually shocked to see Cedric abandoning his dignity and letting his hair down, so openly and so enthusiastically. It was like finding out your strict old maiden aunt wore erotic underwear. Cedric looked around, caught me looking at him, and dropped me a heavy wink. I looked away.

The more I peered around the Wulfshead, the more I seemed to be surrounded by familiar faces. The current Seneschal of the London Knights was there: Sir Perryvale. A large Falstaffian gentleman, he was holding forth to a rapt audience on some of the more secret rituals the Knights got up to when no one else was around. Some of these rituals were extremely old; and some, he freely admitted, he and Jack just made up to see if the Knights would notice the difference. Sir Perryvale had a great mane of silver-grey hair, and a broad ruddy face with huge bristling side whiskers. He was wearing a deafeningly loud Hawaiian shirt over a pair of shorts that were far too short. Especially for a man with legs that hairy. He interrupted himself regularly to drink vintage Champagne straight from the bottle, despite the winces and vigorous protests from more civilised types around him.

He finished off the bottle and tossed it casually over his shoulder. One of the barman snatched it easily out of mid-air and supplied Sir Perryvale with a fresh bottle, already opened. The Seneschal saw me watching, and called for me and Molly to come over and join him, his great booming voice full of good cheer. I looked at Molly, and she nodded, so we made our way through the packed crowd. Sir Perryvale struck me as a useful person to know. You never know when you might need a friend or a favour, among the London Knights. Particularly now that King Arthur was back.

Sir Perryvale clapped me heavily on the shoulder with a big, meaty palm and made a point of kissing Molly's hand. I was a bit surprised she let him; she doesn't normally have much time for the formal stuff. It might have been the man's wide smile, or the roguish glint in his eyes; or she might also have decided she could use a future favour from the London Knights. It's hard to be truly spontaneous in our crowd. You always have to be thinking about what these people might have meant to us in the past, or how they might be useful in the future.

We chatted easily together about the usual inconsequential things, until the crowd Sir Perryvale had acquired drifted away, disappointed that he wasn't telling tales out of school any more. Once he was sure they were all gone, he leaned forward and fixed me with a knowing eye.

"Your uncle Jack and Cedric and I used to go out drinking

together all the time," he said. "More often than not in the sleazier parts of the Nightside, just because we knew we weren't supposed to be there. If you're going to break the rules, go all the way, that's what I say . . . And we used to have regular meetings with all the other servants and factotums, from all the other secret groups and organisations. To share useful information, and to say the things we couldn't say to our own people . . . It's always the most disciplined people who feel the need to let off a little steam, now and again. You wouldn't believe some of the gossip that went back and forth between us . . . But what gets said in the Nightside stays in the Nightside. Mostly. Your uncle Jack always told the best stories. Hell, he starred in a lot of them! I will miss him. I really will. I'm sure some of us will still get together for our little meetings, off the script and under the radar, but it won't be the same without Jack."

"I used to wonder how the Armourer got in and out of Drood Hall so easily, and so often, without being noticed," I said. "Of course, he was who he was, so . . . Now that I know about Cedric, much becomes clearer."

More familiar faces, everywhere I looked. From the Nightside, Dead Boy and Julien Advent. Dead Boy was wearing his usual deep purple greatcoat, with a black rose at the lapel, the coat deliberately left hanging open to show off his autopsy scar. He was drinking something that steamed and bubbled, and telling everyone who would stand still long enough about the times he and Jack went fishing for mermaids in the River Styx, deep down under the Nightside. Might have been true, might not; that was the Nightside for you. And, indeed, Dead Boy . . .

Julien Advent, that time-lost Victorian Adventurer, was dressed in the formal mourning wear of his own period, right down to the opera cloak and the silver-topped walking cane. It suited him, perhaps because he was one of the few people left alive who could still wear such clothes naturally. He made a point of paying his regrets to me and

Molly, while also giving the firm impression that Dead Boy was nothing to do with him. Apparently Julien once talked Jack into giving him a lengthy, no-holds-barred interview for publication in the *Night Times*. I gather drink was involved. Quite a lot of it. Anyway, after Julien sobered up and listened to the recordings he'd made, he quickly realised there was no way he could publish it without starting several wars, so he buried it. "Would have made a hell of an impact," he said wistfully.

From Shadows Fall came those wonderful fictional characters Bruin Bear and the Sea Goat. Shadows Fall is a small town in the back of beyond, where legends go to die when the world stops believing in them. Once upon a time, every child read the many adventures of the Bear and the Goat in the Golden Lands, but the books were no longer published and no longer popular, so Bruin Bear and the Sea Goat now lived only in Shadows Fall. Having marvellous new adventures, of a kind their old readers could only dream about.

Bruin Bear was a four-foot-tall teddy bear, with golden-honey fur and dark, knowing eyes. He wore a bright red tunic and had a bright blue scarf wrapped tightly round his neck. He also had a single gold earring and a Rolex on his wrist. He drank old-fashioned Coke from an old-fashioned glass bottle, and regaled us with happy tales of his times with the Armourer.

Apparently, Jack had once rescued the Bear and the Goat from kidnappers sent by their old publishers, who wanted them permanently disposed of so they could replace them with more modern and relevant versions. Bruin Bear shuddered delicately at the thought, and I felt like joining in. A lot of people paused as they passed, to nod and smile fondly at Bruin Bear. He was just that sort of Bear.

Which was more than you could say about the Sea Goat. Wrapped in a filthy ankle-length trench coat with half the buttons missing, he looked human enough from the shoulders down. Tall and angular, with broad shoulders, he had a huge blocky goat's head, with long curling horns and a permanent nasty grin. His grey fur was soiled and matted, and his eyes were seriously bloodshot. He'd fallen far from grace as a children's favourite, and it showed. He carried a bottle of vodka, which by some kind magic was never empty, and he was cramming his mouth full of the snacks left out in bowls along the bar top. He caught Bruin Bear looking at him and said indistinctly, "But it's the best kind of food! It's free!"

"I'd tell him to pace himself," said Bruin Bear, "but it would only be a waste of breath. *Restraint* is not a word the Sea Goat understands, along with other everyday terms like *dignity, self-control,* and *self-preservation instincts.* It wasn't supposed to be us, you understand, representing Shadows Fall; it should have been Old Father Time. Apparently he and Jack go way back . . . But at the last moment, there was a crisis in the chronoflow. No, me neither. He does hope to look in later, if he can get away. And the universe still exists. Shadows Fall was determined someone should be here to pay the town's respects to Jack's memory, and the Sea Goat volunteered the two of us."

"Did he know my uncle well?" I said politely.

"He saved your uncle's life!" said the Bear. "Didn't Jack ever tell you about that?"

He would have said more, but the Sea Goat chose that moment to pick a fight with the Soulhunter called Demonbane, and the Bear had to hurry over to break it up. Molly and I looked at each other. Sometimes there just aren't any words.

Representing the Ghost Finders of the Carnacki Institute was the Boss herself, the intimidating Catherine Latimer. Sitting quite calmly on a bar-stool, sipping an old-fashioned cocktail complete with a little parchment parasol. Chatting quite happily with Monkton Farley and Waterloo Lillian.

Catherine had to be in her late seventies by now, if not more (and some gossip suggested a lot more), but she still gave every indication of being unnaturally strong and vital. She looked like she could rip your head off and spit down your neck if you were dumb enough to offer to help her across a busy street. Medium height, of stocky build, she wore a smartly tailored grey suit, and smoked black Turkish cigarettes in a long ivory holder. She wore her grey hair cropped short in an unflattering bowl cut, and her face was all hard edges and icy-cold eyes.

Monkton Farley, that renowned consulting detective, shouldn't really have been at the wake. Given that he was the illegitimate son of Jack's brother James, and therefore half Drood. But it was hard to keep him away from any gathering where there was a chance for him to show off. I didn't mind that he solved impossible cases with style and elegance; I just wished he'd stop talking about them. He was dressed in the same old-fashioned outfit he'd worn to the funeral, complete with a starched high collar and immaculate white spats on his shoes. Because he had to make an impression wherever he went. He did look a little bit lost at the Wulfshead without his usual crowd of adoring followers, always ready to listen intently to his latest story and hang on his every word and tell him what a genius he was. Like he didn't already know that.

Waterloo Lillian was dressed as a showgirl, looking almost unbearably sexy and glamorous in dark fishnet stockings, a sparkling basque, and a tall feathered headdress. Presumably because he'd come straight from work. And, as he was wont to say, *Glamour is my life, darlings.* He was currently sipping absinthe from a champagne flute, with his little finger suitably extended.

Catherine Latimer saw me looking, and left the other two talking together so she could come over and join me and Molly. She was a good foot shorter than me, but I still felt like I should be looking up at her. Even Molly seemed a little unsettled in such overpowering company.

"I knew your grandmother Martha well, back in the day," said Catherine. "Girls together, and all that. I watched Jack and James grow up. And your mother, Emily, too, of course, Eddie. Now Martha and James and Jack are gone, and I'm still here. Don't ask me why. The good die young, perhaps. I shall miss Jack. He did a little work for me, you know, on the quiet. Always ready to help out the Ghost Finders with the odd weapon or device, in an emergency. The family never knew, I take it?"

"I'm pretty sure not," I said. "They tend to frown upon such things."

"Jack did have a life outside the family," said Catherine.

"So I'm finding out," I said.

I circulated through the Wulfshead, mingled, made conversation. And the more I heard about Jack, the less I felt I'd ever really understood him. I'd only known him as the Armourer, the old man in his lab coat who hardly ever seemed to leave the Armoury. I'd heard about his earlier career as a field agent, of course, but that had seemed like some other person. More and more, it was becoming clear that I'd known him only at the end of his life, when most of his activities were over. I felt . . . honoured to have shared a few of his last adventures with him. I wished I'd listened to him more, asked more questions when I had the chance.

And finally, because I could no longer avoid it, I just happened to bump into the Soulhunter called Demonbane. I could feel Molly tense at my side. No one really likes or trusts the Soulhunters; they're all crazy. But then, if you had to do their job . . . you'd want to be clinically insane too. Everyone else was giving him plenty of room. Demonbane was a scrawny, wild-eyed, almost feral presence who could have been any age. Wearing a pale lavender suit of eccentric cut, with big padded shoulders and no shirt underneath. His gaze was unblinking, and his constant smile actually disturbing. He bounced up and down on his bare feet before me and Molly and cocked his head to one side, the better to observe us.

"Hello, Eddie! Commiserations on your loss. Let's just hope he stays dead, eh? Molly, darling! Haven't seen you since that nasty business with the Notional Man and the Sleeping Tygers of Stepney. What a night that was . . . You know, you promised you'd call me, but you never did. Why not?"

"Is that a trick question?" said Molly.

I looked at her. "Another of your dodgy exes? Why am I not sur-prised?"

"Because you've got a nasty suspicious nature," said Molly.

"Of course," I said. "I'm a Drood." I fixed Demonbane with a thoughtful gaze. "How did you know my uncle Jack?"

Demonbane grinned. "I could tell you, but then I'd have to nuke the planet from orbit, just to make sure."

"That can't be your real name," I said. "Demonbane . . ."

"Of course it isn't, Shaman. In our game, to know the true name of a thing is to have power over it. And that kind of knowledge in the wrong hands can get you killed. Or worse. So I chose Demonbane as my username. It's harsh, it's brutal, it's . . . me."

"But it's so obvious!" I said. "It's not exactly original, is it?"

"It's still a name you can use to make people wet themselves, in certain circles," he said complacently. "And some things that aren't even a little bit people."

"You're showing off now," I said.

"This, from a Drood?" said Demonbane. "Ooh! Look at me, wear-ing my bright shiny armour!" He prodded me hard in the chest with one finger. Still smiling his unwavering and really unsettling smile. "You need the Soulhunters. To do the dirty work your family doesn't want to soil their precious hands with. And given some of the things you admit to doing, that says a lot . . ."

"Retrieve your finger," I said. "Or I'll tie it in a knot."

Molly moved quickly forward, to stand between us. "What are you doing here, Demonbane? You never gave a damn about the Armourer."

"The Soulhunters wished to express their regret at his passing," said Demonbane. "His death means there's one less of Us. So They are winning."

"You're weird," said Molly.

"You say that like it's a bad thing," said Demonbane. "Besides . . .

our precogs said one of us needed to be here. Because something's going to happen. Right here, at the Armourer's wake."

He turned abruptly and walked away. Molly and I watched him go, and then looked at each other.

"Precogs?" I said. "Since when have the Soulhunters had precogs?"

"Don't ask me," said Molly.

"Even my family knows better than to depend on visions of the future," I said.

"But . . . ," said Molly.

"Exactly," I said. "But . . . this is the Soulhunters we're talking about. Even my family doesn't know much about what goes on inside that group. Though given the kind of work they do, it's probably just as well. I can't believe anything could happen here, though. Not inside the Wulfshead, with all its famous defences and protections."

"Maybe his people just wanted an excuse to get him out of the way for an evening," said Molly.

"Now that I'll buy," I said.

Perhaps fortunately, Molly's sister Isabella called out to us, so we went over to join her and Louisa at the end of the long bar. Isabella was wearing her usual tight blood-red leathers, plus a black choker round her throat that positively bristled with pointy steel things. She'd dyed her spiky hair a flaming red to match her leathers. Her face had the same beauty as Molly's, but in a harsher style. Louisa was wearing a pastel-coloured Laura Ashley outfit, finished off with white plastic stilettos. She was the baby of the family, and her sweetly pretty face looked pleasant enough, until you made the mistake of looking into her eyes. And saw just how deep they went. Louisa was the really dangerous Metcalf sister, and it showed. Her hair was currently peroxide white and fluffed out like a dandelion.

"We could have made it to the funeral," said Isabella, "but we thought it more tactful not to."

"You thought that," said Louisa, sipping delicately at her Bacardi Breezer. "I've never gotten a handle on this whole tact thing."

"Trust me," said Isabella, "we've all noticed."

"One Metcalf witch was enough," said Molly. "To say good-bye."

"We can say our good-byes to Jack more properly here," said Isabella. "Over drinks."

"Over many drinks," said Molly.

"I want a mouse!" Louisa said loudly.

"You've already had three," Isabella said crushingly.

Louisa looked at her sister with big, pleading eyes, until Isabella sighed deeply and produced a small white mouse from out of nowhere. It peered around from Isabella's hand, twitching its whiskers in a charming sort of way. Louisa made delighted sounds, snatched the mouse away from Isabella, crushed it in her hand, and greedily inhaled its essence. Blood dripped thickly between her fingers. She smiled dazzlingly back at all of us—and when she opened her hand, it was empty.

"Can't take you anywhere," said Isabella.

"Did the two of you know Jack well?" I said, just a bit desperately.

Isabella and Louisa smiled. I decided I really didn't like those smiles.

"Your uncle Jack got around," said Isabella. "And not just as a field agent. That man knew how to have a good time. He had his own life, outside your family."

"So everyone keeps telling me," I said. "I'm starting to feel like an underachiever."

Molly quickly cut in, launching into some seriously sisterly discussions, about people and places of interest only to them. I took the hint and moved off on my own. If there's one thing I understand, it's the importance of family secrets. The club seemed more packed and crowded than ever. There was still no sign anywhere of Charles or Emily. I'd been sure they'd turn up for Jack's wake, even if they couldn't show their faces at the funeral.

While I was looking around, I suddenly spotted a distinguished-looking old gentleman making his way steadily through the crowd towards me. I didn't recognise him. He was average height, average weight, in a smart city suit, and he looked professionally anonymous. He seemed old enough to have been a contemporary of Jack's, but a very well-preserved one. His faultless civilised smile was undermined only by his cold eyes, which wanted nothing to do with it. He seemed polite enough, and not obviously dangerous, but I tensed despite myself as he drew nearer. I can always recognise another agent when I see one.

The old man came to a halt a respectful distance from me and gave me a polite bow. Molly drifted forward to stand beside me. I'd been concentrating so much on the new arrival, I hadn't even noticed her, but she'd noticed what was happening. The old man inclined his head to Molly, a bow carefully calculated to be polite without being in any way deferential. He turned his attention back to me, and when he finally addressed me his English was the perfect kind you learned only from books; it had no discernible accent.

"Do I have the honour of addressing the estimable Eddie Drood? And the illustrious Molly Metcalf? Good! Good . . . I am Nicolai Vodyanoi. Retired, ex-KGB, a counterpart of your dear departed uncle Jack. Back during the Cold War. You know my grandsons, I believe?"

I looked at Molly, and she looked at me. Oh yes, we knew them well enough. Thugs, bully-boys, werewolves. We both smiled politely at Nicolai.

"We've met," I said. "Most recently at the Lady Faire's annual do, at Ultima Thule."

He shook his old head sadly. "Ah yes. I understand they disgraced themselves . . . ?"

"You could say that," I said. "They were asked to leave and had to walk home. Did they get back safely?"

"Eventually," said Nicolai. "Such boisterous boys!"

"Boisterous . . . ," I said. "Yes."

"We were always bumping into each other, Jack and I," Nicolai said carefully. "In this city, or that. In this country, or that. Some of which don't even exist any more . . . In secret science cities, or hidden underground bunkers, usually trying to kill each other as we fought it out for the same prize. For what seemed like perfectly good reasons at the time."

Molly and I looked at each other and shared a smile.

"We've been there," I said. "Molly and I were often at each other's throats when we weren't fighting back to back."

"The good old days," said Molly. "Before we settled down and got civilised."

"Well, almost," I said.

I returned my attention to Nicolai, who was waiting patiently. I gave him my best meaningless smile. "So, you and Jack knew each other during the Cold War. Did you know his brother James as well?"

"Oh yes!" he said immediately. Glad to be back on familiar ground. "I knew the Grey Fox. Everyone did, in our line of work. One way or another. James had the reputation, but Jack did good work too. Getting things done in his own quiet way."

He reached inside his jacket, with a heavily wrinkled but still very steady hand, and I tensed for a moment until he brought out a battered leather wallet, from which he produced an old black and white photo. He handed it to me, and I held it carefully so Molly could see it too. The photo showed a much younger Nicolai and Jack, standing side by side in tuxedos, at some glittering ambassadorial ball. They were both smiling for the camera, but their body language suggested a wary and even watchful feel, as though they'd been brought together only by circumstance, in roles that they were required to play in public. They both looked as though they might draw a weapon at any moment. And they both looked so young, and in their prime, with that indefinable glamour so many secret agents had, back in the day, almost despite themselves. When the sides were clear, everybody's reasons were clear-cut, and everyone knew what they were doing, and why.

"This is from the Sixties?" I said to Nicolai. "Thought so . . . I have to say, you don't look nearly old enough for this to be you . . ."

"State secret," he said smoothly, smiling fondly at the old image of himself. "We still have a few left in my country."

"Who's that?" Molly said suddenly, pointing at a figure standing behind the young Jack and Nicolai. "I feel I should know him . . ."

Nicolai studied the image carefully. "Yes . . . I remember him! Something of a mystery man, as I recall. Such an unusual name . . . Deathstalker." He saw me and Molly react, and raised an eyebrow. "You know this man?"

"I know the name," I said.

"So," said Nicolai, taking the photo back from me and slipping it carefully back into the wallet before making it disappear inside his jacket again. "I heard about Jack's wake through the usual unusual channels, so I knew I had to be here. They tell me he died at his work. It's what he would have wanted."

"No, it wasn't," I said. "He wanted to live forever. He was working on something in that line, but . . ."

"He ran out of time," said Nicolai. "Yes. It comes to us all, in the end."

The evening wore on. Many drinks were drunk, many songs were sung, and a great many toasts were made. Men made passes at women holding glasses. Isabella backed Monkton Farley up against a wall. The general mood became emotional, even wistful, as people looked back on their pasts and found they went back further than they realised. Dead Boy and Waterloo Lillian slow-danced together to an old Frank Sinatra song. The Sea Goat cut in, and Dead Boy stepped politely back. Julien Advent and Catherine Latimer sat side by side at the bar, so deep in conversation that no one dared interrupt them. A few people tried to listen in, but were driven away by two sets of very cold eyes.

Demonbane had taken up a position behind the bar, preparing very complicated, very dangerous, and very popular concoctions. Sometimes the stigmata in his palms would drip blood into the drinks he was preparing, but that didn't seem to bother anyone. It was, after all, a very cosmopolitan crowd.

People told increasingly indelicate stories about Jack Drood, from his days in the field right up to the present day. I think most of us would have been shocked at what emerged if we hadn't all been laughing so hard. Nicolai drank neat vodka and smiled and nodded a lot, but it wasn't until I asked him point-blank for his memories of Jack that he smiled and shrugged and looked at me thoughtfully.

"Did you know about Jack's little fling with the Lady Faire?"

"You mean James," I said.

"No, I don't," said Nicolai. "She had both of them! Though not at the same time. As far as I know . . ."

"And let us not forget Jason Royal, back in the Seventies," said Sir Perryvale. "That most debonair of spies . . . There was a lot of talk, you know, as to whether James or Jack was really his father. James took the credit; but then, he always did. Does anyone here know what Jason's up to these days?"

"Last I heard, he was retired," said Catherine Latimer. "Living in San Francisco."

"I suppose he must be of an age to retire by now," said Nicolai. "Though I still remember him as that handsome young man, a peacock of the London scene . . ."

"Didn't I hear he disappeared, rather mysteriously, sometime last year?" said Monkton Farley.

"I thought I heard something like that," said Dead Boy.

"Was it Jack who went looking for the Holy Grail in Old Shanghai?" said Julien Advent. "Or was that James?"

"No, that was Charles and Emily," said Catherine. "Back when they were still doing fieldwork for the Droods. They never had the reputation, but they always did good work. You should be proud of your parents, Eddie."

"I am," I said.

"Though I sometimes wonder why," said Molly.

"Hush," I said.

"But did they ever find the Grail?" said Sir Perryvale.

"I think I would have heard, if they had," said Isabella.

"No," said Dead Boy. "It turned out to be just a false sighting of John the Baptist's head. The Merovingians were always chasing that . . . But in this case it was just Herod's head. Didn't Elvis have the Grail at Graceland?"

"No," said Molly very firmly. "You've been reading those supermarket tabloids again, haven't you?"

Dead Boy shrugged easily. "These days it's the only way to find out what's really going on."

"Here's to Jack!" Sir Perryvale said loudly. He held up his Champagne bottle, and we all raised our glasses in the toast. "To the Armourer, and all his marvellous toys! Including all the ones that did what they were actually supposed to do! And to a few that should never even have been tried. Remember the gun that fired miniature black holes? And the nuclear grenade?"

"That would have worked," I said, "if he could have only found someone who could throw it far enough."

People knocked back their drinks, ordered more, and swapped happy memories of the Armourer's amazing creations. Which led, naturally enough, to stories about some of the more unusual obsessions and enthusiasms of previous Armourers. I couldn't help but smile at discovering that so many of my family's secrets weren't quite as secret as they thought. There was mention of the Time Train, and Moxton's Mistake, and a great many others. No one mentioned Alpha Red Alpha, so I didn't either.

"I've never really understood why you Droods need all these

wonderful guns and gadgets, when you already have such powerful armour," said Sir Perryvale.

"Because the armour can only do so much," I said. "For long distance, for a whole range of other possibilities, and for subtlety . . . you need specialized equipment."

"Besides," Cedric said wisely, "it's never good for a field agent to get too dependent on the armour. To rely on it to do everything for them, and get them out of tight corners. There's always going to be times when the armour just isn't the right tool for the job. Or it might not be functioning . . ."

"Really?" said Nicolai.

"Don't get your hopes up," I said, to general laughter.

"Oh, perish the thought," said Nicolai. "The Cold War is over, and we are all good friends now, yes?" And then he looked at me and said, very casually, "Did your uncle Jack leave you anything, Eddie? Any special bequest, to remember him by?"

"The reading of the will won't be for some time," I said, just as casually. "But he did say he wanted me to have the Bentley."

"Marvellous car, of course," said Nicolai, nodding solemnly. "But nothing else?"

"No," I said. "Why do you ask? Did you have something specific in mind?"

"Not really," said Nicolai. "How was the funeral?"

"Very respectful," I said. "We did the old boy proud. I just wish my parents could have been there to see it."

"Have they still not turned up?" said Sir Perryvale, frowning. "There are too many people going missing these days."

"Like Jason Royal?" said Catherine Latimer.

And then other people started chiming in, offering names of agents and adventurers, and even Major Players, who'd just vanished down the years.

Slowly, a bigger picture began to emerge. As everyone threw in a name, or two or three, the number began to add up. Whatever happened to Tarot Jones, the Tatterdemalion, the Totem of the Travellers? Or the Which Doktor, who specialized in supernatural illnesses? Or Chrome Delilah, the combat cyborg from the future? Name after name, of powerful people who'd just dropped out of sight, without any sign of struggle or foul play. And other, less illustrious names, but still well-known people, even significant ones, in their own spheres of influence. More people gathered around us as the conversation became louder and more worried, and even more names were put forward. It quickly became clear that none of us had realised just how many people had gone missing down through the years. Until we started putting the picture together . . .

Now, people in our line of work have been known to just drop out of sight, for a time, for any number of good or necessary reasons, but . . . I began to wonder if there might be a more disturbing reason behind it all.

"Could someone," I said, "or even some organisation, be culling the super-secret society? Or securing useful people for their own purposes?"

"If it was anyone but you asking, I'd say it was probably the Droods," said Isabella.

"No," I said, "we don't kidnap people."

"No . . . ," said Molly, in a way that made it sound more like *Yes, but.* "On the other hand, your family has been known to disappear certain people, when they've convinced themselves such action would be in the greater good. We've all heard stories . . ."

There was a general murmuring of agreement from all present.

"It's not us," I said firmly. "I'd know."

"It's not us," said Cedric. "I'd definitely know."

The crowd went quiet, as everyone looked at one another and realised we really didn't know what was going on. Until Sir Perryvale cleared his throat, just a bit self-consciously.

"I have heard . . . something," he said, almost reluctantly. "Just a whisper. About a secret and very exclusive Big Game."

"Oh, come on!" I said. "Another Spy Game? I've already been through one of those, courtesy of the Independent Agent. How many of these games are there?"

"More than you'd think," said Isabella. "Casino Infernale isn't the only place where people like us come together to play games. People with powers and abilities like ours do love to show off what we can do. And who better to test ourselves against than each other? How else could we find proper competition? I'm amazed we don't have our own Olympics, with medals and everything . . ."

"I have heard of this Big Game," Nicolai said slowly. "Though not through any official channels . . . It is, as you say, a whisper, a rumour . . . One of the darker mysteries of our hidden community. A contest of champions, they say, where the competitors are secretly abducted and forced to fight each other to the death. No one knows how long it has been going on."

The crowd was very quiet now, everyone frowning hard, thinking. About things they'd seen, or heard, or heard of, that suddenly made a lot more sense.

"How could something this important have been going on for so long, and I never heard of it?" I said finally. "Why hasn't my family heard about it? I mean, we know everything! I'm pretty sure that's in our job description."

"Someone in your family probably does know," said Nicolai. "At some level. But like most of us who think we might know something, we don't like to talk about it."

"Why not?" Molly said immediately.

"Because the Big Game is protected," Nicolai said flatly. "By the people who run it. The Powers That Be."

There was a pause, as everyone looked at everyone else.

"What kind of a name is that?" I said. "It's so vague; it could be anybody! Who the hell are these people?"

Sir Perryvale shrugged uncertainly. "Nobody knows. I think that's the point. In a community like ours, where you can be sure somebody knows something about everything . . . Even so, nobody knows. And that should tell you something. It's not even wise to talk about the Big Game, because you don't want to attract the attention of . . . whoever it is that's in charge of running the Big Game."

"I'm not sure I believe any of this," I said.

Nicolai nodded quickly. "Probably the wisest course."

"I need a drink," said Molly. "I need a really big drink, with an even bigger chaser."

This quickly became a very popular notion, and the crowd broke up as everyone besieged the long bar, shouting their orders to Demonbane and the barmen. Drinking and talking started up again, loud voices competing to drown each other out, as the subject of the Big Game was deliberately left behind. If not necessarily forgotten.

Finally, after hours of heavy talking and even heavier drinking, the wake began to break up. People started leaving. Heading off to their various homes, in their various ways. Julien Advent went off with Catherine Latimer, still deep in conversation—which raised a few eyebrows. Waterloo Lillian departed with a giggling Dead Boy slung over his shoulder. And Demonbane looked at me, muttered something rude about precogs, and departed as sober as he'd arrived. At the end, no one was left in the club but me and Molly. Even the bar staff had disappeared. Literally blinked out when I wasn't looking, now that they were no longer needed. Maybe the Management just put them back in their box. The piped music cut off in the middle of a Deep Fix medley, and a quiet calm settled over the club.

Molly and I sat side by side at the bar, still somehow perched on bar-stools, leaning companionably against each other. Savouring our last drinks before we headed out into the cold, cold night. I couldn't remember the last time I'd allowed myself to get this drunk outside of safe environs. I felt . . . mellow. Decidedly mellow. The funeral hadn't seemed like a proper good-bye to my uncle Jack, and neither had clearing out his room, but this . . . this wake had been more like it. A proper farewell to a man who had always been so much more than just the family Armourer. I turned to Molly to say as much, and saw that she was very mellow. So mellow, in fact, that it was a wonder to me she was still perched on her bar-stool. I smiled at her fondly. I hadn't been trying to keep up with her, because I knew from experience that I couldn't. Nobody could, when she had her drinking boots on.

"I think we gave Jack a good send-off," I said slowly. "I wish he could have been here to see it."

"Now, that," said Molly, "would have been creepy. Also macabre."

"I mean," I said, speaking slowly and clearly to show I wasn't in any way befuddled by the booze, "so he could see just how well loved and admired and respected he was. In the greater community. Not just . . . at the Hall. Or in the Armoury."

"I think he knew," said Molly, nodding wisely.

"I hope he knew," I said.

"Eddie?" said Molly.

"Yes, love?"

"Something's wrong. I can't move. Why can't I move? What the hell have I been drinking?"

"It's not just you," I said steadily. "I can't move either."

"Eddie, what's going on?"

"I don't know."

And just like that I felt stone-cold sober. As though someone had thrown a bucket of icy water in my face. Shock can do that to you. I struggled to move, or even turn my head to look at Molly, but I couldn't move a muscle.

"We've been spelled!" said Molly. "Frozen in place!"

"But my torc is supposed to protect me from all kinds of attack!" I said. "What kind of spell could be powerful enough to overpower Drood armour? And why are we still able to talk?"

"Good questions," said Molly. "I think we're about to learn the answers."

I saw something moving, out of the corner of my eye. I couldn't turn my head to see clearly, but the lights in the Wulfshead Club seemed to just fade away as shadows gathered around us. Bright electric lights guttered and went out, replaced by a bruised, unhealthy candlelight as Nicolai Vodyanoi came forward out of the dark, holding a Hand of Glory. A severed human hand whose fingers had been made into candles. Eerie green flames rose from wicks set into the fingertips, rising straight up, untouched by any breeze or movement. They were the only light in the Wulfshead now. Nicolai walked up to me, and then past me, to sit down at the bar beside Molly. I still couldn't turn my head to look at him, to see what he was doing. All I could do was follow him out of the corner of my other eye. I'd never felt so helpless. I seethed and struggled, pitting all my willpower, and all the power of my torc, against the power of the Hand of Glory, and still I couldn't move. Couldn't protect my Molly from the old monster sitting so casually beside her.

"Normally, not even a Hand of Glory would be enough to hold a Drood in place against his will," said Nicolai quite calmly. He didn't sound the least bit drunk. It occurred to me that while I'd often seen him with a glass of vodka in his hand during the evening, I'd never actually seen him drink from it. Had he been planning this all along? A cold anger surged through me. This was a wake! Neutral ground for all, by long tradition . . . I realised Nicolai was still talking, and made myself pay attention.

"This is no ordinary Hand of Glory. It was made from the severed hand of a dead Drood. Don't ask me his name. This all took place long before my time. Some Drood field agent came to Moscow, overconfident or really unlucky, and my people took him down. Very carefully, so your family never suspected we were involved. He just . . . disappeared. As we were saying earlier, such things do happen, in our community.

"So . . . after he was dead, my people tried to take his torc, to learn the secrets of your armour; but I understand the torc just disappeared. Right in front of them. Very vexing. So they dissected the young man's body, very thoroughly, to see what secrets it held. This was back before the days of DNA, you understand, so in the end they discovered little of any actual use. But they did cut off one of his hands and make it over into this Hand of Glory. Because even then they thought Drood flesh might be used against Drood armour . . ."

"You see?" I said to Molly. "This is why it's so important to completely dispose of a Drood body."

"Shut up, Eddie!" said Nicolai. "I am talking! We could have used the Hand against your family, but those in charge at that time suffered . . . a failure of nerve, a lack of will. They panicked, afraid of what your family might do to them if the truth ever got out. So they destroyed the body and locked the Hand away. Never even tried to use it. Such a wasted opportunity . . . The Hand remained in the KGB vaults for many years, forgotten—until I found it.

"While looking for something else entirely. Is that not always the way? But once I understood what I had stumbled across, I knew my moment had come. I broke into the vaults, took the Hand, and came here. I fear I have rather burned my bridges with my own people, but it was necessary. I had no choice. It was easy enough for me to get in here for your sentimental little gathering; your uncle Jack once brought me here as his guest. All I had to do, then . . . was wait for everyone else to leave. And now, Eddie. You know what I want."

"I really don't," I said.

"Where is it?" said Nicolai. "Tell me!"

"I don't know what you're talking about? Where is what?"

"I want what your uncle Jack left you," said Nicolai. "All these years I've wanted to get my hands on it, all these years I've waited, and this is my chance."

"The Bentley?" I said. "It isn't here."

"Do not play the fool with me, Eddie." There was a cold, very real danger in his voice. "I would hate to have to hurt your Molly. Hate to have to damage such a pretty face."

"Don't you touch her!" I said. "Please! What do you want?"

"You wouldn't dare!" said Molly. "My sisters would hunt you down!"

"Shut up, witch!" said Nicolai. "Tell me where it is, Eddie, right now, or . . ." He slammed the Hand of Glory down on the bar top. It stood upright, balanced uncannily on the wrist stump, green flames still rising steadily from the fingertips. Nicolai produced a slender silver knife and set the edge against Molly's throat. She couldn't even flinch back from it. The edge of the blade was so sharp that contact alone broke the skin and sent a thin runnel of blood coursing down her throat. I almost went mad then, straining helplessly against the power that held me still.

"All right!" I said. "All right . . . Just, take it easy. Don't hurt her. What you want is in my right-hand pocket, contained within a pocket dimension I keep there. You can't just reach in and take it; only I can. That's the way the Armourer made it."

Nicolai considered the matter, still holding the knife to Molly's throat. He could kill her in a moment, and we all knew it. Finally, he nodded slowly.

"Very well, Eddie. I restore to you the movement of your right arm."

And just like that, I could move my arm again. Nothing else. I couldn't even look down as I reached into my right-hand pocket and slowly, carefully brought out the Merlin Glass. I placed it on the bar top before me. Nicolai looked at it.

"What . . . ?" he said. "What is that?"

"It's what you wanted," I said. "The Merlin Glass. I know—you thought it would look more impressive. Everybody does. But that's it. Now, please . . . Take the Glass and let Molly go. You must know that killing her, and me, would be a really bad idea. You'd have my family and her sisters at your back and at your throat, for the rest of your life."

Nicolai surged forward and swept the Merlin Glass off the bar top with one blow from his hand. The Glass fell to the floor, and he pressed the knife back against Molly's throat. Another thin line of blood ran slowly down her twitching skin.

"I don't want that!" Nicolai said, so angry he was almost spitting the words. "I don't care about that! Stop playing games!"

"I'm not!" I said. "I swear I'm not! Just tell me, please; what is it you want?"

"I want the Star of St Petersburg!" said Nicolai Vodyanoi.

"What?" I said. "That . . . thing? It's just a useless piece of crystal! Why would you want that?"

"Please, Eddie," Molly said carefully. "Let's not upset the excitable psychopath with a knife at my throat . . ."

"That wasn't Jack!" I said to Nicolai. "That was James! He took the Star of St Petersburg! Just . . . picked it up, because it was there. He did things like that. The Star . . . it's no big deal! My grandmother used it as a paperweight. It's probably still in the Matriarch's office. Somewhere. Has been for years . . . What's so special about the Star of St Petersburg?"

"You're lying," said Nicolai. "Stop your lying! I'll kill her!"

"I'm not! I swear I'm not!" Cold sweat rolled down my face as I tried desperately to make him understand I was telling the truth. "The Grey Fox took the Star, not my uncle Jack. It's just a crystal! No special powers; we checked. Why do you want it so badly?"

"Because I put my soul inside it," said Nicolai. "I thought I was being so clever . . . I hid it there, years and years ago, for safekeeping. The way witches hide their hearts so they can't be killed. Yes, you thought you were safe, didn't you, Molly? That you were never in any real danger from my nasty little knife. But this is a very special blade. A blade so sharp it will kill you no matter where your heart is!" He laughed suddenly, and it was a harsh, bitter sound. "All these years, you Droods had my soul in your keeping . . . and you never even knew it."

"Look, you can have it," I said. "We don't need it. Let me talk to my family, arrange something. We can still make a deal, a trade. Our lives for the Star. You know my family knows all about making deals . . ."

Nicolai took the knife away from Molly's throat, got up from his barstool, and came over to stand beside me. My stomach muscles unclenched a little, now that Molly was no longer in danger. Nicolai advanced on me, holding the knife out before him. The blade shone supernaturally bright in the gloom. He held the knife up before my face, so close I could almost feel it. But I couldn't recoil. Couldn't pull back a single inch.

"Very well, Eddie," Nicolai said slowly. "I'll trade you and Molly, for the Star. Your family might not care so much about the witch, but they'll want to save one of their own. No tricks, Eddie; your torc can't protect you from this blade, as long as the Hand of Glory still burns."

"I'm going to reach into my pocket," I said. "To get my phone. It's in my pocket dimension."

"Get it out slowly," said Nicolai.

I reached carefully into my right-hand pocket and brought out the Colt Repeater I kept there. Nicolai couldn't see it from where he was standing until it was far too late. I brought the gun up quickly and shot the Hand of Glory. The bullet hit it square in the palm and sent the Hand tumbling backwards. All the flames on the fingers went out, and just like that I could move again. I jumped up from the bar-stool and aimed the Colt Repeater at Nicolai as he stumbled back away from me.

"You really shouldn't have threatened my Molly," I said.

He didn't try to attack me, or Molly; he just turned and ran for the door. I shot him in the left buttock, and the impact sent him crashing to the floor. The silver blade flew from his hand. He gave up then. Just lay on the floor, on his side, an old man weeping angrily. He turned his head back to glare at me.

"Go on, then!" he said through his tears. "Kill me! You know you want to, Drood!"

"No," I said. "I don't do that any more. I'll have my family come here and pick you up. You can have your Star back; we don't want it. And then I think we'll hand you back to your own people. I wonder what we'll get from them for you? A thief, and a traitor . . . Molly, are you all right? Molly?"

I looked around, and saw that Molly wasn't there. Her bar-stool was empty. There was no sign of her anywhere the club. She was just . . . gone. I turned back to Nicolai. He saw the look on my face and tried to crawl away, leaving a trail of blood behind him. I moved quickly forward and bent over him.

"Where is she?" I said. "Where's Molly? What have you done with her?"

"I haven't done anything!" he said, cringing away from me. Holding his hands up before his face, as though that might protect him.

I slapped his hands away with the Colt and stuck the gun right in his face. I pressed the barrel into his left eye. He screwed his eye up and cried out as I pressed harder.

"Where's Molly?"

He was crying openly now, an old man with all his dignity stripped away, broken by what he heard in my voice.

"I don't know! I don't know anything! This is nothing to do with me! Please . . ."

He was so scared, he wet himself. Whatever had happened to Molly, it wasn't down to him. I took the gun out of his eye and backed away. I might have felt sorry for him if he hadn't threatened Molly. I went back to the bar, bent down, and picked up the Merlin Glass from the floor. I looked it over carefully, but it wasn't damaged. The Merlin Glass can look after itself. I held the mirror out before me.

"Find Molly," I said. "Wherever she is."

My reflection disappeared from the mirror and was replaced by a grey blur of buzzing static. I stared at it for a long moment. The Glass had never done that before. The Merlin Glass had always been able to find anyone, anywhere, even in places that were completely out of this world.

"Find Isabella and Louisa," I said. "Where are they?"

The grey blur disappeared immediately, as the Glass showed me Molly's sisters, talking animatedly together. They broke off abruptly as they turned to stare at me. They both looked startled, and not a little angry. Their faces filled the mirror, but I could hear the sounds of another party going on in the background. Isabella glared out of the mirror at me.

"Eddie? What do you want? And how did you find us here?"

"The Merlin Glass," I said. "It can find anyone. Except it can't find Molly. She's been kidnapped, right out of the Wulfshead, and the Glass can't find her anywhere."

"What?" said Isabella. "She's been taken? How could you let that happen?"

"I was distracted!" I said. "Nicolai Vodyanoi just tried to kill both of us. And while I was dealing with that, Molly vanished. Gone, in a moment. No warnings, no signs, no clues. Look, just come back to the Wulfshead. I need your help."

"We're on our way," said Isabella.

"Damn right," said Louisa. "No one messes with the Metcalf Sisters."

"Allow me," I said.

I shook the Merlin Glass out until it was the size of a Door, and Isabella and Louisa strode through it. There was a brief roar of raised voices and raucous music from whatever party they were leaving, cut off sharply as the Door closed itself. Isabella looked back at the Glass, hovering on the air behind her.

"Okay, that was . . . more than usually weird. Your Glass isn't just a Door, Eddie."

"A definite sense of transition," said Louisa. "And it felt like there was someone in there with us . . ."

The Merlin Glass shrank back down to hand-mirror size, shot across the intervening space, and all but forced itself back into my hand. As though it was afraid of the Metcalf Sisters. Which was a common enough reaction to Isabella and Louisa. I slipped the Glass back into my pocket.

"Help me find Molly," I said. "Please."

"Are you sure the Merlin Glass didn't show you anything useful?" said Isabella.

"Just a grey blur, thick with static," I said. "I don't even know what that means."

"It means Someone, or Something, is blocking it," said Louisa.

"I didn't think that was possible," I said.

"I could do it," said Louisa.

"Look, before we all start panicking, why don't I just try the obvious thing?" said Isabella.

She produced her mobile phone and called Molly. While I called myself all kinds of an idiot for not thinking of that myself. We all waited, and waited, but Molly didn't answer. Isabella shook her head, shook the phone harshly a few times just on general principles, and then put the phone away.

"That should be impossible too," she said. "My phone is spelled to find Molly and Lou, wherever they are. In or out of this world. It's the only way I can keep track of them."

"It was worth a try," said Louisa. "Now it's my turn."

She lifted both her feet and sat cross-legged in mid-air, frowning hard, concentrating. Her presence was suddenly overpowering, as though she filled the whole club. One of the many good reasons why so many people are scared of Louisa Metcalf is because no one's sure exactly who or what she is, or what she can do. But in the end, she just shook her head and lowered her feet onto the floor again.

"Sorry. I can't See her anywhere. And that should be impossible as well. There shouldn't be anywhere, in or out of this world, that I can't See into if I put my mind to it."

"Unless Molly has been taken completely out of this reality," said Isabella.

"How could she have been taken at all?" I said. I could tell my voice was rising, which is never a good idea with Isabella and Louisa, but I was so worried I was past caring about anything but Molly. "Who could even touch her, with all her protections? And from inside the Wulfshead, with all its defences?"

"She could only have been taken by something extremely powerful," said Isabella.

"We were talking about the Big Game earlier," I said slowly. "Someone said that it wasn't wise to attract the attention of those who run the Game. The Powers That Be. Could they be behind this?"

"Let's hope not," said Louisa. "Because if they are, I don't have a clue where to start looking."

I looked around for Nicolai Vodyanoi, to try out some more questions on him, but he was gone. Not disappeared, like Molly. Nicolai had left a smeared trail of blood all the way across the floor to the door. He'd made his escape while we were distracted. Let him go. I'd find him later if I needed to. He wasn't important now. I turned back to Isabella and Louisa.

"What do you know about the Big Game? I mean, really know?"

"Supposedly," Isabella said carefully, "the Big Game . . . is only played by people who have made too many Pacts and Agreements, with too many Powers and Dominions. For people who owe far more than they can ever hope to repay. The Big Game offers a way out; beat everyone else—and by that I mean kill everyone else in the Game—and the Powers That Be will pay off all your debts for you."

"But nobody knows for sure," said Louisa. "Because no one has ever come forward to boast of having won the Big Game. But then, I suppose they wouldn't, would they?"

"Molly would never talk to me," I said slowly, "about all the things she thought she had to do, early on in her career; to acquire enough power to strike back at the Droods. To make herself a creditable enemy. She did once say to me, when we were talking about Heaven and Hell, *You'd be surprised who owes me favours.*"

"She never actually sold her soul to anyone," said Isabella. "But she did make a whole series of very unwise deals, with various Powers. Paying for what she got with years off her life. From an old age she never expected to reach anyway."

"And Roger Morningstar," I said. "The infernal, the half-demon . . . He once told me to my face that Molly . . . lay down, with demons in the Courts of Hell. To buy powers she couldn't acquire any other way."

"And you believed him?" said Isabella. "Hell always lies."

"Except when a truth can hurt you more," I said.

Isabella looked at Louisa, who just shrugged. "I don't know. Molly always was the most secretive of us."

"Often with good reason," said Isabella.

"But did she ever talk to you . . . about how she meant to pay back what she owed?" I said.

"She said . . . some things," Isabella said carefully. "But it's not our place to talk about that, Eddie. Not ever. Not even to you. Still, you might want to consider the question of just how she was able to acquire title to the Wood Between the Worlds. And what that cost her."

"Things just keep getting better all the time," I said. "Look, I know she made bargains with the Immortals. Those shape-changing bastards were at my family's throat for centuries. You worked with them, didn't you, Isabella?"

"You know I did," she said coldly. "I also went out with your Serjeant-at-Arms for a while. I don't take sides, Eddie. And why bring the Immortals into this? Your family destroyed them. The few that still exist are a broken force. There's no way they could be involved in this."

"No," I said. "But they might have sold Molly's debt to someone else."

"Ooh! Ooh!" said Louisa, jumping up and down suddenly. "I've just thought of something! Isn't your Merlin Glass supposed to be able to travel through Time? Why don't we just go back, and stop this all happening?"

"The Glass has very limited abilities," I said. "And that's when it's cooperating. Right now, I wouldn't trust it to send a letter into the Past."

"I know! I know!" Louisa was bouncing up and down again. "I know what we need! We need answers—so we need an oracle! I know a really good one in the Nightside that will tell you the absolute truth about anything! If you only threaten it a bit . . ."

"Eddie's banned from the Nightside," said Isabella.

"You really think that would stop me?" I said.

Something in my voice made both sisters stare at me for a moment.

"I do know of another oracle," Isabella said carefully. "Far more reliable, if a little more difficult to get to. At Castle Inconnu, home to the London Knights. Louisa and I couldn't hope to gain access to it, short of a declaration of war . . . But do they by any chance owe you or your family a favour, Eddie?"

"Let's find out," I said.

I took out the Merlin Glass again and told it to find Sir Perryvale, Seneschal to the London Knights. The Glass found him immediately and showed him wearing a long white nightgown, with a floppy white nightcap on his head. He looked out of the mirror at me, startled and a little shocked.

"How the hell did you get past the Castle's defences? Can't a gentleman call his private quarters his own any more? Oh . . . it's you, Eddie. Can't this wait? I'm about to go to bed and work on my hangover."

"I need your help," I said.

I quickly brought him up to speed on what had happened, and he made all the right noises of concern and alarm.

"Poor Molly . . . What can I do to help, Eddie?"

"I need to talk to your oracle," I said.

"Strictly forbidden, where the Droods are concerned," Sir Perryvale said immediately. "But what the hell. Jack was a good friend; I know he'd want me to help. So come on through. But just you, Eddie. Not the Metcalf Sisters. Sorry, ladies, but there are limits. And I think you pretty much define them."

"Understood," said Isabella. "Lots of people feel that way."

"Lots and lots," said Louisa. "Like we care."

"Understand me, Seneschal," said Isabella. "If we find out you didn't do everything you could to find our missing sister . . ."

"Yes, yes, I think we can take the threats and menaces as real," said Sir Perryvale. "When you're ready, Eddie."

"I'll take Louisa into the Nightside," Isabella said to me. "See if we can scare some straight answers out of the oracle there. And don't be proud. If you need backup, call."

I nodded, shook the Merlin Glass out into a Door, and strode through into Castle Inconnu.

CHAPTER SEVEN

# A Knight to Remember. And an Owl.

arrived in a simple bedroom, just big enough to hold an old-fashioned four-poster bed and some elegant if rather battered furniture. The well-used kind, with scratches in the veneer and the sheen worn off, that usually gets handed down as heirlooms because you can't find anyone to buy it. There were no windows in the bare stone walls, and the warm, cheerful butterscotch light came from a single lamp.

There's always a certain element of surprise the first time you enter someone else's bedroom. In this case, the surprised party was the Castle's Seneschal. Sir Perryvale sat on the edge of his bed in his long nightie and floppy nightcap and stared back at me with studied dignity. Defying me to make any remark concerning his choice of nightwear. I just nodded respectfully to him, as befitted his station, and reduced the Merlin Glass down to hand-mirror size, then put it away.

"So," said Sir Perryvale, "the legendary Merlin Glass in action . . . Brought you straight here, without setting off a single alarm. Incredible."

I looked at him sharply. "You didn't shut down the Castle's security systems to let me in?"

"Hardly, old boy. Can't have the Castle left vulnerable, not even for a moment. The London Knights have far too many enemies just waiting for us to put a foot wrong. Besides, I wanted to see what would happen. Don't worry—no one's going to bother us if we take a swift walk round the Castle. Not tonight. But we'd better be quick about our business. We have our very own top-rank telepath in residence, the Lady Vivienne de Tourney. I have reason to believe she's . . . somewhat occupied just at the moment, but that won't last. You need to be done with your business and gone before she notices you."

"You let me in," I said. "Just like that. I'm grateful, of course, but . . . how can you trust me? You don't know me."

"I knew Jack," Sir Perryvale said simply. "He often talked about you. He believed in you. I don't suppose he ever told you that . . . No. He wouldn't. For all his many admirable qualities, he was still a Drood. Emotionally constipated, just like the rest of you."

"But . . ."

"It's not like I'm going to be allowing you access to any of our forbidden areas," he said, riding right over me. "All right, yes, technically speaking, access to our oracle is forbidden to outsiders, but only technically. If the oracle doesn't trust you, you won't be getting any answers, so . . . Don't worry, though. I'm sure you'll find out everything you need to know."

"But . . ."

"Look, you don't mean any harm to Castle Inconnu, do you?"

"No!"

"Well, then! I am the Seneschal. I have every right to decide who is and who is not a threat to the London Knights. So there. If I want to bring in a guest, that's my business. Pardon me a moment."

He reached down and grabbed a heavy brown bottle from the floor beside his bed. He uncorked it, with something of an effort, and knocked back several swallows. He then grimaced, made a truly awful noise, and shook his head unhappily.

"Just a little pick-me-up; it's hard to go straight from the drunk into the hangover without any sleep in between. Damn, I feel rough."

He took another long swallow, and then glared at me. "You were matching me drink for drink at the Wulfshead, Eddie. Why aren't you suffering as well?"

"It's the torc," I said. "It can flush all the poisons out of my system in a hurry, in an emergency. For when I need my mind to be clear."

"Lucky bastard," said the Seneschal. "Why can't our armour do something that useful?"

He took one last drink, slammed the cork back into the bottle, and put it down on the floor again.

"What is that stuff?" I said.

"Disgusting," Sir Perryvale said flatly. "I think it works on the principle that anything that tastes so utterly vile has to be doing me some good. I do feel a little better. I think. Why do the worst emergencies always have to happen when you're never in a suitable state to deal with them?"

He forced himself up onto his feet, swayed a little, and then strode over to a side door and kicked it open, revealing an adjoining self-contained bathroom. He turned on the light, which turned out to be stark, unforgiving electric, glaring back from a lot of white tiling. Sir Perryvale winced and went inside.

"You stay put," he said over his shoulder. "While I get changed into something less comfortable. So one of us can stop being so damned embarrassed. Keep talking! I'll still be able to hear you."

The Seneschal left the bathroom door open while he got changed. He threw his nightcap on the floor and then whipped off his long night-gown, revealing himself to be entirely naked underneath. He pottered around the bathroom, picking things up and putting them down again, entirely unconcerned about his nudity. I took one look at his large Falstaffian figure, broad and heavy and entirely unconfined, and then looked determinedly in another direction. It does seem to be some sort of general rule that the people most keen on casual nudity are nearly always the kind of people the rest of us least want to see doing it.

"I know," said a voice behind me. "I've been trying to get him to diet for ages."

"I heard that!" said Sir Perryvale.

"You were meant to!"

I looked around, but there was no one else in the bedroom with me. Apart from a large, puffed-out owl, sitting proudly on a wooden perch in the corner and watching me intently with dark, thoughtful eyes. I blinked at him a few times, trying to figure out how I'd over-looked him before. His feathers were grey, with long tawny streaks, and he clutched his perch with heavy, powerful claws. I moved over to him and put out a hand to stroke his head.

"Don't get familiar, bub," said the owl.

I withdrew my hand. "Why didn't I notice you before?"

"Because I'm a stealth owl. Finest kind."

"Don't mind him," Sir Perryvale said cheerfully from the bath-room. "Archie is always a bit tetchy, with people he doesn't know."

"I am not tetchy!" said the owl. "I'm just . . . careful. You have to be careful around strangers, because they're always trouble. I keep tell-ing you that!"

"Eddie is my guest," said Sir Perryvale.

"He's a Drood!" the owl said loudly. "I can see his torc! Unnatural thing . . . just looking at it puts my teeth on edge. And I don't even have any teeth!"

"Do I mention your shortcomings?" said Sir Perryvale.

"Frequently," said the owl.

Sir Perryvale came back in from the bathroom to join us. He was wearing the same colourful outfit he'd worn to the Wulfshead—a loud Hawaiian T-shirt over very short shorts. They stank of old booze, ciga-rette smoke, dried sweat, and other party residues. Away from the club, they smelled flat and sad, like the ghosts of parties past.

"Sorry," said Sir Perryvale. He didn't sound it. "If you wanted to see me in my ceremonial robes, you should have given me more warning."

"He's only got the one set," said the owl. "And they're in the wash. Ugly things . . ."

"I knew I should have chosen the talking raven when they offered it to me," said Sir Perryvale.

"What? Edgar?" said the owl. "But he's got no personality! And no conversation!"

"Precisely," said Sir Perryvale.

"Well, really . . . ," said the owl.

Sir Perryvale smiled at me. "How do you like my owl?"

"Fascinating," I said solemnly. "Where did you get him?"

"Mail order," said Sir Perryvale.

I suddenly noticed a handwritten sign underneath the perch, saying *Beware of the Wol.* I looked at Sir Perryvale. He took me by the arm and moved me a discreet distance away.

"Don't say anything," the Seneschal murmured. "He wrote it himself. He's very proud."

My attention was caught by two small photographs in standard silver frames, sitting on top of the dresser. The only photos on display in the room. One showed a handsome young man decked out in a full set of brightly shining London Knights armour. Medieval in style, but obviously new; not a dent or scratch on it. He smiled easily at the camera, with his helmet tucked under his arm. It reminded me of a graduation photo. He looked brave, confident, ready for anything. Sir Perryvale moved in beside me.

"That's my son, Ricard," he said. "He died not long after that was taken. On a campaign against the Elder Monstrosities, out in the Shoals. We won the campaign, but . . . His mother died too, not long after. Just faded away, despite everything I could do. That's her, in the other photo. My Elise."

Elise was a pleasantly pretty young woman, dressed in sweet casual wear, smiling diffidently. She looked very young. She seemed happy enough, with no idea at all of what life had in store for her. I couldn't help noticing that there were no photos of Sir Perryvale with his wife, or his son.

"Now there's just me," said Sir Perryvale. "And Archie, of course."

"Someone's got to look after you," said the owl.

"And the London Knights are family, in their own way," said Sir Perryvale. "We all swore our lives, and our sacred honour, to a greater cause. You can't fight battles without casualties. You're a Drood, Eddie. You understand about duty, and loss, and sacrifice."

"Yes," I said.

"I saw my share of fighting the good fight," said Sir Perryvale. "Riding a great war charger, singing the old battle songs. Fighting side by side with my fellow Knights, on the muddy plains and stinking jungles of other worlds. Striking down monsters, and worse. Good times and bad. Triumphs and victories . . . and all the friends and family who never came home. I'm too old to campaign now, but I still serve. As Seneschal. I like to keep busy."

"Why did you let me in so easily?" I said. "I mean . . . Droods aren't usually welcome at Castle Inconnu. Actually, I'd be hard-pressed to think of anywhere we are welcome . . . But normally I'd have to submit a petition to the Matriarch, spelling out all my reasons, to be passed on to the Castle administration, and then sit back and hope for the best."

"You don't have time for that," said Sir Perryvale. "And I owe your uncle Jack more than I could ever hope to repay." He stopped suddenly and looked at me. "Oh my dear boy, I'm so sorry. I've been wittering on, and all this time you must be out of your mind with worry about your Molly being missing. Do forgive me. What happened to her exactly?"

I filled him in on the details as best I could. He nodded slowly.

"You're right. You do need to consult the oracle. I'll take you there. But Eddie . . . I am taking a chance on you. Don't let me down. You may . . . see things that you mustn't talk about. To anyone, not even your family. Perhaps especially not to your family."

"I'm used to keeping secrets," I said. "Especially from my family. Don't worry, Seneschal. All I care about right now is finding Molly and getting her home safely. And I don't care who I have to walk over, or through, to do that."

"All right," said the owl. "Him, I like."

"You've come to the right place," said Sir Perryvale. "Our oracle is second to none."

"What kind of oracle have you got here?" I said.

"The Metcalf Sisters didn't tell you?" The Seneschal raised an eyebrow and seemed briefly amused. "Ah . . . very well. I think I'll let you find out for yourself. Because you wouldn't believe me otherwise."

"But your oracle can answer questions?" I said. "Accurately?"

"Oh hell, yes," said Sir Perryvale. "Try to stop her . . . She really does know everything."

"*She?*"

"Yes."

I waited, but he didn't have anything else to say. Just stood there, smiling his quietly irritating smile.

"Okay . . . ," I said.

"She sees all, hears all, knows everything," said Sir Perryvale. "Of course, how much she chooses to tell is up to her."

"She'll talk to me," I said. "I don't plan on giving her any choice in the matter."

"Oh, I am going to enjoy this," said Sir Perryvale.

I gave him a hard look. "There's something important you're not telling me, isn't there?"

"There's a lot I'm not telling you, old chap. It's for your own good."

The owl sniggered loudly from his perch. Sir Perryvale addressed him sternly.

"We need to make a start. The clock's ticking. Archie, guard this room while I'm gone. No one is to enter, and no one is to know where I'm gone or who I'm gone with."

"Got it!" the owl said importantly. "Anyone tries to mess with me, I'll have them!" He glared at me. "I will!"

"I believe you," I said.

"Come with me, young Drood," said Sir Perryvale. "Wonders and marvels await."

The Seneschal led me through a labyrinth of empty stone corridors. The first thing I noticed was that the splendid hanging chandeliers of crystal and diamond were all made up of standard electric light bulbs, providing a bright and almost shadow-free illumination. The Seneschal noticed me noticing.

"We are part of the Twenty-First Century here, Eddie. We may live in a castle, but we still have indoor plumbing and central heating, cable and broadband. We're traditionalists, not barbarians."

We moved on. It was good to be moving at last, after so much talking. It felt like I was accomplishing something. I didn't know where Molly was, or what had happened to her, and I needed to know. Good news or bad, I needed to know. Because the strain of not knowing was like a knife in my gut. And yet for all my worries, and all my sense of urgency, I was still fascinated by the interior of Castle Inconnu. I'd read the family's files on the London Knights, compiled down the years from a fact here and a rumour there, but as far as I knew, I was the only Drood ever to be invited inside. Officially. I peered about me as we hurried along, trying not to seem too much like a tourist. I knew my family would expect me to make a report on all this, afterwards. I didn't see that as betraying the Seneschal's trust; I'd already decided I would mention only those things on open display and keep the Seneschal's secrets as my own.

I looked surreptitiously around for surveillance cameras, or any other forms of security system, but I couldn't see anything. Probably still there; just concealed. I didn't say anything to Sir Perryvale; presumably he'd already dealt with everything that needed taking care of.

The great towering walls we passed were all constructed from the same creamy white stone; glowing brightly, spotlessly clean. Each separate stone had been expertly laid into place, set so tightly and perfectly together there was no need for mortar. But no windows anywhere, to provide an outside view, not even an arrow slit. I had no idea where Castle Inconnu actually was. For all I knew, there was nothing at all outside.

The broad stone corridors were decorated with hanging tapestries and colourful pennants, in sharp, vivid hues. Stained-glass windows blazed in the connecting walls, depicting scenes from the lives of the Saints, ancient and modern. I particularly liked the one of Mother Teresa drop-kicking a possessed leper off a tenement roof. Huge silver crucifixes had been mounted at regular intervals along the walls, in a variety of styles from a variety of periods, along with a number of surprisingly tasteful little shrines. The huge open marble floors were covered with intricate mosaics of London Knights in their armour, fighting armies of monsters in the mud and blood of alien battlefields, under strange night skies with unknown constellations. Fighting for their dream. King Arthur's dream. Of might for right, instead of might makes right.

The Seneschal and I passed quickly through a number of elegant stone galleries, huge banqueting halls with long, extended tables that seemed to go on forever, and wonderful indoor gardens with trees and fountains and flower displays that reminded me irresistibly of the Drood grounds. There were even comfortable gathering places with tables and chairs set out in front of bistros and restaurants.

"We do like our morning coffee," said Sir Perryvale, hurrying along. "No better way to start the day than with a chat and a gossip over the morning papers. Nothing like a black coffee, thick as tar, to get your heart started on a cold morning. I wish I had time to give you a proper tour, Eddie."

"I wouldn't be able to concentrate," I said.

"Of course, my dear chap. Molly must come first. I quite understand. But if whoever has taken Molly had wanted her dead, they would have killed her right there in the Wulfshead while you were distracted. And they didn't. Which definitely implies they have a purpose in mind for her. And after all, my dear fellow, she is Molly Metcalf. If there is anything at all to her legend, that young lady can take care of herself."

"Usually, yes," I said. "But this whole business seems to be linked to the Big Game, and the Powers That Be . . . Personages strong enough to break through the Wulfshead's notoriously tough security measures. I didn't think anyone could do that. I'm worried they've taken Molly because they want her to do something for them. And the longer they have her in their power, the more time they've got to . . . persuade her. One way or another."

Sir Perryvale shot me a concerned look. "You have time, Eddie. You must believe that. Or you'll never get anything done."

"But what if they're using that time to . . . do things to her?"

"I refer you to my previous answer," Sir Perryvale said sternly. "That the infamous witch of the wild woods is perfectly capable of kicking the crap out of anyone who upsets her. I'm right, aren't I?"

I smiled despite myself. "There is that, yes."

"You mustn't let a big impressive name like the *Powers That Be* get to you," said Sir Perryvale. "In my experience, the bigger the name people give themselves, the less there is to worry about."

"What if they're not people?" I said. "And what if we gave them that name?"

"Just concentrate on what's in front of you, Eddie," Sir Perryvale said kindly.

We finally came to a halt in a great open space, surrounded by stairways leading up and up, and floors and floors rising around us. For the first time I got a real sense of the scale of Castle Inconnu. It wasn't just a building; it was a whole world in itself.

"Impressed?" Sir Perryvale said calmly.

"Yes," I said. "It reminds me a lot of Drood Hall. But where is everybody? We've covered a lot of ground, and I haven't seen a single soul anywhere. Has something happened?"

"Our Grand Commander, Sir Kae, has led the Knights off into battle against some other-dimensional threat to the Earth," said Sir Perryvale. "Apparently something really nasty is brewing."

I looked at him, frowning. "What threat is that? I haven't heard anything. I'm sure somebody would have said something at the Hall if my family had known . . ."

"We do rather specialize in such things," said Sir Perryvale, in an only faintly patronising tone of voice. "You Droods protect Humanity, but in the London Knights we set our sights somewhat higher. We keep an eye on the bigger picture."

"And who decided that?" I said.

The Seneschal shrugged, just a bit vaguely. "The Knights and the Droods did both start out at roughly the same time in history, give or take a century or two. Doubtless . . . people got together, and agreements were made. As to territory, and responsibilities. To prevent . . . disagreements, and even clashes. It's probably for the best that the London Knights aren't here right now. Most of us don't get on with Droods. Professional courtesy is all very well, but . . . Of course, to be fair, we don't get on with anyone, much. There's nothing like defending this world for centuries, against all comers, highly successfully, to convince you that you're always right. Mind you, we nearly always are. It's a matter of attitude, I suppose . . . You understand, Eddie."

"Of course," I said. "I'm a Drood."

Sir Perryvale chuckled dryly.

"Thank you; for your help," I said. "I do appreciate what you're doing, what you're putting on the line, by letting me in. Helping me. If I can ever do anything for you . . ."

"Well," said Sir Perryvale, "could we, perhaps, have the Drood dragon? We'd be ever so grateful, and I promise we'd take very good care of it. The London Knights have wanted their very own dragon for ages and ages."

"That's . . . up to him," I said. "I will ask him, when I get back, but he seems quite attached to us." A question occurred to me. "Can I just ask: is it true that the London Knights had the Merlin Glass in their keeping for years?"

"Oh yes," said the Seneschal, quite off-handedly. "For centuries, I think."

"The Glass was given to my family, originally, by Merlin himself," I said carefully. "For . . . services rendered. How did the Glass end up in your hands?"

"I'm sure I don't know," said Sir Perryvale. "Ancient history, I'm afraid. Not really my field. We do have a great many items in our vaults, things that originally belonged to Merlin. King Arthur felt it important that we keep them, in case the old sorcerer ever came back to us."

"You think that's likely?" I said. "After all this time?"

"Why not?" the Seneschal said simply. "Arthur did. Our King came back to us, for a time. And what a glorious time that was."

"King Arthur . . . ," I said. There are some names that just give you goose pimples. "What was he like?"

"Everything they said he was," said Sir Perryvale. "And so much more, besides."

"Where is he now?"

"Gone back to his sleep. Somewhere safe. Until he's needed again, for the Final Battle."

"Why did you give the Merlin Glass back to us?" I said bluntly.

"Because your uncle Jack asked for it," said Sir Perryvale. "And no, he didn't say why."

"And you just gave it to him? Didn't that get you into trouble?"

The Seneschal shrugged briefly. "I'm not the only one here who owes a lot to Jack Drood."

"Didn't any of the Knights object?"

"Ah," said Sir Perryvale. "I may not have actually got around to informing all of the rank and file, so to speak."

I gave him a hard look. "Hasn't anyone noticed it's missing?"

"The only way we can all rub along together here, in such a confined space, is for all of us to allow each other our little secrets," Sir Perryvale said sternly. "I'm sure there are things being kept from me . . . Now, let's go see the oracle!"

He led me up a steep stairway, and on through a series of open stone galleries, all of them decorated with impeccable style and taste. Our footsteps sounded ominously loud and carried to me in the constant quiet.

"Is everybody gone from the Castle?" I said finally.

"No, just the Knights. Our wives and families are all gathered safely together in the Great Redoubt, at the heart of the Castle, behind all kinds of protections. They're safe there until the Knights return. Strictly speaking, I should be in the Redoubt with them, but I was damned if I was going to miss Jack's wake. And besides, I can never get to sleep in a strange bed. Not at my age."

"Wives and families . . . ," I said. "Aren't there any female Knights?"

"Not yet," said Sir Perryvale. "Though it is an idea whose time has pretty much come. We do change, Eddie, but only slowly. Is it really very different with the Droods? I mean, how many female field agents do you have?"

"Quite a few," I said. "And my family is led by a Matriarch."

"The London Knights are still mainly a religious order," said Sir Perryvale. "And that kind of organisation is always going to be the slowest to change. By long tradition, the Knights fight, and the women provide necessary backup, here in the Castle. As doctors, teachers, historians, librarians, armourers, and spiritual councillors . . ."

"Servants?" I said.

"What? Our Ladies?" said Sir Perryvale, openly amused. "Hardly! Perish the thought . . . No, no; Castle Inconnu is full of airy spirits that take care of all the everyday, necessary things."

We came to the Hall of Forgotten Beasts. An extremely long hall, whose walls were decorated with the stuffed and mounted heads of all kinds of fantastical creatures, many of whom were no longer part of recorded history. The only remaining examples, in some cases, of hundreds and hundreds of exotic beasts. I slowed down, despite myself, to take a better look. Sir Perryvale slowed too, reluctantly. He looked at me and didn't like what he saw in my face.

"You have to understand," he said as we passed slowly between the two opposing rows of preserved heads on plaques, "that for a long time, hunting was an important part of our Knightly duties. Wiping out creatures whose very existence was considered a real and present threat to Humanity's survival. It is possible that perhaps some of those early Knights got . . . a little out of hand. We don't do this any more, of course. Another slow change."

"And too late," I said, "for most of these creatures."

"Pretty much everything on display here would have killed you quite cheerfully," said Sir Perryvale. "Don't get sentimental, Eddie. And, it has to be said, you're not seeing the Hall at its best. Much of this place was destroyed during a recent elf attack. We had to rebuild the Hall and restore a great many of the exhibits . . . We lost quite a few specimens. Too damaged to be preserved. An irreplaceable loss."

He walked on down the Hall, pointing out particular items of interest. A pure white unicorn's head, with a vicious curlicued horn and crimson eyes blazing madly. It didn't look like anything a maiden might want to ride. A gargoyle, with a bullet hole right in the middle of its flat, broad forehead. A basilisk with no eyes. (Obviously.) A dire wolf with moulting fur, its jaws still snarling defiance. And then I stopped and pointed at one particular head.

"What is *that*?"

"Ah," the Seneschal said proudly. "That is the Questing Beast. You wouldn't believe how many of us it took to track that down. It's an old monster, not much valued and even less missed."

The Questing Beast was an odd mixture of beast and bird. It looked . . . old and tired, and perhaps even a little resigned. As though it knew it had outlived the time it was meant for.

And finally . . . we came to the dragon's head. Just the face, really. If the whole head had been there it would have blocked the Hall. The exhibit wasn't very impressive. Its bottle-green scales were dull and dusty, and the eyes obviously glass. Some of the teeth were missing. It was just the preserved remains of something that had once been great. I looked at it and felt suddenly, coldly, angry.

"No wonder you want our dragon," I said.

"Your dragon, by all accounts, has mellowed considerably since its time in the wild," Sir Perryvale said evenly. "Having your head cut off, and then being left to think about things under a mound of earth for centuries, will do that to you. Your dragon is an almost civilised creature now. In their own time, dragons were nasty, vengeful, and quite deadly beasts. Killers of men, women, and especially children. Destroyers of whole communities. A lot of good Knights went to their deaths bringing this creature down. We thought the breed was extinct, until we learned of your find in Germany, out by Castle Frankenstein."

"What do the London Knights want with our dragon?" I said. "To finish the job?"

"No," said Sir Perryvale. "We wish . . . to honour it. If there's one thing Knights understand, it's the need to do penance."

I looked up and down the Hall, taking in all the heads on display. "You know, in these days of DNA retrieval and forced cloning, it might actually be possible to bring some of these beasts back. Under carefully controlled conditions."

"I'd like that," said Sir Perryvale. "I think a lot of us would."

"So you could hunt them again?"

"No, so they could be returned to the wild. It's a terrible burden to know you're responsible for the extinction of a species."

"I think we could work something out," I said.

"I'll have a word with the Grand Commander when he returns," said the Seneschal. "I think it would do both the Knights and the Droods good to have some project we could work on together."

"It would be good," I said, "to have something in common."

"Oh, there are a few things we can all agree on," said Sir Perryvale, setting off down the Hall again. "If only that the Nightside should be utterly wiped out."

"Couldn't agree more," I said. "Terrible place."

"I don't know what your uncle Jack saw in it," said Sir Perryvale, "but he spent enough time there . . ."

In the end, the Seneschal led me up a long, winding stairway, with frequent rests for him to get his breath back. Finally, he unlocked a door at the very top of the stairs and led me into a great circular stone chamber. Something about the room made me feel as though I was at the top of a tower. Given that there were still no windows to show what was outside, there was no way of confirming it, but that was what it felt like to me. A tower inside a castle? I shrugged mentally. Castle Inconnu was very old, and it kept its secrets to itself.

The chamber was wide and airy and open, dominated by a great circular well that took up most of the available space. A well, inside a tower, inside a castle . . . Good thing I was a Drood. We believe six impossible things before breakfast, just to keep our hand in. The chamber was a good sixty feet in diameter, and fifty feet of it was the well. The containing rim was polished stone, only a few feet high. When I leaned over the rim to look into the well, I was hit in the face by the sharp smell of the sea. And when I looked down, into the murky waters . . . all I could see was endless darkness, falling away forever, looking back at me. Suddenly vertigo hit me, and I swayed on my feet.

Sir Perryvale grabbed me by the arm and pulled me back. I shook my head hard and glared at him.

"What kind of oracle is this?"

"The Lady of the Lake," Sir Perryvale said proudly. "The Lady Gaea herself. Mother Earth."

I had to think about that for a moment. *"Really?"*

"Oh yes. Our Lady of ancient days, the bestower of Excalibur. We serve her, we protect her, we belong to her. And in return she tells us what we need to know. I'm hoping she'll extend that same courtesy to you." He put a steady hand on my shoulder. "I know you're worried about Molly. But our oracle really does know everything. She can help."

I nodded, unable to speak for a moment. Not just because I was finally close to learning the truth about what had happened to Molly, but also because the comforting hand on my shoulder reminded me so much of the Armourer.

And then we both looked round sharply as we heard heavy footsteps hurrying up the stairs, towards the chamber. I looked at Sir Perryvale.

"That sounds a lot like armoured feet to me. You assured me all the Knights were gone!"

"Most of them are!" Sir Perryvale looked unhappily at the closed door. "But of course, a few always stay behind to guard the Castle. Can't leave the old place undefended, can we? I was rather hoping we'd be done and gone before they noticed anything was amiss."

The door slammed open, and a young man in full armour burst in, holding a drawn sword out before him. He studied us both with cold, angry eyes, sweeping his long blade back and forth before him. He dismissed the Seneschal with a contemptuous sniff, and then fixed his glare on me. I really didn't like the look of his armour. It wasn't ceremonial, or a work of art, or in any way symbolic. This was battle armour, designed to keep its wearer alive in the most desperate and dangerous of situations. Gleaming heavy steel-plate armour, covering the young man from head to toe, expertly fashioned and entirely un-adorned. No engravings or decorations, not even a patterned tabard to add a touch of colour. The blunt steel helmet covered his entire head, with just a Y-shaped slot at the front for eyes and nose and mouth.

And the sword he carried was a heavy brutal thing, a butcher's blade, a killing tool.

Sir Perryvale took a cautious step forward, and the sword immediately moved to cover him. Sir Perryvale stopped where he was.

"Sir Bors," he said. "I thought you were occupied with the Lady Vivienne."

"Did you really think she wouldn't notice?" said Sir Bors. From his voice, he seemed to be barely into his twenties, but he still gave every appearance of being extremely dangerous. The sword and armour helped, but this was clearly a man with warrior's training.

"I did hope this confrontation wouldn't be necessary, yes," said Sir Perryvale. "Allow me to present my guest . . ."

"He's a Drood!" said Sir Bors. He made my family name sound like an obscenity.

"Quick, isn't he?" Sir Perryvale said to me.

"A damned Drood!" said Sir Bors.

Sir Perryvale shook his head. "You're going to be awkward, aren't you?"

"Sir Bors," I said, and the cold eyes snapped back to me. So did the sword. I gave the Knight my best charming smile. "Nice to meet you. You look . . . very martial. Do you always wear your armour inside the Castle?"

"Only when we're expecting trouble," said Sir Bors. "Stand still! Don't move!" He glared at the Seneschal. "What were you thinking? You should never have let him in!"

"That was my decision to make," Sir Perryvale said coldly. "My prerogative as Seneschal. My guest is here because he needs to consult the oracle . . ."

"Not going to happen," Sir Bors said immediately. "You know that's strictly forbidden to outsiders. And we definitely don't do Droods any favours."

"Why are you here, Sir Bors?" said Sir Perryvale.

"I'm going to take this Drood away, lock him up somewhere secure, and leave him there," said Sir Bors, "until the army and the Grand Commander return. Sir Kae can make the decision of what should be done with this . . . intruder. And then I'll see you prosecuted for dereliction of duty, Seneschal! I'll see you relieved of your position! You let the wolf in at the gate . . ."

"Just because you're humping the Lady Vivienne," Sir Perryvale said calmly, "don't think for a moment that means you share her exalted station. You weren't her first, and you won't be her last. I'll set my decades of service to the Castle against your calculated outrage any day."

"Excuse me," I said, "but how long before Sir Kae returns?"

"Weeks," said Sir Bors. "Maybe months."

"I can't wait that long," I said. "Molly Metcalf has been kidnapped, and I need access to your oracle to find out where she's been taken. Just let me ask my questions, and I'll be on my way . . ."

"You don't get to make conditions, Drood," Sir Bors said loudly. "Everyone knows you can't trust a Drood! And if your notorious witch has gone missing, good riddance to bad rubbish."

"Please don't kill him," Sir Perryvale said quickly to me. "He's young, and he means well."

"You're right," I said to Sir Perryvale. "He is going to be awkward. And I don't have the time or the inclination to be diplomatic about this."

I armoured up, and Sir Bors fell back a step as my strange matter armour wrapped around me in a moment. Even when you think you know what to expect, your first sight of a Drood in his golden armour is always going to be a heart-stopping experience. Armour supple as flesh, openly unnatural, impossibly strong and fast, and a mask with no features. Not even any eyes. That always upsets people; which is why we do it. I grew a long golden sword out of my armoured right glove, and Sir Bors immediately dropped into a fighter's crouch, his sword extended before him. At least he looked like he knew what he was doing. I didn't want this to be over too quickly. Not after what he'd said about Molly.

I moved forward, and his sword leapt for my throat. I parried it easily with my golden blade. The two swords slammed together in a shower of sparks, and I think both of us were a little surprised that neither blade shattered. We circled each other slowly, studying each other's form.

"Merlin gave your family a Glass," said Sir Bors. "He gave us enchanted swords and armour!"

I cut at his head with my sword, and he parried at the last moment. Our blades flashed back and forth, as we went round and round in the limited space available to us in the gap between the well and the door. Sir Perryvale retreated quickly, out of the way. Sir Bors was a lot more experienced at sword-fighting than I was. I blocked most of his attacks easily enough, but a swift feint caught me off guard, and his sword-point slammed into my ribs. The strange matter held against his enchanted steel, and while he hesitated for a moment, surprised, I stuck my blade into his ribs. His spelled armour held off my strange matter sword in its turn. I swore under my breath. This was going to complicate things.

I looked him over carefully, searching out the weak spots in his armour. The elbows and the knees and the groin, obviously; and the Y-shaped slot at the front of his helmet. But most of those were killing blows, and I really didn't want to do that. Sir Bors was just defending his home.

And I had meant it when I swore I didn't want to kill again.

We circled each other, looking for weaknesses in each other's

stance. This was all taking far too long. Taking up time I needed to locate and rescue Molly. So when in doubt, cheat. My first thought was to
use the Merlin Glass. Take it out, slap it over Sir Bors, and just teleport
him somewhere else. I switched my sword from right hand to left. I was
good enough to hold him off that way for a while. Sir Bors hesitated,
then fell back a step, wary of a trick. I used that moment to reach
through my armoured side with my free hand, into the pocket dimension I kept there. But the Merlin Glass avoided my grasp. The damned
thing refused to be brought out. So instead, I grabbed hold of my Colt
Repeater, brought that out, and pointed the gun at Sir Perryvale.

"Stand down!" I said to Sir Bors, my voice sounding cold and au-
thoritative, filtered through my mask. "Or I'll shoot your Seneschal. I
don't need him to get answers from your oracle."

"Please don't let him shoot me," Sir Perryvale said quickly.

Sir Bors hesitated, looking from me to the Seneschal and back
again. "You wouldn't . . . You wouldn't dare!"

"Of course he would!" said Sir Perryvale. "He's a Drood!"

Sir Bors lowered his sword and stepped back into the open doorway. "And you are still a London Knight, Perry, for all your sins."

"Get out of here," I said to Bors. "Go take a little walk, just long
enough for me to conclude my business with the oracle. And then you
can have your Seneschal back and I'll get the hell out of Castle Inconnu."

Sir Bors nodded slowly, reluctantly. "I'll be back. With reinforcements! And if our Seneschal is harmed, your death will be a slow and
terrible one!"

"Why, Bors," said Sir Perryvale, "I didn't know you cared."

Sir Bors sniffed loudly and disappeared out the door. I listened to
his heavy footsteps retreating back down the stairway, then pulled the
sword back into my glove and armoured down. I realised I was still
holding the Colt Repeater, so I put it away. Sir Perryvale looked at me
thoughtfully.

"I won't ask," he said.

"Best not to," I agreed.

He turned to face the well and raised his voice.

"Lady Gaea, it is Sir Perryvale of the London Knights who calls you! It is the Seneschal of Castle Inconnu, who invokes you! Come forth and speak, for we have need of your knowledge and wisdom! Come to us. In Arthur's name!"

There was a long pause, and then from deep in the well there came a great roaring sound, of something huge rushing towards us. Building and building, with all the strength and power of an approaching tidal wave or tropical storm. I could feel pressure on the air, the sense of a growing presence, of something coming. Something too large to fit easily into our small, fragile, and easily breakable world. A feeling of something condensing itself so it wouldn't overpower or damage our reality. I realised Sir Perryvale had stepped back from the well, pressing his back flat against the wall, so I did that as well. A solid jet of water blasted up out of the well, dark blue-green seawater. It slammed against the stone ceiling overhead and fell back as a shower of rain. The waters formed themselves into a human figure that suddenly snapped into focus, and there, standing elegantly on the still surface of the water in the well, was a beautiful woman. Not a single ripple moved across the surface of the water from where her bare feet made contact. She was wearing a long emerald-green dress, with a bright golden sash around her waist. She smiled dazzlingly at me and the Seneschal, and stepped forward. She placed one foot on the stone rim of the well and reached out a hand to me so I could help her down. I took hold of her hand automatically, and she stepped down to stand before me. I was amazed at how normal, how human, her hand felt in mine.

Because I knew there was nothing normal or human about her. She was Gaea. All the world in a woman. I just knew.

I let go of her hand and studied her openly. She had a classic face, with a strongly defined bone structure. A great mane of night-dark hair, warm blue eyes, and a really nice mouth. I thought she could be any age—until I looked into her eyes. They were old, so old; older than any living thing had a right to be. I dropped down on one knee before her. Just because it felt like the right thing to do. Sir Perryvale was already kneeling, and bowing his old head respectfully. I bowed to Gaea too. She felt like my mother. Like everyone's mother.

Mother Earth.

"Lady of the Lake, welcome," said Sir Perryvale. "Lady Gaea . . ."

"Oh stop that," she said. "And get up. You know very well I've never required any of you to kneel or bow to me."

I got to my feet. I could see Sir Perryvale was having trouble with that, so I helped him up. His knees cracked loudly.

"We don't do it because it is required, Lady Gaea," said Sir Perryvale. "We do it because it's you."

"Call me Gayle," she said. "I haven't used that old name in ages. How many times do I have to tell you? So knock it off! Or I'll get cranky." She looked at me. "Well. A Drood. It's been a while . . . What do you want with me?"

I filled her in quickly on everything that had happened. She was very easy to talk to, nodding in all the right places.

"It seems likely Molly has been kidnapped by the Powers That Be," I said finally. "Do you know who they are? Where they are? Do you know what's happened to my Molly?"

"Of course," said Gayle. "I know everything. And when I don't, I make it up. Though you'd be surprised how often it all turns out to be true anyway. Molly Metcalf has been taken by the Powers That Be, taken out of this world so she can participate in the Big Game. And yes, I know you already know that; I'm just confirming it. As to who the Powers That Be are . . . not all of my knowledge, or all of my secrets, are mine to share."

"Why not?" I said. "Who is there powerful enough to compel you to keep things secret?"

"I am," said Gayle. "I am the world, and the balance must be maintained."

"Am I supposed to understand that?" I said.

"No," said Gayle.

"Just as well," I said. "All right, what can you tell me? Can you See Molly? Can you See where she is?"

"Yes," said Gayle.

"She's still alive?" I said. "She's all right?"

"She's still alive," said Gayle.

I could tell she was being careful about what she said. I wanted to shout at her, demand more information, make it clear to her how much I needed to know this and how angry I was; but I could tell . . . that would be a really bad idea. She really was everything she seemed to be, and more. So I clamped down hard on my emotions and said, very carefully and very politely, "What can you tell me, to help me?"

"Molly can't save herself," said Gayle. "You must go to where she is and save her."

"How do I find her?" I said.

"You need a Door," she said. "To take you to the Shifting Lands. A very special, very powerful Door."

"I have the Merlin Glass," I said.

"You say that like it's a good thing," said Gayle. "If you only knew what's inside that Glass, watching you . . . The Glass can't help you this time. It isn't powerful enough to take you where you need to go."

"There's the Doormouse," I said. "And his House of Doors. He's always boasting he can provide a Door to anywhere . . ."

"To anywhere else, perhaps," said Gayle. "The Doormouse does good work. But the way to the Shifting Lands, and the Big Game, is protected. The only way in is by invitation. And if the Powers That Be had wanted you, they would have taken you along with Molly. There's a reason they take people, Eddie Drood. Have you ever entered into any binding Pacts or Agreements?"

I did think about the deal I once made with the rogue armour, Moxton's Mistake, but I didn't say anything.

"You need to find a Door powerful enough to punch right through all the defences," said Gayle. "And for that you need to pay a visit to the Travel Bureau."

I winced at the name. Sir Perryvale saw me do it.

"What?" he said immediately. "What is this . . . Travel Bureau? And why haven't I heard of it?"

"Because you don't move in those kinds of circles," I said. "I've heard of them. They're a kind of Underground Railroad, for people who need to get away. In a hurry. Before certain other highly motivated people can track them down and express their extreme displeasure with them. The Travel Bureau offers a one-way trip to the destination of your choice. The price is everything you own. Because you can't take it with you, and you definitely won't be coming back for it. The Travel Bureau provides Doors for desperate people who need to disappear without trace. The most powerful Doors to be found anywhere in this world, or out of it. So they say."

"Where are they?" said Sir Perryvale. "Do you know?"

"Of course I know!" I said. "Droods know where everyone is. Or at least that's what I always thought. The Shifting Lands . . . are new to me. Let's hope the Tourist Bureau has heard of them. They have a Departure Lounge, hidden away in a private pocket dimension, in the space between spaces. Tangentially attached to a particular location in London, from where they can access every point in Space and Time. According to their brochure. The problem is you can only get in if you make contact through the proper channels. They'd never willingly admit a Drood . . . but they might let Shaman Bond in. There is a chance their security measures might detect my torc; if that happens my cover identity will be blown. But I'll risk it. For Molly."

We all looked round again, at the sound of heavy armoured feet pounding up the stairs towards us. It seemed that Sir Bors had found his reinforcements. I nodded quickly to Gayle and looked at Sir Perryvale.

"Are you going to be all right if I leave you here to face Sir Bors? He knows you let me in."

"Don't worry," said Gayle. "I'll vouch for Perry."

"You're too kind," said Sir Perryvale.

"Yes," said Gayle, "I am."

I reached into my pocket for the Merlin Glass, so it could make me a Door to leave by, and again it stubbornly avoided my hand.

"Oh come on!" I said. "Don't you dare play up now!"

"It's not the Glass," said Sir Perryvale. "Sir Bors will have reinforced the Castle's security wards. Once they're set to Red Alert, nothing can get in or out. You're trapped here, Eddie."

I thought quickly. "Not necessarily. I can still fight my way out. Through the Knights, through the Castle, all the way to the main entrance. But not without hurting people. I don't want to do that, but I can't afford to be stopped. Not now. Not when Molly is depending on me." I looked at Sir Perryvale. "How many reinforcements can Sir Bors call on?"

"Twenty Knights," said the Seneschal. "That's the full complement left behind to guard Castle Inconnu."

"What about the security people?"

"Those are the security people!" said Sir Perryvale. "Twenty London Knights in their armour could stand off an army. Normally they answer to me, as Seneschal, but I don't think they'll be in any mood to listen to me after everything Sir Bors will have been saying about me."

I was still thinking hard. If I did take on the London Knights, that could start a war between the Knights and the Droods. Particularly if I beat them. I could tell from the look on Sir Perryvale's face that the same thought had occurred to him.

"My family will just have to disown me again," I said. "Declare me rogue and throw me to the wolves, to save the family honour. I can live with that. I've lived with it before. Anything for Molly."

"You really think you can take on twenty London Knights?" said Sir Perryvale.

"I have to," I said.

"Hold everything," said the Seneschal. "I've had an idea. A way out of a very dangerous situation, for all concerned. I am now declaring this a security drill. You are my invited guest, called in by me to test the Castle's defences. To check just how secure this place really is, while the army's away. I'm allowed to do that. Technically . . ."

I looked at him. "Your people will buy that?"

Sir Perryvale shrugged quickly. "They will if you break through them, and leave, and don't get caught. That'll prove my point. But, Eddie, you mustn't kill anyone. Not even accidentally. That would mean war . . ."

"Don't worry," I said. "I don't do that any more."

"Of course, Sir Bors will never believe any of this," said Sir Perryvale. "But luckily no one likes him much anyway. A brave enough fighter, but a stuck-up little prig."

"I may have to get a bit rough with the Knights," I said.

"Fuck them if they can't take a joke," said the Seneschal.

I looked to Gayle. "Will you be getting involved in this?"

"No," she said. "Let the children squabble . . . But I always was a sucker for true love. So go with my blessing, Eddie Drood."

I bowed to her, nodded to Sir Perryvale, armoured up, and left the room.

I charged down the long, winding stairway, and met Sir Bors coming up, accompanied by three other Knights. All in their armour. Sir Bors stopped and gestured quickly for the others to spread out and block the way. They hesitated a moment, impressed by my golden armour, and then moved quickly into place. I stopped and looked down at them from behind my featureless golden mask. Sir Bors levelled his sword at me.

"Surrender, Drood!"

I had to chuckle. "You haven't met many Droods, have you?"

The long sword shot out of my golden glove, and I went down the steps to meet Sir Bors. As I expected, he didn't wait for the others; he just stormed up the steps to confront me. He raised his sword with both hands and brought it swinging down with all his strength behind it. I waited till the last moment, and then stepped smartly to one side. The sword slammed down, missing me easily by inches, and Sir Bors staggered forward, caught off balance. I placed one armoured boot on his lowered armoured shoulder and shoved him back, hard, with all my armoured strength. Sir Bors went flying backwards and tumbled helplessly down the stairs, making a hell of a racket. He slammed into one of the other Knights, who couldn't get out of the way fast enough, and knocked the man right off his feet. The two of them crashed down even more steps, making angry, pained noises all the way. The other two Knights jumped back to the sides, out of the way. And I ran straight through the gap they'd opened up and charged down the stairs, passing the two still-off-balance Knights along the way. A sword lashed wildly out at me as I dashed by, but it didn't even come close. I bolted down the steps, taking them two and three at a time. I could hear some of the Knights coming after me, but they couldn't match my armour's speed, and I soon left them behind.

I reached the bottom of the stairway and sprinted through the open stone corridors, not even breathing hard. I could hear voices calling my family name, and not in a good way, coming from more than one direction. I ran through a portrait gallery, lined with some of the more famous faces from the Castle's long history, all of them depicted in their armour, in a whole bunch of different styles. And as I passed them, each of the images came to life. They turned their heads to watch me go and leaned out of their frames to sound the alarm. I kept running.

At the end of the gallery, three armoured Knights appeared to block my way. They at least had the sense to hold their ground and make me come to them. There was no way past them, and no point in turning back. I had to go through them. And not kill any of them. Though I doubted they'd show me the same courtesy. I was an intruder in their home. I had sworn not to kill anyone, and especially not men like these, who thought they were the Good Guys, but I couldn't allow myself to be stopped. Not while Molly needed me. So I slowed to a walk and went to meet them with my sword at the ready.

I cut at them savagely with my strange matter sword, which could normally cut through anything, but while sparks flared where my golden blade met their spelled swords and armour, they still held their ground. I managed to sneak a few hits past their defences, but my blade couldn't pierce their armour. They spread out, so they could attack me from three sides at once, and only my armour's speed allowed me to hold them off. I knew I couldn't keep that up for long, so I concentrated on putting all my armoured strength into every blow. Just the impact of each blow was enough to send the Knights flying backwards, off balance for a moment. I slammed my shoulder into one Knight, knocking him over, and kicked the feet out from under another. The remaining Knight came straight at me, head-on; I just dodged round him and ran.

The Knights called out angrily behind me, shocked that I hadn't done the honourable thing and fought my way free. I grinned behind my mask. Droods are trained to win. Whatever it takes.

My armour remembered the path I'd previously taken through the Castle, when I was following the Seneschal; all I had to do was trace the route in reverse. I pounded along corridors and down stairs, all of them vaguely familiar, following a glowing arrow floating on the air before me, generated by my armour, seen through my mask. But it didn't take me long to realise this route only led back to Sir Perryvale's bedroom. I needed the way to the main entrance. I accessed the maps stored in my armour's memory, hoping against hope for something useful, and was astonished to find a complete floor-plan for Castle Inconnu. Some Drood must have been here before me after all. Probably my uncle Jack. Another glowing arrow appeared, and I followed it.

I was running at full speed now, pounding through the stone galleries with my arms pumping at my sides, driven forward by my own desperation and my armour's unnatural vitality. Just a golden blur, in the depths of the Castle. I could hear people moving and shouting all around me, but none of them could match my speed, and I soon left them behind.

I passed through a long hall full of classical statues and suits of standing armour set out on display. The statues turned their heads to watch me pass, their empty mouths sounding the alarm. And one by one the suits of standing armour came alive. They lurched forward to block my way, throwing themselves at me, grabbing onto me with their shining steel arms. I threw the first few off easily enough, but more and more of them clung to me with unnatural strength, trying to pull me down. I fought them savagely, and when their heads came off and their arms tore away, I quickly discovered the suits of armour were empty. Just old armour, animated by old magic. Now that I knew I didn't need to hold back, I tore them apart and ripped them off me, one suit at a time. I smashed them with my golden fists and cut them apart with my sword. No one wastes protective enchantments on empty suits of armour. I finally broke free and ran on again, but the time it had used up was all it took for the other Knights to catch up with me.

When I entered the next corridor, a dozen armoured Knights were waiting for me. I barely had time to stumble to a halt before they charged straight at me, yelling their battle cries. They quickly spread out to surround me, so they could come at me all at once from different sides. Glowing swords and battle-axes rained down on me as I dodged this way and that, using my armour's speed to keep them off balance. Moving at my armour's top speed made it seem as though they were all moving in slow motion, giving me plenty of time to anticipate their movements and avoid their attacks. But I was tired, so tired. I was the one who had to move the armour, and I had already done so much. It had been a very long day . . . I was slowing down despite myself, and they were speeding up.

I dodged and feinted, using their numbers against them. They had to be careful not to hit one another in the press of the fight, while for me everyone was a target. A sudden inspiration came to me, and I switched my sword to my left hand. Immediately, the Knights fell back, expecting a trap or a trick. I backed away, just enough that they were all arrayed before me. And then I reached through my armoured side, into my pocket dimension, and brought out one of my uncle Jack's most dependable devices. The portable door. The Knights saw that all I had in my hand was a black plasticky blob, and they started forward again. Which was just what I wanted.

I manipulated the blob, rolling it back and forth in my hand to activate it, but instead of slapping it against the nearest wall to make a door, I threw it onto the floor before me. It immediately expanded to make a trap-door opening, and the advancing Knights fell through it before they could stop themselves, crashing down into the floor below. The sound of their armour landing made a terrible noise, and I grinned briefly behind my featureless mask.

Nice one, Armourer.

I made it the rest of the way without being stopped, or even challenged—all the way to the main entrance door. A pretty ordinary-looking door, on the far side of a great open hall. And there, standing between me and the way out, were six armoured Knights. I was so tired I almost cried at the sheer injustice of it. I was so sure I'd left them all behind. I didn't have the strength left in me to fight my way past one angry Knight, let alone six. I staggered to a halt and tried hard to give them the impression I was studying them thoughtfully from behind my impenetrable mask, while I fought to get my breath back. My chest was heaving, my arms and legs and back ached, and my head was swimming with simple fatigue. I could feel sweat running down my face, under my mask. Drood armour can make a man more than a man, but it's still the man who drives it.

I could tell from the way these Knights held themselves, and their glowing weapons, that they were experienced fighters. Men who knew what they were doing. I was out of strength, out of tricks, and out of time, and they knew better than to come to me and leave the door unguarded. So all that remained for me was to take the fight to them.

*I'm coming to get you, Molly. I swear to God I'm coming for you.*

I strode towards them, taking my time, gathering my strength, and then accelerated at the last moment, forcing my aching legs on. The armour's speed had me in and among the Knights before they could react. I lashed out at them with my strange matter sword, with all the strength my armour could give me. But these Knights dodged my blows, or deflected them with raised swords or lowered shoulders, and stood their ground. The force behind my blows was enough to rock them on their feet, when they landed, but the Knights wouldn't fall, or fall back. Their swords and axes flared brightly, supernaturally fierce, as they hit me from every side. The points and edges couldn't pierce my armour, but just the terrible strength behind their blows was enough to hurt me, inside my armour. The spells laid down on their steel were enough to reach me, and damage me, beyond my armour's protection. And all I could do was take it.

I couldn't kill them. I *wouldn't* kill them.

I lowered my head and struck out with my sword and my fist, absorbing the punishment that came at me from everywhere; forcing my way closer to the door, one stubborn step at a time. The blows came hard and fast, doing real damage, until I wanted to cry out at the pain. Swords and axes rose and fell, driving me this way and that, until I couldn't even see them coming any more. I gritted my teeth to keep from crying out. So they wouldn't know how badly they were hurting me. I could feel blood coursing down inside my armour. Sudden attacks sent me staggering back and forth, but I wouldn't fall. I was damned if I'd fall. Molly needed me.

I could have drawn my Colt Repeater and shot the Knights, trusting to the strange matter bullets to punch through their armour. But that would have meant killing them—which would mean war between the Knights and the Droods. But Molly needed me . . . I couldn't think what would be best. So hard to think, when it hurt so much . . . I lowered my head and bulled forward, into the blows and the pain, forcing my way forward one stubborn step at a time.

An axe came sweeping round impossibly fast and hit me in the side of the head, almost causing me to pass out from the impact. I hurt so bad I fell to one knee, and the Knights immediately crowded in around me, raining blows down on me, scenting victory at last. I punched one of them in the knee, slamming his leg out from under him, and he fell forward across me. I held him there, using him as protection against the blows, trying desperately to think what else I could do. And that was when the owl appeared out of nowhere.

It came sweeping across the open space at incredible speed and hit one of the Knights in the side of the head with such force that it actually dented the metal of his helmet. The impact spun the Knight around on his feet, and he fell to the floor, the sword flying from his hand. The owl spun round in a tight circle and came screeching in again, striking another Knight so hard in the chest that he was thrown over backwards. The owl swept up into the air, hooting triumphantly.

"I am stealth owl! Death from above!"

The Knights scattered, surprised and unnerved by this unexpected intervention, turning desperately this way and that to see where the next attack would come from. The owl drove the Knights away from me and yelled my name as I hauled myself painfully back onto my feet.

"Get the hell out of here, Drood! I'll hold them off! Teach them to look down their noses at me! I am a weapon of war, dammit! I am!"

And while the Knights were still coming to terms with that, I lurched forward and made it all the way to the main entrance without being stopped. I grabbed the handle—and the door was locked. Of course it was locked. And then I heard the lock mechanism work and felt the handle turn in my grasp.

"I always was a sucker for true love," said Gayle.

I pulled the door open and staggered out into a London street, armouring down as I went. The cool evening air was a blessing on my torn and bloody flesh. The door slammed shut behind me.

# CHAPTER EIGHT

# Going Underworld

C old; so cold.

I was back in the world again, and already it was starting to feel like a really bad mistake. I felt cold and tired, and I hurt all over. I looked cautiously around me and gradually realised I'd emerged onto Oxford Street. A familiar enough area to me; part of my old hunting ground when I was the official Drood field agent for London. Traffic was roaring past, taxi drivers leaning on their horns when anyone hesitated even for a moment; and all kinds of people hurried past me, far too busy and preoccupied with their own lives to pay me any attention. The late-evening sky was heavily overcast, and an increasingly bitter rain was slanting down. From an Arthurian Castle to a wet and windy day in London— story of my life, really.

I looked behind me. According to my family's files on the London Knights, there should have been a Green Door, the only real-world access to Castle Inconnu. Instead, there was just a bleak expanse of yellowing wall, separating two quite ordinary and respectable businesses. Presumably with Castle security now on Red Alert, the Door was closed. I turned away and stumbled off down the street before the Door could reappear and spit out a whole bunch of outraged London

Knights charging after me. The Seneschal might be able to justify my presence in the Castle, or he might not. And Gayle might decide to keep the Green Door closed, or she might not.

I staggered through the driving rain, keeping my head well down as I weaved my way through the crowds as best I could, not wanting to draw anyone's attention. Though this was, after all, London; where people are well versed in not seeing people and things they don't want to know about. I was feeling worse all the time. I'd taken a hell of a beating inside my armour, and it was starting to get to me. Stabbing pains jolted through my body with every step, and I was feeling increasingly weaker and more worn down. I braced myself in case anyone should bump into me and make things worse, but somehow nobody did. Which was . . . unusual for a street in London.

Every movement sent more and more pain shooting through me. I'd been too busy concentrating on moving forward while the Knights attacked me to realise just how much punishment I was soaking up inside my armour, and now that I no longer had the armour to support me, the damage was catching up fast. I had to stop, just for a moment. I concentrated on my breathing, pushing back the pain and weakness with an act of iron will. I lurched over to the nearest shopwindow. Shop dummies in sharp city suits stared blankly back at me. Watching coldly, dispassionately. They didn't care how bad I felt, no more than the people passing by did. London can be a cold city.

I made myself concentrate on my reflection in the glass. I looked bad. Hell, I looked awful. Battered and bloody. I was shaking and shuddering all over now, and not just from the cold rain. My left arm hung limply at my side, blood coursing down to drip steadily from my numbed fingertips. I couldn't move the arm at all without risking a pain so bad it almost made me pass out. I hadn't realised how far over I was leaning to compensate and favour my damaged side. Underneath the arm, my whole left rib cage shouted pain at me with every breath I took. The left side of my face was worryingly slack, under heavy mottled bruising. And my left eye was swollen completely shut. A nasty wound jerked across my brow above the eye, and when I touched it gently with my right hand, fresh blood ran streaming down my face. It didn't hurt at all—which was not a good sign.

So . . . my left arm was broken, in at least two places. Most of my left ribs were broken, and from the feel of it, pressing in to pierce the lung. Add to that the beginnings of a really serious concussion as well as any number of internal injuries. Something inside me felt loose, detached, damaged. Blood gathered in my mouth, and when I spat it out, more blood immediately appeared to replace it. Really not good. I felt suddenly hot, and then cold, and then hot again, in sudden sharp flushes. My head was swimming and my legs were trembling, and only an act of desperate willpower was holding me up.

I didn't have time to be hurt this badly. Molly needed me.

I put forward my good arm, placing my right hand flat against the window glass, so I could lean on it. That supported some of my weight, and helped a little. I pushed back the gathering confusion in my head, refusing to give in to it, and tried to work out what I should do next. I could armour up again, and let the strength of the armour carry me until I could reach a place of safety. But that would definitely freak out all the people around me, and give the game away as well. There had been too many sightings of armoured Droods in public in recent years. Most of them my fault. The general public isn't supposed to know that Droods move among them. When people stopped running and hyper-ventilating, they might start worrying about what else might be moving unseen in their midst. And they really wouldn't like the answer.

Besides, the open presence of a Drood in his armour on a London street would be bound to attract the attention of all the wrong people. The kind who would very definitely come running, for the chance to attack a wounded and weakened Drood. I turned and put my back against the window, gritting my teeth against the horrid pains that stirred up. I looked around, but I couldn't see anyone, or anything, immediately threatening. I pushed myself away from the shop-window and moved on, not sure where I was going, knowing only that I had to get away. Get somewhere safe. I needed help; I was no use to Molly like this.

So I gathered up my courage, swallowed my pride, and called on my family for help.

"Kate?" I said, through my torc. "This is Eddie, reporting in. I'm in trouble. I need support, and backup, and a really good medical team. I'm on Oxford Street. Who have you got in the area? Who's nearest? Kate? Kate, can you hear me?"

I couldn't hear anything. Which was disturbing. My controller should have been there, just waiting for me to make contact, in the event I might need something urgently. That's the only reason field agents put up with controllers. I called Kate again, but there was still no response, so I called out to anyone in my family. Anyone on duty, who might be listening. There's always someone on monitor duty. But there was only silence. I tried to make sense of what was happening. Could someone have already told my family about what had just happened at Castle Inconnu? If the Seneschal hadn't cleared me, could my family have already cut me off, abandoned me, to avoid a war? Without even wanting to hear my side? It was possible. They'd done worse to me before. I kept moving. I was on my own. So I had to keep moving, or die.

I weaved ponderously through the packed crowd on Oxford Street, and no one bothered me. No one even glanced in my direction. I looked around, curious. People were avoiding making eye contact with me. I wondered if they were doing that because they thought I was one of the homeless, or because they genuinely couldn't see me. No . . . if I was invisible to them, they'd be trying to walk straight through me. And everybody was giving me plenty of room, even stepping off the pavement and into the busy street if I happened to lurch suddenly in their direction . . . without any of them seeming to realise they were doing it. Just as well; one heavy impact, one crash of bodies, would have been painful enough to knock me out cold.

I felt . . . distanced; not a proper part of the world any more. As though I was drifting between the real and the unreal, suspended between life and death. I didn't understand what was happening. I felt . . . lost. I stopped and stared blearily about me, and realised I no longer had any idea of where I was. My surroundings had changed while I wasn't looking. The street around me didn't look anything like Oxford Street. I didn't recognise the area, or any of the shops, and when I looked up . . . it was into a night sky. Night? How could it be night so soon? Where did the day go? There was no moon, and the stars were like splashes of white paint, sliding slowly down the endless dark of the sky.

I made myself concentrate on the shop-windows around me. All the familiar businesses and tourist traps were gone, replaced by new and unfamiliar places. Like changelings, left in place of a kidnapped baby. The names above these new ugly premises were in languages I couldn't read, didn't even recognise. The things on sale in the windows made no sense. Some of them moved around, or bumped angrily against the inside of the glass. Some changed shape even as I looked at them, their details becoming strange and monstrous. Like in those really bad nightmares, where you can't trust anything to stay what it seems. Neon signs flashed and flared too quickly to be understood, their colours so harsh and overpowering that they hurt my head and made me feel sick. The buildings rearing up around me were now impossibly tall, or broad, or inhumanly detailed, bulging with too many spatial dimensions to be contained in a single shape. Some shops seemed to slide away, backwards and sideways, as though reluctant to meet my gaze. Or to be pinned down to one shape or location, by the pressure of my observing them. Other shops were all too clearly there, staring right back at me, with bad intent.

Come inside . . . Come on in, little Drood, and see what's waiting for you.

When I peered out at the traffic, most of what was passing by looked more like living things than vehicles. Or perhaps vehicles that were living things. The pavement under my feet felt soft and treacherous. As though I might suddenly sink into it and never come out. And the people on the street around me . . . didn't look or sound or act the way I thought ordinary people should. As though everyone was just wearing a people mask and pretending to be ordinary. My heart pounded painfully in my chest. I wanted to just run, blindly, wildly, slam people out of my way and leave all this madness behind. But I didn't know where to go. There was nowhere that felt safe any longer.

I didn't know where I was, though that shouldn't be possible. I was Drood field agent in London for years, had been everywhere, leaned on everyone. So why didn't I know this street, these buildings, these people? I tried to access the street maps stored in my armour, but there was no response. I wondered briefly whether my armour would still come if I called? Or would it defy me now, like the Merlin Glass had? Was I really that alone, that helpless? Where had the Green Door brought me . . . ? I swayed on my feet, cold sweat slick on my face, a nameless horror clutching at my guts. Lost and alone, in a crowd of strange strangers.

Until slowly I became aware that someone was walking through the crowd, heading straight for me. And the crowd was falling back to let him pass. I raised my head slowly, against the pain, and concentrated, and a great rush of relief passed through me. I knew his face. It was the Armourer, my uncle Jack. The one person in my family I knew I could depend on to never let me down. The feeling of relief faded away as the Armourer drew closer, leaving me confused. It seemed to me that something was wrong. That there was something I should remember . . .

Uncle Jack came to a halt right in front of me and smiled at me. Warmly, and kindly. I smiled back. I wondered if I was dreaming. I started to say something, and then my legs buckled and I almost fell.

Jack was immediately there to grab my good arm and hold me up. I leaned on him heavily, unashamedly. He felt reassuringly real and solid. I almost cried out with relief. My legs grew stronger, and I straightened up again. I stepped back to study his face.

The Armourer looked just as I remembered him from the last time I'd seen him. Standing tall and steady in his stained and burned white lab coat. But now he had all his old strength and vitality back. He didn't look tired, or worn out . . . And it was only then, as a slow chill moved through me, that I remembered why that had been the last time I'd seen him.

"Uncle Jack?" I said. "Aren't you . . . dead?"

"Aren't you?" said the Armourer.

I thought about it. "No," I said decisively.

"Well, that's a start," Jack said cheerfully. "Come with me, Eddie, if you want to live."

He started off back down the street, and I went along with him, leaning heavily on his supporting arm. Wondering if I was so ill I'd started hallucinating. I could be imagining it all. But no; if this was all just in my head, I wouldn't hurt so much.

"I went to your funeral, Uncle Jack," I said.

"Did you? That was kind of you, Eddie. Good turnout, was it?"

"So you are quite definitely dead?"

"Oh yes . . ."

I thought about it. "Is . . . Uncle James here too?"

"I'm afraid not," said the Armourer. "Only one guardian angel to a customer. That's how it works. I don't make the rules."

"Who does?"

Jack looked at me. "Do you really want to know?"

"Possibly not," I said.

"It's all right to lean on me, Eddie," said Jack. "You're in a bad way. Someone put the really hard word on you."

"Am I dying?"

"Maybe," said the Armourer. "That's up to you."

"Where are you taking me, Uncle Jack?"

"We're going underground," said the Armourer. "Where all the dead things go. How long you stay there will depend on you."

And then he stopped abruptly, and I had no choice but to stop with him. Up ahead, two large and very determined-looking men were heading towards us. I recognised them both immediately. The Vodyanoi Brothers, Gregor and Sergei. Thugs and bully-boys, villains for hire, werewolves. Tall and leanly muscled, in expensive long black leather coats, with shaven heads and nasty smiles. They crashed to a halt before me, and looked me over with hot, anticipatory eyes. Even standing still they looked violent, and vicious with it. Gregor gave me his best menacing sneer.

"Yes! It is being you! Eddie the Drood, you remember us. Gregor and Sergei Vodyanoi. Very dangerous people!"

"Incredibly dangerous!" said Sergei, determined not to be left out.

"Yes, little brother, but you will be remembering that we did agree I would be the one to do all the talking," said Gregor. "Because I am best at."

"Then get on with it!" said Sergei.

"You always did bolt your food," said Gregor. "It is no wonder you are being a martyr to your digestion." He glared at me. "Our grandfather called us in. Because of what you did to him, at the Wulfshead. The way you treated him!"

"And we are being glad to come here!" said Sergei, unable to contain himself. "Come to make you pay, Eddie Drood, for the way you have always treated us."

"For getting us thrown out of the Lady Faire's Ball!" said Gregor. "We had to walk home! The long way!"

"And when we heard you are being hurt, and injured," said Sergei, "weak and vulnerable, at long last, well! It is all our birthdays come at once."

"Icing on the cake," said Gregor.

Sergei looked at him. "What cake? No one said anything about cake."

I looked at Jack. "Normally I'd find them funny. But today I'm just not in the mood."

"Understandable," said the Armourer.

Gregor Vodyanoi turned the full force of his glare on Jack. "You do not wish to be a part of this, whoever you are. Go now, or we will not be answering for the consequences. We are being werewolves, and very hungry."

"Always hungry," said Sergei. "Go, and let us be about our business. And maybe we won't chase you."

"Okay," I said. "Not funny at all."

I straightened up and moved away from the Armourer, standing on my own, unsupported, doing my best to seem dangerous. I armoured up my right fist and held it out before me. Nasty golden spikes rose from the knuckles. The Vodyanoi Brothers stood very still, looking at the golden glove as though fascinated. And then they looked at me, and from the expressions on their faces I knew that to them at least, I didn't look tired or hurt or vulnerable any more. I looked like a Drood. The Vodyanoi Brothers looked at each other.

"It is still only the one of him," said Gregor. "We will never be getting a better chance, little brother."

"Got to be worth a try," said Sergei.

And then the Armourer stepped forward, putting himself between the Vodyanoi Brothers and me. And just like that, all the colour dropped out of Gregor's and Sergei's faces, replaced by looks of utter shock. They fell back, clutching at each other in their panic, frightened and appalled by what they were seeing. The Armourer was suddenly an overpowering presence in the night, terrible and threatening. I was behind him, so I couldn't see what the Vodyanoi Brothers were seeing, but I could still feel enough of it that all the hairs on the back of my neck stood up. This wasn't the Uncle Jack I remembered. What had happened to him when he died? The Vodyanoi Brothers suddenly turned and bolted, plunging back into the crowd and shouldering people out of their way, until they disappeared in the distance. No one else seemed affected by the Armourer's presence, and when he turned around to smile at me, he was just my uncle Jack again.

"Come along, Eddie. We must be going."

I pulled the golden strange matter back off my fist and into my torc, and almost collapsed. I hadn't realised how much difference just a little of my armour could make, but without its support there was hardly enough of me left to stand upright. I hadn't realised . . . how bad my condition was. I nodded slowly to the Armourer.

"We need to get the hell out of here, Uncle Jack," I said. "Get off the street, disappear, go to ground. Until we can find someone willing to help us."

"No one can help you now but me," said the Armourer.

"All right; I'm hurt! I'm hurt badly, I get it! But there are hospitals, secret underground medical centres, for all the people, and other things, of the hidden world. Places people like us can go when we need help. Somewhere you can be sure no one will ask awkward questions. I'm thinking of institutions like the Sisters of Conditional Mercy, the Hidden Hospice, Médecins Sans Frontières . . ."

I stopped, trying to think where the nearest of these sites might be, and then realised I didn't know. I knew of them—everyone in our line of work did, or at least knew stories about them—but I'd never needed to visit one before. Thanks to my marvellous armour. I knew the odd place or two in Harley Street, because of a case I followed there some years back . . . assuming the Hospice of Saint Baphomet was still there, and that someone had rebuilt Dr Dee's House of Exorcism. . . . but I had no idea how far away they were. I had no idea where I was any more. I looked at Jack, and he shook his head slowly and deliberately.

"None of those places can heal you, Eddie. You're beyond any help they could offer."

"I wish you'd stop saying things like that!"

"Would you rather I lied to you?"

"I'm starting to think so, yes."

"It wouldn't help. You need to come with me, Eddie. I'm your only hope."

"Oh hell," I said. "I'm too tired to argue. Let's go. Before something really nasty turns up to take a bash at me. There's lots of things worse than the Vodyanoi Brothers; the kind who'd give their left nut, or more likely someone else's, for a chance to take down an injured Drood. The kind who won't give a damn about manifesting their unnatural abilities in the normal world and freaking out the natives. I don't want that. First rule of our kind: don't let the innocent bystanders get caught up in our battles."

"Your concern does you credit, Eddie," said Jack, "but we haven't been a part of the ordinary world for some time now. That's how I'm able to be here."

I looked around me. It did seem to me that the people passing by were subtly altered, out of focus. And the roar from the passing traffic seemed strangely muted, distanced. I looked back at the Armourer.

"How did you get here? I mean . . ."

"Because you needed me," said Jack. "Come along, Eddie. You can't put it off any longer. We have miles to go before we can sleep; and one of us has promises to keep."

He started off again. I walked along beside him. It took me only a few moments to realise I was feeling a lot better. As though all my pains and injuries and weakness had been . . . moved away. Not gone, as such, but not troubling me any longer. Jack turned suddenly and strode briskly out into the open road, plunging straight into the oncoming traffic. I hesitated at the curb, automatically, and then just thought *What the hell, six impossible things before breakfast just to give you an appetite* . . . before striding defiantly out into the busy traffic myself.

Jack and I walked straight through the speeding vehicles, passing through cars and taxis and buses as though they were all insubstantial, nothing more than mist. We reached the other side of the street, untouched and unharmed, and I couldn't resist a loud whoop of delight.

"That was fun! Let's do it again!"

"Maybe later, Eddie," said Jack, in that voice uncles use when dealing with the young and easily distracted. "We have somewhere we need to be."

He strode off, and I hurried to catch up with him. The people on this side of the road were still giving us both plenty of room.

"Is the traffic really insubstantial?" I said after a while. "Or is it us?"

"Does it make any difference?" said the Armourer.

I considered the matter. "It might . . ."

Jack chuckled. "You see? You're learning . . ."

He finally brought me to an Underground Station. One I didn't know—though before today I would have sworn I'd at least heard of all of them. It looked old, maybe even Victorian in its style. Lots of grimy bare stone and polished metal. The sign above the entrance simply read ARBITER. No one else was going in, or out, which was . . . odd. Jack marched straight in and started down the bare stone steps. I wandered along behind him, taking my time so I could have a good look around me. The moment we were away from the roar and clamour of the traffic, an eerie silence took hold. Our feet didn't make the smallest sound on the bare stone steps. I stamped one foot hard, experimentally, and I heard nothing. Not a whisper of sound, not even a hint of an echo. The steps still felt entirely real and solid under my feet, though.

*Are they insubstantial? Or is it us?*

At the bottom of the steps we moved forward into a deserted

vestibule, and the ticket barriers opened obligingly before us, even though neither I nor Uncle Jack had a ticket, or an Oyster card. Normally, I would have used my armour to fool the system, but here I didn't need to. Jack and I seemed to be operating under new rules. As though we were expected, invited. A moving stairway took us smoothly down into the station's depths. In fact, the ride was so completely smooth, without the slightest bump or jolt, that this more than anything convinced me we were no longer in the world I knew. We reached the bottom, and moved on through featureless tunnels of a dull grey stone. No posters or ads on the walls, anywhere.

We passed through a tunnel mouth and out onto a platform, and suddenly there were people everywhere, crowds of them, all around us. Well, I say *people* . . . There were men with the heads of birds and animals. Women with no faces. Egyptian mummies with clay-baked features, wrapped in yards and yards of rotting gauze. Young men and women clinging together, weeping hot, bitter tears. And men and women standing alone, with dried blood caked around terrible self-inflicted wounds at their wrists and throats. Staring straight ahead of them with sad, angry eyes.

Through another tunnel mouth, to another escalator, that seemed to just go on descending forever. I leaned out as far as I dared, but I still couldn't see the bottom, or where we were going. So I just straightened up and stuck close to my uncle Jack. Because I trusted him.

We finally ended up on a small platform, this time entirely untroubled by other people. There wasn't a sound from anywhere, and everything seemed almost unnaturally still. No posters or ads on the walls, and the single Destinations board was worryingly blank. Jack led me to a door set quietly away to one side, with a sign written over it in Enochian. The sign appeared to have been written in blood, and quite recently. Enochian is the artificial language created back in Elizabethan times, to allow men to speak directly with angels. Apparently, just speaking the words of this language aloud can lead to permanent changes in your brain chemistry. It seemed to me that I should be able to read and understand Enochian, but although I could recognise the language, the dripping crimson words made no sense to me at all.

Uncle Jack stood before the door and made a pleased sound as he checked out the sign. He gestured imperiously, and the door opened immediately, falling back before us. I followed him through, into a grim grey flickering light, revealing a dull grey tunnel. The door closed itself quietly behind us. Jack didn't seem concerned about that, so I did my best not to be either. At the far end of the tunnel, we ended up standing before another closed door, this time simply marked *Maintenance.* Jack opened it, and we stepped through into what seemed to be a closet. Half full of scarecrows sitting slumped together, wearing British Rail uniforms.

"Don't ask," the Armourer said wisely.

So I didn't.

He reached out a hand to the old-fashioned telephone set on the rear wall. A telephone I was sure hadn't been there just a moment before. Jack lifted the receiver and spoke firmly into it.

"Going down."

The dull grey wall split in two before us, from top to bottom, both sides grinding slowly apart in jerky, shuddering movements, to form yet another long narrow tunnel. The Armourer strode forward into it, but I hesitated. There was something . . . bad, up ahead. I could feel it. Something dangerous. Jack realised I wasn't with him, stopped, and looked back.

"Come along, Eddie! This is where you have to go."

"Why?" I said, not moving an inch.

"Because you have to go all the way down, and all the way through, before you can come out the other side."

"That doesn't even make any sense!"

"It will," said the Armourer. "Probably. Trust me, Eddie. Please."

And what could I say to that? I nodded and went after him.

The bare walls of this new tunnel were blood-red, hot and sweaty, and almost organic. Like passing through an open wound in the body of the world. The sourceless light was dim and murky. The place smelled of ancient corrupt perfumes and flowers crushed underfoot. There was a constant background murmur of many voices, rising and falling, along with snatches of music that faded in and out, like so many competing radio signals from other worlds. Somewhere a cloister bell was ringing. It sounded like . . . a bell made of ice, ringing sadly in the middle of a deep dark forest. It sounded alone, so alone . . .

We emerged suddenly onto another platform. Another completely deserted scene, with nothing to show that people had ever been allowed access. I had the oddest feeling that dust was falling, silently, continuously, though I couldn't see or feel it. The single Destinations board on the far wall was filled with names I didn't know. Old stations, lost stations, forgotten stations. *Ludd's Gate, Darkchapel, Thamesfleet, Cemetery Wharf, Cain's Causeway.* None of them sounded like anywhere I wanted to go.

I moved forward, to the very edge of the platform, and looked down. And discovered something decidedly unique about this new station. A river ran through it. Dark waters filled the space where the train tracks should have been. Dark and impenetrable and completely still. Not a ripple, not a movement anywhere on the flat black surface. And no reflection at all. Without looking back at Uncle Jack, I raised my voice.

"What the hell is this?"

"The River Styx," said the Armourer. "Some say, a river in Hell, made from the tears of suicides. Or a symbol of the way between the worlds. A transition point, between Life and Death. Don't expect me to pin it down, Eddie; we're in legendary territory here. This is your journey, so it's up to you to decide what the symbols mean."

"If three Christmas ghosts turn up," I growled, "I am going to kick the crap out of all three of them. And that goes for Tiny Tim too. Never did like ukulele music. Uncle Jack, what am I doing here?"

"You're on the brink, Eddie," said the Armourer. "You could go one way, or the other. It's up to you. I'm helping you as much as I'm allowed, but . . . if you want to be forgiven, you have to forgive yourself. If you want to move on, or be renewed, you have to leave your sins behind you."

I thought about that. "All my sins? Even the sins of omission? Things I should have done but didn't?"

"Oh, I think those most of all," said the Armourer.

I turned then, to look at him steadily. "Why have you brought me here?"

"I'm the Armourer. An engineer. I fix things that need fixing. It's what I do. And it's the last thing I can do for you."

We both looked round sharply, as a voice emerged from somewhere deep in the right-hand tunnel mouth, mournfully singing "Somewhere Over the Rainbow." A long, narrow barge drifted slowly out of the tunnel mouth, old-fashioned and basic, made from dark cedar wood, propelled by no obvious engine or action. It glided silently through the dark waters towards us, and I made the connection immediately. The barge of ancient legend that transported the living to the land of the dead. But instead of Charon at the helm, it was Dead Boy. In his long deep purple greatcoat, still hanging defiantly open to show off the ragged stitching on his autopsy scar. He looked up, saw Jack and me, stopped singing, and brightened up. He pushed his floppy wide-brimmed hat onto the back of his head, and I saw that his corpse-pale face looked even worse than usual in the uncertain light. His eyes were dark and fever-bright, but his smile was marvellously uncomplicated.

"Hello, Eddie! Jack!" he said loudly. "Hey, you wouldn't believe who I had in the back of my barge just the other day! So, two tickets to Tartarus, is it? One way or a return trip?"

"Do I need to give you a coin?" I said, just to show I was keeping up. "That is traditional, isn't it? A coin to pay the ferryman?"

"Your uncle Jack already paid in full," said Dead Boy. "Climb aboard! Sit anywhere you like. Don't trail a hand in the waters if you like having fingers, and if things should get a bit choppy try to get some of it in the bags provided."

I stepped aboard the barge, followed by Jack, and we arranged ourselves as comfortably as we could on the bare wooden bottom of the boat. The barge didn't rock even a little under our weight. Dead Boy produced a gondolier's pole from out of nowhere, thrust it down into the dark waters with a dramatic gesture, and started the barge moving. We headed steadily towards the left-hand tunnel mouth, while Dead Boy sang "Let It Be."

We passed through the dark, gaping mouth and on into a new tunnel, whose walls shone with a pearly gleam. The dark waters dropped away before us, sloping sharply, carrying us deeper and deeper into the earth. Going down, all the way down. I looked back over my shoulder, and already there was no sign of the tunnel mouth. Clouds of birds fluttered silently overhead, black bunches of feathers slamming into one another and off the tunnel roof.

"Crows," Dead Boy said wisely. "Indentured security for the place of the dead. They can sometimes be persuaded to carry messages out of the underworld."

I looked at him. "If this is . . . the place of the dead, have you seen my parents? Charles and Emily Drood?"

"Like you," said the Armourer, "their future has yet to be determined. Concentrate on what's in front of you, Eddie." He paused. "How do you feel?"

I considered the question. To my surprise, I discovered that I felt pretty good. No pain, no weakness, everything working perfectly. I looked at the Armourer.

"I feel great. Now tell me the truth, Uncle Jack. Am I dead?"

"Not necessarily," said the Armourer. "You're feeling better because you've left your earthly cares and woes behind to come to this place in search of judgement and forgiveness and renewal. A new chance at life. You do want to return to the world above, don't you?"

"Yes," I said. "I have to. Molly is depending on me."

The Armourer grinned. "You always were very single-minded. I approve of Molly. She's good for you. Don't ever tell her I said that. She'd hate to think she was a good influence on anyone."

The dark waters suddenly levelled out, and our descent slowed and stopped. The barge eased to a halt beside a new platform that had suddenly appeared out of nowhere. Dead Boy grounded his long pole and leaned on it, nodding to me companionably.

"Okay, this is it. Even I can't go any farther. See you around, Eddie. Hopefully." He nodded to Jack. "Good seeing you again. I enjoyed your wake. Oh, sorry . . ."

"That's all right," said the Armourer. "I was there, in spirit."

I stepped carefully up out of the barge and onto the platform, and the Armourer quickly joined me. Everything looked . . . perfectly ordinary, but once again there was no one around. The long, empty platform was bathed in a flat, characterless light, and the Destinations board consisted of just two arrows—one pointing up and the other pointing down. Some symbols are so obvious they're not even really symbols. More like a slap round the back of the head. I turned to Jack and did my best to sound off-handed and confident.

"Okay, what are we doing here?"

"You're here to face the Arbiter," said Jack. "To tell the truth, at last; because nothing less can save and redeem you. It's judgement night."

I really didn't like the sound of that. Particularly when I became aware that the flat light was fading steadily all around us. I looked back at the black river, but Dead Boy and his barge were already gone. Gloom closed in on Jack and me from all sides, until finally there was just a spotlight, sharp and clear and concentrated, falling out of nowhere onto me and Jack. Pinning us in place, like specimens mounted on a board.

"I'm on trial, aren't I?" I said.

"Yes," said the Armourer.

"By this . . . Arbiter? Who put him in charge? Who gave him authority over me?"

Jack smiled. "You did, Eddie."

I sniffed loudly. "I've never liked authority figures. Even when I was one."

A second spotlight stabbed down, abruptly illuminating a dark human silhouette sitting on a bar-stool not far away, facing me. A bar-stool that looked just like the one I'd been sitting on, not so long ago, at Jack's wake in the Wulfshead Club. The dark figure leaned forward suddenly, and his face came into the light. It was, of course, me. Smiling.

"Yes," said the Arbiter. "The one person you know you can't lie to."

I looked to my uncle Jack. "Is it too late to request a change in venue?"

"It was too late for that before we even came down here," said the Armourer. "Some things just have to be faced, Eddie."

"Who knows you better than me?" said the Arbiter. "Who can you trust to give you fair judgement, if not me? There can be no lies between us, no prevarications, no justifications. Just the truth. At last."

"You must confess your sins, Eddie," said Jack. "If you want to be forgiven. If you want to survive this. You were dying, up there, but this . . . is your chance to be reborn. If you're worthy of it."

I thought hard. This mattered; I could tell. I'd been hurt bad, by the London Knights. It was quite possible my broken body was lying huddled somewhere on Oxford Street, quietly bleeding out, while people just stepped over me and kept going. While my soul was . . . here. Wherever or whatever here was. I looked to Jack. He seemed realer than anything else. And if I was going to die, I couldn't think of better company to do it in.

"All right," I said. "For you, Uncle Jack."

I turned to face myself, to face the Arbiter, and began my confession of sins. I talked about my career as a Drood field agent. Of the man I'd been, and the man I'd wanted to be; and the man my family had tried and failed to make me into. About the things I was ordered to do that sometimes I agreed with and sometimes didn't, until finally the family turned on me, for all my loyalty. I talked about how I ended up running the family, to save its soul, to save it from itself; and how I stepped down because I honestly believed I was getting good people killed, because I wasn't up to the job.

"I know all this," said the Arbiter coldly. "I'm you, remember?"

"It's important to me to talk it through," I said just as coldly. "To be clear about it all. To understand the context . . . You want sins, and confessions of guilt, and mea culpa? Then let's start with Charles and Emily. My father and my mother. I understand what they did, and why they did it, a lot better now . . . But still, I can't forget how they made me feel. By going away and leaving me. Leaving me to the family. That's why I've been so desperate to find them. So I could talk with them, and get the truth out of them. But really . . . facts won't help. Won't make any difference. Inside, I'm still the small boy abandoned by his parents. All I can do is understand that they did what they thought was best under the circumstances. So I forgive them."

"Good start," said the Arbiter. "Continue."

I scowled at him. "I'm really not very good at all this head-shrinking, touchy-feely crap."

"Of course not," said the Arbiter. "You're a Drood. Continue."

"I never forgave my grandmother Martha, for not loving me. Or at least, not loving me the way I thought she should. She tried to have me killed! But she had pressures and responsibilities I couldn't understand until I tried to do the job myself. And in the end I took everything away from her. I changed the family until she couldn't recognise it. I caused her husband, Alistair, to die horribly. We came to a meeting of minds, at the end . . . but it could be said I blamed her not for what she was but for not being what I wanted her to be. And that, again, is a child's viewpoint. So I forgive her too."

"Not bad," said the Arbiter. "Continue."

I talked about all the people I thought I'd let down, from all my various cases and missions. The people I tried to save, and couldn't. The people who trusted me, and died still trusting me. I remembered all the bodies, all the dead Droods coming home from my failed attack on the Hungry Gods. I remembered the CIA agent Honey Lake, dying in my arms. I remembered . . . so many names, so many faces. And I forgave myself—because looking back, I realised I really had done my best.

I finally ground to a halt. Exhausted. Like I'd just run an emotional marathon. I honestly hadn't realised I'd thought so much about my past, or blamed myself for so much. I was shaking, worn down and worn out, from the strain of remembering so many old emotions.

"Continue," said the Arbiter.

"What?" I said. I looked at him angrily. "What else is there? That's it!"

"No, it isn't," he said. "Why don't you want to live, Eddie? Your injuries are bad, but you've come back from worse. Why do you think you don't deserve to live? Why have you decided you're not going to kill ever again?"

"Because it shouldn't be that easy!" I shouted at him. "I just decided that little shit at Uncanny deserved to die, and he did! All right, he probably wanted to die. Suicide by Drood. But . . . I should have found some way to save him. He was Arthur's grandson, just like me. He was family."

"Good," said the Arbiter. "You didn't kill him; he killed himself, using you as the weapon."

"I still don't want to kill again."

"That's the future. That's between you and your conscience. We're dealing with the past here. With forgiveness and absolution. Continue."

"There's nothing else!"

"Yes there is. Continue."

"No!"

"Say it. Speak the truth at last. What's the one thing left, that you can't, won't, forgive yourself for?"

"No!"

"Say it! Say you're sorry!"

I spun round to face the Armourer. "I'm sorry, Uncle Jack! I'm so sorry! I went away and left you to die alone! I wasn't there when you needed me! I should have been there with you!"

"I know," he said. "I know, Eddie."

He opened his arms, and I stumbled over to him, and hugged him hard. He held me in his strong engineer's arms, held me close, while I buried my face in his lab-suited shoulder and cried like a child. Hot tears streamed down my face so hard I could barely breathe. He patted me comfortingly on the back, with his big engineer's hands.

"I'm sorry, I'm so sorry . . ."

"Hush, hush," he said. "It's all right, Eddie. Really it is. Forgive yourself, Eddie. For being a man, and fallible. Not even a Drood can be everywhere at once, be everywhere he's needed. You did the best you could. So forgive yourself; and then go save Molly. And Charles and Emily. As for me . . . Do you really think I wanted you there to watch me die? Why would I want to put you through something like that?"

I stepped back from him, sniffing back the tears. He was smiling kindly.

"But you died alone, Uncle Jack."

"We all die alone, boy. But . . . there was someone there with me, at the end. So forgive yourself. So we can get this over and done with and move on."

"I shouldn't have done it," I said. "But I couldn't have done anything else. So, yes, I forgive myself."

"Good man," said the Armourer.

He hugged me again, one last time. And put his mouth right next to my ear.

"I have always been so proud of you, Eddie. You are the son I should have had."

He let me go, and I let him go, and we stood apart. I mopped the drying tears from my face with a handkerchief, and turned to the Arbiter; but he and his bar-stool were already gone. The trial was over. Guilty, but human; and forgiven. It felt . . . like a bright new morning after a very long night.

Jack led me up, out of the underground. Just a simple stairway this time. Didn't seem to take nearly as long. The need for symbols was over. I stepped out of the Underground Station and onto the street; but Jack didn't come with me. I stopped, and looked back.

"Uncle Jack?"

"I've done all I can, Eddie. The rest is up to you now."

"Good-bye, Uncle Jack," I said. "It was so good to see you again."

He smiled, and turned away, and walked back into the dark, back down into the underworld.

I looked around, and found I was standing outside the Green Door—access to Castle Inconnu. Right back where I'd started from. Had any of it really happened? Had any of it been real? I flexed my left arm, and then my side, increasingly vigorously, until people passing by in the street looked at me curiously. I didn't hurt any more. I felt good; I felt better than good. I felt . . . healed, inside and out. One last gift from my uncle Jack.

And now it was time to go find whoever had taken Molly. And make them sorry they'd ever heard of her, or me. I might have given up killing, but I hadn't given up protecting those I cared about. I strode off down Oxford Street, and people took one look at my face and hurried to get out of my way.

# CHAPTER NINE

# No One Ever Comes Back to Complain

I made contact with my handler, Kate, through my torc and was pleasantly surprised when she answered me promptly. I could still remember the chill in my heart and my soul when I had reached out to Kate and my family and no one answered. But this time Kate's cheerful voice sounded in my ear immediately.

"Hello, Eddie! Yes, of course I'm here; why, is anything wrong? You sound a bit . . . concerned."

"I just thought I should apologise for being out of contact for so long," I said.

"Okay, this isn't like you," said Kate. "It's an improvement, but it isn't like you. It's been hardly any time at all since we talked. You'd have to be off the air and off the grid for a lot longer than this before I even started getting worried about you. Though . . . apparently, we are just starting to get complaints coming into the Hall, about your conduct at . . . Castle Inconnu? What the hell were you doing there? Eddie, why have you upset the London Knights?"

"It needed doing," I said.

"Good for you," said Kate. "Stuck-up bunch of prigs. Don't snigger,

Eddie. You know very well I said 'prigs.' Oh, Eddie, please tell me you haven't killed any of them!"

"Of course I haven't killed any of them! I keep telling you, I don't do that any more."

"Just checking," Kate said airily. "You do have a reputation, you know . . . Not that any of us here gives a damn about the London Knights, you understand. If they want, they can make an official complaint about you to the family. And then we can have the fun of officially ignoring it."

I filled Kate in on everything that had happened during my visit to Castle Inconnu. Including my conversations with Sir Perryvale and the Lady Gaea. Even including the things that might have made me look a bit bad. Kate immediately went all swoony at the very thought of talking with Mother Earth in person. She pressed me for details on exactly what was said, what the Lady looked like, and what she was wearing. But I was already forgetting most of what had passed between us. Which was probably just as well. Mortals aren't supposed to get used to talking with living goddesses. I did explain to Kate why I had to fight my way out of the Castle, and then I stopped. She didn't need to know how badly I'd been injured. And she really didn't need to know about Uncle Jack and the underworld. That was nobody's business but mine. And Jack's.

So instead I told Kate about my lead on finding Molly through the Travel Bureau and its infamous Departure Lounge.

"I can have armoured backup on the spot to assist you in under an hour," said Kate.

"No," I said quickly. "I can't wait, and we can't risk word getting out that I'm heading their way. The Travel Bureau must have their own ear to the ground, to be able to run an operation like theirs, and it would only take a whisper that the Droods were involved to put the wind up them. They might shut everything down and do a runner, or destroy all their records—and there goes my only lead to Molly. No, Kate, I think it's safer I do this alone, as Shaman Bond. That is what he's for, after all."

"Don't be proud, Eddie," Kate said quietly. "If you do need help, yell for it."

"Understood," I said. It was a way of agreeing without agreeing, and we both knew it.

I strode along Oxford Street, half wishing I hadn't left the Bentley back at the Hall. Everywhere I was thinking of going was in walking distance, but that still covered quite a lot of ground and meant quite a bit of walking. I didn't dare try using the Merlin Glass openly anywhere in London; it would have been like blasting a great spotlight through the dark, and be bound to attract all kinds of unwelcome attention. Even assuming I could persuade the treacherous little object to do what I needed it to.

I realised I was walking with a distinct spring in my step. I felt better than healed; I felt strong and sound again. As though I'd put down a cripplingly heavy weight that I hadn't even realised I was carrying. I still wasn't sure what really happened down in the underworld, or even if anything actually had . . . but I didn't want to think about that right now. I'd had enough of mysteries; I wanted answers. Starting with who the hell had taken Molly, and where they had taken her. And that meant striking a deal with the Travel Bureau for use of their Departure Lounge. As quickly as possible.

I'd never been to the Travel Bureau before, but I knew about it. I knew about a great many things and places and nasty practices that went on in London that I'd never got around to checking out in person. There's just too much weird shit going down in this city for even a Drood field agent to keep up with. As long as most of them didn't make waves, or draw attention to themselves, I was usually ready to leave them be so I could concentrate on the things that needed stamping on. The twilight side of London isn't so much a maintained peace as a constant juggling act between what we Droods can actually do and the threat of what we might do if we became sufficiently upset. Drood authority helps to keep the lid on things, but there's always going to be a lot bubbling away underneath.

I looked around surreptitiously as I continued down Oxford Street, but it all seemed normal enough. Crowds of people everywhere, traffic moving slowly and bad-temperedly along, and a general sense of people hurrying off to do things that needed doing even though everyone knew it was already too late. That's London for you. I took time to stop and browse in the occasional shop-window, not because I was interested in any of the contents but because there's nothing so useful as studying the reflection in the glass to help you check out the people behind you. And there's nothing like stopping suddenly, to catch even the most professional tail off guard. But even though I took my time, and looked very carefully, I couldn't spot anyone out of place. Not a single familiar face, and no appearance anywhere of suspicious behaviour. No one was watching me, and no one gave any indication of giving a damn about me. Which was . . . reassuring.

When I was sure I wasn't being followed, or observed, I set off again and plunged suddenly down an unofficial short cut into old Soho, where twilight meets sleaze and together they make a profit off all the marks and suckers. Most of old Soho is gone now; after the most determined cleanup in generations. But there's always some sin left, if you know where to look. I headed down a particular side street that's always underlit, and well off the beaten track, and entered an area where no one ever stopped to browse the windows. People came this deep into old Soho only in search of quite distinct things and places. People walking these streets kept their heads well down, and never looked at one another, because they didn't want anyone to look at them.

Eventually I came to a familiar little cybercafé, part of the information underground. The silicon subterraneans. This particular quiet establishment used to be part of the Electronic Village chain, but was far too independent to bow down to anyone for long. It was currently called the Mighty Argus.com. Which was . . . cute. Argus was the Greek god of a thousand eyes, who saw everything. Someone knew their classics. I didn't; I got the reference only because I used to be very fond of an old Eddie Campbell comic about the Greek gods called *Deadface.*

This particular information-highway pit stop was open twenty-four hours a day, especially for twilight people like Shaman Bond. People who tended to need access and information in a hurry, and a hell of a lot of privacy. The storefront's single window had been thoroughly whitewashed over, and the neon sign above the door hadn't worked in ages. The café didn't believe in publicity, and its patrons didn't want to be disturbed . . . while they did illegal and quite possibly immoral and unnatural things with their computers. This was not a place to just wander in and look around, in the hope of making new friends.

I strode right up to the door, and it opened before me as it recognised me. The café and I go way back. Or more exactly, the café and Shaman Bond go way back. If this place even suspected the Droods knew about it, it would probably vanish in a puff of green smoke. I stopped just inside the door to give my eyes a chance to adjust to the deliberately maintained gloom. The café's patrons valued their anonymity. There were tables and chairs and computers waiting for use— and absolutely nothing else. You didn't come here for comforts.

The establishment's manager came drifting forward out of the gloom to greet me, smiling weakly. Willy Fleagal has been around the information market for what seems like forever, always a part of the scene while owing allegiance to no one, always happy to facilitate a meeting or a deal or . . . anything else, really—for a consideration. Willy was a tall, gangling middle-aged hippy; with gold-rimmed bifocals, a really high forehead, and a long grey ponytail. He wore a grubby T-shirt over very grubby jeans and sneakers, and always looked like he thought he knew something you didn't know. His T-shirt bore the simple message *Yes, I Know.*

Willy gave me his best smile and a weak handshake. He always looked like he was short of a few good meals, but no one ever gave him any trouble. He was protected. And the fact that none of us knew by whom, or even what, just made that all the more impressive. Willy knew Shaman Bond as a fairly regular customer, with certain special privileges guaranteed by the café's mysterious owners. Whoever they might be. For a café dedicated to the uncovering and passing on of important information, there was a lot about the place that remained deliberately obscure. Hell, I'm a Drood, and I don't know. There's a lot of businesses like that in old Soho.

It didn't matter. All Willy and I needed to know was that an agreement had been made on my behalf so that Shaman Bond was never challenged. I frowned, briefly and inwardly so as not to upset Willy, as I remembered what Uncle Jack had said: *It's all about Pacts and Agreements* . . . While I was thinking about that, Willy produced a highly up-to-date handheld scanner and ran it over my body, checking for listening bugs and other inquisitive things that might have been planted upon my person without my knowledge.

Willy was always pleased enough to see me; in the past, I had dropped the occasional hint that Shaman Bond was a local source for a number of well-regarded investigative journalists, all of them dedicated to sticking it to the Man; and Willy loved that. He did a quick, professional job with the scanner, and I let him do it because it gave him a false sense of security. I knew I didn't have any bugs on me—my armour would have detected them immediately. And I knew Willy's scanner wasn't powerful enough to detect my torc, or any of the toys and surprises I kept about me; otherwise I wouldn't have let him scan me. Willy finished the scan with a flourish, put the thing away, clasped his bony hands together over his sunken chest, and gave me another of his weakly assertive smiles.

"All part of the service, Mister Bond. And always good to see you, of course. Have we been smiting the ungodly again?"

"I make them pay," I said solemnly. "From those who have shall be taken, and serve the greedy buggers right."

"Will you be wanting your regular private room, Mister Bond?"

"That's what I'm here for, Willy." I paused, and considered him thoughtfully. "Has anyone been . . . asking around, about Shaman Bond?"

"Not that I've heard of," said Willy, blinking at me owlishly through his bifocals. "And I'm sure I would have heard something if there'd been anything worth the hearing. I mean, that's what I'm here for."

He led me between the packed tables, each in its own little pool of light, with people hunched over their computers like priests at prayer, only not quite. No one looked up at us, even for a moment. Willy unlocked a door at the rear of the café and led me into the private room with its single table, chair, and computer. The hanging bare bulb turned itself on as we entered—a bitter yellow light that somehow banished every shadow in a moment. I nodded my thanks to Willy, and he immediately backed out, nodding bashfully as he closed the door firmly behind him. I sat down before the computer. I didn't bother with the keyboard. I was probably the only person in the café who knew that this particular machine was just a shell, containing nothing but a preprogrammed scrying ball, provided by my family. (Reverse-engineered alien tech, rather than a mystical artefact, for whatever difference that makes.)

I spoke aloud, giving my real name, and identified myself officially by armouring up one hand and placing the golden palm flat against the monitor screen. The machine immediately came to life, chattering quietly to itself in half a dozen languages at once, while it made up its mind who it was today. I armoured down again. I didn't think anyone would get past Willy to take a quick peek in through the door, but it's always best not to take chances you don't have to. The monitor screen turned itself on, and I spoke up quickly before it could start reeling off all its various options and services. AIs do so love to show off. Like actors working as waiters who insist on declaiming all the day's specials.

"I don't need any of the usual contact protocols for my family," I said. "Or any of the diagnostic or investigative tools. Just give me a standard interface, with information and communication skills."

There was a pause, and a certain sense of sulkiness from the machine, that it wasn't going to be allowed to demonstrate all of its many wondrous skills; then a metal face appeared on the screen before me. All harsh, angled lines and old-fashioned character. Like the Man in the Iron Mask, with all the human elements removed. I recognised it immediately. It was Robot Archibald, a mechanical adventurer from the Sixties. *Robot for Hire: A Hard Man for Hard Times.* I still had one of his business cards somewhere; a souvenir from one of Uncle James' old cases. The glowing eyes in the metal face fixed themselves on me.

"Yes? What do you want? Speak up! It's your own time you're wasting, you know. I don't have to be doing this . . ."

"You're a standard interface?" I said.

"I'm moonlighting," said Robot Archibald. "Atomic power batteries don't pay for themselves, you know. So I hire out. Apparently I'm cheaper than running and maintaining an AI. Who knew? What do you want, Eddie?"

"I want you to make contact with the Travel Bureau on my behalf," I said. "Concerning Shaman Bond and his current urgent need to make use of the Departure Lounge. But this has to be set up so they can't tell where the communication originates, or that there's any connection whatsoever with the Droods. This is strictly Shaman Bond business. I also need this message to be just interesting enough to intrigue them without giving them any reason to worry about me. And I don't want them to be able to track this message back here. Can you do all of that?"

Robot Archibald sniffed loudly, no mean feat in itself for a metal face that didn't even have a nose. "Teach your granny to suck batteries. Of course I can do it! I thought you were going to ask for something difficult."

He set things in motion quite efficiently, establishing contact with the Travel Bureau on Shaman Bond's behalf, using all the very latest code phrases and contact protocols. The Drood family prides itself on keeping up on all the latest passwords, etc. Droods know everything, remember?

Robot Archibald suddenly disappeared, replaced by another artificial face, this time a computer-generated visage representing the Travel Bureau. All flat lines and no character; almost Art Deco. The eyes didn't blink, and the mouth didn't move as the face spoke to me.

"You have reached the Travel Bureau," it said, in a polite but entirely impersonal voice. "Your first step, for when it becomes necessary for you to make that much-needed hurried exit. Please be patient; your money is important to us. Please note, if you cannot afford to pay for First Class service, we recommend you do not waste your time or ours. If you can afford it, how may we be of service to you at this time?"

"This is Shaman Bond," I said, doing my best to sound urgent and affluent. "I am currently in deep doo-doo, and I need to disappear. Very thoroughly, and very quickly. I was told you could help me."

The artificial face paused, and seemed to look at me thoughtfully. "Shaman Bond. Processing . . . Your name and reputation are known to the Travel Bureau. We feel obliged to ask, therefore, are you currently solvent enough to be able to afford our Departure Lounge services?"

"Yes!" I said. "I am now! That's the problem! That's why I need to disappear!"

The face gave me an address in Denmark Street and an appointment. Along with a stern warning that the appointment was good only for its half-hour slot. Any earlier or later and I would not be admitted. The face disappeared, and the monitor screen shut down. Presumably so I wouldn't be able to bother Robot Archibald with any more requests. I sat back in my chair, thinking. I recognised the address. It was that part of Denmark Street which edged onto old Soho. Where the really wild things still hung out. Modern-day London likes to say it's cleaned everything up, and driven all the sin underground. Unknowingly, they're describing the situation very accurately. There's a lot goes on beneath the streets of London that those above are much better off not knowing about.

I arrived at the Travel Bureau with time to spare. The area seemed open and ordinary enough, mostly business premises and retail chains and ethnic restaurants. And the kind of pubs you wouldn't want to enter on your own without an invitation. The streets were brightly lit, full of the kind of people who are always in a hurry, and ready to walk right through you if you don't get out of their way fast enough. Much like most London streets, really.

I hung around outside the Travel Bureau, looking the place over while waiting for just the right time to go in. From the outside, it looked very perfectly commonplace and everyday. Just another Bucket Shop, offering cheap and cheerful getaways to the usual suspect destinations, to the kind of people who looked like they could use a good holiday. The shop even had *Travel Bureau: Ask About Our Special Departure Lounge!* written across the top of its main window, which was packed full of gaudily-coloured posters and brochures. Featuring the kind of tanned and healthy happy-smiley people you only ever see in holiday posters and brochures. Nothing like hiding in plain sight . . .

I braced myself, as I finally walked in through the main entrance. I could See all kinds of pretty powerful defences and protections in place, every one of them ready to do something thoroughly unpleasant and downright devastating to me if they decided I presented any kind of threat. More than enough to stop anyone who wasn't a Drood. I was a little concerned they might detect my torc and blow my cover identity. But nothing happened as I strode through the door, and I made myself relax. I should have known, should have trusted my armour. Ethel always does good work.

Inside, the shop seemed almost offensively ordinary. Full of ads for familiar vacations, at quite reasonable prices. The best cover is always going to be a real(istic) cover. Everyday people bustled around the shop, hurrying back and forth between the posters and the information desks, trying to squeeze a few more extras out of the money they had to work with. They chatted cheerfully with the information staff, paying me no attention at all. My gaze was drawn to a massive poster on the rear wall, bearing the official motto of the Travel Bureau, and its Departure Lounge: *No One Ever Comes Back to Complain!*

I walked straight up to the main reception desk, and introduced myself to the happy-smiley young lady sitting behind it. She didn't even blink at the name Shaman Bond, or when I told her I was there to make use of the Departure Lounge, right now. A part of me wanted to wink significantly at her, but that would have been over-egging the point. I still felt one of us should make an effort . . . The receptionist nodded easily to me.

"Welcome, Mister Bond. We've been expecting you." She gestured to a door at the rear of the room that I would have sworn hadn't been there just a moment before. "If you would care to pass through the door marked *Private,* one of our personal assistants is waiting to talk to you."

I stood my ground and scowled at her unhappily. "You were expecting me? How did you know I was coming here?"

"You made an appointment with us, Mister Bond," the receptionist said patiently.

"I know!" I said. "I just don't like people knowing things about me in advance. Like, where I'm going to be. That kind of information should be strictly need-to-know. It can be very dangerous to my well-being in my line of work."

"I wouldn't know," said the receptionist. "And I really don't give a damn. Please go through the door marked *Private*, where one of our people is waiting to help you with your problems. Or don't. See if I care. Let some other firm help you with your problems."

"There isn't anyone else who can help me!"

"I know!" the receptionist said brightly.

I sighed loudly and headed for the door marked *Private*. Of course they knew I was coming; but I needed to establish my suspicious credentials as Shaman Bond. I slammed open the door and strode into a very smart, very comfortable private office. Nice carpet, nice prints on the wall, all the usual distractions. A smart young lady in an exquisitely cut suit stood up behind her desk to greet me. The door shut itself quietly as I moved quickly forward to shake the young lady's hand. She was a hard-faced sort, with understated makeup and a business-like air, and a wide and utterly impersonal smile. Her steady grey eyes studied me carefully, like an angler who's just felt a sudden pull on his line. I did my best to look like a sucker.

"Good to meet you, Mister Bond," she said. "We've been expecting you."

"Getting really quite tired of that line," I said.

"With the name you chose, you must get it a lot," she said, entirely unmoved. "So, Shaman Bond. I am Miz Smith. I know your name, of course, and the reputation that goes with it. One does hear things, after all."

"Nothing good, I hope," I said.

"Don't waste your famous charm on me, Mister Bond. I don't find humour funny." And quite suddenly there was a small but really quite nasty gun in her hand, trained very professionally on me. "Please stand still, Mister Bond. It's a security thing."

I raised an eyebrow, and my hands. I wasn't in any danger, of course, but I didn't want Ms Smith to suspect that. The door behind me opened, and a large and very muscular gentleman came in and stood beside me. He was so big he could have made two of me, and his plain grey suit strained to hold it all in. He had the usual shaved head, and enough steel piercings in his face to make him a danger to stand next to during thunderstorms.

"Good evening, sir," he said, in a flat basso profundo voice. "I will be your threatening presence for this meeting. Just think of me as Mister Genuine Muscle, here to facilitate the deal and ensure that everything goes smoothly. Or to dispose of the body, should it prove necessary. It is necessary that I frisk you now."

"Not going to happen," I said. "Not unless you like gumming hospital food."

Ms Smith came out from behind her desk to better aim her gun at me, and flash me another of her bright professional smiles.

"It's all standard business practice, Mister Bond. Please don't take it personally. We do occasionally find it necessary to disappoint people, some of them very desperate and dangerous people, and we have to be prepared for when they become . . . upset. So please stand extremely still and allow yourself to be searched, or Mister Genuine Muscle will do it while you're unconscious. And that might involve cavity searches."

I shrugged resignedly, and raised my hands just a bit higher. Mister Genuine Muscle frisked me with professional thoroughness, and found nothing of any interest to him. He didn't find any of my weapons or useful toys, because I kept all of those in my pocket dimension. And while the Merlin Glass was currently resting in my coat pocket, he didn't find that either, because it evaded his hand with all its usual perversity. As I'd thought it would. And neither Mister Muscle nor Ms Smith could even see my torc. You'd have to be the seventh son of a seventh son, outside my family, and Family Planning has pretty much put an end to that.

Mister Muscle finally finished, and nodded briefly to Ms Smith, before stepping away from me. Ms Smith nodded back to him and he left, closing the door quietly behind him. Ms Smith put her gun away and sat down behind her desk again. She gestured to the visitor's chair, and I sat down facing her. Projecting just a little injured pride, as befitted Shaman Bond.

"Was that really necessary?" I said.

She smiled again. It didn't improve. "Think of it as professional courtesy, Mister Bond. Now, I need to take down your details. Starting with how did you hear about the Departure Lounge? We don't exactly advertise."

"Harry Fabulous told me," I said.

She nodded immediately. Harry's name was always going to be a safe enough bet. Everyone even remotely connected with our line of business either knows or knows of Harry Fabulous. Your special Go-to Guy, for absolutely everything unusual that's bad for you. Knock-off Hyde, Martian Red Weed, smoked black centipede meat . . . Harry might have developed something of a conscience in recent years, after encountering something he still won't talk about in the back room of a Members Only club in the Nightside. . . . But he's still your main man to go to when you want something out of the ordinary. And everyone knows it. Harry would definitely have at least heard about the Departure Lounge. I find a lot of the business of being a good field agent lies in knowing just the right name to drop, and just the right moment to drop it.

"Sorry to have to ask these questions, Mister Bond," said Ms Smith. "But we do have to be very careful."

"I understand," I said. "But that thing with the gun; don't ever do that again."

She looked at me sharply, hearing something in my voice, but elected to move on.

"Now why exactly do you need our very special services, Mister Bond? And what makes someone like you believe you can afford it?"

"I have stolen something," I said flatly. "From the Droods. Yes, I thought that would get your attention. To be exact, I am now in possession of the legendary and quite priceless Merlin Glass."

She reacted immediately to that name. She just couldn't help herself. She sat up straight behind her desk, forgetting the paper she'd been filling out, and leaned forward suddenly, her eyes glowing with pure unadulterated greed.

"Details, please."

"Trust me," I said, "you don't want to know exactly how I got it. Look . . . it was a mistake, all right? I didn't realise what I was getting myself into, or that I'd end up with the whole damned Drood family chasing after me! I've already tried going to ground in a dozen different places, that I would have sworn were perfectly safe and secure. . . . But I've been chased or scared out of all of them. These people are inhuman! They know everything! They really are taking this far too personally . . . They want the Merlin Glass back, and they want my head. Not necessarily in that order. I'd give them the bloody Glass back, if I thought they'd just take it and let bygones be bygones. But they do seem to be very angry indeed. Look . . . I am prepared to give you people the Merlin Glass in return for one of your guaranteed one-way tickets to someplace where the Droods can't find me!"

"I'm not sure where to recommend," Ms Smith said slowly. "Is there such a place?"

"I have heard of one," I said. "The Shifting Lands."

Ms Smith looked at me sharply, and then sat back in her chair and regarded me thoughtfully with her cold grey eyes.

"It is supposed to be one of the few places outside of Drood jurisdiction," I said after a while. "You do know about this place?"

She shook her head suddenly. "Sorry, Mister Bond, I think I'm going to have to pass this one further up the chain of command. So stay put. Don't move from your chair and don't touch anything while I'm gone. You are being watched."

She all but ran out of the office, she was so keen to pass this hot potato on to someone else. She didn't want to be the one who lost out on the Merlin Glass, but on the other hand, she really didn't want to be the one who got the Droods mad at the Travel Bureau. I looked around the room for hidden surveillance cameras. There were only a couple, blindingly obvious to anyone with a torc. Hardly state-of-the-art equipment. I reached out to them through my armour and over-wrote their signal so anyone watching would only see Shaman Bond sitting quietly in his chair. Standard operating procedure for any Drood in the field. How else do you suppose we stay hidden in this age of electronic surveillance? Just let everyone see what they expect to see, and they're perfectly happy.

I got up out of my chair, and wandered around Ms Smith's desk to take a look at her laptop. It was all very basic. I armoured up one hand, and sent golden filaments of strange matter burrowing into the computer. I soon had it purring like a contented tabby cat as I bypassed all its security protocols and had a good rummage through its files.

I knew I should have been patient, and taken no unnecessary risks. Just play the game and not risk the deal . . . but I couldn't. Not while Molly was still missing. I had to believe Jack was right; that whoever it was and wherever they had taken her, Molly Metcalf was still perfectly capable of taking care of herself. But . . . I couldn't help but remember the vicious beating Molly had taken at the hands of Crow Lee's soldiers after she and I underestimated them. It doesn't matter how good you are; there's always going to be someone tougher, and nastier. Not knowing what was happening with Molly was driving me insane. I couldn't just sit and do nothing while there was something I could be doing to hurry things along.

My armour opened up the laptop easily enough, but it had only limited access to company business. I was still surprised to discover just how many people had made use of the Departure Lounge in recent years. The Travel Bureau had done a lot of business, with hundreds of names, many of which I recognised. Nobody particularly big or important, but all of them known faces on the scene. Where I had occasionally wondered *Whatever happened to . . . ?*

I heard someone coming. I whipped the golden filaments out of the computer, armoured down, and settled myself comfortably in the visitor's chair again. Looking innocent. Or at least as innocent as Shaman Bond could be expected to look.

A smooth salesman type came in, a cheerful young fellow, already prematurely balding, wearing a smart blue blazer over white slacks. With an Old School Tie from a very minor public school. Of course, that didn't mean as much as it used to, not when you can find anything on eBay these days. The new arrival seemed very businesslike, all tanned and plausible, and he went out of his way to give me his most polished professional smile. I stood up just long enough to have my hand gripped in a brief professional handshake (quick and hearty and utterly uninvolved), and then we both sat down on either side of the desk, facing each other.

"Hello, Shaman!" he said cheerfully. "I am David Perrin, at your service. So pleased to meet you at last. I know your reputation, of course, but I never thought we'd ever actually meet in person. We do move in such different circles, after all!" He smiled again, to show that this was a joke, but he couldn't quite keep the superiority out of his tone. I just stared back at him, and he moved quickly on. "Your reputation does rather precede you, Shaman, so I trust you'll understand when I say I need to see the Merlin Glass for myself. Right here and now, in person. In the flesh, so to speak. Before we can go any further."

I just nodded, reached into my coat pocket, and took out the Glass. I'd known they would insist on seeing it for themselves at some point, so before I even approached the Travel Bureau I removed the Merlin Glass from my pocket dimension. It wouldn't do for anyone here to discover that Shaman Bond owned something like a pocket dimension. Questions would be asked . . . So I carefully wrapped the Glass in the cloth Jack had provided. (I'd hung on to the cloth, on the grounds that the old Armourer wouldn't have chosen just any old cloth to wrap the Merlin Glass in. That it would be bound to have some useful properties . . .) And then I slipped the Glass into my coat pocket, and just hoped the Travel Bureau's protections wouldn't go ape-shit if they detected it.

David Perrin watched my every movement with hot and eager eyes, until I finally placed the silver-backed hand mirror on the desk between us. I was careful to handle the Merlin Glass as though I was very respectful, and not a little scared, of the thing. As Shaman Bond would be. (Hoping all the while that the bloody Glass wouldn't play up again.) Perrin was actually breathing hard by the time I'd finished, his fingers twitching visibly. But he still had enough self-control, and enough self-preservation instincts left, not to touch the Glass himself. He just sat there and stared at it for a long moment; and then an old-fashioned eyepiece, like a jeweller's loupe, suddenly appeared in his hand from out of nowhere. It jumped up into the air and screwed itself firmly into Perrin's left eye socket, where it glowed a whole series of unnatural colours as he studied the Merlin Glass through the lens. Perrin leaned forward over the table, positioning his face right over the Glass until his nose was almost touching it. He examined the hand mirror from end to end, still careful to keep his hands well away; and even more careful not to look at his own face in the mirror's reflection. Eventually, the eyepiece stopped glowing. Perrin slowly straightened up again, his back creaking loudly as he sat back in his chair. The loupe dropped out of his eye socket, fell down, and disappeared in mid-air. Neither of us mentioned it; we were, after all, professionals. There was a faint sheen of sweat on Perrin's face. He looked . . . concerned, but determined.

"It is the real thing," he said, his voice just a little strained. "And we do very definitely want it. How the hell did you get hold of a really powerful piece like this, Shaman?"

"It was an accident!" I said loudly. "I just happened to be somewhere, and helped myself to a certain sealed container that had been left just lying around, almost entirely unprotected. When I finally got the box open, I nearly had a heart attack! I wasn't expecting the bloody Merlin Glass. I don't want the damned thing . . . Or the whole Drood family coming after me! Look, you want it, it's yours. If you can get me to somewhere safe. You can get me to safety, can't you?"

"Easy, Shaman, easy," murmured Perrin. "You have nothing to worry about here. We have the best protections in the business. And yes, we can send you somewhere safe."

"It has to be now!" I said. "I'm pretty sure I shook the Droods off my trail, but you know as well as I do that they could turn up here any time. You know what they're like. You don't want them here, do you?"

"No," said Perrin. "We very definitely don't." He looked thoughtfully at the Merlin Glass, and then at me. "Ms Smith said you wish to be sent to . . . the Shifting Lands. That's . . . not somewhere most people have heard of. I have to ask, Shaman, how did you come to learn about the Shifting Lands?"

"I was at the Wulfshead Club," I said. Which was safe enough. Everyone knows Shaman Bond drinks there regularly. "Janissary Jane was holding forth about this place so out on the edge that even the Droods can't get there. She'd had a few, but . . . Look, if I haven't even heard about this place, it must be well off the beaten track!"

Perrin nodded slowly. "That sounds . . . plausible. You've always known all the right, or more properly, wrong people. Very well, then, Shaman; I think we can accommodate you. A trip to the Shifting Lands, in return for the Merlin Glass."

I snatched the Glass up off the desk even as Perrin reached for it. I sneered at him openly as I quickly wrapped the hand mirror in the cloth.

"You don't even get to see this again, until right before I'm ready to leave. I'll only hand the Glass over at the last possible moment. Nothing personal, you understand, but this is my only bargaining chip. And don't think you or any of your people could just take it from me. The Merlin Glass has its own built-in protection and defences."

"Of course it has," said Perrin. "We expected this . . . behaviour. You are Shaman Bond, after all. Very well; come with me. And be prepared for the trip of a lifetime."

He took me straight to the Departure Lounge, through a door at the back of the office, which I would have sworn wasn't there before he indicated it. I was getting just a bit annoyed about that happening. I used to be able to spot hidden entrances and exits as a matter of course. But I kept my face carefully calm and neutral, and followed Perrin through into the Departure Lounge.

At first glance it was just another room, containing nothing but a single bog standard dimensional Door, standing alone and upright and entirely unsupported in the middle of the empty room. I've seen a lot of dimensional Doors in my time. But there was something very . . . wrong, about the room. I didn't like the way it looked, or the way it looked back at me. The walls seemed to recede whenever I looked at them directly. Only to sweep back in again to a more respectable distance, when I looked away. The room seemed to grow and shrink in sudden spurts, as though its size and volume were just a matter of choice. I shook my head, and swallowed hard. Perrin nodded understandingly.

"Take a moment, Shaman. Get used to our Departure Lounge. We're really very proud of it. You and I are actually standing inside a pocket dimension, created and maintained by the presence of this really quite remarkable Door. The room contains an awful lot of space, so you might say its physical dimensions have become somewhat . . . stretched, to contain it all. Concentrate on the Door, Shaman. That is what we're here for."

I nodded silently, and slowly approached the Door. A great slab of polished and veneered dark wood, with no hinges, no handle, and no knocker; just a combination dial set into the wood. After you turned the dial to choose the correct Space/Time coordinates, the Door would open onto whatever destination you'd selected. And yet this Door didn't feel powerful enough to be able to do all the things Perrin claimed for it.

"We can deliver you anywhere," said Perrin. "Strictly one-way, of course. That's the point, so no one can track you, or follow you. And you can't return, because the Door only exists from our side. We've sent all sorts of people to all sorts of places, and they must be happy there, because no one ever comes back to complain!"

He laughed easily, at the familiar company joke. And while he was busy doing that, I leaned in for a really close look at the Door, and its combination dial. With my back to Perrin, I was able to send a trickle of golden strange matter up to my face from my torc, to form a pair of golden sunglasses over my eyes. And then, I was able to study the Door's true nature. It took me only a moment to determine that the Door was quite genuine, but the combination dial was a fake. It was jammed on one setting, one location. No one had moved it in ages. Which suggested . . . that the Travel Bureau people had been taking their clients' money, opening the Door to the only place it could go, and then . . . pushing them through if need be and slamming the Door shut again after them.

It was a con job. Of course it was a con. First rule of the confidence trick: if it seems to be too good to be true, it is too good to be true.

I subvocalised my activating Words, and my armour leapt out of my torc and surrounded me in a moment. I spun round to face Perrin, and he cried out in shock to see a Drood in his armour suddenly appear before him. I moved steadily forward, and Perrin screamed like a little girl. He turned to run for the exit door. I grabbed him by one shoulder, my golden fingers sinking deep into his flesh, and he cried out again. He fought me like a cornered rat, shouting and crying and striking at my armour with his bare hands. Hurt him far more than it hurt me. I let him get it out of his system, and then shook him hard, once. He stopped fighting, sniffed back tears, and called me a bastard. I dragged him over to the dimensional Door. When he saw where I was taking him, he started crying again, and kicked and struggled all the way.

I slammed him up against the closed Door, with enough force to shut him up. The Door didn't react at all. I thrust my blank golden face into Perrin's, and when he saw his own terrified face in the reflection, he almost passed out. Anyone else, and I might have felt a little ashamed of myself. But if what I suspected had happened here was right, he deserved far worse.

"What did you do?" I said, not even trying to hide the anger in my voice. "What did you do with all the people who trusted you? That Door only goes to one place, so none of them ended up where they thought they were going. Where did you send them really?"

Perrin swallowed hard. "I don't know! No one here knows. We acquired the Door at an auction. Blind bid; no details, no history. That's why we were able to afford it. But it works! We send people through and we never hear from them again. We've been sending people through the Door for years. Can't be that bad a place; no one ever comes back to complain . . . And none of them are the sort of people who'll be missed, so . . ."

"You have no idea at all where they've gone?" I said. "Or what might have happened to them? You took everything they had, took advantage of them when they were at their most vulnerable, and then just . . . threw them away! Justify yourself!"

"Justify myself?" said Perrin. "To Shaman Bond?"

"I'm Eddie Drood," I said. "I just borrowed Shaman's identity to get in here. You didn't really think the Droods would leave a valuable item like the Merlin Glass just hanging around, did you? Now talk to me! Justify what you've done here!"

"I'm a businessman!" Perrin said loudly. "Providing a service! They all wanted to get away, and never be seen or found again, and we made that possible!"

"Except you didn't," I said. "You sent them to their deaths—and perhaps worse than that."

"You don't know that!"

"You don't know that."

Perrin gave me his best pathetic look. "Are you going to kill me?"

"No," I said. "I don't do that any more. I'm an agent, not an assassin."

"Oh good," said Perrin.

And he twisted suddenly, breaking free of my grasp with an effort. He ran for the exit door, screaming at the top of his voice for help and reinforcements. The door burst open just as he reached it, and a whole bunch of people came running in, armed with a whole assortment of weapons. I recognised Ms Smith and Mister Genuine Muscle among the many angry faces. Perrin fought his way to the back of the crowd and hid behind them, trying to explain to everyone what had happened, but it was obvious they already knew. I should have looked for more surveillance cameras. The crowd fanned out, to better cover me with their various weapons, but I wasn't worried. All they had were guns. Perrin yelled for the others to kill me, to shut me up, to stop me from telling the world what they'd been doing here in the Departure Lounge. Most of the crowd took one look at my Drood armour and looked for someone else to tell them what to do. Some tried to hide behind others. Ms Smith stepped forward.

"Can we make a deal?"

"No," I said. "I don't think so."

"Most of us just work here!"

"You knew what was going on. You all profited from the lie. From all the people missing, presumed dead. You're all guilty."

"Get him!" Perrin shouted urgently from the back. "Kill him! He knows everything; he'll tell! For God's sake, somebody get him!"

But nobody moved.

I grabbed hold of one side of the Door with both my golden hands and pulled hard. The Door made loud creaking sounds of pain and distress, almost like a living thing, and then it swung slowly open, unable to resist the sheer power of my armour. I stepped back, pulling the Door all the way open, and looked inside. There was nothing there. Just a blank blur that hurt the eyes to look at it. No sound came from behind the Door, not even a breath of moving air. There was nothing at all on the other side of the Door except a horribly empty gap.

I looked back at the people watching me from the other side of the room. Most of them were staring, fascinated, as though they'd never seen the Door open before. And most of them probably hadn't. But that hadn't stopped them from using it to profit from the fear of desperate people. The only one not looking at the open Door was Perrin. He'd eased his way back through the crowd, to face me again. He had a formidable-looking futuristic gun in his hand, pointed right at me. An energy weapon; alien tech, or at the very least, alien-derived. The odd metal thing glowed and shimmered and twisted in his hand, as though it couldn't quite decide what it was supposed to be. I turned to face Perrin, and he fired the gun at me.

Howling coruscating energies flared up all around my armour, blasting the floor at my feet and scorching the ceiling above me. Harsh energies crawled all over me, spitting and sparking as they tried to force their way in. I stood my ground, trusting my armour, and soon enough the energies fell away, defeated. And then I advanced steadily on Perrin. Everyone else fell quickly back, out of my way, scattering across the room. Perrin swore savagely at his fellow businesspeople as they abandoned him to me. He kept firing his gun, but the energies had less and less effect. When I was finally close enough, I snatched the gun out of his hand, grabbed him by the shoulder again, and dragged him back to the Door. I think he guessed what I meant to do, because he kicked and fought every inch of the way, screaming shrilly to the others for help that never came.

"Did your clients call for help?" I said. "Did you listen?"

I turned Perrin round to face the awful emptiness inside the open Door. He didn't want to look at it, but I made him.

"This is the last thing a lot of people saw in this world. Before you took everything they had and forced them through," I said. "Did you force them? You must have; I can't think anyone would walk willingly into . . . that. Even I can't tell what lies on the other side of this Door. You took everything they had and gave them nothing. So I think it's time for some old-fashioned justice."

I threw him through the open Door. He disappeared into the blur, his last horrified scream cut suddenly short. I waited, but that was it. I turned back to the others.

"Is that what usually happens?" I said. "Give or take the scream?"

A few heads nodded, here and there.

"All right," I said. "Time for some more justice."

"I thought you said you didn't kill!" said Ms Smith.

"I'm giving you a chance," I said. "The same chance you gave your victims."

I held up one hand, to show off the energy weapon I'd taken from Perrin. I aimed it at them, and they scattered. I blasted the exit door with the gun, and the raging energies sealed it shut. I crushed the gun in my golden hand and let the pieces fall to the floor. There was a loud babble of voices, as the Travel Bureau people realised they were trapped in the Departure Lounge with me. And the open Door. Some of them beat on the exit door with their bare hands, but they couldn't budge it. Some yelled at me, saying it was all nothing to do with them, that they just worked here.

"You all knew," I said. "You all profited. You're all guilty."

And I grabbed them one by one and threw them through the open Door. Some of them fought me, and some of them tried to run, and some of them just cried miserably. It didn't make any difference. There was no room left in me for mercy. Some of them fired their guns at me, and some thrust other people forward in their place, shouting *Take her instead of me!* Some offered me money, or information, or threats—anything they thought I might want or fear. I just kept grabbing them and throwing them in.

Mister Genuine Muscle walked through of his own accord rather than fight a Drood. He had his dignity. The others, mostly, didn't. I had to chase the last few round the Departure Lounge, but there was nowhere for them to go, nowhere for them to hide. The last few sobbed and pleaded, their voices like those of frightened children. But all I could think of were the missing people. Some of whom I'd known, and some of whom I hadn't; but all of them deserved better than this. Until finally, I was the only one left in the Departure Lounge.

I stood looking into the terrible emptiness of the open Door and raised my voice.

"Well?" I said. "Any complaints?"

No one answered me. And the cold rage that filled my heart wouldn't let me feel bad about it.

I considered the open Door thoughtfully. I did wonder . . . whether I might just stick my head through, to see what was on the other side. Trusting to my armour to protect me. It might not be that bad . . . and it would only take a moment. I could place both hands on either side of the door frame to brace me, and keep from getting sucked in. Just one quick look, so I could know for sure . . . where I had sent so many people. But in the end I decided not to. There was something about the Door. It felt surprisingly inviting, like a trap. Or perhaps, a trapdoor spider. So I took a firm hold on the Door and forced it shut again.

Justice, of a sort, had been done. Now that my anger was starting to fade away, I wasn't so sure about what I'd done. But I had saved other people from being taken advantage of by the Travel Bureau, and I decided I'd settle for that. What mattered . . . was that I was no nearer getting to Molly. I'd just lost my only lead. How was I going to get to the Shifting Lands now? And then I stopped, as I remembered how easily my armour had hacked Ms Smith's computer. I looked thoughtfully at the coordinates dial on the Door. It might be stuck on one setting; but I'd back my armour against a Door any day.

A dimensional Door creates a momentary break in Space and Time, connecting two places and slamming them together just long enough for someone to pass through from one location to another. The coordinates decided what place the Door opened onto. So I set my armoured hand on the dial and let golden filaments burrow deep into the mechanism. The dial fought me, but it was no match for Ethel's marvellous strange matter. There was a sudden sense of the Door throwing up its hands and going *Oh hell, have it your own way*, and the dial spun madly round and round under my hand before settling on the destination I wanted. The Shifting Lands. The Door started to swing open, and I stepped back.

The terrible emptiness was gone, replaced by brightly shining mists that curled and twisted before me. I called out to Kate through my torc, and she answered immediately. I brought her up to date on what had just happened and what I intended to do next.

"No, Eddie!" she said. "You can't just dive straight in! Don't trust the Door! Let me send some engineers in to inspect it first."

"I have to do this," I said. "It's the only way to Molly."

"At least wait for backup! You don't have to do this on your own, Eddie!"

"Yes, I do," I said. "Molly's expecting me."

And I strode forward, through the Door and into the Shifting Lands.

# CHAPTER TEN

# The Rules Are What We Say They Are

When I think of all the Doors I've walked through, often with only a suspicion of what might be on the other side, or where I might end up, it frankly astonishes me that I'm still around. It's like rolling the dice while wearing boxing gloves, knowing they're fixed but hoping whoever did it owes you a favour.

The moment I passed through the Travel Bureau's Door, the swirling mists glowed a dozen different colours, and then just disappeared, like curtains drawing back so the play can begin. I stood braced in my armour; ready for action, ready for anything. Except. . . . the scene before me.

I was back on the grounds of Drood Hall. The familiar grassy lawns stretched away into the distance under a bright Summer sun. It was all very calm, very peaceful. I felt a bit of an idiot, standing there in full armour with absolutely nothing threatening in view, so I relaxed just a little and armoured down. My first thought was to wonder whether my family might have interrupted my journey and brought me home by force. They'd done it before, when they disapproved of something I intended to do. I smiled, and just knew it wasn't a pleasant smile. I was going to find and save my Molly and no one was going to stop me, not even my family. Perhaps especially not my family.

I looked around for someone to yell at and discovered that the Door had disappeared from behind me. The Travel Bureau people had been right; the Door existed only from the other side. And the next thing I noticed . . . was that while everything in the grounds looked exactly as it should, there was still something wrong, something . . . off, about my surroundings. I looked around me slowly, frowning. The grounds were deserted. Where was everybody? It all seemed unnaturally quiet and still. At this time of day there should have been any number of people out and about, but there were no security patrols, no gardeners, no happy young things taking a break just to enjoy the Summer day . . . No autogyros or flying saucers or winged unicorns sweeping by overhead. None of the familiar sights of home. I couldn't even hear the usual harsh cries of peacocks and gryphons. There wasn't a breath of moving air, and no scent of freshly cut grass. And when I finally looked up, into the bright blue sky, I realised none of the clouds were moving.

It was like standing in a photograph. Or perhaps a moment clipped out of Time and preserved.

Drood Hall was gone. My heart lurched sickly as I realised that while I was looking straight at where the Hall should have been nothing but empty open space was there, just wide, grassy lawns sweeping away forever. I looked frantically around me, but there was no sign of the Hall anywhere. The grand old manor house that had stood for centuries, protecting the family within as they protected the world . . . had been wiped out of existence.

I remembered coming home once before to find Drood Hall completely destroyed. A burned-out ruin, full of dead bodies. Of course, that turned out to be some other-dimensional Drood Hall, from some other reality, but still, that had been bad. This was worse. I wondered . . . whether someone might have activated the old dimension-travelling apparatus deep underneath Drood Hall, the enigmatic Alpha Red Alpha mechanism. Could the new Armourers, Maxwell and Victoria, have meddled with something they only thought they understood, and rotated the Hall out of this reality? No. That wasn't it. There were too many things wrong with this picture. It wasn't just the Hall that was missing; there were no trees, no ornamental lake, no hedge maze . . .

I wasn't where I thought I was.

These weren't the real Drood grounds, just some place that looked like them. Good enough to fool me, but only for a moment. No wonder there was no Hall, no people. Far too difficult to counterfeit convincingly. This was just a familiar-looking trap. And with the Travel Bureau's Door gone, I had no way of leaving.

I looked down at my feet. Something else was bothering me. The grass looked real, and the ground felt solid enough under my feet, but something was missing. It took me a moment to realise that although the sun was shining brightly overhead, I wasn't casting a shadow. I looked quickly around me, and even lifted each of my feet in turn, as though my shadow might be trying to hide from me, but there was nothing. No trace of a shadow anywhere. Which was . . . disturbing. I could feel all the hairs standing up on the back of my neck.

What kind of a place had I come to?

I was sure my armour had fed the correct Space/Time coordinates into the Door. It should have delivered me straight to the Shifting Lands. So where was I? And why did I keep trusting Doors, anyway? And then I jumped, just a little, as I suddenly discovered I did have a shadow. A perfectly ordinary respectable shadow, that moved when I did. As though someone had realised I'd spotted a mistake in the design of this new reality, and had moved quickly to correct it. Which implied that someone was watching me . . .

I called out to Kate, through my torc. There was no response. I wasn't surprised. The Shifting Lands were supposed to be beyond the reach of the Droods. That was the whole point. I was cut off from my family, and completely on my own. I couldn't help but grin. If that was supposed to shake me, or undermine my confidence, whoever was watching didn't know me at all. I've always done my best work on my own, without my family butting in to stop me from doing things they disapproved of. I bounced up and down on my feet and looked speculatively about me. Whoever thought they could trap me here was in for a really nasty surprise when they found they had an angry Drood by the tail.

And then someone close at hand cleared his throat, quite politely, and I looked round sharply.

Standing calmly before me was a familiar figure, with a face I knew only too well. Walker. He looked to be in really good condition, for a man who died years ago. Or at least, was supposed to have died. This was Walker, after all. As always, he looked very smart, like someone big in the City, in an expertly tailored three-piece suit. Right down to the gold pocket-watch chain stretched across his patterned waistcoat, the rolled umbrella, and the bowler hat. Not a young man, Walker, not for some time—though clearly full of energy and purpose. A man past his best days, perhaps, but still a man to be reckoned with.

Walker was the ultimate authority figure: straight back, patient stance, and cold, cold eyes. He used to run the Nightside, that dark and dangerous place, inasmuch as anyone could. And did it with a ruthless efficiency that inspired respect in gods and monsters. He was much admired, even more feared, and liked by . . . remarkably few people. Not that he ever gave a damn about that, of course. He leaned nonchalantly on his rolled umbrella now, bestowing on me his most enigmatic smile. As though he knew far more than I did. More than anyone did.

Daring me to try something.

I have to say, I felt a little shocked to see Walker standing so easily and so freely on Drood family grounds. Even if this wasn't the real Drood grounds. Walker and I might have been allies on occasion, and even worked together once, to bring down the Independent Agent, but even so, he had no right to be here. Walker was far too dangerous a man to ever be allowed in Drood territory. And besides, if my family were banned from the Nightside by long-established Pacts and Agreements, it seemed only right and proper that all the creatures of the Nightside should be banned from setting foot in Drood territory.

"Hello, Eddie," Walker said easily. "Welcome to the Shifting Lands. So good of you to join us."

I glared at him. "Doesn't anyone stay dead any more? This seems to be my day for being bothered by ghosts with familiar faces. Memories from my past. Am I supposed to be glad to see you? It's been a long time since you and I were on the same side . . ." And then I broke off as a sudden insight struck me. I stabbed an accusing finger at him. "Except, you're not really him, are you? You're not Walker! You're whoever or whatever pretended to be Walker, back when I was caught hovering between Life and Death, trapped in the Winter Hall, in Limbo's waiting room. You tried to pressure me into giving up important information, personal and family secrets . . ."

"Perhaps," said Walker, entirely unmoved by my accusations or my anger. "But I feel I should warn you, Eddie; you don't come to the Shifting Lands for certainties. This face will do as well as any other."

"All right," I said. "What are you doing here, Walker? I don't have time for games. I have business of my own to be about."

"I am here because the Powers That Be require me to be here," said Walker. "And now they want you."

"Where's Molly?" I said.

"Oh, she's around, somewhere," said Walker.

"Where?"

"Around," said Walker. "Somewhere. Don't get testy with me, Eddie. You're in no position to make demands; not here. You're on the same footing as everyone else in this place. Molly is . . . waiting, preparing to take her place in the Big Game."

"Molly was kidnapped!" I said, and the cold anger in my voice would have been enough to warn off anyone else. "Taken from the Wulfshead and brought here against her will." I gave Walker my best slow, threatening smile. "What makes you think you can hold Molly Metcalf? Especially now I'm here."

Walker sighed, as though faced with a particularly difficult, and not very bright, small child. "It doesn't matter how anyone gets here, Eddie; they all stay of their own free will. Ready, and indeed eager, to participate in the Big Game in the hope of winning a way out of the terrible and awful obligations they agreed to when they first made Pacts and Agreements at the beginning of their career. Obligations that are now coming due; promises made that must be paid. And your Molly did agree to so many things, to acquire the power she needed to take on your family. She wanted, needed, revenge for the Droods' murder of her parents. And she didn't care what she had to do, or agree to, as long as it would get her the power she needed.

"And then . . . she fell in love with you. A Drood. Funny how things work out, isn't it? Of course she must have known, even if she never discussed it with you, that she could never hope to pay off everything she owed in one lifetime. So what do you think will happen to her after she dies? And all those debts come due? I really don't like to think about it. She made promises to Heaven and to Hell, to so many Powers and Dominations. They'll tear her soul apart, arguing over who has the best right to it."

He stopped as he saw the look on my face. "Of course, if you were to support her, she would stand a much better chance in the Big Game."

I took a step towards Walker, my hands clenched into fists, and then stopped myself. This was what Walker wanted, what he did; he got people angry, and off balance, so they'd be that much easier to out-think and manipulate. For his own ends. So I stood my ground and stared coldly at him.

"You always did have a taste for blackmail, Walker."

He shrugged easily, unmoved. "Stick with what works, that's what I always say."

"I have been told," I said carefully, "that Molly was taken by the Powers That Be. And that if they'd wanted me, they could have just as easily taken me at the same time. So if they didn't want me then, why are they so keen I should take part in their Big Game now?"

"Because you're the first one to break in," said Walker. "The Powers That Be admire that. They're impressed, and that really doesn't happen very often. Trust me . . . They're fascinated to see what you might do next."

"What if I decide I don't want to take part in their damned Game?" I said. "What if I'm just here to break Molly out?"

"You can't," said Walker. "With or without your family, or your quite remarkable armour, you're no match for the Powers That Be. This . . . is their world. They made it. Everything here answers to them. The very rules of reality in this place change from moment to moment, according to what the Powers That Be want them to be. And I have to tell you, Eddie, Molly doesn't want to leave. She wants the way out that winning the Game offers her. She knows what's waiting for her, at the end, all the awful things in store for her . . . and even the infamous wild witch is sensible enough to be scared of that. It's one thing to take on such an appalling burden when you're young, and driven by rage and revenge. It's quite another to see the awful things you've condemned yourself to drawing nearer day by day, and to know there's no way out."

"My family have entered into a great many Pacts and Agreements of their own," I said. "They have power to call on that could be used for the cancelling of debts . . ."

"Not here," said Walker. "We're a long way from anywhere your family has influence or power. You're all Molly's got, Eddie."

"Always," I said.

I took another step forward, until Walker and I were practically face-to-face. He didn't flinch, didn't fall back.

"Where's Molly?" I said. "I could make you tell me . . ."

"No, you couldn't," said Walker.

I started to reach for the Colt Repeater at my hip, in its hidden pocket dimension, and then I hesitated, and stopped myself. The real Walker had a Voice that could not be resisted or denied. That could make you do anything, anything at all. There are those who say he once made a corpse sit up on its slab in the mortuary to answer his questions. And there was always the chance . . . that this was the real Walker. People in the Nightside don't follow the usual rules about anything, including Life and Death. Walker could have faked his own death, for reasons of his own. He'd done stranger and sneakier things, in his time. If my uncle Jack could come back . . . If he had come back . . . I took my hand away from my side, away from my stash of hidden weapons and dirty tricks. I didn't want to reveal all my cards, all my nasty little secrets, just yet. Not until I had a better understanding of the lay of the land, and the rules of the Big Game.

I looked at Walker, and he looked calmly back at me. As though he knew everything I'd just been thinking. Which was very Walker . . .

"So," I said, "is it just you, or have you brought a few friends and colleagues with you? Like John Taylor, or Shotgun Suzie?"

"Perish the thought," said Walker. "They're far too busy running the Nightside in my absence. And the Powers That Be are very careful about who they let into this world. Those two would wreck the place."

"What gives these Powers authority over you?" I said. "I didn't think anyone could order you around. You've faced down gods and devils in the Nightside, in your time."

"Oh, I have," said Walker. "Really. You have no idea. But this . . . is different."

I waited, but that was all he had to say on the matter.

"The real Walker would never put up with that," I said.

"You're right," said Walker. "He wouldn't. Unless, of course, it served some hidden purpose of his own."

"Okay, you're making my head hurt now," I said. "Which is the best argument yet that you are the real deal."

I looked around me, at the green grass and the blue sky, the bright Summer sun and the unmoving clouds. The empty grounds, and the utter silence surrounding us. More than ever it all looked like a stage set. A simple background for the play to come. I thought about the sheer power it would take to make a world like this. To create a whole separate reality, just to have somewhere suitable to play your Game. Unless . . . Walker wasn't telling me the truth. Or all of the truth.

"Where are we, really?" I said. "These aren't the actual Drood grounds."

"Of course not," said Walker. "They're just here to help you feel at home. To put you at your ease."

"Definitely not working," I said.

"We're in a private pocket dimension," said Walker. "A world created specifically to hold the Big Game. The Shifting Lands, far from everywhere and of their own unique nature. Because nothing less would do."

I took that with a pinch of salt. There was always the chance the Powers That Be had simply discovered the Shifting Lands and taken them over for their own use. I didn't trust anything about this deceitful world that had lied to me from the moment I arrived. And I definitely didn't trust Walker. Of course, he knew that when he started telling me things . . .

"So," I said, "what does this place really look like, when it isn't pretending to be Drood grounds?"

"Don't ask me," said Walker. "I'm just a visitor, like yourself. Only with rather more privileges. Think of me as the umpire. Feel free to come to me with all your little problems."

"You really are pushing it now," I said.

"I am, aren't I?"

I thought for a moment of the subtle realms, of the soft world where I met Melanie Blaze. That had been a private pocket dimension too, where the world changed according to the wishes of those who lived there. Could I be back there and not know it? It seemed to me that ever since I'd walked through that damned Travel Bureau Door, I hadn't been able to trust anything.

"Who are the Powers That Be?" I said.

"Ah," said Walker, "that would be telling."

"Do you know?"

"Of course I know. But you don't . . . How unusual. I thought Droods knew everything. No doubt the Powers That Be will tell you when they want you to know."

I decided I'd had enough, and so I armoured up. Golden strange matter flowed out of my torc and covered me in a moment, and just like that I felt stronger and faster, more awake and more certain. Walker fell back a step in spite of himself. Not surprising, really. The last thing a lot of people ever saw in their life was an angry Drood in his armour, advancing on them. Coming for them. I lifted one golden fist and let Walker see the heavy spikes rising up from the knuckles. And then, quite suddenly, someone else appeared, to stand between Walker and me. The sheer impact of her presence stopped me in my tracks—and there aren't many who can do that. Walker peered out from behind her, and smiled easily.

"This is my protector. The Somnambulist. Isn't she splendid?"

I looked her over carefully. I could sense the power burning in her, the dangerous strength and speed, even though she was quite clearly fast asleep. Her eyes were tightly closed, but the eyeballs still moved. Rapid Eye Movements. The Somnambulist was dreaming.

She had a sharp chin and prominent cheekbones, a formidably pretty face, packed full of character, and more than a hint of ethnic Gypsy about her. She could have been anything from her twenties to her forties. Dark russet hair fell in thick ringlets to her shoulders and beyond. Her arms lay limp and unmoving at her sides, but still managed to suggest they were ready for action at a moment's notice. She had large, bony hands, with heavy knuckles, weighed down by a great many gold and silver rings, set with strange and unfamiliar gems. She wore traditional Romany clothes, Gypsy chic, complete with a hell of a lot of necklaces, bangles, and bracelets. She stood almost unnaturally still, between me and Walker, blocking the way. Walker smiled easily at me over her shoulder.

"This is my personal assistant," he said.

"You mean bodyguard," I said.

"That too!"

"Why would Walker need a bodyguard?" I said. "When he never needed one in the Nightside, possibly the most dangerous place there is? After all, with or without his Voice, Walker was always an extraordinarily dangerous person in his own right. So I have to ask, who or what do you need protecting from in the Shifting Lands?"

"They do things differently here," said Walker. "Not all the dangers in this setting are immediately obvious. The Somnambulist . . . is quite extraordinarily powerful. For as long as she sleeps, she has the strength of dreams. She was once Carrys Galloway, the legendary Waking Beauty of that small but significant country town, Bradford-on-Avon."

I nodded, remembering the story Molly had told me of her visit there, and her encounter with Carrys. The woman who never slept. Had never slept, for centuries upon centuries. Molly and her sister Isabella helped Carrys break her long-standing pact with the elven Queen Mab so she could finally sleep again.

"And now she's sleeping hard, making up for lost time," said Walker. As though he'd been listening in on my thoughts. "But she still has to pay off her debts to the Powers That Be for brokering the original deal those many years ago. Now she protects me from all threats. Until she wakes up."

"Why?" I said. "Why do you need her?"

"The Game has been known to get a bit boisterous sometimes," said Walker. "The players aren't always willing to accept a decision that goes against them. Not when there's so much riding on it."

"Since when does the mighty Walker need an enforcer?"

"It is the nature of the Shifting Lands that they are constantly changing," said Walker. "Particularly during the Game. I can't be everywhere at once. But she can. Because she's dreaming and therefore not bound by the limitations of the waking world."

I nodded slowly. That sounded almost reasonable. So why didn't I believe it? I looked at the Somnambulist, and then back at Walker, still standing carefully behind her.

"I want answers," I said. "And I want Molly. And I'm going to get them, one way or another."

"Typical Drood," said Walker. "Subtle as a sledgehammer."

"Stick with what works," I said. "That's what I always say . . ."

I advanced on Walker, but the Somnambulist didn't move. Just stood there, quietly blocking the way, eyes shut. Her face was a complete blank, as though she was thinking about something else. Or perhaps more properly, dreaming about something else. I put one hand on her shoulder, gripping firmly, to steer her out of the way, but she didn't move. I pushed again, harder, and I still couldn't move her. It was like trying to shift a brick wall. I put both my hands on her bony shoulders, and set all my armoured strength against her; she didn't even notice. Which was unheard of. A Drood in his armour can move a mountain if he puts his mind to it. I clamped down with my golden hands to pick the Somnambulist up bodily, and her hands came flashing up with impossible speed. They grabbed my arms just below the elbows, picked me up, and held me in mid-air, with no effort at all showing in her sleeping face. And then she just threw me away.

I shot through the air, tumbling helplessly end over end, until finally I crashed to earth again, some distance away. I hit hard, digging a deep trench in the grassy lawn, and rolled to a halt. The repeated impacts knocked all the breath out of me, even inside my armour, and for a while I just lay there, gathering my wits. It had been a long time since I'd been humiliated so easily.

Slowly and painfully, I hauled myself out of the deep hole I'd made, and straightened up. I was actually shaken at being dismissed so easily. As though I was nothing. I was also starting to feel seriously angry. Bad enough that Walker stood between me and Molly, but a sleeping woman as well? I felt a very definite need to prove I wasn't going to be pushed around. I strode back across the lawns to face the Somnambulist again. It took me a while. I hadn't realised she'd thrown me so far . . . Walker was still standing behind the quietly waiting Somnambulist. As I closed in on her, he shook his head at me, more in sorrow than in anger.

"You wouldn't hit a woman, would you, Eddie?"

"Hell yes," I said. "I'm a Drood."

I walked right up to the Somnambulist and threw a punch at her head. She slapped the fist aside easily, even though she couldn't have seen it coming with her eyes closed. I tried again, aiming the punch right between her eyes, with all of my armour's strength behind it. For anyone else, that would have been a killing blow, enough to tear her head right off, but by now I was convinced the Somnambulist wouldn't even notice anything less. This time she stopped my hand in mid-blow, her hand closing hard over mine and bringing it to an abrupt halt. I was almost thrown off balance at having my attack anticipated and stopped so effortlessly. I might even have fallen if her grasp hadn't held me so firmly in place. I tried to pull my hand back, and found I couldn't. Her hand clamped down fiercely on mine, the heavy ringed fingers crushing my armoured hand.

I had to grit my teeth to keep from crying out under my mask. My armoured glove was no protection against her unnatural strength. I could feel the bones of my hand grinding together, and the pain was almost unbelievable. She had to be applying tons of pressure per square inch to reach my hand inside the glove, and that just wasn't possible. I put all my armoured strength into resisting her, fighting to pull my hand free—and couldn't.

"I'd surrender," said Walker, "if I were you. Even the world of the Shifting Lands is no match for the world of dreams."

"What does that even mean?" I said angrily, fighting to keep the pain out of my voice.

Walker shrugged. "It's your hand. You tell me."

"All right!" I said harshly. "I give up! I surrender!"

The Somnambulist let go of my hand. I staggered back a few steps and armoured down, holding my aching hand to my chest. It throbbed painfully, but it didn't feel like anything was broken. The Somnambulist hadn't wanted to injure me, just to teach me a lesson. Except . . . if she was asleep, how could she make decisions like that? I looked past her, at Walker, the legendary puppet master of the Nightside. He patted his sleeping enforcer on the shoulder, but she didn't seem to notice. I flexed my hand, trying to drive out the pain and the weakness.

"Told you," said Walker. "She has the strength of dreams. Which means she can be as strong as she dreams she is."

All right, I thought, When in doubt, when all else fails, cheat. Or engage in lateral thinking, if you like.

I stepped forward, thrust my face right into the Somnambulist's, and shouted *"Wake up!"* as loudly as I could. "Wake up! Bedtime's over! Wakey wakey!"

The force of my breath was enough to disturb her long hair, but her expression didn't change in the least. Even though I was shouting at the top of my voice, screaming right into her face, she didn't react at all. No ordinary sleeper could have stayed asleep, but she did. I stepped back again, shaking my head. Walker grinned at me, as though pleased at my choice of tactics, and sportingly joined in, shouting right into the Somnambulist's ear. Still nothing. Walker shrugged easily.

"She can't hear us," he said. "She's asleep. Far beyond the reach of mortal voices. She only hears what the Powers That Be want her to."

I considered some of the nastier weapons and dirty tricks I still had scattered about my person, that might be of some use against her, or Walker . . . but I couldn't justify using anything like that against Carrys Galloway. She wasn't the villain here; she was just the villain's weapon. And besides, I didn't want to reveal all the aces I had hidden up my golden sleeves, not this early. It was bad enough I'd allowed Walker to provoke me into using my armour against the Somnambulist, and failing. No . . . there were other ways of getting information out of people besides brute force. I looked thoughtfully at Walker.

"She won't always be around to protect you."

"Yes she will," he said calmly. "As long as I have need of her, she'll always be here. That's what she's for. She's paying off her debts, Eddie. I wonder what poor Molly will be made to do to make good on all her promises?"

"Don't go there," I said. "Really. Don't."

And there must have been something in my voice, because he looked at me for a long moment. "What if you could pay off her debts for her? To Heaven, and to Hell? Would you be prepared to do that, Eddie? Suffer her torments and punishments? How much would you be prepared to sacrifice, and how far would you go? For Molly Metcalf?"

"Forever and a day," I said.

I meant it, and I could see he knew I meant it.

"That's my boy!" he said genially.

To my surprise, he seemed genuinely pleased with my response. As though that was the answer he'd been hoping for. He came out from behind the Somnambulist and leaned companionably against her, shoulder to shoulder, as he smiled at me.

"You need to come along with me now," he said. "So you can meet the other players in the current Big Game. Before everything kicks off and it all gets a bit rowdy."

He turned abruptly and walked away, striding out across the open grassy lawns. The Somnambulist turned and followed him, ignoring me. I hesitated, and looked around me. There was nothing to keep me here, and nowhere else for me to go. Nothing else to do. At least Walker seemed to have some idea of what was going on. So I just shrugged, and went after him.

The three of us strode along together, across the Drood grounds that weren't really Drood grounds. The Somnambulist quickly took up a position between Walker and me, keeping us apart even though she was still clearly fast asleep. I wondered how she could see where she was going with her eyes closed. But then, there was a lot about her I didn't understand. So I ignored her, if only because her presence up close was creeping the hell out of me.

"In the Winter Hall," I said finally to Walker, "back when I was floating between Life and Death; that was you, wasn't it? Why did you interrogate me there? Why were you so determined to get answers out of me, to learn my secrets and those of my family? Who sent you there, and who told you to ask those questions?"

"The Powers That Be," said Walker, not looking round.

"Getting really tired of that answer," I said. "Who are they? What are they?"

"I would have thought that much was obvious," said Walker. "Just from the title they've given themselves."

And the really annoying thing was, Walker really did seem to feel

I should be able to guess, from the clues available. I frowned fiercely as we walked along, considering the matter, though Walker seemed quite unconcerned. Was he hinting at something, or trying to distract me, keep me pointed in the wrong direction? I've never been good at puzzles. When you wear a suit of armour that can punch holes through the world, mostly you don't have to be. Other people will normally fall all over themselves to tell you everything you need to know. The Somnambulist started to snore quietly. Walker elbowed her discreetly in the ribs, and she stopped.

The Drood grounds seemed to just go on and on forever, much farther than they ever could have in the real world. Nothing but empty open lawns, stretching away into the distance. No landmarks anywhere; no trees or lakes or flower gardens. Nothing to help me judge distances. Nothing living moved anywhere in the grounds, apart from the three of us. I wondered whether this was a living world, or just an artificial construct. Time didn't seem to change either. When I first arrived here, through the Departure Lounge Door, it had felt like midday, and it still did. Even though we seemed to have been walking for ages. I wanted to ask Walker if he felt the same way, but I knew he'd only say something evasive and deeply irritating, and I was damned if I'd give him the satisfaction.

And then change did set in, quite suddenly, almost as though I'd triggered it by noticing its lack. The green lawns lost all their colour, all their detail, everything just dropping away until the three of us were walking across endless grey dust plains. Still no landmarks, still no sign of where we were, or where we were going. Great plumes of dust rose with every step we took, then fell slowly back to the ground again. Our footsteps made no sound at all, as though we weren't really there. Just ghosts, passing through. It wasn't hot or cold or anything much. I glanced back, and saw that the lawns we'd been walking through had vanished, replaced by endless plains of grey dust that looked like they'd always been there. A world of nothing but dust, because everything else had died long ago. The sky was full of static. And then the world changed again; and again; and again.

Walker took it all in stride, and just kept going. I gaped openly around me, like a tourist. The Somnambulist didn't seem to notice anything.

We were walking through the dark, rain-slick streets of the Nightside. I recognised them immediately, from when I'd visited them before, with Walker. The dark, hidden heart of London, where it's always three o'clock in the morning, always the hour that tries men's souls. With its forever night sky, packed full of unfamiliar stars and a hugely oversized full moon. I didn't like that moon; it looked like it might come crashing down on me at any moment.

Hot neon signs burned fiercely on every side, sweet and gaudy as Hell's candy and twice as tempting. Shop-windows displayed things no one in his right mind should ever want. Barkers outside nightclubs with ever-open doors yelled their price lists for the awful and unnatural practices to be found inside, and there never seemed to be any shortage of punters. Women lounged around on street corners in all their fetish finery, offering love for sale. Love, or something like it. And gods and monsters went walking hand in hand.

I couldn't keep from glaring at the scene around me. I've always hated the Nightside, where morality is relative, and Good and Evil work side by side and seem quite content to do so. I didn't belong here, and not just because I was a Drood, and therefore banned. I've always needed to know where I stand, what matters and what doesn't. The whole dark and sleazy setting set my spiritual teeth on edge.

People hurrying up and down the crowded streets turned their heads to watch the three of us pass by, as though they could tell we didn't belong. The looks they gave us weren't in any way friendly. I was tempted to call on my armour, but I couldn't escape the feeling that was what they wanted. To give them the excuse they needed to fall on me. Like a pack of rabid rats. For daring to disapprove of them. I stared straight ahead, ignoring them all, but after a while even the brightly lit windows in the towering office buildings came to feel like watching eyes. Observing the three of us with bad intent.

Interestingly enough, no one seemed surprised to see Walker. Even though he was supposed to be dead.

Sunlight suddenly blasted in, driving back the endless dark, dazzling me for a moment. I had to raise an arm to shield my eyes. Walker didn't seem at all bothered by the harsh light, and neither did the Somnambulist. Of course, she already had her eyes shut. When I was finally able to see clearly again, the Nightside streets were gone, as though they'd never been there. The three of us were striding down a pleasant country lane. Low dry stone walls slouched on either side of us, pockmarked with age and long exposure to the elements. To my left stood a huge field of gently waving corn, so brightly golden it was almost painful to look at. To my right, a great open field full of grazing cows. And then the hair on the back of my neck stood up, as one by one the cows lifted their heads and turned to look at us. Until all of them were staring right at us, with cold, fixed intent.

The sunlight was bright, even fierce, but I couldn't feel it on my skin. I didn't feel hot, or cold, or anything much. On an impulse I reached out and trailed my fingertips along the nearest dry stone wall. It felt hard and solid, and reassuringly rough to the touch; indisputably real. But I still couldn't hear any footsteps, as the three of us walked along the road. The ground felt hard and solid enough underfoot, but I wasn't sure I trusted it to stay that way. I checked for shadows, but we all had them.

As though my checking was the last straw, the world changed again, and we were walking along the bottom of the ocean. Sand crunched and slid treacherously under my feet but still didn't make a sound. The waters were dark, but I could see our surroundings quite clearly thanks to great shafts of light filtering down from far above. I waved a hand back and forth before me, and slow, fat ripples moved through the water ahead of me, but I couldn't feel any of the expected resistance from the water.

Clouds of clashing technicolor fish swam endlessly around us, sometimes sweeping in for a closer look but never getting close enough to be touched. Their mouths opened and closed in an eerie synchronisation. Some of them glowed in the dark, carrying their own lights within them. Which made me wonder just how deep we were. I was relieved to find I was breathing quite normally, but I didn't feel any of the expected deep cold or pressure. Massive dark shapes passed by, to either side and overhead, vast and ponderous, observing the three of us from a safe distance. There were whales the size of mountains, and massive squid with huge, bulging eyes and tentacles that seemed to trail away for miles. There were other things too, not so easily identified. Just huge shadows, darker than the waters, watching with great unblinking eyes the size of houses. I really wanted to put on my armour now, but I knew I couldn't afford to seem weak or scared in front of Walker. He was looking straight ahead as he strode along, but I had no doubt he was keeping an eye on me. He seemed entirely unmoved and unaffected by the whole underwater experience, while in my case it was only pride that was keeping me from being a gibbering wreck. An underwater wreck. Heh.

I had no idea where I really was, or where I was going. I felt, simply, lost. And that was a strange new feeling, one I wasn't used to at all. In my armour I always knew exactly where I was, and where everything else was. But now there was no way out and no direction home. I really didn't like this new feeling. I stuck close to Walker—or as close as the Somnambulist would allow. At least Walker still seemed to have some idea of where he was going. And if he had some idea of how I was feeling . . . he had the decency to keep it to himself.

Change again, and the three of us were trudging up the steep side of a mountain, heading for a far-off summit. All of us bent right over, staring down at the rocky ground before us, just to keep our balance as we fought our way upwards against the steep incline of the mountain. Even the Somnambulist had to lean forward, and she wasn't even looking where she was going. I glanced back, and down, and saw that the sheer steep drop fell away behind us. The base of the mountain was far below, lost to view, hidden among thick clouds. I felt a sudden stab of vertigo and had to turn away. The air seemed authentically thin, and cold. I looked up and saw that the mountain plunged up into the sky. The snow-covered summit was only occasionally visible among slowly drifting clouds.

I think Walker sensed I was losing patience and about to start demanding answers to questions again, because he just started talking, without having to be prompted. Still staring straight ahead, and stepping casually over and around the many broken stones littering the way.

"The entire structure and substance of this world," Walker said cheerfully, "this pocket reality called the Shifting Lands . . . is made up of psychegeography. That is, the whole physical environment shapes and reshapes itself constantly, to reflect the needs, wishes, and even hidden desires of the people who move within it. We are the world . . . if you like. Nothing here can be trusted to stay the same for long. But a word of warning, Eddie: the more you try to control your surroundings, through willpower and concentration . . . mental discipline . . . the more control will evade you. The Shifting Lands respond better to mood and emotion than to logic and common sense."

"So we create the world as we walk through it?" I said.

"Perhaps," said Walker. "Or it might all be down to the Powers That Be. Testing and toying with us, for their amusement."

(And again I remembered the soft world of Melanie Blaze, where everything changed constantly . . . That had to mean something, something important; but what?)

"Which means," said Walker, "this world can be anything at all. A cobbled street in old Paris; a Gothic castle; a giant chessboard with living pieces. I have seen them all, or something very like them. This is a place of visions and nightmares, fever-dreams and wild imaginings, and the worst impulses in man."

"Why?" I said. "Why would anyone want to make a world like that?"

"Because they can," said Walker.

"The Powers That Be can't control everything that happens here," I said. I was starting to get short of breath from the climb.

"No . . . ," said Walker. "But they can and do decide what will best serve the Game, and its players. They always take a keen interest."

"While you're in such a helpful mood," I said, "tell me, is there anything in particular I should look out for?"

"Parts of this world can break away," Walker said carefully. "And form themselves into specific, individual people. Apparently separate living beings can appear in this world, under the urging of hidden thoughts or needs from the Game's competitors. Sometimes you can't tell the players from the playing pieces. The players from the played. It's that kind of place, and that kind of Game."

"Terrific," I said.

"So remember, not everything you encounter is necessarily going to be who, or even what, it seems." Walker broke off, smiling, apparently quite pleased with the thought. "Or even who they believe themselves to be."

"Including you?" I said, perhaps just a bit spitefully.

"Of course!" said Walker. "Now you're getting it . . . It's not unknown for old friends and enemies, the living and the dead, to appear to take part in the Big Game. Some will be real, and some won't. Good luck figuring out which is which. And which of them you can trust."

"Should you really be telling me all this?" I said. I was finding it hard to get my breath now, from the climb and the altitude. Walker didn't seem at all bothered by the climb or the conditions. Neither did the Somnambulist. Walker considered my question carefully.

"Perhaps," he said finally. "Perhaps not. Who can tell? If I'm not really me (and I have to say, it does feel like me), then perhaps the Powers That Be made me too well. In which case, I am Walker. Particularly if I'm dead everywhere else."

"If you were to leave here," I said, "and step outside the Shifting Lands, would you still be Walker?"

"What a fascinating question!" He actually stopped for a moment, to think about it, and the Somnambulist stopped with him. I stopped too, glad of a chance to get my breath. If the mountain wasn't real, climbing it felt real enough. Walker smiled briefly. "I suppose it would depend on who and what I really am. Though it would be one hell of a way to find out I'd guessed wrong . . ."

"Why did the Powers That Be take Molly?" I said. "Do you know? I mean, there must be any number of people who've got in too deep and owe too many people . . . Why choose her, out of all of them? When the Powers That Be must have known that the infamous Molly Metcalf has friends and family who will never stop looking for her?"

"The Powers That Be don't explain themselves to me," said Walker. "They don't need to. They move in mysterious ways because they can. But I am convinced they have a purpose in everything they do. Maybe, quite simply, it was her turn."

He shot me a quick glance over his shoulder as he set off again. "Come on, Eddie. Nearly there."

"Nearly where?" I said testily, forcing myself onward again.

Everything changed again, and we were walking through the massive nave of an impossibly huge Cathedral. A building so big I couldn't see the beginning or end of it. The farthest walls seemed to be miles away, the ceiling unbearably high. The sheer scale of the building was staggering. The Cathedral was a city, a world, in its own right. Far too huge to be anywhere real, or even historical. Warm sunlight spilled in through massive stylised stained-glass windows. But when I looked closely at the designs on the nearest wall, I discovered the depicted

Saints were all Droods I knew. James and Jack, Arthur and Martha, Cedric and William, all wearing golden medieval-styled armour, with old-fashioned circular halos around their exposed heads. They were all fighting hideous demons, and losing.

I deliberately turned my head away. The interior space of the Cathedral was impossibly huge, a space too large for the human mind to comfortably comprehend. Walker just strode forward across the bare stone floor in an unwaveringly straight line, looking neither left nor right, with enough confidence to suggest he knew where he was going. The Somnambulist followed him, and I followed her. Our feet made no sound at all on the stone floor. But at least we all had shadows.

After a while, I made out a small group of people up ahead, standing in front of an oversized altar. They seemed to be waiting for us. Still too far away for me to be able to make out any of their faces, but it did seem to me there was something decidedly familiar about the way one of them was standing. Something in the way she held herself . . .

She stepped forward, away from the others, and called out my name. Her voice echoed through the great open space, hanging on the air. My name, spoken in a voice I knew like my own. I broke away from Walker and the Somnambulist, running past them, sprinting across the great open space of the nave, and Molly came running towards me. It seemed to take ages before we finally met and crashed into each other. We hugged and held each other tightly, crying out each other's name, tears on our faces.

"Oh Molly, my Molly," I said, fighting to get the words out past the ache in my heart, "I am never letting you out of my sight, ever again."

We finally let go of each other, and stood back to look into each other's face, our hands still on each other's shoulders. We were both laughing and crying at the same time, and not giving a damn. I wiped the tears from her face with my hand, and she did the same for me.

"I thought you'd never get here," said Molly. "Where's the cavalry?"

"You're looking at it," I said.

Molly actually looked a little outraged. "No Iz, or Lou? Not even some of your appalling family?"

"It's been really hard to track you down," I said, just a bit defensively. "And even harder to get here."

"Not as hard as it is to escape from," said Molly. "And believe me, I've been trying."

There was a polite clearing of the throat, and we both looked around to find that Walker and the Somnambulist had caught up with us. Molly and I stood side by side to face them. Molly sniffed loudly.

"I see you've met two of our jailors. A dead man and a traitor. After everything I did for you, Carrys!"

"She can't hear you," I said. "She's asleep."

"I know!" said Molly. "It's so infuriating, not to be able to give the ungrateful cow a piece of my mind. You wait till you wake up, my girl . . ."

"I'm not even sure she can hear me," said Walker. "And I'm supposed to be able to give her orders."

"Have you tried?" I said.

"Not as such, no . . . She is very good at anticipating. For someone who's fast asleep."

I looked at Molly. "Have you met the people in charge here yet? The Powers That Be?"

"No," said Molly. "None of us have. They're keeping themselves well in the background. Only make their wishes known through Walker. Which leads me to think . . . We might just know them, if we saw them."

"Well," I said, "it's not like we have a shortage of enemies."

"I know!" said Molly.

I had to smile. She sounded so proud. Molly looked down her nose at Walker, hovering nearby.

"Why can't you stay dead?"

"Too much to do," Walker said calmly. "Come along, Eddie. There are people waiting up ahead that you're going to want to meet."

Molly surprised me then, by nodding and smiling in agreement. "You really won't believe who's here, Eddie."

Walker led us across the vast nave to the small group of people waiting in front of the oversized altar. Two of them stood hand in hand, as though they belonged together. The other three stood stiffly on their own. Because of the sheer size of the nave, it took a while to reach them. Molly stuck close by my side, her arm tucked firmly through mine, as though determined not to be separated from me again, even for a moment. The Somnambulist brought up the rear, perhaps to keep any of us from falling behind, or escaping.

But when we finally got to the altar, I recognised the couple standing together. My heart lurched in my chest, and for a moment I couldn't get my breath. I knew this older man and woman, knew their smiles. They looked so happy to see me.

"Mum?" I said. "Dad?"

I ran forward, and Molly let me go. Though I didn't realise that until later. I ran to my parents and hugged them both in turn, and they held me close, held me the way I always wanted my mother and father to hold me, when I was a child, left alone with the family. I had to fight for self-control, but eventually I let go and stood back, and looked them over carefully.

My father, Charles. A calm, self-possessed middle-aged man, completely bald but with a bushy salt-and-pepper beard. He had sleepy eyes and an easy smile, but there was still a definite presence to the man. Something about him suggested he could still be dangerous if the need arose. He wore a casual suit in a careless manner. My grandfather, the Regent of Shadows, originally introduced him to me as Patrick, the best weapons master the Department of Uncanny ever had. Apparently the engineer's gene ran in my side of the family, though it seemed to have bypassed me. Uncle Jack did try to teach me some basic skills when I used to hang out in the Armoury as a child, but nothing ever took.

"I have to ask," I said quietly, "do you happen to have any of your nasty little tricks about you? Like your famous protein exploder?"

"Unfortunately, no," said Charles just as quietly. "We're only allowed what the Powers That Be allow us."

He didn't ask whether I had anything about me. But we did exchange a look before I turned to my mother, Emily.

Originally presented to me as Diana, one of the Regent's very Special Agents. She spoke with a clipped, aristocratic accent that I knew for a fact never came from any of the standard finishing schools, because Droods don't go in for that sort of thing. Emily was a calm, poised middle-aged lady, good-looking in a classic way. She wore an elegantly cut tweed suit, with a creamy panama hat crammed down over her long grey hair. And a flounced white silk scarf at her throat. She sparkled with charm and grace, without even trying.

Without being asked, she shook her head. "No, Eddie. I've tried repeatedly, but the Powers That Be have suppressed my shadow-dancing skills. Just as well, or I'd have grabbed your father, dived into the nearest shadow, and disappeared from this awful place so fast it would have made their heads spin. I didn't think anyone could interfere with my abilities, especially after everything I had to go through to get them; but then, I didn't think anyone could kidnap your father and me against our will either."

"So you've been here all this time?" I said.

Charles and Emily looked at each other, quickly picking up from me that more time had passed during their absence than they'd thought.

"Not by choice," said Charles.

"We were abducted," said Emily. "Snatched out of our hotel room, past all the Casino's defences, between one moment and the next."

"No warning," said Charles. "No way to avoid it. A most professional job."

"I have so many questions to put to you," I said. "But first, I have some bad news. You've been gone for months, and bad things have happened. The Regent of Shadows is dead. Murdered."

Emily and Charles made low, shocked sounds and held each other's hands. They looked like they'd been hit.

"How?" said Emily. "My father had Kayleigh's Eye! How could anyone hurt him while he had that?"

"The Drood in Cell 13 found a way," I said. "But my grandfather has been avenged. His murderer is dead. And I'm sorry, but that's not all. The Armourer, Jack, is also dead. A heart attack."

Charles and Emily embraced each other tightly, as though they were holding each other up. They looked suddenly older, and frailer.

"But I just saw him!" said Emily. "He seemed fine!"

"You've been gone a lot longer than you think," I said.

"Have we missed the funeral?" said Emily. "We have, haven't we. Bastards!"

"And the wake," said Charles. "After we were forced to miss James' wake, we swore we'd be there for Jack's. Someone is going to pay for this."

We would have talked more, but Walker insisted on interrupting so he could present the other players in the Big Game. I turned reluctantly away to study the three other people standing at the altar. Walker started with Tarot Jones, the Tatterdemalion. A tall, lean, and almost indecently young-looking man, though years of experience showed in his eyes. He wore the traditional mix of travellers' clothes: rags and woollens, leathers and jeans, bangles and beads. Strangely constructed stick figures clung to his back, as though they were catching a lift. He had a great mass of curly black hair, and a long, bony face dominated by a beak of a nose and a big, toothy grin. His occasional sudden gestures were surprisingly graceful. There was a certain otherworldly, almost fey quality to him," like a woodland creature, only superficially civilised.

Tarot Jones looked wildly out of place in the Cathedral setting, with his patchwork outfit and almost feral presence, but then, I would have been hard-pressed to name anywhere the Tatterdemalion would have seemed at home that didn't involve a whole lot of trees. I put forward a hand for him to shake, but he declined, studying me thoughtfully.

"I am the Totem of the Travelling Tribes," he said finally. "Their protector and spiritual leader. I stand between them and the violence of the town people. I sold my soul, repeatedly, to gain the power I needed to look after my people. So I could hide them away in isolated natural settings, far from anywhere civilised. Where no one could find or reach them to punish them for being different. And for enough power to defend them from any threat. You probably don't remember the bad old days, when Thatcher sent her stormtroopers against us. The blood, and the horror . . . I swore then: Never again."

"But to sell your soul . . . ," I said.

"Over and over again," said Tarot Jones, suddenly grinning broadly. "What's a soul or two between friends, eh? I knew what I was doing. I did it of my own free will. It is the old way, after all. The King sacrifices himself; for the good of the Tribe. But it seems none of the power I bought so dearly is enough to get me out of here. Out of this awful, unnatural place. I have to get home, to look after my people! They need me!" He glared at Walker. "Why did your Powers choose me?"

"They don't tell me things like that," said Walker. "But I have heard it suggested that just possibly, the players of the Game choose themselves. Because they're so desperate to avoid the fate awaiting them."

Tarot Jones looked at Walker for a long moment, and then looked away.

Next we were introduced to Chandarru, Lord of the Abyss and Seeker After Truth. Chandarru made a point of adding these titles themselves, stressing the capital letters. He bowed to me, rather than taking my hand. He was a robust, comfortably padded Oriental gentleman, wearing a smart formal tuxedo, with top hat and swirling opera cloak. He also had the traditional long moustaches, painted-on devilish eyebrows, and a tarred pigtail. When he spoke, it was in considered formal phrases, as though English wasn't necessarily his first language. He gave the impression of a man holding everything within, giving nothing away.

"I used to be big on the stage," he said. "One of the last authentic Oriental conjurers to tread the boards. London, Paris, New York. Such days! But as I grew older I decided I'd had enough of tricks, and went in search of the real thing. And I was never the same after that. I have made many deals in my time; and many promises, to Powers and Principalities, in return for secrets. And power, of course, because once you have secrets, other people want to take them from you. I never really believed I'd have to pay the many debts I amassed, because I was always careful to play my various debtors against each other. But eventually I ran out of tricks. I was actually on the run when I was contacted."

"So you weren't kidnapped?" I said.

He gave me a quick, meaningless smile. "No. I was offered a chance to earn my salvation, through participation in the Big Game. And I jumped at the chance."

I gave him a meaningless smile of my own. With a sudden insight, I realised that Chandarru was a performer. What he was showing us was just a role he played. No more him than the man he was onstage. He hadn't told us a single real thing about himself.

The Sin Eater was a large black American with a big round face, close-cropped white hair, and a gaze so direct and unblinking it was a challenge to meet it. He wore the blindingly white suit of a Southern preacher, complete with a dog collar, and held himself as though he expected to be attacked at any moment. And was more than ready to give as good as he got. He refused to shake my hand, or even to give me his real name.

"Sin Eater," I said. "Interesting title. A very old, very heretical practice, condemned by all sides of the Christian Church. Consuming the sins of others, to allow them forgiveness . . . Why would anyone do that?"

"It's what I am," said the Sin Eater, in a dark, rich voice that sounded more used to addressing and intimidating a large audience. "I gave up my old life, gave up everything, to become what I am now. I have allowed myself to be possessed, many times, exorcising the demons out of the afflicted, and then locking them up inside me. Making a cage for them out of my body and my soul. Partly so I could save the cursed and demon-ridden, and bring peace to the persecuted. But also so that I could take the demons for myself . . . draw on their hellish powers and make them mine."

"There are demons inside you?" said Molly. "Why would you want that?"

"So I can use Hell's power to fight Hell's agents," said the Sin Eater, smiling for the first time. It was not a pleasant smile. "So I could use demonic power to strike down Evil wherever I found it. It isn't difficult to find these days. I save those worth saving, protect those worth protecting."

"Whether they want saving, or protecting, or not?" said Molly.

"It is my duty before God," the Sin Eater said coldly. His voice was flat and uncompromising. "What else is there that matters?"

"Then what are you doing here?" I said.

"I was ready to pay the price, or so I thought," he said slowly. "Until I got old. And tired. It has become . . . more difficult to contain the demons inside me. They are always whispering in my ear, tempting me . . . They want me to do things, and sometimes I do. I wake up with blood on my clothes, and worse." He suddenly pulled back his left sleeve to show us the length of barbed wire wrapped around his arm. The barbs had dug deep into his flesh, and there was dried blood caked around the wounds. Some of them looked to be infected, but I knew better than to say anything.

"I mortify the flesh," said the Sin Eater, gently running his right hand over the barbed wire and patting it fondly, like a favoured pet. Before carefully pulling the sleeve down again. "I control myself, through pain and punishment. So I can still do what I need to do. Be the Sin Eater; and bring salvation to those who need it most. Because what we do in Heaven's name has Heaven's strength."

"He's very conflicted," Walker said quietly.

"So!" I said, smiling easily about me. "We're all here to play the Big Game! For the entertainment of the Powers That Be . . . Does anybody know what this Big Game actually entails? What the rules are? What we have to do?"

"No one's said anything yet," said Molly, scowling impartially around her. "Nothing useful, anyway."

"How long have you been here?" I asked.

"Not long," said Molly. "Hardly had time to swap names and backgrounds. Of course, it helped that everyone here had heard of me . . ."

"Witch!" said the Sin Eater.

"Exactly!" said Molly and turned her back on him. "I couldn't believe it when I met your parents though, Eddie. I mean, what were the odds?"

"Yes," I said. "I was thinking that . . . You and Charles and Emily were kidnapped. But not the other three . . ."

"They were contacted, in various ways," said Walker. "And offered a way out of their problems. They agreed, and were brought here. They all considered themselves lost, you see, damned, and running out of time and hope. Now look at them—almost giddy with relief at the chance of a last-minute reprieve."

"You are not Walker," Chandarru said suddenly. "Walker is dead."

"That's no problem here," said Walker. "But you're quite right, of course. I look like Walker, because someone here wants me to. I wonder who, and why . . ." He looked happily around the small group, and they all looked thoughtful, as though any of them might have their own reasons.

Unless, I thought, Walker is just pretending not to be Walker, for reasons of his own. I wouldn't put it past him.

I turned to Molly. "Sorry it took so long for me to get to you."

"What are you talking about?" said Molly. "It's only been a few hours since they grabbed me from the Wulfshead."

I looked at her, and then at the others. They were all nodding in agreement.

"It's only been a few hours for us," said Charles. "Since we were abducted from the hotel in Nantes."

The others all chimed in, saying the same thing. No matter how long they'd been gone from the world, as far as they were concerned they'd been in the Shifting Lands only for a few hours. Everyone turned to Walker for an explanation.

"Time is a matter of choice and intent here," he said, just a bit grandly. "Like Space, Time is made to serve the purposes of the Powers That Be. You were all taken from your world at different positions in Space/Time, but arrived here at the same moment. Because that's what the Powers That Be wanted."

I turned to Molly. "He must be finished, because he's stopped talking, but I can't say I feel any wiser. Do you feel any wiser? No? Thought not." I glared at Walker. "Just tell us what we need to know! Tell us what the Big Game is, and what it's for."

"And what the rules are," said Molly. "If only so I can have the fun of breaking them."

"There is only one way out of the Shifting Lands," said Walker. "A Door is waiting, to take you home. But it will only open once, for one person. So the only way to be sure of winning the Game, of freeing yourself from your obligations and returning home . . . is to kill everyone else in the Game." He smiled about him, into the sudden silence. Everyone was thinking hard, and looking at one another speculatively. Walker carried on. "Let me be very clear; there can only be one winner, one survivor. If you want your debts paid."

"No," I said immediately. "I won't do it. I won't kill for you. I don't do that any more."

"Not even to save Molly?" said Walker.

"I don't need saving!" said Molly.

"Or your parents?" said Walker, still looking at me. "Though of course, in the end, you could only save one of them. Would you give up your life for the parents who abandoned you? And if so, which one would you choose?"

I gave him my best cold smile. "Like Molly said, rules are made to be broken. I've spent my whole career winning games by kicking over the board and scattering the pieces."

"But you never played a Game like this," said Walker.

Everyone else in the group was still staring at one another, weighing people up and judging the competition.

"You're a Drood," Tarot Jones said to me suddenly. "I can See your torc. My people have heard of you. The authority figure's authority figures. You maintain the status quo, by any means necessary. I don't think I'd have any problem killing you to protect my Tribe."

"Butt out, hippy," said Molly.

"I have a mission and a cause to return to," said the Sin Eater. "Nothing can be allowed to stand in the way of that."

Chandarru remained quietly thoughtful, as though still considering the odds, and the possibilities.

Charles and Emily looked at each other and smiled over some

shared secret thought. They took each other's hands, and turned to face Walker.

"Screw the rules," said Emily. "We won't kill our son, and we won't kill each other."

"You can't make us play the Game if we choose not to," said Charles.

"Damn right," said Emily. "Any debts or obligations we may have incurred, we'll take care of ourselves."

"We defied the Droods," said Charles. "Do you think it bothers us to defy your precious Powers That Be?"

"You can't leave here except through the Door," said Walker.

"Then we'll stay here together," said Emily. "To protect our son."

"Damn right," said Charles. "We understand duty, and sacrifice."

"We're Droods," said Emily.

Molly shot me a quick grin. "All right, Eddie . . . Your parents have style!"

I looked coldly at Walker. "I can see why everyone else is here, but why my parents?"

"They made deals," said Walker. "To be able to leave the Droods and remain undetected by your family."

Emily nodded slowly to me. "We had to disappear completely, Eddie. Become entirely different people, to protect you."

"Some people might have put pressure on you," said Charles, "if they thought we were still alive. To get us to return."

"Or they might have hurt you, even killed you, to get at us," said Emily. "Your grandfather, as Regent of Shadows, was able to hide us away in his organisation, but only as long as we were someone else."

"Patrick and Diana," I said.

"Exactly," said Charles.

"So we entered into Agreements," said Emily. "To make sure you could never be put in danger."

"Who did you make these Agreements with?" I said.

Charles and Emily looked at each other and didn't say anything.

"We were so mad at you," said Molly. "Or I was, anyway, thinking you'd just run away from Casino Infernale . . ."

"We were abducted!" said Charles. "Right in the middle of our mission!"

"Right in the middle of our game plan," said Emily.

"You do know," Charles said to me apologetically, "that we lost your soul, as well as our own, gambling at the Casino?"

"I did find that out, yes," I said. "Don't worry; I won them all back again and broke the bank."

"Of course you did," said Emily. "You're our son."

"We were a little concerned," said Charles. "About being trapped here, and leaving you in the lurch."

"Our game plan would have worked," said Emily, glaring at Walker, "if we hadn't been interrupted!"

I gave him one of my best glares too. "What is to stop any or all of us from working together to win the Game?"

"Nothing," said Walker. "But in the end, the Door will still only open once, for one person."

"Hah!" Molly said loudly. "I never met a Door I couldn't unlock."

"I never met a Door I couldn't force open," I said. Which wasn't strictly true, but Walker didn't need to know that.

He just smiled easily, apparently entirely unmoved. "The rules are different here. Because the Powers That Be decide what the rules are."

Chandarru suddenly stepped forward and thrust out a hand at me. Savage green lightnings sprang from his extended fingertips, but I already had my armour in place, reacting instinctively to his movement. Magical lightnings crawled all over my armour, trying to force their way in, only to fall away defeated. Chandarru immediately turned his lightnings on everyone else, and the rest of the group scattered to avoid them. Somehow, Tarot Jones was never where the lightnings struck. The Sin Eater stood firm, protected by a magical circle. Emily grabbed Charles' arm and stepped back into a concealing shadow, re-appearing only after the lightnings had passed. She grinned, de-lighted.

"My abilities are back! I'm a shadow dancer again!"

"Somebody must want you to have them, for the Game," said Charles.

"More fool them," said Emily.

And of course, none of the lightnings got anywhere near Molly. She just stood her ground and faced them down, until Chandarru lowered his hand and the lightnings stopped. He bowed briefly to Molly and to me, and smiled inscrutably, apparently completely unembarrassed by his sneak attack. I armoured down.

Tarot Jones turned angrily to Walker, who had quietly stepped behind the Somnambulist until the attack was over.

"Is that allowed? Can he just get away with that? Attacking us without warning, before the Game has even started?"

"The Game started the moment you all arrived," said Walker.

"We should kill the conjurer now," said the Sin Eater. "All of us, together; while we have the chance. We can't concentrate on winning the Game if we have to worry about being stabbed in the back all the time."

"That's part of the Game," said Walker.

Chandarru just smiled around at us. "You are, of course, welcome to try . . ."

"But some or all of you might find you have need of his particular talents, at some point in the Game," said Walker. "Shifting allegiances is a standard tactic amongst the most powerful players."

"Whose side are you on?" I said.

"Nobody's," said Walker. "That's the point."

"Why is the Somnambulist here, really?" I said. "To enforce fair play among the participants?"

"Hardly," said Walker. "She's here to enforce the rules. You must play the Game, all of you. No complaints, and no way out. Fight and win, or die. The Powers That Be must have their amusement. And their pound of flesh. If anyone refuses to participate in the Game, the Somnambulist will kill them."

"No!" said Molly. "Carrys wouldn't do that!"

"Possibly not, but Carrys isn't here right now," said Walker. "She won't know anything about it until she wakes up. She might be very upset at that point, but it will be far too late to do any of you any good."

"Who are you really?" I said.

"Who do you want me to be?" said Walker.

And I have to say, that did sound a hell of a lot like the real Walker.

# CHAPTER ELEVEN

# That's Not Playing the Game

E verything disappeared. As though the whole world had been taken away. I couldn't see or hear anything, couldn't even feel whatever it was I was standing on. I waved my hands back and forth in front of me, and there wasn't even the pressure of resisting air on my palms. I called out to Molly. My voice sounded flat, diminished. It didn't carry and it didn't echo. There was no reply. My hands clenched into fists. I was almost out of my mind with rage. I couldn't have lost Molly again, so soon after finding her.

Light rose up around me, slowly and uncertainly. Details of a new world appeared, fading in and out of the gloom. I was standing somewhere in the midst of a desolate empty moor, bathed in a foul leprous moonlight. Just the look of it made me feel unclean, and I almost flinched as the light touched my bare face and hands. I looked quickly around me. The moor was a dim, deserted setting, nothing moving, not a sound anywhere. Nothing to suggest there was a single living thing present apart from me. A cold wind blew from no direction in particular, hardly disturbing the air, but enough to chill me to the bone in a moment. I hugged myself tightly, and stamped my feet hard on thick, glutinous mud. The moor stretched away in every direction.

A whole world of mud and dirty water, bubbling bogs, and the occasional tuft of unhealthy-looking vegetation.

This was no real, material setting. I could tell. Someone had made this place, brought it into being through an act of will imposed upon the chimerical nature of the Shifting Lands. And then, that same someone had dropped me in it.

It all seemed solid enough. I could even smell the mire. A ripe stench of fermenting gases, oozing and bubbling up through the thick, viscous mud. And when I crouched down to study a stunted tuft of grasses close up, I could make out each individual blade of grass in the blue-white moonlight. At least this time, all the details had been filled in. A living world. Real enough to die in . . .

The ground beneath my feet collapsed without warning, the solid earth becoming saturated mud, a sucking bog, pulling me under. I yanked my feet free of the mud with an effort and lurched forward, forcing my way across the mire. But I just sank in deeper with every step. I struggled on, mud already lapping up around my thighs, but I couldn't seem to find my way to solid ground. There didn't seem to be any, anywhere. Or at least nothing strong enough to support my weight.

I was soon waist deep and sinking fast. The harsh, urgent noises I was making as I fought my way forward sounded clearly on the quiet. I didn't like the sound of them. They sounded dangerously close to panic. With my next step I plunged down even further, almost falling forward onto my face. I fought fiercely to regain my balance, but I was quickly chest deep in the mud; and it took all the strength I had just to keep moving forward, pressing against the resisting mire with all its slow strength and tenacity. I didn't dare stop; I couldn't feel anything solid under my feet.

I was breathing hard now, my heart hammering in my chest. The stench of gasses bubbling up grew even worse, disturbed by my progress through the bog. It filled my head till I couldn't seem to think straight. I clapped a hand over my mouth and nose, and breathed through my fingers. That seemed to help. I made myself concentrate on my situation.

I was sure I'd read somewhere that you could actually swim through quicksand, if you took it slowly and carefully and kept your wits about you. I eased myself slowly forward, spreading my weight out across the surface of the mud, but it didn't help. Within moments my whole body was submerged, and the mud was lapping up against my chin. My neck ached from holding my head up. I could hear myself making harsh animal noises as I struggled. My arms and legs thrashed helplessly, unable to gain any traction in the enveloping mud. I was still sinking, if only a little more slowly, and I'd stopped making any forward progress.

I didn't want to armour up. I was pretty sure the weight of it would drag me under. And while my armoured mask would let me breathe under the mud, there was no telling how deep the mire was. I might just sink and sink and sink . . . But as the mud crept up over my chin, and lapped against the underside of my bottom lip with its cold, clammy touch, I didn't see what other choice I had.

I subvocalised my activating Words, and the golden strange matter swept over me in a moment. Sealing me in, protecting me from this awful, sucking world. And the moment I took on my armour the mud suddenly became hard as concrete, solid and implacable, holding me in place. As though it had just been waiting for its chance. I fought it with all my strength, yet couldn't move at all. I had nothing to push against; no traction, no leverage. But I was still sinking, very slowly. Going down, into the mud, into the dark.

I stopped fighting and lay still. My heart was pounding like a jack-hammer, but I concentrated on slowing my breathing as I made myself think. Walker had said something to me . . . about the Shifting Lands. That the psychegeography of the world responded to the wishes and the needs of the people in it. That it didn't matter who created whatever world you ended up in; you could still affect or change your environment through an effort of will. Make it be what you needed it to be. So I closed my eyes, focusing my mind on just one thing, one definite objective. I needed something to stand on. I needed to stand up.

And just like that, I wasn't lying flat in the mud any more. I was still buried up to my chin, but now I was standing bolt upright; and there was something wonderfully solid under my feet. I might not be able to see it, but I could definitely feel it. Thinking hard, I visualised another step, just like the first; and slowly I raised my left foot through the thick mud and stepped onto it. The mud still resisted my every move, but it wasn't strong enough or solid enough to hold me. Not now. I visualised more steps, and one step at a time I rose up out of the clinging mud, until I was standing on the surface of the mire once again.

Thick, dark foulness dripped off my gleaming armour, falling away in sudden slurps and rushes. I shook myself hard, and more of it flew away. I cried out, in triumph and relief, and thrust both my arms up, into the shimmering moonlight. It felt so good to be able to move again.

I glowered about me, my hands clenched into fists, ready to lash out at anyone. This had been a deliberate attack. A world designed to kill me, slowly and horribly. If my willpower hadn't been up to the job . . . But I was a Drood. And self-control is one of the first things my family teaches its children, from a really early age. Self-control is vital if you're going to live with your armour. One of my competitors in the Big Game must have made this place just for me, one of the few kinds of death trap that might just work against a man in armour.

I frowned. A place like this couldn't have come from anywhere inside me, could it? Not even subconsciously . . . Walker said the Shifting Lands took their shape and direction from conscious and subconscious needs and wishes, but even so . . . I shook my head firmly. In my current circumstances, in the middle of the Game, self-doubt was just a distraction. I made myself concentrate again, on the one thing that really mattered to me.

"Molly!" I said loudly. "I want Molly! Where is she?"

A door appeared before me. A perfectly ordinary-looking wooden door, standing alone and unsupported, about a dozen feet away. It seemed almost to hover on top of the mud, barely touching the surface, but it didn't have the look or the feel of a dimensional Door. I studied the slowly heaving mud, bubbling away between me and the door, and didn't trust it. I visualised a series of steps, lying on the mud in a straight line between me and the door, and immediately there they were, gleaming golden in the unhealthy moonlight. Like so many stepping-stones. Solid and firm, as though they'd always been there. I walked steadily forward across the stones, trusting my weight to them one step at a time, and they didn't give at all.

The moment I drew near the door, it swung open before me, and bright, healthy sunlight spilled through, pouring into the gloomy moor from the world beyond the door. I laughed aloud. The sunlight spoke of a sane and normal world, and I wanted it. I strode forward, though a small part of me was still thinking, *Another damned door that could lead absolutely anywhere. Getting really tired of that* . . . I stepped through the door, and fell into an ocean.

I dropped into the waters like a lead weight, plunging under the surface in a moment, sinking deeper and deeper. I thrashed helplessly as the weight of my armour pulled me down, and the bright light from the surface quickly faded away, becoming a dull green haze. I swam with all my armoured strength, kicking for all I was worth, but it did no good. The sheer weight of my armour worked against me, overcoming all my best efforts.

The green light became steadily darker, the deeper I went. I soon lost all sense of direction, even which way was up. Panic burst inside me, at being so lost, and helpless. I had nothing to orientate me, nothing to see or hear or touch in the cold, empty dark. It was like a bottomless sensory deprivation tank. I could feel my heart racing, hear my ragged breathing, because they were inside my armour. I felt so alone . . . it was actually peaceful. Such a relief, to have nothing to fight any more. Nothing to disturb me, nothing I needed to do . . . But there was. I couldn't rest, couldn't give in, not while Molly still needed me. My thoughts snapped back into focus, and I grinned despite myself, under my golden mask. Whenever I weakened, whenever I lost my way, I could always rely on Molly to rescue me.

My armour was the problem. It was allowing me to breathe, but it was dragging me down. It couldn't help me, so it had to go. I armoured down, and immediately the terrible freezing cold of the dark waters hit me like a hammer blow. The shock of it was nearly enough to kill me. I thrashed my arms and legs, trying to swim, but the cold was inside my head, numbing my thoughts, and I couldn't think what to do. I tried to concentrate, to make something solid under my feet, solid enough to stop my descent, as I had in the mire . . . But the cold was so awful, so overwhelming, it dominated my thoughts. I couldn't seem to concentrate on anything else. My thoughts raced in a dozen different directions, and got nowhere. And I had only a little breath left in my lungs, to get me back to the surface.

I seized on that thought. Keep it simple, keep it practical . . . I let a little air seep out of my mouth, and felt the bubbles bump against my face as they rose past it, heading for the surface. Now I knew which way was up. I forced the last of my strength into my legs, and kicked hard. I felt my descent slow, and stop; and then I began to rise up through the waters. New confidence forced more strength into my arms. I could barely feel them through the freezing cold, but I made them work through sheer willpower.

I swam up, and up, and the green light returned. It seemed to take forever, fighting my way up out of the dark and back into the light, my heart slamming painfully in my chest, my lungs fighting me, demanding I open my mouth and take in a breath I knew wasn't there . . . but once again Drood self-control kept me going. I shot up through the brightening green light, and then my head burst through the surface of the ocean, and I could breathe again.

Bright sunlight dazzled me as I drew in air, and for a while all I could do was just bob there, struggling to keep my head above water, breathing in that glorious air. Still half dead from the awful cold, frozen to the bone, my body was wracked with terrible shakes and shudders, enough to endanger my attempts to stay afloat. But soon enough my vision cleared and I looked around me. I was floating in the middle of an ocean that seemed to stretch away forever. The sun beat down on the peaceful waters, out of what seemed like a clear Summer sky. Though if there was any warmth in the sunlight, I couldn't feel it on my numb face.

A voice called my name. It seemed to me that it might have been calling to me for some time. I slowly turned around in the water to look—and there was Molly, standing precariously in a small rowing boat, some distance away. She waved vigorously at me, once she saw she had my attention, and then had to stop and fight for balance as her boat rocked dangerously. She didn't seem to have any oars, or any way of moving her boat closer to me. Which was typical of the situation I'd found myself in so far. I sighed heavily. Tired, exhausted, and frozen to the bone as I was, I would have to go to her.

I swam steadily towards the rowing boat, carefully doling out the last of my strength. *There had better not be any sharks in this ocean,* I thought. *Because the mood I'm in right now, I'd eat them.* I lumbered slowly through the water, fighting to keep my head up, and finally got to the boat. I clamped one hand onto the side, and then just hung there. I looked closely at my fingers, to make sure they were holding on tightly, because I couldn't feel them. I was so damned tired . . . Molly knelt down in the boat, talking to me, but her words made no sense. I couldn't even answer her. In the end, she had to haul me out of the water and over the side.

I collapsed in the bottom of the boat, as it rocked uneasily back and forth from the violence of our movements. I tried to say something to Molly, but couldn't force it past the chattering of my teeth. She lay down in the bottom of the boat with me, saying my name over and over, and hugged me fiercely to her; pressing the whole length of her body up against mine, so she could share her body warmth with me. I was so cold I must have hurt her, but she never said a word. And slowly, blessedly, the cold left me. The shakes stopped, and feeling returned. I grimaced at the pins and needles, but I welcomed them too; they were a sign of life returning. After a while, I got my breathing under control again, and was able to sit up in the boat, with Molly's assistance. She sat back and looked me over carefully. I managed a small smile for her.

"We have got to stop meeting like this."

"Ho ho ho. Where the hell have you been?"

"Sinking, mostly. Where is this place? Did you make it? Why did you choose an ocean?"

"Of course I didn't make this!" said Molly. "I don't even like the seaside. The Cathedral disappeared on me, everything went dark . . . I tried to call on my woods, but when the light returned I was here. I suppose I should be grateful I appeared in a boat. Even if the bloody thing doesn't have a sail or a motor."

I remembered Walker saying that the Shifting Lands responded more to mood and emotion than to willpower. I also remembered, now that it was far too late, strolling along the bottom of the ocean floor with Walker and the Somnambulist, and being able to breathe perfectly normally. I should have concentrated on that while I was underwater, but the cold had been so bad, so overwhelming . . . Just because the world you're in isn't real doesn't mean it can't kill you if you let your guard down. Worth remembering.

"Still!" Molly said cheerfully, "At least we're back together again. I knew if I just concentrated hard enough, I could fashion a door that would find you and bring you here."

"Hold on," I said. "I made that door!"

"Yeah, right," said Molly. "Pull the other one; it plays the Bells of St Mary's. Maybe we could use the door to get out of here!"

But when we looked there was no sign of the door anywhere. While we were distracted, it had softly and silently vanished. First rule of the Shifting Lands: if you don't keep concentrating on things, they disappear.

"I could call it back," said Molly.

"I rather doubt it," I said. "And even if we did, I'm not sure we could trust it. A door like that . . . there's no telling where it might take us. We need to do better than that."

"Like what?" said Molly. "Wish up a motor for the boat? I've already tried, and got nowhere. It would probably help if I had some idea how an outboard motor works . . ."

"No," I said. "We need to think bigger. We need to change this world for a better one."

I'd stopped shivering almost completely now, and it suddenly occurred to me that there was no need for me to be soaking wet any longer if I didn't choose to be. One hard thought later, I was bone-dry. Molly saw me do it, swore briefly, and made all the damp disappear from her clothes, from where she'd hugged me. She grinned at me.

"There are advantages to being stuck in an artificial world," she said brightly. "I wonder if I could call up a whole new wardrobe . . ."

"Let's concentrate on what's right in front of us for the moment," I said carefully. "This is a Game, and the other people playing in it will kill us, given half a chance. Now, I am looking around and I don't see land anywhere. I intend to change that. I shall start by calling for an island."

I sat cross-legged at the bottom of the boat and concentrated,

focusing all my thoughts on the one idea. There was a sudden distur-
bance in the waters under the boat, and it rocked crazily from side to
side. Molly and I had to cling to the sides to keep from being thrown
overboard. Molly peered over the side, and made a startled sound.

"Take a look, Eddie. You really need to see this."

I looked over my side, to help balance the boat. Something from
far below was rising up through the dark waters, something really big.
And it was heading straight for us. I tried to think of some way to move
the boat, but it was so hard to concentrate with that huge shape sweeping up out of the depths . . . It slowed at the very last moment, to press
hard against the underside of the boat. Lifting it up out of the waters.
And then it stopped. The boat grew still. It was clear I'd called something from inside my mind, and brought it into this world, but what? I
looked at Molly.

"You need to hold my legs."

"I do? Why?"

"Because I need to lean right over the side of this boat, to see what
it's currently resting on. And I don't want to take any chance of falling
out until I knew what's what."

Molly grumbled under her breath, but took a firm hold of my legs
as I leaned out over the side and looked down. And then, back and
forth, taking in the familiar and very suggestive shape of what had
risen up beneath us.

"Ah," I said.

"Ah?" Molly said suspiciously. "What do you mean, ah?"

"It's . . . a whale," I said. "Very large, and very white. I have an awful feeling . . . it's Moby Dick."

"What? You're kidding!"

"Apparently not," I said. "I can see the shape of it quite clearly. It
would appear my subconscious mind moves in mysterious and only
slightly helpful ways . . ."

"How is this going to help us?" said Molly, just a bit dangerously. "What is a whale going to do? Swim us to land somewhere? Except there isn't any land that I can see!"

"Good point," I said. "I want an island, dammit!"

I concentrated again, taking a firm hold on my thoughts. I frowned until my forehead ached, and when I opened my eyes the waters were receding, rushing away in every direction. And when I looked over the side of the boat again, the white skin of Moby Dick was gone, replaced by what gave every appearance of being a sandy white beach. The boat was now resting on a small tropical island. Not a very big island; more the kind you see in a cartoon, just big enough for the two people necessary for the joke. White sand, and a handful of coconut trees. The ocean had pulled back, but it looked to me like it would just love to sweep straight back in again if I let it. I gave it a stern look, told it to behave itself, and then turned to Molly.

"Welcome to my island!" I said grandly. "Take a walk; stretch your legs."

I lifted her up and put her over the side of the boat, lowering her carefully onto the white sands. She kicked at the ground suspiciously, and then glared about her.

"It's not much of an island, is it?" she said. "I mean, I could walk around the thing in under a minute."

"Well," I said, "it is my first island. It's . . . traditional."

"Underachiever," said Molly.

She walked over to the nearest coconut tree and looked up. A dozen or so nuts were clustered under the broad leaves, all of them well out of reach. Molly kicked the tree trunk, hard. A single nut broke free, and dropped obligingly into her waiting hands. She then realised she didn't have anything to cut it open with, so she smashed the nut against the side of the tree. The nut obligingly broke open, to reveal that it was empty. Hollow, with not a scrap of meat or a drop of water. Molly gave me a disgusted look and threw the nut away.

"I guess I didn't imagine the place clearly enough," I said. "It's all in the details . . . Come on, though; be honest! It's still an island. And islands have one very useful advantage over boats."

"Oh yes?" said Molly. "Like what?"

"Islands very rarely sink."

"All right, you've got a point there." She looked around her, hands on her hips. "We still need something more . . . useful. This whole world feels like a trap to me. I say we get the hell out of here. Go somewhere else completely!"

"Sounds like a plan to me," I said. "All right, brace yourself. I think I may be getting the hang of this."

I concentrated again, and felt the world move under me. It was like flexing a muscle I hadn't known I had. And when I looked again, the boat and the island were gone, and Molly and I were standing in a London street.

And not just any street; we were standing on Oxford Street, with all its familiar shops and settings . . . not far from where I'd left it earlier. I allowed myself to relax a little, happy at being in a place I not only recognised but one that gave every indication of being entirely unthreatening. I did stamp my feet on the pavement a few times, surreptitiously, just to check that it wasn't going to suck me down. I'd had enough of that. Molly slipped her arm through mine to show I was forgiven, and grinned at me.

"I know this! Oxford Street, right? Have you transported us back there? Out of the Shifting Lands?"

"No," I said. "I'm pretty sure this is just another fake. Something that only looks like Oxford Street. Pretty damn close, though. All the details seem right."

"It'll do," said Molly. "But why did you choose this street, in particular? Did you want to go shopping?"

"I was just here," I said. "I'd been visiting Castle Inconnu."

Molly gave me a hard look. "What the hell were you doing there, with those stuck-up little prigs?"

"A story for another day," I said.

My voice trailed away, as I realised something was wrong after all. Something was very wrong with Oxford Street. There were no people, no traffic, no noise or movement or signs of life anywhere. Why hadn't I noticed that immediately? The whole street was horribly still and silent. Like a stage setting before the play has begun. Molly's grip on my arm tightened as she realised it too. She looked quickly about her, and then took a deep breath, regaining control of herself. She gave me an encouraging smile. It looked cheerful, but strained.

"You're starting to get the hang of this, Eddie. It just needs . . . a little more work." And then she stopped, and frowned. "Actually, you know . . . this does sort of remind me of something. Do you remember Casino Infernale, when I played the game of World War with the Bones Man? We created familiar backgrounds for us to fight in. This is the same sort of thing, but on a much larger scale. We can do this, Eddie! We just need to practise . . ."

I shook my head. "I'm not playing any Game for the Powers That Be. Where they get to decide what the rules are, and change them when they feel like it. That gives them far too much of an advantage for my liking."

"But there isn't any way out," said Molly. "The only way to leave the Game is to win it. And that means . . ."

"I know what it means," I said. "And I don't do that any more."

"Then what . . ."

"I'm still working on it, okay?" I looked up and down the long, empty street. "Where is everyone? Where are the other competitors?"

"I thought you didn't want to play the Game?" said Molly, amused.

"I don't," I said. "I'm mostly concerned with finding Charles and Emily . . . But I do think we need to locate the other three players.

Before they find us. If they can force their way into this world, who knows what control they might have over it? Change the setting, change the rules, find new ways to attack us . . . Can you use your magic to find any of them?"

Molly scowled, looked down at her feet, and then shook her head reluctantly. "My magic's gone. I've been trying to access it ever since I arrived in the Cathedral, but nothing works. I think the Powers That Be did something to me, the bastards!"

"They took your magic away?" I said. "Why would they do that?"

"Perhaps to give you more of a reason to fight," said Molly. "If I can't defend myself in the Game, you would have to get involved. To protect me."

"Damn," I said. "You're right."

"Well, I'm sorry to be such a burden to you!"

"You know I didn't mean it that way . . ."

But she just turned her back on me and folded her arms tightly, sulking. Molly can take the strangest things personally.

Trees shot up out of the pavement and the road, hundreds of them, blasting up all around us. Huge, towering trees, soaring into the air, until Oxford Street was gone, overgrown and replaced by a dark, brooding forest. Broad-boled trees with wide-stretching leafless branches, set unnaturally close together. Nothing between them but patches of forest gloom.

At first I thought this might be Molly's doing, that because she was upset she'd summoned a setting she could feel more comfortable in. But it quickly became clear we weren't anywhere in Molly's familiar wild woods. This was a darker, far more threatening place. The light falling in heavy shafts through the overhead canopy of intertwined branches was trying to be golden sunlight, but it was curdled, spoiled. As though the whole forest setting was somehow corrupt. No wildlife anywhere, not even the smallest living thing moving among the trees.

Not even any shrubs or grass, and the dark earth at my feet looked more like mud and ashes. As though the trees were growing out of dead matter. Molly and I moved quickly to stand close together, ready for any attack.

The trees seemed to crush in around us, with no obvious path or way out. The air was thick with the stench of rotting mulch. Wrinkled bark on the trees looked like the faces of mad old men, with staring eyes and hungry mouths. Long, gnarled branches reached out incredibly far, their curling ends seeming to clutch and grasp. They moved restlessly, though there wasn't a breath of wind in the forest to disturb them. Roots churned slowly in the dark earth, like great dreaming worms.

We were surrounded.

"Really don't like the feel of this," said Molly. Her voice was hushed, little more than a murmur. As though the trees might be listening. "Can you get us out of here, Eddie? Maybe back to Oxford Street?"

"I'm not even sure how we got here," I said. "I didn't call these woods. Did you?"

"Of course not!" Molly turned up her nose at the surrounding trees. "Wouldn't be seen dead in a place like this. Could you summon another door?"

"Can't you?"

"I can't think straight!" Molly scowled unhappily, avoiding my gaze. "Something about these trees just . . . gets to me."

I could hear a definite note of fear in her voice. And that worried me. I wasn't used to seeing Molly afraid, or this close to panic. I had to wonder whether the Powers That Be might have . . . damaged her when they took her magic away. It was so much a part of who and what she was . . . Unless this was what she was really like, without her magics . . . No. I couldn't believe that. I tried to concentrate on a door, to get us out of the forest . . . but I just couldn't seem to visualise a door in this setting. It didn't belong here, didn't seem right. And if I couldn't believe in it . . . I turned to Molly.

"This is more your kind of world than mine. Can't you reshape it, turn it into something more pleasant?"

"This is nothing to do with me!" said Molly. "It's not my woods, not my world."

"No," said Tarot Jones. "It's mine."

We both looked round sharply, and there he was, lounging at his ease between two tall and twisted trees. He was smiling at us, with his big, horsey grin, and not in a good way. Tarot Jones, the Tatterdemalion, the Totem of the Travellers. A raggedy man, with an air of the wild things about him, he looked perfectly at home in the dark forest. As though this was where he belonged. I wondered if this was how he saw all wild places, all the time.

He looked down his long nose at Molly. "You know nothing of the true wildness of the woods. The sleeping power of the dark face of Mother Nature, red in tooth and claw and loving every moment of it. There was a time I didn't; but I had to give up my innocence, put it aside and leave it behind so I could become wise enough, and strong enough, to protect my people. To defend my Tribe from all those who threatened them."

"We're no threat to your people," I said carefully.

"Of course you are. You're a Drood."

"Try not to be so literal in your thinking," I said. "You're the hero of your story, and I'm the hero of mine."

He looked suddenly older, and oddly sad, for a moment. "I'm no hero. Not any more. I wanted to be, but I had to give all that up to become the guardian and protector my Tribe needed. When they come with weapons to move us on, I have to face them with worse things than weapons. I stand between my people and a cruel and vicious world, and they must never know, never find out, all the awful things I've had to do on their behalf. To keep them safe. I am teeth and claws in the night, the fever that burns in dark places, the terror and horror of abandoned places. There is blood on my hands, but I do not regret one drop of it. You'd understand that, being a Drood."

I nodded slowly. "Like I said, we have some things in common. So why don't we put our differences aside, just for the moment, and work together to get out from under the hands of the Powers That Be? You can go back to your Tribe, and I can go back to my family. We don't have to do this. We don't have to fight and kill, play the Game, for the amusement of others."

He cocked his head on one side, studying me with bright eyes. "Fine words, for a Drood. When did you ever turn away from violence? You kill for your family. I kill for my Tribe."

"No," I said, "I don't do that any more."

"Good," said Tarot Jones. "That will make this so much easier."

He gestured with his left hand, and all the trees around us tore themselves free of the dark earth. They rose up on their roots, lurching and swaying, and plunged towards us, thrashing branches reaching out with clawed and clutching fingers, to rend and tear. A savage power moved in the trees, ancient and unstoppable. There was a harsh anger in their movements, as though this was what trees dreamed of all the time, in their long, deep sleep. Of revenge on men, for what they did with saws and axes and fire . . . The trees advanced from every side, with deafeningly loud creaks and cracks, their roots churning up the dead earth. I looked quickly about me, but there was still no way out.

"I have had enough of this!" said Molly. "I am never defenceless! Never!"

She produced an aboriginal pointing bone from somewhere about her person. That nasty old night magic that can kill with a gesture. She stabbed the discoloured bone at the nearest tree. Anywhere else, the kind of curse magic bound into that bone would have been enough to blast the tree into kindling, but nothing happened. Molly swore briefly, and threw the bone aside. Her left hand was immediately full of an ancient arthame, a witch dagger. The leaf-shaped blade was deeply scored with old runes and sigils. Molly spoke a Word of Power over it, but the blade didn't burst into flames as it should have. Molly looked shocked. She shook the blade hard, as though that might help, and tried again, but it remained just a knife. Molly threw that away too, and pulled a leather pouch out of her pocket. She poured a purple powder out into her hand and scattered it on the air before her, but it didn't glow, or scintillate, or do terrible things. It just fell harmlessly to the ground and lay there. The pouch fell from Molly's trembling hand. She looked at me, and her eyes were full of frustrated tears she wouldn't give in to.

"I can't even command my armoury any more! What have they done to me?"

"Take it easy," I said. "And stay back. I've got this."

"Of course you have," she said, smiling slightly. "You're a Drood."

I armoured up and went to meet the trees. Wrapped in my golden armour, I felt strong and fast and sharp, more than a match for a bunch of trees with bad attitude. I laughed aloud as they reached for me with their long, gnarled hands, because their woody strength was nothing compared to my armour. I snapped off branches and threw them aside, stamped on roots until they broke, punched great holes in tree trunks until they split from end to end. I kicked trees out of the way and pushed them over, tore them to pieces with my golden hands. Heavy branches closed around me, snapping tight with inhuman strength, crushing me. But they couldn't hurt me, and they couldn't hold me. I shrugged and the branches broke; I ripped them from me and threw the pieces away, and went on. I grabbed one tree with both hands, tore it out of the dead earth, and upended it, swinging it effortlessly like a great club, striking down all the other trees and smashing them apart, until I'd opened up a great clearing all around me.

Trees toppled silently, and thrashed helplessly on the ground.

Branches broke and roots snapped, none of them of any use against me. I knocked over trees and shattered others, and when I finally stopped, not even breathing hard, I had opened up a great wound in the heart of the forest. I looked around and the remaining trees stood back. Afraid to approach me. I dropped the tree I was holding, and looked at Tarot Jones. Standing on his own.

"I knew it," he said. His voice was flat and cold, not from lack of emotion but because what he was feeling was too big to put into words. "Just another Drood bully-boy. The despoilers of the forest, destroyers of the wild. But I have more than trees to set against you. I command the elements."

He drew himself up and raised both hands to the heavens. He spoke Words I didn't understand, older than any language I knew, and massive storm winds blasted into the clearing I'd made from a dozen different directions at once. They hit me hard, battering and bludgeoning me, but I stood my ground in my armour, and they couldn't move me. Broken and fallen trees were lifted up and thrown around, and many of them slammed into me, but they couldn't knock me off my feet. I didn't even bother to slap or shoulder them aside; I just stood there and took it, staring implacably at Tarot Jones from behind my featureless golden mask. Molly crouched behind me, for shelter from the storm, both arms wrapped around my golden legs to keep her from being carried away.

The winds died down, and lightning struck. Long, jagged lines of elemental power, fierce and vivid, blasting sharp electric illumination through the forest gloom. Lightning bolts hit me again and again, but my armour just soaked them up. Scraps of lightning crawled over and around my armour, crackling and spitting, trying to force a way in, only to fall away, defeated. I glanced down, to make sure Molly had retreated out of range, and of course she had.

Tarot Jones actually danced on the dark earth, out of his mind with rage, and then he stopped abruptly and made a series of gestures. Heavy roots burst out of the dark earth, white as corpses, and wrapped themselves around me, trying to pull me down. I tore them apart with my golden hands and let the pieces fall back to the ground.

Tarot Jones turned his back on me to show off the stick figures that clung there. And one by one they turned their shapeless heads to look at me, before dropping down from his back and landing lightly on the forest floor. Strange twisted shapes, just twigs bound together into almost human things. Full of dark malignant passions. They scampered across the broken earth towards me, and then changed direction at the last moment and went for Molly. Because if they couldn't hurt me, they could still hurt the thing I cared for most. They saw her as an easier target. They should have known better.

Molly grabbed up the stick figures and wrenched them apart with her bare hands, dismantling their knotted shapes, and scattering the pieces around her. She stamped them under her feet; smiling nastily all the while. Even without her magics, Molly Metcalf was still a very dangerous person. A few of the figures escaped her, and I ground them to pieces under my armoured feet. They broke easily.

I don't know whether they were really alive, in any way. I hope not.

Rain slammed down, thick and cold and heavy, soaking Molly immediately. I moved quickly to stand over her, sheltering her as best I could. The ground beneath our feet was quickly waterlogged, becoming deep mud in moments. My armoured feet sank into it, but I had been there before. I visualised a solid surface underneath Molly and me, to hold us up, and it was there in a moment. And all the rain in the world couldn't affect it.

The rain cut off. Molly crouched beside me, gasping for breath, soaked from top to bottom and looking like a drowned rat. I made the moisture disappear from her with a single hard thought, and she grinned at me, gave me a thumbs-up, and then glowered fiercely at

Tarot Jones, who was still standing alone in his rags and tatters, among the ruins of his forest. I started towards him. I'd had enough of being reasonable and holding back. He really shouldn't have attacked Molly. Tarot Jones held his ground as I advanced on him, and shot me his best arrogant grin.

"I am the Totem of the Travellers, and the Spirit of the Woods! I am the Green Man!"

"That's nice," I said. "I'm Eddie Drood, and I'm mad as hell."

He reached out to two trees still somehow standing on either side of him. Their branches dropped down and wrapped around him again and again, like a cocoon, and then lifted him up into the air, until he was lost to view. The two trees slammed together, fusing themselves into one great living thing. A tree forty or fifty feet high, with a roughly human shape and powerful arms and legs. A face appeared in the wrinkled bark that was very like Tarot Jones. A massive tree with the face of a man and all the strength of the forest, driven on by one man's fury. It stomped heavily towards me, and the ground jumped and shook under the weight and impact of every step.

I concentrated on my armour, and turned my golden gloves into buzz saws. The vicious blades roared loudly as they spun, and I walked forward to meet the Green Man. My howling blades dug deep into his wooden body, ripping and tearing, sending splinters flying. The great face in the bark screamed. The huge wooden hands beat at me, and I didn't even feel them inside my armour. One hand tried to pick me up, and I cut it off with my saws. I dug deep into the wide trunk, splitting it open and carving it out, and all the ancient strength of the wood was nothing, set against my armour. I opened up the heart of the Green Man, and there was Tarot Jones, nestled within. I turned my saws back into gloves, and tore him out of the wood. I clubbed him down with a single blow, and he fell unconscious to the ground before me. The Green Man fell backwards, stiff and unwieldy, no longer animated by one man's will, to ponderously measure its great length on the forest floor. The sound of the impact carried on and on, but the massive shape did not move again.

I armoured down, and stood over Tarot Jones' motionless body. I looked at him for a while, and then I raised my head and addressed the unseen watching audience.

"I won't kill him! Do you hear me, you Powers? I don't kill! Not for you, or anyone!"

I waited, but there was no response. I didn't think there would be. I just wanted to make a point. Presumably, as long as I was playing the Game, for whatever reasons, the Powers That Be were happy. As long as I was providing a show . . . Molly came forward to join me.

"He would have killed you," she said finally. "And me."

"That's not the point."

"What is the point?"

"Not dancing to someone else's tune. I did what I had to, but I don't feel good about it. You know, Molly . . . it's not enough, just to escape from the Shifting Lands. I am going to put a stop to this Game, hunt down the Powers That Be and bring them down. Hard."

"Of course you are," said Molly. "I wouldn't expect anything less from Eddie Drood. But can we at least try to get out of this Game alive first?"

"Perfectionist," I said.

Molly looked at the unconscious form on the ground before us. She gave it a good hard nudge with her boot, just in case.

"What about him?"

"He'll keep," I said.

The light darkened as the forest shut down all around us. Wood cracked and creaked loudly, as the remaining trees slumped and sagged forward, rotting and decaying, falling apart. The forest was dying without the will of Tarot Jones to sustain it. What golden light remained shrank in on itself, darkening like spoiled treacle. Somewhere up above the forest, the sun was going out. It was already growing cold, as the life bled out of Tarot Jones' world. Molly shot me a concerned look.

"What happens to us if we're still a part of this world when it dies?"

"I think we're probably better off not knowing," I said. "We need to move on. Replace this world with one of our own choosing. Something we decide on."

"We?"

"I think we'll stand a better chance of getting what we want if we both concentrate on the same thing."

"Too late," said Molly. "I've already thought of something."

The forest disappeared in a moment, swept away like a passing fancy. I expected Molly to replace the dark forest with her own preferred wild woods, but instead, we were suddenly standing on a street that could only have been part of the Nightside. Hot neon, night sky, good and evil rubbing shoulders and stabbing each other in the back. Business as usual, in the night that never ends. I looked reproachfully at Molly, and she shrugged briefly, not even a little bit embarrassed.

"It's what came to mind . . ."

A thought struck me. I looked down at my feet, but Tarot Jones' unconscious form hadn't made the transition with us. We'd left him behind, in his dying world. I hoped he'd get out okay.

I looked around me, trying not to appear too openly disapproving. All kinds of people, and some things not even pretending to be people, hurried up and down the rain-slick pavement, carefully avoiding each other's eyes. All in search of the driving passions that might not have a name in polite company, but most certainly had a price list. The night sky was still crammed full of unfamiliar stars, and the huge, overbearing full moon. Traffic rushed by without ever stopping, or even noticeably slowing down. Not everything on the road looked like a vehicle; in fact, some of them were eating each other. I was pretty sure this wasn't the same street I'd walked down with Walker and the Somnambulist earlier, but it looked pretty damned similar.

Something large flapped slowly across the night sky, so huge the moon actually disappeared from view for a moment as the creature passed in front of it. I looked away. Nothing in the material world should be that big. A shuddering bass beat caught my attention, blasting out of the open door of a nearby nightclub. Music reduced to its most basic, seductive and compelling. A barker in a chequered suit strode back and forth before the open door, loudly proclaiming the joys to be found inside. I really hoped he was exaggerating. Molly noticed my interest, and grinned.

"We could pop in for a moment, if you like. It's been ages since we went dancing."

"No thank you," I said. "I've heard of what goes on in Nightside clubs. Where the drinks may be free, but the cover charge is your soul. Or someone else's. Where the band never stops playing because the Management have a lifetime contract. Put on the red shoes and dance till you bleed . . ."

"You can be such a stuffed shirt sometimes," said Molly.

I remembered Walker saying that whatever you end up with in the Shifting Lands could be the result of conscious or subconscious desires. I had to wonder what it said about Molly that we'd ended up here.

An old woman dressed as the Lone Ranger, complete with black silk mask, tottered up to me from out of the crowd and grabbed one of my hands. She held on to it with impressive strength, despite my efforts to pull it free, and cackled loudly.

"Cross my palm with a silver bullet, dearie, and I'll tell you your future!"

I wrested my hand free of hers with an effort. "Do I look like a tourist?"

"Oh, come on," she said, dropping me a roguish wink. "Live a little!"

"Not today," I said.

She spat on the ground between us, turned her back, and tottered away. At the last moment, she turned to glare back at me. "You don't have a future! He's coming for you, from the other side of the mirror, and oh he's so angry! Doctor DOA is coming for you!"

And then she was gone. I looked at Molly.

"Haven't a clue," she said.

You hear the damnedest things in the Nightside.

I looked around me, hoping to spot either the Sin Eater or the magician Chandarru, but there was no sign of either contestant. Given how easily Tarot Jones had found us, I didn't think it would be long before one or the other, or even both, turned up here. But there was nothing in the street to present an obvious threat; it was just another disturbing scene from the Nightside. I really wanted to armour up, if only to keep from catching something nasty . . . but that would attract attention. This might or might not be the real Nightside, but I was pretty sure Droods would still be banned here. And the one thing absolutely guaranteed to bring all the disparate elements of the long night together would be the chance to gang up on a Drood.

Something that might have been a Yeti, with heavy eye makeup and false eyelashes, stomped past, hauling along several naked old men on leather leashes. Half a dozen nuns had hiked up their skirts in order to give a street mime a really good kicking. And a pack of small children tottered past, their bulging oversized heads tattooed with demonic script and their eyes blazing with hellfire. They saw me watching, and chattered among themselves in harsh inhuman voices. I wanted to do . . . something, but I knew there was no point. I couldn't hope to change anything for the better—not here. Molly patted me comfortingly on the arm.

"Leave it, Eddie. It's the Nightside."

*And you chose it,* I thought, but had the good sense not to say out loud.

"We can't just stand around here, doing nothing," Molly said briskly. "That would make us conspicuous, and it's never a good idea to stand out in the Nightside."

"I'm almost sure this isn't the real Nightside," I said, trying to sound casual.

"It might be," said Molly. "You'd be surprised how many places are attached to the long night, one way or another."

"But we haven't finished playing the Game," I said. "I don't think the Powers That Be would let us go anywhere we might escape from. So if this is another fake . . . there might not be anywhere else for us to go. This street could be all there is to this world, this setting."

"All right," said Molly. "Maybe I could summon one of my favourite watering holes here, if I put my mind to it. Strangefellows, say; or the Hawk's Wind Bar and Grill."

I knew both of those appalling locations by reputation, and suppressed a shudder. "They still wouldn't be the real deal. And I have a strong feeling that any place here could be full of nasty surprises, courtesy of our subconscious."

"How right you are," said Crow Lee.

And there he was, standing before me, grinning unpleasantly. The Most Evil Man in the World, by popular consent. A large, broad-faced, powerfully built man, perfectly at ease in a long white Egyptian gown with gold trimmings. He had a shaven head, dark piercing eyes under bushy black eyebrows, and enough sheer presence for a dozen men. He gave me his best hypnotic stare, and I glared right back at him.

"You're dead!"

Crow Lee shrugged easily. "You should know, you killed me. But you should also know by now that's no drawback here. One of you called me back. I wonder who, and why?"

I drew my Colt Repeater, and shot him between the eyes. His bald head snapped back in a flurry of blood, and he crumpled to the pavement and lay still. I shot him twice more, in the chest, just to be on the safe side. None of the people passing by so much as glanced down at the body, even when they had to step over him. I put my Colt away again, and realised Molly was staring at me.

"I thought you'd decided you weren't going to kill any more . . . ," she said carefully.

"Some shit I just won't put up with," I said. "Even if it does comes from my subconscious. Perhaps especially from there . . ."

"But . . ."

"I won't kill people. He was just . . . scenery."

"Quite right," said Crow Lee, from the pavement. But by the time I'd looked down, he'd disappeared.

And then, quite suddenly, all of the people hurrying up and down the street slammed to an abrupt halt. They stood still and silent for a long moment, and then they all turned their heads to look at me, and Molly. Hellfire burned in all their eyes, infernal flames dancing in their eye sockets. They were all wearing exactly the same smile. As though they were looking forward to something. I didn't need to look around me to know we were surrounded. Hundreds of men and women, and some that might have been both or neither, were staring at me and Molly . . . with Hell's eyes and bad intent.

"They're possessed," Molly said quietly. "Every damned one of them."

"I had spotted that, yes," I said.

"But who could possess that many people all at the same time?"

"Him," I said, pointing.

The Sin Eater was hanging on the air above us, in his shining white preacher's suit. Arms outstretched as though crucified, nailed to the night, blood dripping thickly from the stigmata in his wrists and ankles. He smiled down at us, looking very pleased with himself.

"Don't make a fuss, please," he said. "There's no need for this to get unpleasant. Just admit you're beaten, and it will all be over very quickly. I can't promise it will be painless, but I can make it quick. You should have known you couldn't win, not against me. I walk in Heaven's sight, with Heaven's strength. I have released all the demons contained within me and sent them out to occupy these passing sinners. My own little army. And since they aren't really people, but as you have already pointed out, merely animated scraps of scenery . . . the demons can't do any real damage, or hope to escape my control. I can have them do my bidding and then just call them home again. Where they belong. After they've dealt with you two. Why should I get my hands dirty when I already have so many burdens weighing down my poor benighted soul?"

"Just once," said Molly, "I really would like to meet a villain who doesn't feel the need to lecture us, or impress us with how clever they're being."

"Never happen," I said. I looked thoughtfully at the Sin Eater. "All . . . of your demons?"

He smiled. "Well, perhaps I kept a few back. To keep me warm inside."

The possessed army surged forward, lurching and staggering, as though the things inside them were still getting used to their new bodies. Bitter yellow flames rose from their staring eyes, and their hands had clawed fingers. Many of them tore at their own flesh, giggling as they disfigured their helpless hosts. Blood fell from their wounds, to hiss and steam on the pavement. Many of them produced weapons; it was the Nightside, after all.

"Leave it to me," said Molly. "I've got this."

She stepped forward and carefully pronounced several disturbing Words of Power, but nothing happened. Molly scowled, and tried a whole series of impressive gestures, some of which I'd seen tear the material world apart before . . . But to no avail. She called down the elements, as she had so many times in the past, but nothing answered her. Molly stamped a foot in sheer frustration and looked at me with tears in her eyes.

"They've left me nothing!"

A man stepped up to her and pointed a gun at her head. Molly leapt on him, punched him out, and grabbed the gun from his hand as he fell to the ground. A woman with cat's eyes and long, curving fingernails jumped at her, and Molly shot the woman dead. She shot three more of the nearest possessed before the cat woman hit the ground, and then turned to smile happily at me.

"Now that's more like it. Good to know there are some things you can still depend on. Oh, don't look so disapproving, Eddie. None of these people are real! Half of them probably wouldn't be even if this was the real Nightside!"

"They're real enough to kill us," I said. "But I take your point."

"Definitely stuffy," said Molly. "What do I see in you?"

I armoured up, and once again altered its configuration to suit the situation. My golden gloves morphed into two oversized machine guns, and I opened up on the ranks of possessed before me, mowing them down. Without hesitation or mercy. The golden guns fired strange matter bullets, and even the possessed had no defence against them. Their bodies blew apart in messy explosions, thrown this way and that by the impacts, and bodies hit the pavement faster than the crowd could advance on me. I turned around in a slow circle, raking my guns back and forth, shooting everything I could see. Molly moved quickly to keep behind me, picking off the odd target herself, just to keep busy. I could hear her laughing.

"Hardcore, Eddie! This is more like it!"

*They're not real,* I told myself. *I'm just destroying scenery.*

But when I'd finally finished, and ran out of possessed people to shoot, the dead bodies piled up around me still looked real enough. With their gaping wounds and shredded flesh and so much blood, pooling thickly. Some of the bodies were still twitching, as though the demons within were still trying to manipulate them, but they were all clearly dead, and one by one they stopped moving. I let my guns turn back into gloves and then called out to the strange matter bullets to return. They ripped themselves free of the bodies, and shot back through the air to sink into my armour. I wasn't leaving any strange matter behind for someone else to get their hands on.

With their hosts fallen, destroyed past the point of usefulness, the demons abandoned the bodies. They rose up, like so many blood-coloured ghosts or spectres, and streaked through the air to re-enter the hanging body of the Sin Eater. His face twisted and grimaced as his hellish children came home, but whether from pain or pleasure I couldn't tell. I was genuinely shocked that there were so many of them, contained within one man, who still claimed to serve the Good.

I walked over to him. Molly hung back. I looked up at the cruciform figure, hanging on the air above me. He stared down coldly.

"You haven't won," he said. "I haven't even started yet."

"You have to stop this," I said steadily. "Now. While you still can. Before it's too late."

"It was too late long ago," said the Sin Eater. "Don't you think I know that? So many demons; it's like I'm full of razor wire, scraping against my soul . . . What I've done to myself, for what seemed like good reasons at the time . . . Fight fire with hellfire . . . I'm damned. I know that. Unless I can win this Game, and have all my sins forgiven. Or at least, adjusted. It won't bother me to kill you, to sacrifice two more innocents for my holy cause. Especially since you aren't really innocents, are you? A Drood and a witch? I've no doubt you deserve everything that's coming to you. So there's some comfort in that. I'll just be sending you where you were bound to end up anyway."

The ground in front of me cracked open, and I stepped quickly back. A jagged split shot across the street, from side to side. And it was only then that I realised all the traffic on the road had disappeared. Not needed any more to set the scene. A deep crevice opened up, full of blood and fire and heaving molten lava. With darks shadows moving in it. The Sin Eater laughed briefly.

"There you are, Drood! An express route to Hell, just for you and your little witch!"

Terrible things came crawling up out of the flames and the lava, hauling themselves out of the crevice. Awful distorted shapes, sickening to look at. Sins given shape and form, sculpted in flesh and blood and bone. Foul things from out of the Pit, all of them smiling with anticipation as they headed for me, and for Molly. She moved quickly forward to stand beside me.

"They aren't the real thing," she said.

"You'd know," I said.

"And if they're not really hellspawn . . ."

"Then they're just more scenery."

My gloves became guns again, and I opened fire. The demons looked startled, even shocked, as my strange matter bullets tore into them and blew them apart. The sheer firepower I generated stopped them in their tracks, and then drove them back. I wasn't sure I was really hurting them, but I was causing more damage to their material forms than they could hope to repair. I raked my guns up and down the length of the crevice, forcing the creatures back into the flames. Molly danced delightedly beside me, whooping and howling with glee. The Sin Eater cried out in frustration. I finally stopped, lowered my guns, and looked down into the crevice. Foul things stared back at me, unwilling to leave the flames, afraid to face me.

"I'm not afraid of you," I said to them. "Whether you're real or not."

I walked forward, across the crevice, defying the fall. I walked across the wide gap as though it wasn't there, and didn't even feel the heat from the flames. The demons flinched back from me, cringing away from my act of faith. The crevice slammed shut, shutting off the light from the leaping flames in a moment. And every strange matter bullet I'd fired returned to my armour.

The Sin Eater glared down at me, his face full of rage and fear and desperation.

"Take him!" he said loudly. "All you demons within; I give him to you! Possess the Drood!"

They oozed out of his flesh, seeping through his white suit like so much congealed blood, forming into twisted demonic shapes in mid-air. More and more of them boiled out of the Sin Eater to hang on the night, before and around him, snarling and hissing, but not one of them moved forward to possess me. They preferred to stay where they were, forming a protective barrier around their host. He raged and roared at them, ordering them to obey his instructions, but they wouldn't. They waited for me to come to them. So I walked slowly, steadily forward, until I was standing directly before the Sin Eater. He was breathing hard now, his ragged voice silenced by sheer frustration. The demons stared silently at me.

"You think your precious armour will protect you, Drood?" said the Sin Eater. "After everything you've done?"

I thought about it, and then armoured down. The demons murmured uneasily among themselves. I stood there before them, in nothing but my bare flesh, and stared steadily back at them. Real or not, they still scared the crap out of me, but I wasn't going to let that stop me. They looked away from me, unwilling to meet my gaze. I turned to the Sin Eater and held his gaze with my own.

"I have faith in me," I said. "Because my uncle Jack had faith in me. And I have always valued his opinion and his judgement. While I may not always be sure about me, I have no doubt he was a good man. I have done my duty, to my family and to Humanity. And to the cause I have always believed in, to be a shepherd to the world. I have fought the good fight, and done my best not to stain my honour too much in the process. I have tried to do the right thing, even in the worst situations. Judge me, you demons. If you dare."

And one by one they turned away and forced themselves back into the Sin Eater. Even as he raged and ranted, cursing and screaming at them. They ignored him, choosing to go home, where they felt safe.

Where they belonged. And as he finally realised that, the Sin Eater fell silent.

Molly moved in beside me. "Hardcore, Eddie," she said respectfully.

The Sin Eater looked down on me, his eyes full of spite and desperation. "You can't stop me! I have Hell's strength on my side!"

"Shouldn't that be Heaven's strength?" I said. "For someone who claims to walk in Heaven's sight?"

The Sin Eater tried to say something and couldn't. Caught and held by an insight he couldn't deny any longer. Caught in the terrible contradiction of the life he'd made for himself. The demons within sensed him wavering and tried to seize control. His face writhed and contorted, as other faces tried to take its place. Hellfire shot up from his staring eyes, and disappeared just as quickly. He shouted, and screamed, and spoke in tongues. A blasphemous halo of buzzing flies formed around his head . . . but only for a moment, before they fell silent and dropped dying to the ground. As the Sin Eater fought the forces within him. One last battle—to be the man he'd always meant to be. His own face re-emerged, and the demons fell quiet. Cowed, for now. The Sin Eater looked down on me.

"It was all my doing. All my fault. Everything . . . I take full responsibility for all my actions. For my pride, and arrogance. All my sins. I was such a fool . . . such a damned fool."

His eyes closed and he collapsed, falling out of the night sky like a wounded bird. He hit the ground hard and lay still. I hurried forward to kneel beside him. I called his name, but he didn't respond. His eyes were open, but they saw nothing. He'd gone inside, to face his demons, and now he was trapped in his own thoughts, struggling to resolve his contradictions. I wondered how long it would be, before he came out again, if he ever did. Molly knelt down beside me and pressed the barrel of her gun against the Sin Eater's head. I grabbed her wrist, and forced the gun aside. Molly fought me for a moment, and then pulled her hand free. We stood up, facing each other. For a moment I thought she would aim the gun at me, but she didn't.

"Why not?" she said harshly. "Why not kill him? After what he would have done to us?"

"Because that would mean playing the Game," I said steadily. "I won't kill, Molly. And I won't see anyone killed. Not for them."

"Not even for me?"

"He's no danger to us now," I said.

She sniffed loudly and lowered her gun. "Odds are he'll try to kill us again, the moment he wakes up."

"Then we'll just have to beat the Game before he wakes up."

We both looked up sharply as a great shadow fell across us, blocking out the street lights and the blazing neon signs. The shadow kept spreading, covering the whole street. Because up in the night sky, the huge full moon was growing steadily larger. Falling at last, crashing towards us, descending with increasing speed to destroy everything beneath it.

"Oh, come on!" said Molly. "Who's doing that? I'm not doing that!"

"I think the Powers That Be are annoyed with us," I said.

"Sore losers!" Molly screamed at the rapidly descending moon.

"It's time to go," I said. "You'd better let go of this world so we can move on to a new one."

"I can't!" she said. "I don't know how! I'm trying, I'm concentrating, but nothing's happening!"

I tried too, but I couldn't seem to concentrate on anything but the huge moon dropping out of the sky onto me. Which was probably the point. So I looked up at the massive white pock-marked face and met its gaze steadily.

"All right," I said. "We'll do it the hard way. Pay attention. *I don't believe in you.*"

And the falling moon exploded into an incredible fireworks display. Bright burning colours, shining and sparkling, shot across the night sky. I braced myself, expecting a shower of burning meteors, or crashing moon fragments, but it was all just lights in the sky. Putting on a good show for the Powers That Be. Molly *oohed* and *aahed*, and clapped her hands delightedly. And when the last of the lights died down, I looked around and discovered that the world had changed again while I wasn't looking.

Molly and I were standing together, side by side, in a place that made no sense at all. I couldn't even be sure what we were standing on. There were shapes and structures and surfaces all around us that made me think of some freakish three-dimensional maze, or maybe even four or five dimensions. I couldn't tell what anything was, or even how it all connected. Just looking at the shapes that made up this new world made my head hurt. Nothing stayed the same from one moment to the next. It was all shifting, changing . . . There were huge floating objects that seemed to turn themselves inside out as I looked at them. There were things that might have been buildings, or at least structures, with too many sides and too many angles. Things came and went, without any clear purpose or meaning. It was like being caught in a nightmare, trying to force yourself awake, and finding you can't.

Whose world was this? Who made this? Who would want to make something like this? I was sure none of it came from anywhere inside my head. I was less sure about Molly, but it seemed unlikely. She'd always been very practical and level-headed, for a witch. And then I made myself pay more attention to my immediate surroundings, as I realised there were living things, or things that looked like they might be alive, crawling over some of the nearer surfaces. Things that might have been creatures, or people, or people becoming creatures . . . that I could only see out of the corners of my eyes. When I looked at them directly, they weren't there. But they did seem to be sneaking closer.

Great Voices boomed from Above, and terrible sounds rose from Below, while flaring colours exploded around strange structures I couldn't even put a name to. This ever-changing world threatened to take my mental breath away, but I could cope. I'd had Drood training, and I'd been around. I'd visited other worlds, other dimensions, even other realities. If all of this was supposed to throw me, they didn't know anything about my family. I'd survived growing up in Drood Hall, and if you could cope with that, you could cope with anything.

I thought about armouring up, but decided not yet. It might look like an admission of weakness, or even fear. And while this new world was quite definitely as weird as all get-out, I hadn't seen anything yet that struck me as a real threat.

Molly clutched at my arm, and I jumped, just a little. When I looked at her, I was surprised to see real distress in her face.

"Eddie, I don't like this. Do something . . . I'm scared!"

For the first time, I was really worried. Because this wasn't like Molly. Unless she was Seeing something I wasn't. I put a comforting arm across her shoulders and held her close. She felt reassuringly real and solid, in this place of ever-changing things. And then someone said my name, and I looked up.

And there he was. Chandarru; dressed in flowing and highly decorated Oriental robes, to accompany his traditional Chinese look of long moustaches and pigtail. The look an old-time theatrical audience would have expected from a Chinese stage magician.

He floated effortlessly before us, sitting perfectly at ease on a throne made of monstrous bones held together by rotting threads of flesh. Some of them were still steaming, as though only recently pulled from the insides of dying things. It was hard to tell how far away Chandarru was. Hard to judge any distance in this place. He could have been close at hand or far away, both or neither.

He smiled benignly down at us, in a really irritating way.

"This is where I came in search of enlightenment. To this place between places, where nothing comes from and everything returns. I journeyed here to study with the Hidden Masters, in their spiritual redoubt. You might say this is what Space and Time look like when seen from the other side. This is where I learned many amazing truths and much secret knowledge. Most of it not in the least what I was expecting. The true nature of reality isn't at all what I was hoping for. Came as something of a shock, in fact. I'm afraid it is necessary that you die now, Drood. And your little friend. I can't let you stop me. Not when I still have so much more to learn."

"And then what?" I said, cutting across what promised to be another long explanatory lecture. "What will you do? When you've finally learned all you can, all that the human mind can encompass? What then?"

"That is one of the things I have yet to learn," Chandarru said serenely. "Maybe I'll just take a good look at the way our world is going, and then wipe everything clean and start over, with something better."

"You haven't learned a damned thing," I said.

Chandarru looked startled, even shocked, by the hard certainty and judgement he heard in my voice. For the first time he looked uncertain. He sat up straight on his throne, as though challenged. He glared at me, pulling his dignity about him, and I ignored him to look at Molly.

"How are you doing?"

"Better, thanks." She grinned at me cheerfully. "Sorry. Something about this place just got to me, for a moment. I'm back. What do you need, Eddie?"

"You have more experience with the odder realms of magic than I do. Does this place seem . . . I hesitate to use the word *real*, but I suppose it will have to do for want of anything better . . . Does all of this look real to you? Are we where we appear to be; or are we still in the Game?"

"Hard to tell," said Molly, peering dubiously about her. "It seems authentic enough, but then it would, wouldn't it? But the bottom line is . . . I can't believe a second-rate conjurer like Chandarru has the power to take us out of a world created by the Powers That Be. So this is almost certainly just some place he's called into being because he feels important and powerful here. We're still in the Game. Still being watched by the Powers That Be . . . no doubt waiting eagerly to see what we'll do next. If I knew which direction they were in, I'd flash them."

"Have any of your magics returned?" I said carefully.

"Not yet," said Molly, scowling fiercely. "Right now I couldn't pull a hat out of a rabbit."

"Enough muttering!" snapped Chandarru. He sounded peeved that we weren't paying any attention to him. "It's time for both of you to die! There can only be one survivor, one winner, in this Game."

I turned unhurriedly back to face him. "You really think you can take down a Drood? We don't die easily. That's the point."

Chandarru gave me his best smug smile. "But you're in my world now. And that makes all the difference."

"No, we're not," I said.

"What?" said Chandarru.

"If you were half the sorcerer you claimed, you'd know that," I said. "Except you do know that, don't you? Or you wouldn't still be concerned with winning the Game. Nice bluff, conjurer, but we have to deal with reality. What really matters."

"What?" said Chandarru. *"What?"*

"Look, we don't have to do this," I said. "We don't have to fight and die to entertain the Powers That Be. We can work together. Find our own way out of this mess."

"No," said Chandarru. "We can't. You're a Drood, you see. I could never trust you. Or, for that matter, the infamous Molly Metcalf. After everything I had to promise, all I had to swear myself to, to pay for my terrible learning . . . I really can't afford not to win this Game."

I did my best to remain calm and reasonable. "Listen to me, Chandarru . . ."

"No! No more talking! I am the amazing Chandarru, Master of the Occult and Lord of the Abyss! And you are in my power!"

"Knock it off!" I said. "No you aren't, and no we aren't. This is all just another trick."

"What?" said Chandarru.

"All you ever are is a collection of tricks," I said. "A stage magician who desperately wanted to be something more. So you reinvented yourself. Went on the road, talked to all the right people, immersed yourself in weird shit like this . . . But even after everything you claim to have learned, you're still just running tricks in front of an audience. All of this . . . is just another stage setting. None of it's real. So the powers you claim to derive from this place can't be real either. But this armour I wear, it's real."

I armoured up, and concentrated . . . and a set of steps appeared before me, floating on the air, leading all the way up to Chandarru on his bony throne. The steps glowed golden, just like my armour. Chandarru gestured frantically at them, trying to make them disappear, but his willpower was no match for mine. I ascended the steps towards him. He stood up abruptly, and threw handfuls of his crackling green lightning at me. They flickered and flared all around me, spitting and sparking as they sank into my armour and were absorbed without trace. I never felt a thing. Chandarru drew himself up, and threw change spells, disappear spells, and distortion spells at me . . . and they all just detonated harmlessly against my armour. Chandarru hesitated as I kept heading straight for him, and then he hit me with the strongest curse magic he had. It rebounded from my armour and struck him down.

The throne disappeared, leaving Chandarru floating unconscious in mid-air. His Oriental costume disappeared, and he was back in his formal stage outfit. He looked smaller, less impressive—and strangely peaceful now he wasn't having to pretend all the time. I stood over him and armoured down. Molly hurried up the steps to join me.

"I suppose you won't let me kill him either?"

"No," I said. "Does this mean we've won the Game? I mean, we've run out of competitors."

"No," said Molly. "It's not over yet."

The world snapped off, and for a long moment there was nothing but an impenetrable darkness. I reached out blindly for Molly, and her hand found mine. We held on to each other tightly, until light flared up again, dazzlingly bright. When I could see clearly again, we were standing in the main entrance hall of Drood Hall. I think it's fair to say, it was the very last place I was expecting to see. Molly gave my hand a reassuring squeeze, let go, and looked quickly about her.

"We're back in Drood Hall? Does that mean we're out of the Game? Out of the Shifting Lands, at last? Eddie! Have your family intervened and brought us home?"

"Doesn't seem likely," I said. I stood very still, carefully studying my new surroundings. "I'm not in contact with my current handler, so there's no way anyone in my family could know where I am. The whole point of the Shifting Lands is that they're out of the Droods' reach, remember? And anyway, even if my family had somehow tracked me down . . . they wouldn't override a field agent in the middle of a mission and just yank him out of trouble. It's not the way we do things. No, Molly, this isn't real. It's a fake Hall, like the fake grounds I originally appeared in. I think the main clue is it's far too quiet. Listen . . . there's not a sound anywhere. The Hall is many things, but it's never quiet. There's always people around, hurrying back and forth on family business. And by now the Serjeant-at-Arms would have burst out of his private office, demanding to know how we got in here without setting off all the security alarms. And probably challenging my very right to be here, because that's what he does."

I walked over to a nearby table, picked up a heavy silver platter, and slammed it down hard on the tabletop. It made a hell of a racket. The sound carried loudly in the quiet, echoing on and on. But there was no response anywhere. I waited till the last echoes had died away, and then turned to Molly.

"Told you. Nobody home."

I glanced at the silver platter, prior to replacing it on the table, and then I stopped and looked at it more closely.

"What's wrong?" said Molly.

"It's just an ordinary platter," I said slowly, turning it back and forth. "No engravings, no decoration, nothing to suggest a significant history . . . It's just . . . ordinary. And Droods don't bother with ordinary things. This is blank, unfinished. As though the details haven't been filled in. Like a stage prop."

"Another clue?" said Molly.

"Right . . ."

I put the platter down on the table. Molly looked it over.

"It's still silver," she said brightly. "If I had a big enough pocket, I'd take it with me."

I had to smile. "You must be feeling better."

Molly shrugged, and looked quickly about her. "It all seems real enough. Familiar, in all the right ways. But then I suppose it would, if it's come from your memories."

I didn't say anything. I didn't think I was responsible for this setting. I hadn't called for it. But I supposed it could have come in answer to some subconscious need to replace the dark void left by the removal of Chandarru's world.

"Maybe we're here because you felt the need to be somewhere safe," said Molly.

"Safe? Here? In Drood Hall?" I said. "You must be joking. You should know better than that, Molly."

"Well, this isn't going to be coming from my mind, is it?" Molly said sharply. "You know I can't stand this place! So what do we do now? If you don't like it here, I suppose we could take a look outside."

"No," I said. "I've already seen the fake grounds, and they aren't up to much. I think we were brought here by someone else. For a reason. And almost certainly one we're not going to like. There must be something here that matters, something significant to the Game."

"All right," Molly said resignedly. "Let's take a look around, see what there is to see. Maybe I can find a few useful items small enough to fit into my pockets."

I suddenly realised Molly was holding the gun she'd acquired in the Nightside. "Why have you still got that gun, Molly?"

"They took away my magics," she said, not looking at me. "I have to have something."

I felt as though I should say something, but I couldn't think what. In the end, I just nodded. She had a point.

I strode off down the hallway, Molly trotting along beside me. Taking a close look at everything that seemed as though it might be valuable. I thought about fairy gold, which turns to leaves when returned to the real world, but I said nothing. The more I saw, the less the Hall felt right. I checked to see that we both had shadows, and that our feet were making the right kind of sounds on the waxed and polished wooden floor. Everything was as it should be . . . but I couldn't escape the feeling that something wasn't right.

When you know you're in a trap, the Devil is always going to be in the details.

And while I knew this wasn't the real Hall, there was no getting away from the fact that part of me wanted it to be real. To put all this madness behind me, and be home again.

I glanced at the line of portraits of old, dead Droods, the honoured departed, that stretched all the way down the long wall, from our oldest paintings to the most recent photographs. When seen out of the corner of my eye, they all seemed strangely blurred, only to snap into sharp focus whenever I looked at one directly. And sometimes it seemed to me that a face here and there would turn to follow me as I passed. Everything else seemed dependably real and solid, and properly detailed. But I couldn't shake the suspicion that something important was missing.

On a sudden impulse, I moved quickly over to a side door and slammed it open, and there on the other side was the room I'd been heading for. But it shouldn't have been there, behind that door. I ran down the hallway, with Molly hurrying to keep up, loudly demanding to know what was wrong. I kicked open the door at the end of the hallway, and there was the room again. Only this time, it was where it should have been. Molly looked back down the hall, and then back at the end room, and shuddered briefly.

"Okay, that is spooky. Someone is playing games with us, Eddie."

"Of course they are!" I said. "That's the point!"

"Well, pardon me for breathing! Don't you snap at me, Eddie Drood, or I will slap you one and it will hurt!"

"Sorry," I said. "I really don't like being messed with, in what looks like my own home. It's like someone is meddling with my memories. Sniping at me from behind the scenes."

I looked out the window opposite, and for a moment I saw faces looking in. Strangely familiar faces, though they were come and gone so quickly I couldn't place them or put a name to them. I hurried over to the window and looked out, but nobody was there. Molly quickly forced her way in beside me and studied the sweeping green lawns.

"What? What did you see, Eddie?"

"You didn't see them?"

"See who? I wasn't looking."

"It doesn't matter," I said.

I turned my back on the window and scowled at the room around us. The almost exact familiarity of the Hall was giving me the creeps. Like a monster hiding behind the mask of a friendly face.

"We didn't choose this setting," I said. "Someone else did. Which means this is a trap. I think we need to get the hell out of here."

"Are you sure?" said Molly. "If we keep going, we might flush out our hidden enemy, force him to reveal himself."

"We're going," I said. "I won't play their Game."

But of course it was never going to be that easy. Whichever way I went, whichever route I chose, it never led us outside. When I strode back down the hallway and out the main entrance, I found myself walking back into the hallway through the end door. I tried a dozen different ways out, running up and down side corridors and kicking open side doors, but somehow Molly and I always ended up back in the hallway. And when I finally lost my temper and tried to dismiss the whole setting by shouting *I don't believe in you!* at it . . . Nothing happened. It's hard to really concentrate when you're feeling that angry.

Which was almost certainly the point.

It was actually a relief when someone opened fire on us from hiding. Out of the corner of one eye I caught a brief glimpse of movement, and armoured up immediately. Bullets slammed into my chest in a steady tattoo, and my armour absorbed them as fast as they arrived. Molly ducked behind me in a moment and used me as cover to return fire. Whoever our attackers were, they were really well hidden. I couldn't even see the muzzle flashes, let alone movement. And with my mask in place I should have been able to see . . . something.

"We can't stay here, Eddie!" said Molly, shouting to be heard over the staccato bursts of gunfire. "We're too exposed!"

"Where are they shooting from?" I said.

"Can't you see?"

"No!"

"Then how do you expect me to be able to?"

"They're very good," I said. "Professionals."

"We need to move, Eddie! Now!"

"All right!" I peered quickly around. "Do you see that alcove to my left, with the really ugly statue of Bacchus in it? I'm going there. Right now. Try to keep up."

I sprinted for the alcove, though still careful to keep my armoured body between Molly and the gunfire. Bullets followed me all the way, and every single one hit me somewhere, tracking back and forth and up and down as though searching for a weak spot. I didn't feel any of it, of course, but it was starting to get on my nerves. I reached the alcove, grabbed Bacchus and threw him out, and then Molly and I squeezed into the narrow space, pressed close together. More bullets slammed into the walls on either side of us, chewing up the wood panelling . . . But they couldn't reach us, and that would do, for the moment.

We couldn't stay in the alcove. All the enemy had to do was change position, and he'd have a clear shot. I had hoped he would reveal himself, doing just that, but I still couldn't see anything. I needed to take the fight to the enemy, but I couldn't just run off and abandon Molly. She was almost defenceless without her magics. Without me. I had to protect her, even though I knew she'd deny needing it. There was a sudden pause, a worrying hush.

"Must be reloading," said Molly. "Quick, where can we go next? We need more room to move, and better protection. And preferably some-place where we can launch our own attack."

I peered down the hallway, and spotted an ironwood table. "There. That's our best bet."

Molly looked. "That's a table!"

"Ironwood. Trust me."

"You'd better be right about this, Eddie."

I charged out of the alcove and sprinted down the hallway to the table, with Molly pounding along and crowding my heels all the way. The gunfire started up again, a deafening fusillade of bullets. It was like running into horizontal steel rain. I got to the table, overturned it, and then grabbed Molly and pulled her down so we could both shelter behind the heavy wood. Massed firepower slammed into the table, and the ironwood absorbed it all, quite complacently. It didn't even budge under the repeated impacts. Molly grinned at me.

"Some table! I love this table! Where did you get it?"

"From the future," I said. "A present from the Deathstalker."

Molly shook her head. "You and your family."

As though annoyed they couldn't blast their way through the ironwood, the heavy stream of bullets turned its attention to the portraits of my ancestors on the walls. Old photographs and older paintings were chewed up and shredded, centuries of family history destroyed in moments. Scraps of old canvas floated on the air. I knew they weren't real, weren't the real thing, but I was still mad as hell. This was a cold act of contempt, against my family. Molly put a hand on my golden arm.

"You stay put, Eddie. They're doing this deliberately, to get to you. To upset you enough that you'll break cover, so they can get a clear shot at you."

"Let them," I said. "I have my armour."

"And they must know that," said Molly, doggedly patient. "Which suggests they have even nastier weapons, held in reserve. Something they think can get to you."

And while I was considering that, a large, chunky grenade came rolling down the floor towards us, from out of nowhere. I saw it coming, grabbed Molly, and wrapped myself around her as completely as I could. The grenade rolled to a halt just on the other side of the table, and exploded with a roar so loud it actually deafened me inside my armour. The ironwood tabletop absorbed a lot of the blast, but the sheer impact was enough to send the table skidding down the hallway, pushing Molly and me ahead of it. Black smoke filled the hallway. I approved of that; it should hide us from the enemy, for a while. I grabbed Molly by the arm and hauled her up onto her feet. She clung to me for a moment, half dazed by the explosion, so I picked her up and ran for the far end of the hallway.

I pushed my armour's speed to its limit, till I was just a golden blur hammering through the black smoke, my armoured feet punching holes in the wooden floor. The smoke was already clearing as I approached the end door. Bullets followed me down the last part of the hallway, but couldn't catch up. Other statues in alcoves blew to pieces, shattered by gunfire; furniture was destroyed; and priceless antiques were smashed and shattered. Even though I was sure my surroundings weren't real, I still felt hot flushes of real anger, and guilt at seeing such familiar objects lost because of me. I reached the far end of the hallway and skidded to a halt before the door. I put Molly down, though she still clung to one of my arms. I was worried she might have been hit and wounded, but she didn't seem to be. Just shocked. Which wasn't like Molly. What had the Powers That Be done to her? I tried the door; it was locked. I lowered one golden shoulder and slammed it open. It sprang back, accompanied by the sounds of rending wood and a broken lock. I plunged through into the next room, turning all the while to protect Molly with my armour from the continuing hail of bullets. How much ammunition did the bastard have? I grabbed the door, and forced it back into place. The heavy wood immediately jumped and shuddered, as gunfire slammed into it.

"Whoever our attackers are," I said, just a bit breathlessly, "they are really well armed. Guns and grenades, and an apparently endless supply of ammo . . ."

"Could be worse," said Molly. "They might have incendiaries."

"Hush," I said. "Don't give them ideas."

She was standing on her own now. I looked her over. The colour had come back into her face, and her eyes were tracking again. She glared at the door, then stepped smartly to one side, just as the first bullets punched right through it. Our enemy had found some heavier ammunition.

"Speaking of ammo," said Molly, "I'm almost out. Hey, why don't you morph your hands back into machine guns? Give the bastard something to think about."

"I've been trying," I said. "But I'm getting nothing. It's hard to concentrate, with everything that's happening. And it might be because I'm back at Drood Hall, where I was always taught that such adaptations were unacceptable inside the house."

"But it's not really the Hall!"

"I know! But I'm having a really hard time convincing my subconscious of that!"

"Terrific . . . ," said Molly. "All right, let's go down to the Armoury. Where your family keeps all the really powerful weapons and nasty devices. There's bound to be something there we can use. Something to let us turn the tables and take the fight to the enemy."

"Would those weapons really be there?" I said, frowning. "Assuming this fake Hall has a fake Armoury?"

"It'll all be there, if you believe it will," Molly said firmly. "Just because you didn't summon this place it doesn't mean you don't have any influence over it. Okay, that sentence got a bit out of control, but you know what I mean! Whoever it is out there, you must know the Hall better than they do. Your certainty should override whatever they're thinking."

I didn't want to go down to the Armoury, though I wasn't prepared to admit that to Molly. I was afraid I might meet a fake Uncle Jack there. And I didn't think I could cope with that, so soon after our recent encounter. But since I couldn't say that to Molly, I just nodded brusquely.

"The only problem is, the entrance to the Armoury is right over on the other side of the Hall."

"Not necessarily," said Molly. "Not if you don't want it to be. Concentrate on a short cut."

I looked at the closed door. There were almost more jagged holes in it now than there was wood holding it together. I concentrated hard, screwing up my face till sweat ran down it, and a door appeared in the wall opposite. A sign on it said simply, *To the Armoury*. I relaxed, shaking just a bit from the exertions.

"I think I'm starting to get the hang of this. If I wasn't so annoyed with absolutely everyone involved, I could get to like this Game."

"Famous last words," said Molly. "Move!"

I opened the door, and we went straight through into my family's Armoury.

It looked exactly as it should. A huge stone cavern, full of work-benches and computer stations, assorted high tech, shooting ranges, and testing grounds. But all of it was unnaturally still, and silent. Utterly deserted. It felt eerie, with no Armourer and none of his lab assistants working away. Nothing dangerous or explosive or worryingly unwise going on. But before Molly and I even had a chance to look for new weapons, gunfire opened up on us again. The attack came from the far end of the Armoury, a concentrated firepower that tore through the computers and workstations to get to Molly and me. Experimental tech exploded, things caught on fire, and delicate equipment simply vanished in sudden bursts of shattered silicon and shrapnel. I grabbed Molly and hauled her behind a tall piece of standing machinery. It rocked and shook under the repeated impacts of the heavy-duty bullets, but did good work as a shield.

"Don't grab me!" said Molly, pulling free.

"Sorry!" I said. "How the hell did our enemy get here first? How is that even possible?"

"It's the Game," said Molly. "Whoever creates the setting has control over the setting. They can be wherever they need to be."

"Really?" I said.

"I don't know!" said Molly, her voice rising sharply. "I'm just guessing! Do I look like I've got a copy of the rule book on me?"

The tall standing machinery rocked dangerously on its base, as our attacker concentrated his fire. Molly and I knelt down and put our shoulders against the machinery to steady it. The sheer rate of firepower slamming into our only protection was impressive, and just a bit worrying. We couldn't stay where we were, but I couldn't think where else to go. I could go—I hadn't seen anything yet that looked like it could damage my armour—but I couldn't leave Molly behind. Which was almost certainly what our attacker was counting on.

"Look," said Molly, "you must have some control over the environment here, because you know this Armoury like the back of your hand. And he doesn't. So work with that."

"All right," I said. "If I concentrate on certain things being where I want them to be . . . If I decide, for example, that this drawer right here contains a personal force shield . . ."

I glared at the drawer in front of me, which I was almost sure hadn't been there a moment before, then hauled it open and looked inside. And sure enough, there was a personal force shield. Score one for lateral thinking under pressure. I took the chunky metal bracelet out of the drawer and handed it to Molly. She slipped it on, worked the controls, and a six-foot-by-three-foot shield of crackling energy appeared on her arm. A force screen that would serve as an actual shield. Another present the Deathstalker had left us. Molly grinned widely, then stepped out from behind the tall piece of tech. Heavy gunfire immediately targeted her, hundreds of rounds slamming into the force shield. Molly grinned delightedly, as not one bullet got through. She fired her gun around the edge of the shield a few times, just to make a point, and then ducked quickly behind the standing piece of machinery again. She dropped me a wink.

"I feel so much better now."

"Thought you might," I said.

A second burst of gunfire opened up, joining the first, hitting the standing machinery from a different direction. Confirmation, for the first time, that we were facing more than one attacker. The standing tech was taking a hell of a pounding. I didn't know how much longer we could depend on it. And our enemies weren't sparing the rest of the Armoury either. Whole sections were being demolished by the continuous firepower. Great jagged holes appeared in the stone walls of the cavern, and lengths of chopped short electrical cable hung down from the ceiling, jumping and sparking. I was just relieved that the bullets hadn't found anything explosive or really dangerous yet. It was only a matter of time, though. Whoever our enemies were, they had really powerful weapons. And hiding from them wasn't getting me anywhere. Now that Molly was safe behind her force shield, it was time for me to show our attackers what a man in Drood armour could really do.

I stepped out from behind the standing machinery, and it seemed like every gun the enemy had opened up on me. I stood there, letting my armour soak up the bullets and hoping I might at last catch a glimpse of who our attackers were, or where they were. I could see muzzle flashes now, from the far end of the Armoury, but they kept changing position. I still couldn't see the enemy themselves. I concentrated on my armour, forcing a change in it through sheer willpower. My golden gloves became machine guns again. It probably helped that I was in the Armoury now, where such weapons were not only allowed but actively encouraged.

I opened fire, raking the far end of the Armoury with pulverising firepower, blasting apart absolutely everything in front of me. Everything that stood between me and my enemies. Workstations blew up, equipment was blasted apart, and the rest was just blown away in all directions. It still disturbed me to see such familiar sights destroyed, but I hardened my heart and kept firing.

And then an energy beam hit me square in the chest. It came out of nowhere, catching me completely by surprise, almost blasting me off my feet. I fell back several steps, but still kept my balance. The impact had been so great I actually felt it, inside my armour. I looked down, and was relieved to see that my armour had held—but only just. There was a great dent in my golden chest, right over my heart. It slowly straightened itself out. But while I was still gathering my wits about me, another energy beam hit me dead on—and another. My armour rang loudly, like a wounded gong, and great golden ripples spread out across my chest, as though a stone had been thrown into a pool.

I was sent staggering backwards, and very nearly did fall this time. I had to fight to stay on my feet. Whatever this new weapon was, it had to be incredibly powerful to almost breach my armour. So powerful as to be almost unheard of. There shouldn't have been anything like it in the Armoury. The Droods had never made such a weapon, strong enough to destroy Ethel's work . . . as far as I knew. A lot goes on down in the Armoury that no one else ever knows about. For the good of the family. I looked up and saw another energy beam heading my way. I seemed to have all the time in the world to watch it coming towards me, and no time at all to evade it. I wondered if this would be the one that killed me.

And then a tall black woman appeared out of nowhere, to stand between me and the energy beam, with her own personal force shield on her arm. The crackling energy field soaked up the energy beam as though it was nothing. And the woman who'd just saved my life turned to smile at me. She was taller than me, Amazonian, with dark coffee skin and close-cropped blonde hair. She wore a tight-fitting white jumpsuit under a long white fur coat, with thigh-high white leather boots. She looked impressive as all hell—but then, she always did.

"Come on, Eddie," said Honey Lake. "Shape up! You want to live forever?"

We both jumped back behind the tall piece of standing machinery, as more energy beams came howling our way. The tech took a hell of a battering, but stood firm. Perhaps because I had faith in it. I patted it fondly, like a good dog. Molly gave Honey Lake a long, hard look and then gave me an even harder one.

"Who . . . is this?"

"Oh, Eddie," said Honey, still smiling broadly. "You mean to say you never told her about me? Honey Lake, superspy for the CIA? About the special work we did together, and how close we became, on our shared mission to take down the Independent Agent? That short but action-filled time when we played the great spy game? You never told her about all the things we might have been to each other, might have meant to each other . . . if only you hadn't got me killed . . ."

"That's not what happened," I said.

"Hold it," said Molly, looking Honey over carefully. "You're dead?"

"As a doornail, darling," said Honey Lake. "I'm only here because Eddie called me up to save him. Subconsciously, I'm sure. He needed someone to save him from certain death, and he knew he could depend on me."

"He has me for that," said Molly coldly.

"If he'd really believed that, I wouldn't be here," said Honey.

The firepower from the energy weapons was becoming utterly savage now, blasting away at the sides of the standing machinery, whittling the tech away as it rocked dangerously back and forth. Honey Lake stepped out from behind the machine, using her personal force shield for cover as she reached for a gun on her hip. An energy beam punched right through the force shield, through her chest and out her back. She made a shocked, surprised sound and sat down suddenly, like a small child who's just run out of steam. Her force shield flickered and went out. I grabbed her and pulled her back behind the shelter.

There wasn't any blood. The great wound had been cauterised by the energy beam. A little steam rose from it, but that was all. And a smell of burned meat. Honey's eyes were wide, and she tried to say something to me, but all that came out of her mouth was a dribble of blood. I held her in my arms. She felt very real. She shook and shuddered, as though she was cold, and then she smiled shakily up at me.

"Here I go again . . ."

Honey Lake lay dead in my arms. Again. I expected her to disappear, but she didn't. I cradled her in my arms for a while, her head resting on my armoured chest like that of a sleeping child. And then I laid her gently down on the floor. I knew she wasn't real, that her second death wasn't real, but the anger I felt was real enough. Molly started to reach out to me, to say something, but she must have seen something in my body language through my armour, because she pulled back her hand and said nothing.

"She was an old friend," I said. "A respected colleague. She might . . . have meant something to me if things had been different. But they weren't. I don't believe I summoned her here. Someone else did it, to mess with my mind. I will make them pay for that. This world we're in responds to my thoughts, my beliefs . . . and I believe my armour is better than anything they've got."

I stood up and stepped out from behind the standing machinery. The enemy's energy guns targeted me in a moment and hit me with everything they had. Beam after beam slammed into me, but I stood firm. My armour remained untouched, and I was unaffected. I had faith in my armour. I could feel it changing, taking on a new shape and design as it responded to the rage boiling within me. It became . . . something monstrous, perhaps even demonic. And I didn't give a damn. I heard Molly gasp behind me. I didn't look back. Didn't look down to see what my armour had become. I just strode forward, into the energy beams.

I walked in a straight line, smashing through everything in my path as though it was nothing more than cardboard. Workstations and heavy equipment crumpled and fell apart, and none of it slowed me down for a moment. The world can be a very fragile thing, to a Drood in his armour.

I raked my machine guns back and forth, strange matter bullets ploughing through everything in my way. I completely destroyed one side of the Armoury, and then the other, and my rage was a cold, cold thing. I kept firing, maintaining a steady pressure, forcing my enemies back and back. Denying them any cover they could use to make a stand. I drove them back the whole length of the Armoury, until finally I could see the two of them moving, retreating from one blown-away protection to another. But I still couldn't see who they were. Finally I came to a halt.

"I know this Armoury better than you ever could," I said, my voice carrying clearly in the hush left by neither of us firing. "And I say that there's nowhere left for you to go. The Armoury ends here. So come out. Or I'll just destroy everything that's left, and you with it. Come out! Now!"

My parents stepped out from behind their place of shelter and stood together facing me. Charles and Emily Drood had been my attackers, trying to kill me and Molly, all along. They didn't look guilty, or ashamed, or afraid. They kept their energy weapons pointed at the floor, but didn't actually drop them until I ordered them to. I was so shocked, so full of contradictory emotions, that I could barely speak. Even after they'd dropped their weapons, they didn't take their eyes off me for a moment. They didn't look like beaten opponents, or cornered animals; they looked like professionals experiencing a temporary setback. Just waiting for me to make a mistake, or have a lapse in judgement, so they could jump me. I didn't know what to say. I heard Molly come forward to stand beside me, picking her way carefully through the wreckage I'd made of the Armoury. I didn't look at her.

"Oh, Eddie," she said, "I'm so sorry."

"You tried to kill me," I said to Charles and Emily.

"And me!" said Molly.

"Why?" I said. Not quite shouting it.

"It's the Game," said Charles.

"You have to play the Game, to win," said Emily.

"And we needed to win," said Charles. "With what we owe . . ."

"I knew we couldn't trust them," said Molly. "They abandoned you as a child. Hid from you for years. Traded away your soul, at Casino Infernale! Remember?"

"Yes," I said. "But . . ."

"Look at them!" said Molly. "They've made up their minds! They'll still kill you, first chance they get. There's only one way this can end, Eddie. Only one way you and I can be safe. You have to kill them. Right here, right now. While you've got the upper hand."

I was so shocked that I actually took my eyes off my parents for a moment. "I can't kill them! I can't kill my mother and my father!"

"You have to!" said Molly.

"No," I said. "I won't play the Game. And I won't kill. I don't do that any more."

"You have to," said Molly. "If you won't do it for yourself, do it for me."

"I can't believe you're asking me to do this! And I don't believe my parents would do this . . ."

That was when the insight hit me. I stepped back, so I could watch Molly as well as Charles and Emily. So I could cover all of them with my machine guns. I looked from Molly, to Charles and Emily, and then back again. So shocked and sickened now that I could barely get my breath.

"You're not my parents," I said. "And you; you're not Molly. You're all just . . . parts of the environment, brought to life. But why?"

Charles and Emily stood very still, looking at me with blank faces and empty eyes. Like actors who couldn't be bothered to play their parts any longer. Molly looked puzzled, as though I'd just cracked a joke and she didn't get it.

"That's why you don't have any magic," I said to her. "Because an animated scrap of scenery couldn't fake that. It's why you've been acting so out of character, needing me to protect you. The real Molly never needed to be protected by anyone. And she would never have tried to pressure me into murdering my own parents."

"Eddie, come on . . . ," said Molly. "This is me! Really! Stop this. You're scaring me."

I glared at Charles and Emily. "I don't believe in you. *I don't believe in any of this!*"

And the wrecked Armoury just faded away, like a bad dream. Taking Emily and Charles, or the things that looked just like them, with it. All that remained was a featureless grey plain, stretching away forever. It didn't even try to feel like a real location. It was just a place for Molly and me to be, as we stood facing each other. I did wonder, briefly, if this was what the Shifting Lands really looked like when there was no one around to give them shape and purpose and meaning. I looked at Molly, and she looked back at me.

"Stop it, Eddie!" she said. "It's not funny. Stop it right now. I'm Molly. Your Molly. You know that!"

"Stop pretending," I said.

"I'm not pretending! I'm Molly Metcalf!"

I remembered Walker saying how the people made from the Shifting Lands could sometimes actually believe they were what they'd been made to resemble. But this wasn't Molly. This thing might look like her, but it didn't act like her. Not really. So even though it broke my heart, I looked her right in the eye, and denied her.

"I don't believe in you," I said.

She screamed something at me, but she was already disappearing, fading away. Her scream vanished along with her, leaving me standing alone, in the middle of nowhere. And the rage in my heart, for what had been done to me, and for what they'd tried to make me do . . . was a very cold thing indeed.

I could feel my armour returning to its normal shape and configuration as I regained control of myself. I looked at my hands, and they were just gloves. I had sworn never to kill again, but it had been close, so close. Killing things that looked like people, that I had been sure weren't people, had weakened my conviction. Which was, of course, the point. I armoured down. I didn't want any distractions from what I was about to do. I lifted my head and addressed the grey and empty space around me.

"I know who you are, now. Who you have to be. Walker was right; the clue was in the title you gave yourselves. The Powers That Be . . . Only one people I know of would be that arrogant. I encountered a setting like this before, not so long ago. On a smaller scale, but . . . A soft world, out in the subtle realms, inhabited by elves. The only people who would feel at home in such a place. The only people arrogant enough to want a whole world that would do what it was told. So come forth, you Powers. Come forth and face me, King Oberon and Queen Titania."

A new world appeared around me, sinking into place with a cold and cheerless authority. An elven setting, with ancient stone and coral buildings whose long sweeping lines seemed more organic than functional. I was standing in a rose garden, but I knew better than to try to touch the blood-coloured flowers. I knew from experience that the dark, bitter green leaves would have razor-sharp serrated edges. The thick, pulpy flowers pouted and pulsed rhythmically, as though they were breathing. Gathering up their venom, to spit at anyone foolish enough to come within range. Statues stood scattered about the garden, in alarmingly naturalistic poses, elves caught in mid-motion, as though transfixed by a Gorgon's gaze.

The grass was a faded green, as though the life had been sucked out of it. The sky was almost unnaturally blue, flat and featureless, without a single cloud. The sun blazed fiercely, but shed little warmth. A great circle of massive standing stones surrounded the rose garden, sealing it off from the rest of the world. The stone henges looked oddly new, as though they'd only recently been hauled into position. But then, everyone knows the elves are far older than anything mankind has to offer.

King Oberon and Queen Titania stood before me, tall and regal and imposing. Oberon was a good ten feet tall, bulging with muscles, wrapped in a long blood-red cloak and leggings, the better to show off his milk-white skin. His hair was a colourless blonde, hanging loose around his long angular face, which was dominated by golden eyes with no pupils. He smiled a smile with no humour in it. His bone structure was subtly inhuman, and he had sharp pointed ears. He looked effortlessly noble, and regal, but worn thin, by age and hard times. He had taken his throne from Queen Mab through intrigue and violence, and it showed.

Titania wore a long black robe with outré silver patterns, and wore it with a casual, brooding elegance. She was lovelier than any mere mortal woman could ever hope to be, and she knew it, and didn't give a damn. She was a few inches taller than Oberon, though her musculature was leaner and more aesthetic. But still inhumanly powerful. Her skin was so pale that blue veins showed clearly at her temples. She wore her blonde hair cropped severely short, and her dark gaze was cold and calculating.

They both wore simple crowns of beaten gold, and held themselves like the immortal royalty they were, and always would be. Because they had nothing else.

Walker stepped out from behind them. He leaned casually on his furled umbrella and tipped his bowler hat to me, mockingly. And then the glamour he was wearing dropped away, and there was Puck. A shorter, sturdy figure, almost human-sized, though the sheer looming scale of Oberon and Titania made him seem smaller. His body was as smooth and supple as a dancer's, but the hump on his back pushed one shoulder forward and down, and the hand on that arm had withered into a claw. His hair was grey, and his skin was the colour of old yellowed bone. He had two raised nubs on his forehead that might have been horns. He wore a pelt of animal fur, which blended seamlessly into his own hairy lower body. His legs ended in cloven hooves.

Puck—fool and trickster, spy and thief and joyful killer. The only elf who was not perfect.

He smiled at me. "Lord, what fools these mortals be . . ."

"Get a new line," I said.

I looked away from the elves. There were others present in the rose garden. The Somnambulist stood to one side, along with Charles and Emily, and Molly. I only had to look at them once, to know they were the real thing. And faced with the real Molly, I had to wonder how I could ever have been fooled by her colourless replacement. In my defence, the Game had done its best to keep me distracted . . . The four of them stood crammed together, inside a circle burned into the grass. It was clear from the way they held themselves that they couldn't leave the circle.

I nodded and smiled to them, and then turned back to the elves. "I've had enough of your Game. It's over! It's time now to tell the truth."

"The truth?" said Puck. "Well, there's a time for everything, I suppose. Why not? With your majesties' permission . . . Good, good. The truth is, dear little Drood, that you were on your own from the moment you left the Cathedral. Everyone you encountered was just a part of the environment you were dropped into. You never met any of the other competitors; they were all busy fighting their own separate Games. I regret to inform you that Tarot Jones, Chandarru, and the Sin Eater are all dead. They died at the hands of illusions generated by their own minds. At least they can take comfort from knowing they died entertainingly."

"What about Molly? And my parents?" I said.

Puck shrugged. "They refused to play."

"The Game is not over," said Oberon, and there was still enough strength and majesty in his voice that everyone immediately looked to him. "The rules are clear. The Drood has to kill everyone else in order to win."

"We control the only way out of the Shifting Lands," said Titania, in her cold and effortlessly commanding voice. "And we alone decide whose obligations will be excused, and wiped clean. If you want our favour, Drood, you must earn it."

"Screw your rules," I said. "And stuff your favour."

I turned my back on them again and went over to the circle burned into the grass. Molly put up a warning hand.

"Don't get too close, Eddie! And don't touch the circle; the magic running through it is strong enough to rip the soul right out of you and enslave it to the elves forever."

"You know what?" I said. "Like everything else in this Game, I don't believe it."

I armoured up my right hand, reached down, grabbed hold of the circle, and tore it easily off the grass. It immediately broke under my rough handling, twisting and writhing in my grasp like a petulant snake. It tried to curl around my arm, but I crushed it in my armoured grasp. It fell apart into a hundred pieces, falling to the faded grass like hundreds of dead petals. I armoured down and smiled at the others.

"Time to go home," I said.

"Loving the confidence," said Molly. "But how?"

"I think," I said, "that if we all put our minds together, we could break any hold the elves have over us. The Shifting Lands have no loyalty to anyone." I turned back to Oberon and Titania. "What do you think?"

"You Droods," said Oberon. "Always more trouble than you're worth. Very well. We agree."

"The Game is at an end," said Titania.

"It's been fun, but that's all, folks," said Puck.

Molly whooped, punched the air, and hugged me tightly. She felt very real in my arms. Charles and Emily took it in turns to clap me approvingly on the shoulder. The Somnambulist snored lightly. I didn't take my eyes off the elves. This wasn't over yet.

"I thought you were bound to Shadows Fall these days," I said. "By your own need and wishes?"

"We are," said Oberon. "But Shadows Fall is large, and touches many places."

"Are the Shifting Lands then a part of Shadows Fall?" I said.

"No," said Titania. "We told you. This is a place we made, long ago, for our own amusement. Where we could play, unobserved and uninterrupted."

"Elves just want to have fun," said Puck.

"How did you get Carrys Galloway to be your Somnambulist?" said Molly, moving in beside me to show that she wasn't going to be left out of anything.

"Their Majesties knew all about her pact with Mab," said Puck. "Elven magic made it possible, so of course they knew immediately the pact was broken. And they took advantage of her. It's what they do."

"They?" I said.

Puck shrugged. "Family. You know how it is . . ."

"Well," I said, "now she's free of you, and your Game. She's coming home with us."

"You presume . . . ," said Titania.

"Yes," I said. "I do."

Oberon smiled briefly. "And we admire that. But don't push your luck, Drood."

"How could you pay off debts owed to Heaven and to Hell, and other Principalities?" I said.

"Because elves are old," said Oberon. "We have Pacts and Agreements that go back further than anyone else."

"It is a small thing," said Titania, "to barter what we owe, and are owed."

"All this?" I said. "For a Game?"

"We're easily bored," said Puck.

"How long have you being running this Game?" said Molly, scowling. "Playing with people's lives?"

"What is Time to an immortal?" said Titania.

"Enough fun and games," I said. "The Big Game ends here, and now."

"This Game," said Oberon.

"All Games," I said.

"You lack the power or authority to enforce such a thing, little Drood," said Titania. "We are ready to indulge you over this Game, because you have brought something new into it, and we do so love to be entertained. But you do not dictate to us, Drood."

"You think I'm afraid of you?" I said. "I faced down Mab once, in her own Court!"

"Yes," said Puck, "but she was crazy. You can't hope to stand against us."

"Perhaps not," I said. "But I think I know someone who can."

I reached out through my torc, calling out to my family . . . but not to my handler, Kate.

*Ethel!* I said. *Come to me! I need you!*

And she came, drawn to my torc. She manifested in the rose garden in her usual soft red glow, suffusing the whole world with a new, invigorating sense of life and good humour. Oberon and Titania cried out together, shocked and outraged.

"You dare?" said Oberon.

"How can you be here, in this place?" said Titania.

*My Drood's torc is made of strange matter,* Ethel said calmly. *And that is my physical presence, in this reality. Where it is, I am! Nice pocket dimension; love what you've done with the place . . .*

"I will see you destroyed for this intrusion!" said Oberon.

*Really don't think so,* said Ethel. *Eddie, I need your armour.*

I armoured up, and she concentrated her presence around me, her red glow sinking into my armour until it shone like a ruby. It glowed so brightly that everyone had to turn their heads away, including the elves. Oberon and Titania were the first to turn back, forcing themselves to face me. Puck hid behind them. Or perhaps he was just getting out of the line of fire. The King and Queen of the elves spoke a single Word together, and all the huge standing stones surrounding the rose garden went shooting round and round in a great circle, speeding faster and faster.

"This is our world," said Oberon and Titania, speaking together. "Our Game . . . The rules are what we say they are. Do your worst, Outsider. You cannot fight a whole world."

*Oh, stop showing off,* said Ethel.

I raised my ruby-red arms, and her power surged through me. I glared at the stones, and they slammed to a sudden halt. And then they disappeared. And then the old buildings, and the elven statues, and the rosebushes . . . and King Oberon and Queen Titania and Puck began to fade away too.

"Stop!" said Oberon. "We surrender!"

"We defer to you, and your power," said Titania. "Restore us and we agree that the Games are at an end."

"Even immortals must bend the knee to a living god," said Puck.

They stopped fading and became clear and solid again. I armoured down, the ruby glow already fading from my armour. Ethel's rose-red light disappeared too, as she returned to Drood Hall. She wasn't one to wait around and crow over her victory; she'd made her point. Oberon looked at me thoughtfully.

"You win the Game, Drood. In the only way that matters. Your obligations, and those of your companions, will be taken care of. Because the elves, at least, understand honour."

"Though if you ever do find out who and what your Ethel really is," said Titania, "and why she's staying with your family . . . you may come to feel differently about her."

"What a terrible thing it is," said Puck, "for mortals to fall into the hands of a living god."

"We return to Shadows Fall," said Oberon. "Do not trouble us again."

"My lords and ladies, our revels now are ended," said Puck. He dropped me a quick wink. "Be seeing you . . ."

And just like that, they were gone. And the rest of us were standing in the open grounds of Drood Hall.

They were definitely the real thing this time. Full of life and energy and happy, familiar noise. I hugged Molly to me, picking her up off her feet and swinging her around. She laughed and kicked her heels merrily. Charles and Emily looked about them, smiling. The Somnambulist was still snoring quietly. I set Molly down again and she clung to me happily.

"What happens to the Shifting Lands now?" she said. "Who's to stop the elves, or anyone else, from making use of them again?"

"The Shifting Lands are gone," said Ethel. "I've taken care of them."

"How?" said Molly.

"I ate them," said Ethel.

"Never ask her questions," I said to Molly. "Even when you do understand the answers, they'll only upset you. Right, Ethel? Ethel?"

But she was gone, not even the faintest trace of her red glow remaining. Molly frowned.

"That's it?" she said. "No one's going to punish Oberon and Titania and Puck for everything they did? For all the people who died in their Game?"

"We put a stop to the Game and sent them home humiliated," I said. "For elves, that's a real punishment. Sometimes you have to settle for what you can get."

Emily and Charles were looking at Drood Hall. Standing close together, arm-in-arm. It was hard to work out the expressions on their faces.

"Home again . . . ," said Emily. "It's been a while."

"Wonder what they'll have to say to us after all this time," said Charles.

I couldn't help but grin. "I can't wait to find out."

Carrys Galloway's head came up with a snap, and her eyes shot open. "Oh! Hello! I've just had the strangest dream . . ."

"Me too," I said.

*Shaman Bond*

*Will Return*

*in*

# DR. DOA